THRACE

Propontis
(Sea of Marmora)

Samothrace

Hellespont

MT. ATHOS   Imbros

Lemnos   Sigeum   Troy   PHRYGIA

TROAD

Tenedos

The Ionian Coast

Gulf of Adramyttium

Aegean Sea   Methymna

Eresus   Pyrrha   MYSIA

Mytilene

Scyrus   LESBOS

Psyra   LYDIA

EUBOEA   CHIOS

Clazomenae

Colophon

Andros   Samos   Ephesus

Tenos   Icaria

Miletus

0   10   30   60
Scale of Miles

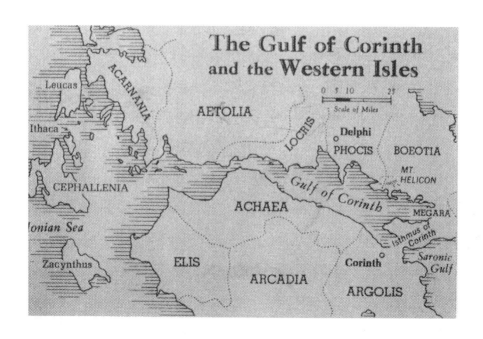

The Gulf of Corinth
and the Western Isles

ACARNANIA

Leucas   AETOLIA   0   5 10   25
Scale of Miles

LOCRIS

Ithaca   Delphi

PHOCIS   BOEOTIA

MT.
HELICON

CEPHALLENIA   Gulf of Corinth

ACHAEA   MEGARA

Ionian Sea   Isthmus of Corinth

Zacynthus   ELIS   Corinth   Saronic
Gulf

ARCADIA

ARGOLIS

The Laughter of Aphrodite

The Laughter of Aphrodite

A Novel about Sappho of Lesbos

Peter Green

UNIVERSITY OF CALIFORNIA PRESS

BERKELEY   LOS ANGELES   OXFORD

*First published in 1965 by John Murray; American edition by
Doubleday & Company, 1966.*

University of California Press
Berkeley and Los Angeles, California

University of California Press, Ltd.
Oxford, England

© *1993 by*
The Regents of the University of California

>   *Library of Congress Cataloging-in-Publication Data*
Green, Peter, 1924–
  The laughter of Aphrodite   :   A Novel about
Sappho of Lesbos   /   Peter Green.
      p.   cm.
  "First published in 1965 by John Murray"—T.p. verso.
  ISBN 0–520–07966–3 (alk. paper)
  1.   Sappho—Fiction.   2.   Lesbos Island (Greece)—History—
Fiction.   3.   Greece—History—To 146 B.C.—Fiction.   I.   Title.
PR6057.R348L38   1993
823'.914–dc20   92–12431
>   *CIP*

Printed in the United States of America

CONTENTS

For

WILLIAM GOLDING

— ὁσσάκις ἀμφότεροι
ἥλιον ἐν λέσχῃ κατεδύσαμεν —

THE LAUGHTER OF
APHRODITE

I

TWO nights ago I went to the cave once more, hoping against hope. The sky was sharp and clear, star-pricked, yet holding the first hints of approaching winter. I knew the signs: what islander does not? There had been a sultry stillness at noon, with clouds gathering across the straits, eastward from Mytilene: monstrous storm-dark chimaeras that crouched, like mating lions, along the mountain ridges of Ionia. I walked in the garden, by the stump of the great fig-tree—memories, memories—and watched them. A flicker of summer lightning scrawled itself across the sky, as though the branching pain in my head had swollen to embrace the whole universe. I could feel the muscles flickering in and round my left eyelid—always the left, the unlucky side, the dark lobe of the brain.

My throat was raw, parched: yet I could not drink. Every sense in my body, each fold of skin and flesh seemed naked to the nerve beneath. All nature was a mirror to my passion and my despair: those obscene clouds spoke to me of more than winter. I shivered and sweated as though I had a fever, and the light linen robe I wore— too late for turning autumn—burnt my skin. It was ridiculous and humiliating, and the worst of all was—is—that I can no longer laugh at myself. Nothing frightens me more than that. All through my life one part of me has stood aside, amused by my own passions and inconsistencies, ready to prick the bubble of pretentious self-pity. But no longer. I am being pretentious and self-pitying now; I know it; there is no help for me.

The afternoon brought thunderous gusts of wind from the north-east, ripping down through streets and alleys with a noise like a split and bellying sail. I could hear, high above the city, the subdued roar of the great forest, and thought of other days when we had climbed the ridge, under a blue autumn sky, to gather fallen chestnuts and pine-cones.

(So still on the needle-carpet, the light slanting between tall tree-trunks, catching and glinting suddenly on a golden shoulder-clasp, the flush of a young girl's cheek, the wildness of blown hair.) The wind whipped up hard granular particles of dust, stung my face and lips: and with the dust came a few random rain-drops, hot, heavy, ominous. But by sunset all was clear again, and the wind had dropped. I called Praxinoa and put on a light shawl, and together we walked down to the headland. Lanterns flared on the quayside below us: the black boats bobbed at anchor still, and fishermen called to each other across rows of barrels. I could smell tar and seaweed and the faint tang of fish. Praxinoa glanced at me, troubled, eyes half-shadowed in the fold of her hood. But she said nothing.

The sun was melting-crimson now, spreading over the dark water like coloured oil. In a soft lemon sky the evening star, Aphrodite's star, gleamed out clear. Now it seemed baleful, curse-laden; yet how often in past years had I not taken it as the very embodiment of fulfilled passion, the gatherer-home of beast, child, and lover? Aphrodite, Aphrodite, it has taken me a lifetime to see what lies behind that still, enigmatic smile. And now I know it is too late: the trap is sprung, my own remembered words mock my helplessness:

Some say a host of cavalry or guardsmen,
And some a fleet, is the finest sight of all
On the dark earth; but I declare the best
Is what you love.

I turned my back on the headland and the harbour, and the winking lights of Mytilene that lay beyond: still in silence we walked up towards the house. There was a smell of thyme and hay in the air, and when I looked out over the dark-glinting water I could see, where the male lion clouds had crouched, a refulgence, a radiance under the dazzled stars. I touched Praxinoa's sleeve, and we stood there in that stillness till the moon's rim thrust up over the mountains and swung clear, riding full and silver-pale, stippling the straits with its cold, colourless fire. I glanced up at the black ridged mountain rising inland above us, seeing in my mind's eye that familiar twisting path between rocks, smelling the scent of pine and rosemary, the dark, close goatish odour of the cave. With a shiver, I walked on,

[2]

Praxinoa following, up the long, stony land by the pine-grove. The owls were hunting early: there came that faint, whickering, unearthly cry and the small squeal of some trapped animal. (*Ghosts, lemurs, witches, avoid this house:* the formula muttered three times, the furtive gesture with finger and thumb, the rosemary and garlic. My Ionian friends worked hard to dispel my island superstitions about owls. They never quite succeeded.) Burning, burning. Down the shoulder of the hill, beyond the apple-orchards and the first farmsteads, the lights were springing out over the city.

Praxinoa had the big key, worn with long use, and stepped in front of me, a black, subdued shadow, to open the garden-gate. The wards rasped harshly: the gate itself was peeling, its rusty iron studs matched by the weeds clustering under the wall. We passed inside and walked down the flagged alley to the fountain. Here I paused again for a moment, listening to the soft chuckle of the water, observing the black-and-white chequerwork thrown up by marble in moonlight: all familiar as my own body, yet now strange, alien, disturbed, and disturbing.

Like my own body.

From the dark house came a flicker of light, a snatch of broad-accented island song. I recognized a lullaby: the new dark girl in the kitchens, with the smudged, searching eyes and the fatherless two-year-old child. *A runaway, Lady Sappho,* Praxinoa had said, disapprovingly. *A slut. She should be sent back to her master and branded.* Sometimes, after nearly forty years' intimacy, Praxinoa can still surprise me. But do I know her at all? What unimaginable thoughts can one woman conceive who belongs, body and soul, to another, who is at once her servant, her protector, her guardian, and her slave? Yet I cannot begin to conceive a world in which Praxinoa would have no place. This, too, frightens me. What is left beyond the familiar landmarks? Over what sheer ocean must I set out while autumn turns to winter? Too late, too late.

As we approached the house I heard old Apollo stir and growl, with a rattle of his chain. He was a Cretan mastiff, ten years old now and the ugliest beast conceivable, with grey-flecked jowls and a rheumy, sour expression that never changed, even during his moments of slobbering, over-demonstrative affection. It was Cydro, in one of her more irrepressible moments, who had had the notion of giving him his grotesquely unsuitable name—and of installing as our porter and doorkeeper a Scythian near-dwarf who bore the most disconcerting resemblance to him. It was, I must confess, somewhat

[3]

entertaining to watch the reactions of visitors when confronted with Apollo and old Scylax for the first time, simultaneously. But now the joke had gone sour, and I found myself hating dog and slave with equal violence for their dumb, patient, submissive loyalty.

Scylax heaved himself up awkwardly in his cubby-hole as Praxinoa and I approached: the big house-door still stood open, and the lamps were ready for us, wicks fresh-trimmed. He scuttled sideways, like a big black crab, with those odd, pale-blue Scythian eyes that seemed so incongruous in the seamed, leathery, toothless face. He was hoping, I knew, for a word, a joke, a quick pat on the shoulder: behind him Apollo uncoiled in equal expectation. Really, I thought, in a gust of irritation, they not only *look* like each other: to all intents and purposes you can treat them identically.

With the briefest of nods I took the lamp he gave me and went straight through the lobby, past the little shrine of Aphrodite—the candles were flickering down in their sockets, the smile on the Goddess' face was shadowed, foam-cold, with (I thought) the cruelty of the sea in it too—not stopping, not thinking, barricading my mind against the silence and the memories, up the staircase where little Timas' statue stood forlorn in its niche, and the tapestries still hung that Gongyla had brought back from Colophon, along the corridor to the two big rooms at the end that were my private sanctuary from the noisy, imperative clamour of the heart.

In the study all was still. I paused a moment on the threshold; one shutter had blown to, and the moonlight cast a cold, latticed beam on the shelves of scrolls, the plain white walls, the oddments that littered my writing-table—a glittering quartz-crystal picked from the river near Pyrrha, a sea-urchin's shell, a Lydian scent-bottle, a pair of golden knuckle-bones, four or five wax tablets, a new papyrus-roll (untouched for a month and more), an onyx ring. I carried the lamp in, and sat down. The first thing I noticed was a sealed scroll carefully placed where I was bound to find it: for an instant my heart swooped upwards, breath catching, and the tremor began to run through me again, wave upon wave, till I held the lamp closer and saw the seal and recognized the device of a merchant whom I disliked intensely and who—till recently—had always been only too ready to supply me with imported goods on credit—the alabaster lampstand from Egypt, that only revealed its pattern when light shone through it; the bale of flowered silk, the Syrian ear-rings, the striped cushions; the pair of inlaid chairs with the running deer pattern (I was sitting in one of them now); the ivory-faced dining-couches, the

[4]

Asian rugs, the creams and scents and lotions—yes, I knew, all too well, what would be in *that* letter.

There was a discreet tap on the door, and Praxinoa appeared, a nervous slave-girl (Thalia, was it? Erinna?) at her heels. I told them to light the lamps in my bedroom and heat the water for a bath. No, I said, I would not eat. Praxinoa shook her head sadly. There was a fine dish of quail waiting for me, she said. I suddenly felt weak and small and childish. No, I said, *no,* and Praxinoa caught the edge of hysteria in my voice and whisked the girl away. I heard them talking together quietly in the bedroom next door, and then the chink of metal, the sound of water being poured, a crackle of twigs as the fire was lit under the great copper pan in the bath-house beyond. Presently Praxinoa came out again, and I heard the soft, familiar pad-pad of feet moving away down the corridor towards the stairs. The girl, still in the bath-house, began, shyly at first, to whistle a haunting little tune that was quarried from my earliest childhood memories: I had first heard it in Eresus, sung by women as they worked at the loom. I sighed, got up, and moved into the bedroom like a sleep-walker.

On either side of my dressing-table, like sentinels, the great seven-branched candlesticks stood, a candle burning clear and steady in each branch, light glinting on gold scrollwork and wrought iron. They were not the gift I would have asked for, and the giver—though long dead—still had the power to make me uneasy in retrospect with the lingering memory of his harsh, half-hostile, uncompromising masculinity. When Antimenidas came back from service with the Babylonian king in Judaea, the candlesticks had been a reconciliatory gesture, but a challenge, too. From some looted Jewish temple, he said carelessly, black eyes flicking from me to the enlaced, five-pointed stars worked into the juncture of branch and stem. There was supposed to be a curse on them: something to do with the spilling of priests' blood. But that was idle gossip: common soldiers, old market-women. It was difficult to tell, from his tone, which category he despised more.

But the magic was in them, running from stem to branch like Dioscurean fire: Antimenidas knew it, and so did I. He knew, too, that between pride and covetousness (they were beautiful and unique objects) I would never get rid of them. I remember him striding to and fro in the south colonnade, iron-shod boots ringing on the flags; a tall, powerful, awkward figure with his close-cropped greying hair and the white puckered sword-scar down one cheek, a braggart soldier

[5]

who (like all his family) would frequently, and without warning, slip into a mood of delicate, perceptive seriousness that caught one unprepared after the roughshod cynicism or political rant which had preceded it. I liked him better than either of his brothers: which, I suppose, was not saying much. But one thing that he told me, on that spring morning nearly a quarter of a century ago, has stuck in my mind ever since.

"You find a people's roots in odd places, Sappho," he said. His voice had an abrupt, jerky quality, as though he were consciously trying to subdue its natural rhythms. "Six years as a mercenary teach you a lot. Books—" He broke off, fumbling for words, leaving the unspoken sentence to hang derisively in mid-air. "You and my beloved poet-brother can tell me all the old stories about our Pelasgian ancestry. But I have *seen*—" He stopped again, fists clenched, frowning. "I served with Cretans, you know that. Hill-Cretans."

I nodded. I knew all about Antimenidas and his private obsession with Crete: to hear him you would have thought every noble family on Lesbos descended from King Minos in person. A strange legend he had pieced together, from soldiers and merchants and wandering minstrels, from beggars on the waterfront, from any Mediterranean traveller who would talk for the price of a drink. He told us of great maze-like palaces built in the old days, of black ships and strange goddesses, of fire and rapine and a terrible tidal wave roaring inland over harbour-works and cities and the proud, rich, peacock-elegant nobles in them. Some—not many—escaped, sailing northwards, away from that vast convulsion, bringing their knowledge and art and leisured way of life to the coast of Ionia and the islands.

Few people believed Antimenidas, especially since he seldom spoke of these things unless he was far gone in wine. But sometimes I wonder, still. It is true (and a thing which foreign visitors frequently point out to us) that our freedom and elegance and individualism compare very well with conditions elsewhere in Greece—especially as regards women. When I heard Antimenidas speak of those magnificent Cretan court ladies—legendary perhaps, but vital and believable—who were the equals of men and in ways more than a match for them, I found no difficulty in imagining such beings. How should I, when the freedom I enjoyed so nearly matched their own?

I said: "Hail, brother-Cretan."

Antimenidas seemed not to have heard; he was pursuing some private path of thought, and finding it unexpectedly stony. At last he said: "When we were fighting in Judaea they didn't like it, my

Cretans. There wasn't much you could put your finger on. Just a feeling in the air. But I found out finally."

He stopped again, frowned, rubbed his nose, and said: "They had a tradition that these men of Judaea were their kin, that they'd sailed to Crete, generations back. Interesting, don't you think?" The black eyes met and held mine. "A tenuous thread, perhaps. But then so was the thread that Ariadne paid out in the labyrinth; and *that* led to a bull. Or a king. Or perhaps both. I wouldn't presume to argue with you on such matters, my dear."

It was a sunny day: but my hands and feet seemed suddenly ice-cold.

So, last night, I sat between the candlesticks and stared at my shadowy, flame-tinted image in the great bronze mirror. Night was kind to me, hiding the grey streaks in my thick, wiry-springing black curls, smoothing out the lines from nostril to mouth, the fine web of laughter-wrinkles round my eyes. *What unimaginable blood runs in my veins, what history has gone to make up this I, this time-bound self?* The robe scorched my flesh, as though it were Deianira's. Too-swarthy skin, irregular features in a wedge-shaped face, small bird-boned body. I smiled bitterly. *How could this two-cubit I ever touch the heavens?* The question—and the answers I had sought to it— echoed mockingly in my mind.

I raised both hands to my cheeks, as though protecting myself against—what? Self-knowledge? Time? Despair? The rings on my fingers glinted in the candle-light, each a wrought, tangible reminder of past passions: the entwined gold snakes, the great cold sapphire, the double signet with the lapis inlay, the dark Egyptian scarab. At my throat hung the necklace of gold pomegranates, a family heirloom so old that no one now knew its history. How many Persephones, I wondered, had worn it down to the cold abyss before me?

I loosened the girdle of my robe, and let it fall in a heap at my feet as I stood up between the candlesticks, naked and burning. *Changed*, the voice whispered, *all changed*. No, I cried silently, *no: I am what I was*—and my hands flew up, touched my breasts, seeking reassurance, knowing them high and firm as they had always been, seeing the nipples dark and neat in the mirror before me, my hands moving as though of themselves, as though they were the hands of some other person, over my still-slender hips and firm, smooth, gently curving belly. The fire raged in me, I was quicklime. *Tonight. It must be tonight*, I thought.

[7]

I remembered, hot with shame, the words I had scratched on a scrap of papyrus a week before. *Come now. Quickly. Quickly*—buying love-charms like any village girl, humiliating myself to that filthy old hag—oh yes, she knew, she knew too well who I was—intriguing with contemptuous, moon-faced sluts for nail-parings and scraps of hair, open utterly now in my extremity of desire, a scandal to put my brother's in the shade. *Wryneck, wryneck, draw that man to my house*—the crucified bird flickering on its wheel in the firelight, the spells and burnt herbs and small, obscene sacrifices, there is nothing I have left untried, no shameful trick to which I have not stooped. But if the Goddess has betrayed my devotion and my trust, where else can I turn? She is cold and capricious as the foam from which she was born, and her eternally renewed virginity the cruellest deception of all.

The moon was at the full now. My skin prickled: I knew, without looking, that the slave-girl—Thalia, yes, I remembered: how could I have forgotten?—had come softly through to the curtained archway from the bath-house, and was standing there in the shadows, watching me. Perhaps that is the answer, I thought: to drive out fire with fire. I sat down again and called softly: "Thalia."

She caught her breath, startled. "My lady," she whispered. She was behind me now: I heard the crisp rustle of her skirts, and the sound of her sandals padding across the floor. In the bronze mirror I glimpsed a young, nervous face, eyes two great questioning smudges, hair braided in a heavy coil. She had no idea what to do with her hands: she either clasped them frantically, as though in agony, or else let them hang, awkward and inert, at her sides. I picked up the pot of lanolin and began to wipe off my make-up.

"Is the bath ready?" I said.

"Yes, my lady." The same choked, breathy whisper. What was she feeling? Shyness? Fear? Embarrassment?

"Shall I bring your bath-robe, my lady?"

I paused, stretched luxuriously, and yawned like a cat: I could feel a quiver run through her as I did so, like the ripple moving over a field of green barley, the spring breeze that sets leaves dancing and stipples a calm sea with fugitive shadows.

Desire? Surely not. And yet—

"Thank you," I said, and turned to watch her move across the candle-lit room, picking her way with neat, short steps to the big press in the corner, beside my bed. She was slighter than I had thought: there was a touching fragility about her movements. She had to reach up on tip-toe to fetch down the saffron-and-green striped robe, and memory stirred uneasily in me as I watched. *Atthis, I* thought: *of course;* yet the realization came without surprise, or indeed any violence of emotion. Atthis as an awkward schoolgirl, eyes starred with tears, waving good-bye to me on the quayside at Mytilene; Atthis, a chrysalis no longer, but the small, brilliant butterfly who burst on my senses when I came back from my five years of Sicilian exile. Even the coil of hair—and then I stopped short, remembering the miniature that hung in my study alcove, seeing the pathetic imitation of it that Thalia had achieved.

She came back with the robe, smiling shyly, her great brown eyes anxious and adoring at once. I turned back to the mirror and let her wait while, very slowly and meticulously, I wiped the last traces of make-up from my face. Then our eyes met in the mirror and I nodded, leaning back as she slipped the robe over my arms and wrapped it about me. Her hands—how well I knew the symptoms!— hesitated at each physical contact, in an agony of uncertainty. I smiled to myself, and then thought, disconcerted: It is not only the Goddess who is cruel. So many years her votary, and can I hope to have escaped her nature?

I walked through to the bath-house, beckoning Thalia after me. The water was steaming, fragrant with pine-resin. I lay back in it, letting the heat work through me, watching Thalia as she stood there, fingers unconsciously stroking out the folds in the heavy linen robe. I smiled at her, feeling nothing except the blessed warmth of the water, conscious of my power.

"Now," I said, "you may wash me."

She came to the side of the marble bath—slowly, very slowly— and I saw her tense her muscles to hide the trembling of her hands. She washed my back, and all the time her breath was coming faster and shallower. I felt nothing, nothing, nothing. Then I lay back again, and waited, smiling, still. As she touched my breasts the tremors ran faster and faster through her till she could hardly stand, and she snatched her hand away as though the water had suddenly become scalding hot.

Not yet. Wait. Be cruel.

She wrapped me in a heavy warm towel, and we went back to the bedroom again. I sat on the side of my bed, still in the towel, while she unpinned and brushed out my hair.

"Now the powder," I said, and almost purred as she dusted my shoulders and feet with the fine-smelling talc Iadmon had given me in Samos.

Time enough, I thought, and took her hand in mine, and shook a little talc over my breasts, and guided her fingers to smooth it out. She was sobbing silently now, the tears streaming down from wide eyes, and I slipped my other hand inside her robe, caressing the high young breasts till they rose under my touch and her lips reached out to me blindly, and I tasted the salt of her tears. Nothing still. Nothing. You cannot drive out fire with dead ashes. Suddenly I felt active disgust surging up through the emptiness and the boredom— disgust with myself, with her, with the whole absurd situation. I flung her off me violently: she lay on the floor with hurt, bewildered eyes, staring up at me, terrified by this sudden change of mood. I wrapped the robe round me again, and found, to my astonishment, that I was shivering.

"Get out," I said. "Out of my sight."

"I don't understand—I thought—"

"You thought, you *thought*—what right have you to *think?*"

The dry tinder of my frustration flamed up in sudden fury. It must have been a comical sight: two small women, inarticulate with rage and fear, drifting rapidly towards physical violence.

"I love you, my lady." It was a thin, supplicating whisper, almost inaudible.

"*Get out!*" I screamed, my last shred of dignity blown away. *How dare this nothing behave like a human being, blackmail my senses and my emotions with her cheap tricks?* My fingers crooked themselves in an atavistic reflex, became long-nailed claws; and the girl fled. I heard the frantic patter of her feet down the stairs, the slam of a door in the servants' quarter.

Well, I thought grimly, Praxinoa should know how to deal with *that* situation by now. I took a deep breath, willing the rage in my body to subside. Little by little the blood began to pulse slower through my veins, the violent pounding of my heart sank to a quiet, regular beat. I walked across to the window and flung the shutters wide. Cold and pure, the moonlight streamed down over the mountain: somewhere an owl whickered, and from a tavern by the harbour there came the distant sound of singing, the plangent thrum of a lyre.

The moon is high, I thought; but where is Endymion? My flesh crawled with desire and humiliation. This last time. This time he must come. Aphrodite, cruel goddess, I implore you, make him come now, quickly. Now before it is too late.

A dog barked: strung out across the strait I could see six faint dots of light, where the night-fishers were waiting for the shoals to rise. Slowly, like a sleep-walker, I pulled on a heavy woollen robe and my black travelling-cloak. Slowly I pinned and braided up my hair, binding a single sprig of rosemary into it. But I put on no scent, and left my face bare of cosmetics. The day he first kissed me he said, laughing: "Why do you paint yourself like an old whore?" My hand had flown out at him before I thought; he caught both my wrists, imprisoned them with strong, callused fingers, and held me at arm's-length from him, like a child or a doll. "Wipe that damned mess off," he said at length, and let me go. The wind blew through his thick brown curls. "Whores need it. You don't." And tears of rage and gratitude stinging my eyes, I did as he told me.

I walked out into the silent corridor, down the stairs, across the courtyard. There were no signs of Praxinoa: presumably she was comforting the wretched Thalia. I tiptoed quietly through the lobby, Scylax was nodding in his cubby-hole, though I knew very well he was awake: we played an elaborate conventional charade on such occasions to preserve the domestic proprieties. Apollo twitched and snuffled, curled up at the old man's feet, hunting long-dead hares up the hillside of his dreams. I slipped through the front-door, taking care to leave it open, and walked back past the fountain and the shrine to the garden-gate. Once outside, however, I turned away from the town, and set off up the mule-track into the mountains.

The moon shone down on me as I moved, and my shadow danced, faint and fluttering, over the silvered stones. When I stopped for a moment I could hear the minuscule sounds of small nocturnal creatures in the brushwood, and, away to the right of me, the cool clear chatter of water on rock. My footsteps, as I crunched over loose shale, sounded preternaturally loud. But presently the path was swallowed up by the pine-forest, and here I walked ghostly-silent, on a thick carpet of fallen needles, with only the occasional random moon-beam to light my way.

The cave lies about half-way up the ridge, close beside a little spring. It is not really a cave at all, but a hollow formed by three gigantic rocks, tumbled together earthquake-fashion against the steep fall of the mountain. Others besides us must have used it: the floor of the hollow is covered with a thick layer of dried grass. The spring gushes out from the rock-face into a worn stone basin, bright with green weed, and spills over down a narrow, stony runnel. There is a tiny shrine beside it, sacred to the Nymphs, a whitewashed niche with a lamp and some cracked clay figurines and, sometimes, a withered bunch of flowers.

When I got there all was still and the cave empty, as I knew it would be. But it was early yet. The lamp in the shrine was flickering; I took the oil-jar from the ledge where I had hidden it, and filled the lamp. The wick needed trimming: that took up a little more time. Then I prayed to the Nymphs, who are kindly deities, and have always been near me in country places: but my words seemed to echo through a great emptiness, as though the tutelary spirits of this place were either gone, or sleeping, or indifferent to me. So I dipped my face in the stone basin, bracing myself against the shock of the icy water, feeling my skin tauten and glow at that astringent touch. I drank a little, remembering, as I did so, that I had not eaten all day. Yet I felt no hunger: indeed, at that moment I could not have stomached food of any sort.

When I had drunk I came back, sat myself down at the mouth of the cave, wrapped in my cloak, and waited.

The pines were sparser here, and I had a clear view of the moon and stars overhead. He must come now, I thought: he must, he *must*. At every crack of a twig, each faint rustle in the darkness, I started up, tense with expectancy. For eight days now, nothing. Not even a letter or a message. No explanation, no apology. People shrug and make evasive answers to my enquiries. I can see the pitying contempt in their eyes.

Time passed; the moon moved inexorably across the sky, and the Pleiades followed. It was after midnight now, and still I kept my vigil alone.

When the first grey was streaking the eastern sky I walked quickly down the mountain track, numb, not letting myself think, a dead husk. A kitchen-maid at the well behind the courtyard stared at me as I came in, and I saw her furtively gesture with finger and thumb against the evil eye. Thin, hot wires of pain twitched under my eyelids, behind my temples: the skin seemed drawn tight over a burning skull, and fiery granules rasped through every nerve.

I lay down on my bed as though it were a rack, while the mocking light lanced through the shutters, and cocks began to crow in chorus, and day swung up, bright, autumnal, full of false promise. Let me sleep, I prayed, let me sleep or let me die. Then I remembered the small, iridescent glass phial that Alcaeus had brought me from Egypt, and which (for reasons I can only surmise) I had hidden away at the bottom of a cosmetics-chest, and forgotten for twenty-five years. Now his words came back to me, the hard yet epicene malice in his grey eyes as he said: "For you, my dear, nepenthe: the blessed gift of forgetfulness. A paradox, you think? Now, perhaps. All your senses are open to the sun: you turn lightwards like a budding flower. But later—later you will understand. Not, I fancy, that you will be grateful for my thoughtfulness on your behalf. The gods have bestowed some rare gifts on you, Sappho, but gratitude is hardly one of them."

"Nepenthe?" I repeated, too bemused by his smooth, barbed words to be angry as I should. (I was not so young and foolish then, either: it was, I recall, just before my twenty-fifth birthday.)

"Yes indeed. Homer's true prescription. You should be flattered, my dear: this little bottle cost me more than I care to think about."

"You must have had some good reason of your own for giving it me, then," I said spitefully. Alcaeus' closeness with money was notorious.

"Perhaps so," he agreed, a gleam of amusement in his eye. "You must exercise your admirable wit on determining the motives behind my generosity. I may say it works extremely well. It was sold me by a quite *terrifying* priest in Memphis, and I would no more have dared ask him for proofs of its effectiveness than have desecrated an Egyptian tomb. But I tried it on young Lycus the other day, with most spectacular results."

I took the glass phial from him awkwardly, embarrassed despite myself at the reference to Lycus, a black-eyed creature whose dark, lustrous hair was as long as a girl's, and who could hardly have been more than fourteen when Alcaeus picked him up on his return from Egypt. Lately, too, he had—out of sheer mischief—been encouraging the little beast to make eyes at my young brother Larichus.

"I haven't told you the dosage yet," Alcaeus said, watching me closely. "That, as you'll realize, is rather important. Three drops in a little wine will give you a good night's sleep. Five drops will make you pass out for twelve hours. Ten drops"—he gestured expressively—"is a really lethal dose. It need *never* be repeated, my dear. So be sure to have your coin ready for the ferryman before you take it."

Now, years later, I turned the glass phial over and over in my hands, resenting the cold insight which it symbolized, the curious malice that had governed its giving, yet unable to deny my need

for the forgetfulness it held. I took the little jug of wine which Praxinoa had left on my bedside table (when did *that* start? four years
ago? five?) and poured out some into a cup, and mixed it with
water. Then I opened the phial and sniffed: the very odour was
sweet, drowsy, soporific. Carefully I measured the drops: one, two,
three. An imperceptible pause. Four. Five.

Why not? Now. Quickly. Without pain.

No. It would give *him* such satisfaction. To be proved right after
a quarter of a century, what exquisite delight! *No.* With a decisive
gesture I put the stopper back. Then, before I could change my
mind, I took two quick steps to the window and flung the phial out.
I heard the small, brittle, final sound as it smashed on the flags
below. So much for that. I picked the cup up, conscious now of
my utter exhaustion, of the dry, burning agony in my bones and
nerves. Sleep. I must sleep. But another thought struck me, and I
went quickly out, down the corridor towards the silent, shuttered
room that belongs to my daughter Cleïs. I had not thought of her
all yesterday, or for several days before that: it is a week now since
she went to stay with Megara, in the square grey house on the citadel, and I feel as though some stranger, a casual guest, had departed,
leaving no trace of her presence behind. Because she has rejected
me, I must, in self-defence, erase her from my consciousness.

Ah, Cleïs, my lovely one, it was not always this way. You were
like a golden flower, and we loved each other, Cleïs, the hatred, and
the violence and the terrible unforgiving, unforgettable words had
not happened. Guilt, jealously, bitterness: is this all the harvest of
our sweet spring together?

Everything was still in place—the bedspread with its chequered
pattern of green, yellow, and black, the carved obsidian toad with
the jewelled eyes, the portrait you painted of Atthis just before my
illness (no, I must be honest, *that* always made me uneasy: what
could have been going on in your mind, even then?), the scattered
rugs and carelessly rolled books.

But then I looked closer, and saw—why only now?—that you had,
after all, taken some things with you, all fragile, personal, private
possessions: your birds' eggs; the purple scarf Hippias gave you (not
that, I can't face that yet; give me time: must we always acknowledge
our guilt?), a few small trinkets of no particular value, your worn,
much-scribbled-on copy of the *Odyssey*, with your own pictures in
the margin—do you remember how amused I was by your Polyphemus?
So irresistibly like Pittacus after his third bottle—and what else I

could not be sure: the room was there, on the surface it was the same, and then the small twinges of absence would begin to nag at my mind, another missing piece fall into place.

It was broad daylight by the time I got back to my own room. Once again I sat down on the edge of the bed and picked up the cup of drugged wine. This time I took a sip, realizing as I did so that I was very scared indeed. I had nothing but Alcaeus' word for the nature of this drug, and it would not be the first time he had played an embarrassing practical joke on me. But something obstinately drove me on: whatever else, I was not going to, could not, let that man intimidate me.

I took another sip.

The only effect I noticed at once was a very faint numbing of the tongue. The taste (which the wine could not disguise) was intriguing: heavy, sweetish, yet with a dry, musty-fresh underflavour that put me in mind of a threshing-floor at harvest-time.

Just as I was nerving myself to swallow the rest I heard a vague commotion down below: old Scylax expostulating, an indistinguishable gabble from Praxinoa, and a third voice—high, edgy, irritable—which I instantly recognized as belonging to my brother Charaxus. After a moment or two there came footsteps on the stairs: my defending forces had clearly been routed. He strode in without even bothering to knock, sniffed, blew out his lips disgustedly, and flung the shutters wide open. We looked at each other for a moment without saying anything.

Though for years I refused to admit the fact to myself, I have always had an instinctive and total antipathy towards Charaxus. It is ironic that the one action in his life which (however infuriating at the time) at least convinced me he was a real human being should, by a series of misunderstandings, have merely driven the wedge deeper between us.

I stared at him now, observing the unhealthy little paunch he carried before him like some oriental badge of office, the squat barrel-body set on short, slightly bowed legs, the plump fingers with their expensive, vulgar rings. Though it was autumn, the walk up the hill had left him sweating: he mopped his forehead and grunted. His little argument with Scylax could not have improved matters, either. He really is a hog, I thought, with tranquil loathing. A white, larded, bristly hog, rooting after truffles, and evil-tempered when disturbed. Then it occurred to me that my own appearance must leave much to be desired just at that moment, and, unexpectedly, I giggled.

[15]

Perhaps I was a little hysterical. Or perhaps that Egyptian drug had unexpected properties.

His eyebrows went up, and he looked at the half-full wine-cup. For once he seemed to be enjoying himself in my company: there was a lip-licking air of anticipatory relish about him. He sat down, wrinkling his nose, savouring his undeniable position of advantage. Well, I thought, two can play at that game. I settled myself back against the pillows, sipped at my drugged wine, and waited.

Having made his point about my drinking habits, Charaxus proceeded to scrutinize first my face (with obvious disgust) and then the bed and the linen-press, as though expecting to find a lover hidden there, or at least some unmistakable evidence of my gross debauches. This, I had to admit, was rather effective. But then he ruined the whole thing by saying: "This room smells like a whorehouse." My brother can be relied upon to produce the appropriate platitude for all occasions.

I smiled (poor booby, it was like taking sweets from a child) and said: "My dear Charaxus, how travel does broaden one's experience."

He flushed, and rubbed the back of his hand across his nose: a sure danger-signal. A warm, delightful torpor was stealing through my body: I had all the time in the world before me.

Charaxus said: "Now listen to me. I don't propose to argue about what happened in Egypt. That's my affair—"

"It was a family affair."

"And so is this."

I shrugged, and drank a little more wine.

"Your position," said my brother, "is extremely vulnerable. I would have preferred to avoid such plain speaking, but you leave me no alternative—"

"What a liar you are, Charaxus. You came round here with one idea in your head: to humiliate me."

"I see there's no reasoning with you. Very well, then; I shall give you some facts. One: your recent behaviour has alienated all responsible people in this city, including your friends. You have disgraced the class to which you belong. You have caused grave scandal in our society. These are not small things."

He paused, apparently expecting a comment.

"Go on," I said. "I prefer the speech whole, not in installments."

"There is also the question of your financial position."

Ah, I thought. Now we come to it.

"I am right in saying—am I not?—that you now have no assets whatsoever apart from this house." His whole voice and manner changed when he was talking about money, became quick, shrewd, authoritative. "The capital which your husband left you has been spent, and there is very little to show for it. You no longer derive any income from your—guest-pupils." His tongue curled unpleasantly round that last word. "You are living very largely on credit—I think I could tell you just how much you owe in the city, and to whom."

"Naturally," I said. "Tradesmen have no secrets from each other."

He shrugged: he could afford not to take offence if he felt so inclined.

I said: "You are forgetting my patrimony. I still have a share in the family estate."

"That," Charaxus observed smoothly, "is a debatable point. I agree that according to our father's will the four of us were left equal shares. But Eurygyus died as a minor, and so his share reverted by law to the eldest male descendant—"

"The eldest descendant," I said. "There is no distinction of sex."

"The court, you will recall, decided otherwise."

"I also recall who the judges were."

Charaxus said: "You are, of course, at leisure to reopen the case if you wish. It will be a long and costly business, but—" He spread his hands expressively.

I said: "There is my own share." I knew what was coming.

"In a manner of speaking, yes. But there are two points again, which I really must remind you of. A clause in our father's will specifically places your share of the estate under my administration from the day I come of age—"

"It also guarantees me a proportionate income from the vineyards and olive-groves."

"Just so." Charaxus rubbed his hands. "But since you chose to mortgage your share to me when you were regrettably short of ready money, that provision no longer applies."

He cocked an enquiring glance at me, half-triumphant, half-apprehensive, as though expecting an outburst of fury, perhaps a physical assault: but the drug was taking firm hold of me now, and (in any case) I had used up most of my temper on poor Thalia. When I made no comment, Charaxus said: "You are in an unfortunate position, sister."

I sighed wearily. "All right," I said. "What are your terms?"

Charaxus placed his fingertips together and stared at the floor.

"You can keep this house," he said. "No, don't start protesting; if

every merchant you owed money to foreclosed—*and they well might*
—the place would be sold over your head."

"I see," I said; and indeed the picture was all too clear.

"Furthermore, I will cancel the mortgage on your share of the estate and pay you an agreed income from the profits on all sales."

"Are you quite sure you can afford to?" I asked tartly. The un-
precedented—and, I must admit, most uncharacteristic—way in which
he had squandered money on Doricha in Egypt had made dangerous
inroads into the family capital.

"Oh yes," he said, mildly: "I can afford to—now."

An unwilling flicker of admiration rose in me. It is not every man
who can recoup his own extravagance with so sure a hand as my
brother (an exceptional vintage helped, but it was his knowledge that
placed the exports); nor, indeed, every merchant who travels the Aegean with his own cargoes, as far afield as Egypt too, in search of
good markets—especially if he is nearly fifty. But money always has
had the most extraordinary effect on Charaxus, ever since I can remember.

"Now," I said, "you had better tell me your conditions."

"Very simple, my dear." But he looked ill at ease as he said it.
He got up and stared out of the window, with his back to me. "There
is only one condition: you must give up this fellow, this boatman or
whatever he is. I must have your word that you will never see him
again."

I said nothing: there was nothing to say.

"Think," said Charaxus. "You will have a house and an adequate income. The scandal will soon die down if you do nothing to encourage
it. It seems a very generous arrangement to me. You will have ample
time for your writing. There may be some pain at first—I know that,
who better? But you have Cleïs still, my dear. A daughter's love is
truer, more deep and enduring, than some vagrant lust for a common
fisherman."

I stared at him, realizing that he *meant* it, that he was full of self-
congratulation on having found so reasonable a solution to a vexing
family problem. This was how his mind worked. Yet the malice was
there, unacknowledged: "vagrant lust," whether he remembered it or
not, had been the phrase I used to describe his own liaison with Doricha. And how much did he know about the breach between me and
Cleïs?

"I'm sorry," I said, and in a curious way I *was* sorry: the whole
situation lay so far beyond his comprehension. "But I can't promise

you that. It's blackmail, Charaxus. Besides—" I broke off, unable to justify or explain myself: how could I talk to my brother of dignity, self-respect, words that for him were smooth, debased coins, rubbed into a meaningless blur by much handling?

In the silence that followed I could hear his heavy breathing, with the faint catarrhal wheeze that never seemed to leave him, winter or summer.

"Then I am sorry too," he said at last. "I had hoped to give you some sort of free decision. But whatever your choice, the end will be the same."

A cold trickle of terror ran through my body, eclipsing momentarily the numbing effect of the drug.

"No," I whispered, "no, no, no," like a child who has dropped some fragile, beautiful toy and tries to will the moment back, make things as they were before.

Charaxus said: "Your young friend has been—how shall I put it?—somewhat *indiscriminate* in his favours. So I had a friendly little chat with him. He proved more amenable than I expected."

"You bribed him," I said dully.

"Not at all. I told him that one or two well-connected citizens were considering whether to lodge charges of adultery against him—which, I may add for your benefit, is quite true. I also told him that if he were to leave the country voluntarily, the matter would go no further."

Whether from the shock (though I had known in my heart, surely I had known) or the increasing effect of the drug, I felt a total physical paralysis spreading through my body. Every muscle seemed stiff, sluggish: it was as though Charaxus had become some obscene male Medusa, gorgonizing me into brittle grey stone.

"I see," I said, but my lips scarcely moved.

"The young man shipped as a deck-hand on a cargo-vessel two days ago." Charaxus smiled complacently. "I have a certain influence with the harbour authorities. Everything was arranged in the most discreet way."

The last hope. "This ship," I whispered. "Has it—"

"Sailed? Indeed yes." He might have added: Would I have been here otherwise?

Two words, like slow bubbles, formed themselves on my lips.

"Where?" I whispered. "When?"

Charaxus stared at me, and for the first time I thought I saw an expression of genuine pity on his face.

"Yesterday, at dawn. The long haul to Sicily."

It was one of his own vessels, then. Wine to Sicily, grain on the homeward run. Sailing south of the Peloponnese, by Crete and Cythera, to avoid haulage-dues at the Isthmus, with an underpaid crew and the constant risk of savage storms across the Ionian Sea.

As though reading my mind, Charaxus said: "Not all my ships go down, you know: give me credit for a little business sense. Besides, that particular young man is much more likely to end with a knife in his back."

I said: "Go away now. Please go away."

He hesitated, shifting from foot to foot.

"You must see the whole thing was hopeless," he said at last.

"Oh yes. Quite hopeless. I knew that." My eyelids began to sink.

"You've had a shock. Of course. But you'll soon get over it."

"I expect so."

"You ought to start writing again. It would take your mind off things."

Perhaps I will, I thought. Perhaps I will. But not as you suppose. This time it is different. This time I must take the shattered pieces of my life and see them whole. I must purge my suffering with words, cast out the pain visibly, cauterize to heal. There is nothing else left for me.

I tried to smile. "Thank you, brother," I said.

"Everything will be all right. You'll see. I'll attend to all the legal details today. There's nothing for you to worry about."

I closed my eyes, and seemed to plummet down a sheer black vortex, an engulfing throat of darkness. But before I could open my mouth to scream, or catch my breath, I was asleep. I never heard Charaxus go.

I was wrong to mistrust the Egyptian drug Alcaeus gave me. I slept, as he said I would, for twelve hours: it was dark when I awoke. I stretched till my muscles cracked. It had been months since I felt so buoyant. Then the mists cleared, and I remembered. But the pain had lost its rawness: it was as though during my drugged sleep a fine protective skin had grown over the nerve.

He was gone, irrevocably, and I remained.

Over, finished, broken.

I was forty-nine years old—very nearly fifty, indeed—and now the Goddess, herself eternally young, eternally virgin as the new spring came round, had played her last, most merciless trick on me.

But my body refused to acknowledge the words, or their meaning:

unaccountably that sense of euphoria, of sheer physical well-being, persisted and spread. Had Alcaeus foreseen this too?

I took a lamp, walked through to my library, and unlocked the great chest that stands beside the south window. Here, tumbled in hopeless confusion, lay the fragmentary record of my life—bundles of letters, invitations, love-tokens, half-finished drafts of poems, old bills, journals (I never had the patience to keep one for more than a month or two at a time), the trivia that every woman accumulates, quite unconsciously, and finds a recurring surprise whenever she spring-cleans or moves house. I stooped and prodded into this musty con-fusion of papers, smelling the camphor-wood, the dusty, faded tang of old documents, old emotions, all a dead past. Well, I thought wryly, here's material enough to raise the dead, indeed. And as the words passed silently through my mind, my fingers closed over that old, bat-tered silver locket. I lifted it out and sprang the catch, knowing what I would find, seeing the blue ribbon and the lustrous curl of dark auburn hair through a sudden dazzle of tears. *I loved you once, Atthis, long ago, when my own girlhood was still all flowers*—the heartbreaking awkwardness, thin arms and legs like a colt's, the great grey eyes and the ridiculous dusting of freckles. Atthis, Atthis, my true spring love, what has become of us?

I closed the lid of the chest: the hinges creaked, and fine dust flew up as I turned the heavy key. Tomorrow, I thought, tomorrow I will begin to find the answer. I went back to my bedroom feeling curiously at peace. When I got there my supper was waiting for me on the bed-side table, and my finest Coan nightdress, with the tiny embroidered roses round the yoke, had been laid out for me. It was only then I noticed I was still wearing the bath-robe in which I had fallen asleep.

In the shadow beyond the lamp a slight, timorous figure stood, hands folded, waiting.

"Thalia," I said, and at the note in my voice she stepped forward, breathless—eager, into the light. "Thalia—" And then she was in my arms, sobbing and shaking, her warm, sweet-smelling hair against my cheek, while I stroked and soothed her as though she were some small, frightened animal. I said: "Did Praxinoa send you?" and she nodded, unable to speak, still trembling violently. *A small, ungainly child.* I held her closer, feeling the hardness in my own breast break, loosen, flow free in a warm flood of tears, the deadness quicken, memories crowding my mind, the past of a sudden spring river, lit with unlooked-for sunshine. Tomorrow the search would begin. But tonight, at least, I had a brief, sweet reprieve.

II

I T IS hard—harder than I would have thought—to detach myself from the present. What am I conscious of, at this moment, sitting in my library with the mementoes of the past scattered over the desk in front of me, pen in hand, committed to my voyage of personal discovery? The sound of a cock crowing in the valley below. The thin distant note of a trumpet: the morning watch taking over on the city walls of Mytilene. The taste of the apple I ate for breakfast, the pattern of the small silver fruit-knife I used to peel it. Thalia's smile, the touch of her fingers—gentle still, but firm and confident now—as she combed and braided my hair. The smell of wood-smoke from the kitchen ranges, and of baking bread, and of fresh earth after that brief, violent storm that came whipping against the shutters of my bedroom in the small hours. The touch, the exquisite touch on my skin of clean pleated linen and silk. The sight of sunlight dappling the fig-trees below the terrace.

The beautiful pleasure and agony of the senses. For this there is no time, no sequence of remembered events: only a series of vivid images, caught from time's flow, held and treasured. I walk in the gallery which is my past, pause by this or that picture, smile or sigh, and move on. When I try to recall my earliest childhood what I am most conscious of, always, is sunlight: sunlight everywhere, dancing motes of dust, the lizard iridescent on the wall between gnarled vine-branches, shadows a mere emphasis of universal brightness.

I am in Eresus again, walking through a sea of head-high, whispering green barley, below a sky so intensely blue that all colour seems drained out of it. Or I am perched on a white stone wall, in one of those steep, winding streets below the citadel: looking down I see a huddle of red-tiled roofs, the merchantmen with their brown patched sails riding at anchor, the sea crawling, grape-purple or viridian, round the harbour's embracing arms. Or I am standing with my nurse in one of the great bakeries, where the famous white barley-bread of Eresus is made. There is a smell of dust and flour and chaff; from outside comes a creaking and a grinding, a monotonous nasal dirge as white-powdered, muscular slaves heave at the great quern; and gigantic cats come sidling round me, purring like mountain lions, rubbing themselves against my back and legs. Then the oven door is flung open, the loaves are slid out on a long wooden paddle like a winnowing-fan, and all other smells are eclipsed by the crisp earthy richness of hot bread. My teeth bite into a crust, I see the steam rise from the torn loaf.

Now I am in the walled garden of our house, a little way out of Eresus itself along the coast road. There is a tall pine by the fountain, a favourite haunt for summer cicadas, and in the orchard beyond, apples are reddening. The mountain stream which runs past has dwindled to a mere summer thread among white stones. But the banks are shady with tamarisk, and in my mind's eye I can see a herd of black and white goats concentrated into one small pool of shadow. Across the stream, in our big vineyard, the air is fluid with heat: my eye travels into the mountains, pine-clustered, mysterious, the white dusty road that winds away to the unimaginable world beyond.

Here in the garden it is still and cool: the wind stirs a little in the cypresses, the bees are busy, and the fountain drips, quietly, *drop-drop-drop*, into its green-stained marble basin. When I look up I can see a kite, wings outspread, circling, waiting. From beyond the wall, like sounds heard in dreams, come the *krrk* of a partridge in the corn-field, the bark of a shepherd's dog, the tinkle of goat-bells, the sudden agonized, sawing bray of a donkey. I am lying on sweet-smelling pine-needles, watching the ants scurry to and fro, gleaming black, each with its twig, its seed, its minuscule social burden. Then my mother's voice cuts through this glass bell of stillness, and the pieces shatter, and I am a small, frightened child, jumping up, brushing pine-needles off my dress, ready to face the world of her arbitrary laws and unpredictable commands.

It has taken me a good part of my life to understand just how much my mother and I detested one another. For her, I think, the antipathy began with my conception rather than my birth. She was a fiery, poverty-stricken aristocrat, with an itch for organizing people. She married my father in a fit of political idealism which hardly lasted beyond the honeymoon: *her* ideas on the subject were practical, direct, and (as I can now see) to my father's way of thinking regrettably brutal. My father was a great reader and talker, whose prime aim in life was the evolution, by peaceful and legitimate means, of a benevolent aristocracy—an idea which, perhaps, seemed a little less impractical then than it does now. My mother, I think, secretly hankered after the good old days when Mytilene was ruled by the Penthilid clan, with young bloods going round the streets clubbing the opposition into silence wherever it raised its vulgar head. Not that she had any time for the Penthilids themselves, despite their impressive genealogy: one way and another, she was decidedly hard to please.

At any rate, she must have taken it very hard when Melanchros' seizure of power in Mytilene—backed by the merchants and business-men, who disliked upper-class attitudes to trade—found her not only miles away in Eresus, but also eight months pregnant. The storms and scenes, I am told, were really memorable. My mother spent a good deal of her life under the impression that she could bully or cajole the world into doing what she wanted: but on this occasion at least, nature proved a match for her. She swore at my father for his in-action (though she could hardly have expected him to ride off and depose Melanchros single-handed); she swore at the steward when he brought her the month's bills (she was, among other things, quite extraordinarily close-fisted with money, at least as much on principle as through necessity); she broke a full pitcher of water over the cook's head after some idiotic argument about pepper; and she insisted on picking olives—to show the slaves how slow they were, she said—the day before her confinement. The result, of course, was an extremely difficult birth, which took far longer than it should have done and broke even my mother's iron will.

Some of this I pieced together, years later, from Praxinoa, who had known the midwife and had got the whole story out of her before she died. But there was not much I needed to be told. Only that my mother had, at last, thrown her self-control to the winds and screamed, screamed, screamed as though she would never stop. For that alone she can never have forgiven me. That I was born a girl rather than a boy, small and puny, bruised by my mother's tormented struggle with her own body—all this must have paled into insignificance beside the shame of her surrender to pain. Yet she felt obscure guilt, too, of the inner, corroding kind that is never openly expressed: guilt that I was so small, so swarthy (as though this had been willed by her in the womb), guilt at her own hatred and resentment, guilt that she had borne me at all, and thus proved herself human, fallible, subject to the common frailty of her sex. My dogged, unbreakable love for her must have been maddening almost past belief.

Morning broke ominously today, with long ribbons of scarlet-shot grey cloud on the horizon: while I was writing the wind got up again, and rain came whipping down in silver gusts through the orchard. A high sea, white crests driving on the rocks. Where will he be now? Past Andros and Euboea: that much is certain. Looking out at the bleak, black-charged sky, with its threat of autumn storms to come, I find my mind turning to the grim challenge he must soon face: the long haul south of Cape Malea, across those treacherous, deceptive-quiet, reef-strewn wastes of water, where in a few moments murderous gales can spring up, even on the clearest, calmest day. Poseidon, great Lord of the Waters, be merciful to him: grant him a peaceful passage and safe landfall, all that his heart desires.

I obstinately (but understandably) continue to think of my father as a very tall man. In fact he was of middle height, it seems, and slightly built. He wore his thick, fair hair rather longer than was fashionable, even in those days, and passed for something of a dandy. When I try to picture him I remember three things above all: the brilliant clarity of his grey eyes, the length and delicacy of his fingers (surprisingly white in so sunburnt a man) and the sweet smell I caught from his beard when he kissed me, a smell of violets and something else, something I could not identify.
He was always very gentle with me: even at that age I could sense the difference in character between him and my mother. He seldom raised his voice, and never, so far as I know, lost his temper— least of all during one of my mother's incandescent tirades, when he would become steadily quieter, more reasonable, more patient, the longer the scene lasted. Once I thought this an admirable trait: now I am not so sure. The portrait of him that hangs before me as I write shows a handsome young man, with a dreamer's eyes: but there is something elusive and irresolute about the mouth, and I cannot, I must confess, look at the picture for long without experiencing a vague uneasiness. There is (as I am at last coming to realize)

[25]

more of my mother in me than I ever supposed: I can see now, dimly, what lay behind those storms and tantrums and bursts of violent aggression. For the first time in my life, the thought of her stirs me to compassion rather than hatred or resentment.

If Pittacus were alive still he could tell me so much about those days. If he wanted to. Or if he decided, for once, that the truth might be more amusing than his aphoristic half-lies and Nestorian platitudes. Truth lies at the bottom of a well. And there *is* the well, the image springs unbidden to my mind, that deep wide well with the stone coping and moss-stained wooden shutter, under the big plane-tree beyond the kitchens. Close by—yes—there is the hen-run, and two of our dogs are somewhere, on the midden perhaps, fighting over scraps. A midsummer afternoon, with the sunlight slanting down into those green mysterious depths, a wavering reflected disc of light below me, my head and shoulders silhouetted on its surface.

Then—I remember—as I gazed down, lost in my green dream, another head appeared beside mine, and for an instant I froze, my two worlds in collision. Slowly I straightened up, blinking. Another little girl was standing there: a gangling, leggy seven-year-old with freckles and short, boyish hair. Her hands were scratched and filthy, and her dress had a badly mended tear in it.

"Hullo," she said. "Didn't hear me, did you?"

I shook my head.

"I could have pushed you in, you know." She sounded very matter-of-fact about it. "I'm a Thracian scout. Papa says never trust Thracian scouts, they'll knife you in the back for a week's pay. What's your name?"

I told her. She had odd hazel eyes, not quite matching: one glinted green in certain lights, the other could pass for brown.

"I'm Andromeda." She put out her grubby hand and clasped mine firmly. "How old are you?"

"Five. Nearly six."

"I'm seven." She pulled her hand away—I hadn't been quite sure what I was meant to do with it—and scratched her short black curls vigorously. "What do you like playing?"

This question took me unawares. The truth of the matter was that I played almost entirely by myself: Charaxus, at three, was too young to play with, Eurygyus was only one, and my mother did not encourage neighbouring parents to let their offspring loose in our gardens. The idea of venturing outside on my own had simply never occurred to me.

[26]

"I don't know," I said lamely. "Just playing."

"Not much fun hanging over a well," Andromeda said. "Pooh, it smells. Did someone die down there?" When it became clear this question was going to remain unanswered, she picked up a stone and shied it, with remarkable force and accuracy, at our big rooster, who was sunning himself in the back yard. He gave an outraged squawk, and vanished. I was impressed, despite myself.

"Who taught you to do that?" I asked.

"Papa, of course."

"Oh." It occurred to me that this was not something I was likely to learn from my own father.

"Come on," said Andromeda, tugging at my arm, "let's go out."

"Out? Where?"

"Down to the sea, of course."

"But—" I was about to say I wasn't allowed out, and then decided this would sound rather silly. "They might see us."

They.

"Oh no they won't. Papa's very busy talking to your mother and father indoors. We can slip out the back way."

"All right," I said, weakly, and we did. We paddled, and climbed rocks, and threw stones at a piece of driftwood that Andromeda said was an enemy ship. She hit it nearly every time.

"I wish I was a boy," she said.

"Why?"

"More fun. Besides, girls can't fight."

"Do you *want* to fight?" I asked. We were lying side by side on the sand, in the shadow of a big rock, both temporarily exhausted: it was very hot indeed.

"Yes," she said, and her visible eye glowed green, as though someone had put a pinch of salt in the flames. "Of *course* I want to fight. Don't you?"

"No. No, I don't."

"Oh well," Andromeda said magnanimously, "you're only five." But she sounded disappointed.

"What sort of fighting, anyway?" I asked.

"Here. On the island. We're going to kill the other side in Mytilene. You mustn't tell a soul. It's a deadly secret."

"How do *you* know?"

"I overheard Papa one day." Andromeda giggled. "I hid in a cupboard."

This really left me speechless.

[27]

"Then I had to sneeze, and of course Papa heard. He was so cross, you wouldn't believe. He beat me half silly, right in front of all those men. Then he made me swear I'd never tell anyone—"

"But—"

"Oh, you're different. You don't count. I mean, your Papa's in the secret too."

For a moment the world seemed to stop. The white, heat-drained sky hung over me, huge, menacing. I felt sick with fear. When I tried to get up, everything wheeled round me. I swallowed, staggered, put out one hand to steady myself. Andromeda stared at me.

"Feeling all right?" she asked. I nodded. How could I explain? The idea of my father being involved in any sort of violence, let alone killing people, was unthinkable. And where there was killing—no, no, *no*. "We'd better get back," I said. "They'll miss us."

"All right." She sounded suddenly bored, indifferent.

But when we slipped in cautiously through the garden-gate my mother and father were both there, strolling to and fro under the shade of the great pine-tree beside the fountain, and with them another man, a burly, broad-shouldered, muscular, bearded giant whose bellowing laugh echoed through the garden.

"That's Papa," Andromeda whispered. We looked at each other. I felt terrified.

"Do you think they've missed us?" I whispered.

"Sure to have," Andromeda said cheerfully.

"Oh dear—"

And at that moment they saw us. The strange man seemed to take in the situation, with all its implications, at once. He looked from us to my parents and back again. Then he strode across and scooped up Andromeda, with a bearlike hug and a ringing smack on the bottom. She shrieked with pain and delight, and wriggled on to his shoulders.

"So you two have made friends, I see," he said. Close to, he was enormous, with thick black hair on his legs and forearms, and a wide, flat nose like a boxer's. He was sweating heavily and smelt of stale wine.

My mother came forward, bristling. But all she said was: "The child's a problem. You can see that for yourself."

The man ignored this remark completely. He said: "Cleïs, would you mind introducing me to this charming young lady?"

"Who—what—oh, you're *impossible*," my mother protested; but there was a warm, teasing note in her voice I had never heard before.

[28]

With her strong, sculptured features and high complexion she was always a striking woman: now suddenly she looked beautiful as well.

"This is my daughter Sappho," she said.

The giant put out one huge hand and enfolded mine very gently.

"I hope for your better acquaintance," he said, and twinkled. "If you take after your mother, I shall have to walk warily with you." (In after years I was to remember that phrase with a certain ironic relish.) From her perch on his shoulders Andromeda grinned at me conspiratorially.

My mother said, with a flash of her normal spirit: "I can't think what the nurse was doing, letting them run loose like that—"

"Now, Cleïs, love," said the giant, "you're not to waste that splendid temper of yours on wretched house-slaves. Save a bit of it for those who appreciate you."

There was a faint burr to his voice, a rough edge that teased and eluded me. Even at five I had an incoherent feeling that his alien accent, his hairiness, the general impression of coarse, perspiring vigour, added up to what my mild-mannered father would describe as "not quite a gentleman"—his most positive term of condemnation.

"What's your name?" I blurted out, quite forgetting my manners; Andromeda must have had more effect on me than I knew.

The giant grinned. "My name," he said, as though to an equal, "is Pittacus. Rather outlandish, don't you think? They know it better in Thrace than on this island."

"But that," said my father drily, "will soon be remedied." He had been standing by, very silent and watchful, during this little exchange, his eyes on each of us in turn. The three of them exchanged quick glances.

"Well, now," Pittacus said, "we must be on our way. We've a long ride ahead of us."

"But I thought you'd stay the night," my mother said: you could almost see the colour and sparkle draining out of her. "Oh, Pittacus— you've only just come, and in the heat of the day—your horse is done in—and think of the child—"

"Andromeda," said Pittacus, "is a glutton for punishment: she makes me feel positively self-indulgent sometimes." He glanced up. "Well, poppet: can you face another long ride today?"

She nodded vigorously. The greenish glint showed in her right eye; there was a secretive, adult quality about her that I found most disconcerting.

"That's that, then," said Pittacus. "I'm sorry, Cleïs"—he took both her hands as he spoke—"I really am. But one way and another it's advisable, you know. Until—" He left the sentence in mid-air.

"Until what?" I asked, innocent-curious.

"Until—next year," he said, and grinned. "Next year we'll all come, and you can play with Andromeda as much as you like. You might teach her to read while you're at it; your mother's been telling me what a prodigy you are."

I flushed with vexation and embarrassment. "All right," I said awkwardly.

"In any case," Pittacus said, "you may be coming to Mytilene before then. How would you like that?"

"To live, you mean?" I turned to my father, who nodded. "If all goes well," he said.

"But I don't *want* to live in Mytilene," I said in dismay. "I want to stay here."

They all laughed, and Andromeda loudest of all. Then we walked through to the stables, and a groom brought out Pittacus' big, stocky black stallion with the white blaze on its nose, and he swung himself easily into the saddle, his hands gathering up the reins as though they were an extension of himself, and he part of the horse. The sun was behind him over the stable roof, filtered through the leaves of the plane-tree, and for a moment he looked like a centaur. I had never seen a centaur, but I knew this was how they must be.

He settled Andromeda in front of him, shook hands with my mother —a little more formally than I had expected—and then turned to me.

"Good-bye, Sappho," he said. "We shall be good friends, you and I and Andromeda."

He was Chiron, the wise Chiron.

"Good-bye, Chiron," I said breathlessly.

He paused, and looked at me in a way I have never forgotten.

"I accept the compliment," he said, "and the omen. Thank you, my dear." He spoke as to an equal. I remember thinking, in a puzzled way, But I should be *afraid* of this man. He's going to kill people. He wants to make Papa kill people. Why *doesn't* he frighten me? Yet all I could feel was the sheer comforting warmth of his presence.

Looking back, from my own middle age, on his extraordinary subsequent career, I think a good measure of the success he achieved can be attributed to that almost physical sense of strength and security which radiated from his presence. People *wanted* to trust him; they could not help themselves. Besides, when this first meeting of ours took place he was still a year or two under thirty, and had not yet developed those exaggerated tricks of speech and behaviour which his enemies were so quick to pick on when they wanted to ridicule him.

"Good-bye, Scamandronymus," he said gravely to my father. "Till our next meeting." (And that was oddly formal, too, because hardly anyone, except on official occasions or at first introduction, called my father anything but Scamon—the accepted, traditional abbreviation of his really tongue-twisting name.) Then Pittacus was gone, with a clatter of hooves and a raised hand, galloping eastward, the sun slanting behind him, into the thyme-patched gorges where rocks rear like angry purple Titans, along the mountain track that sidles down, eagle-haunted, to the smooth waters of the inland gulf. Andromeda and I waved at one another till we were out of sight.

Odd, how of all the crowding small complexities and incidents that filled my childhood, I remember that scene so clearly. It may be that I have given it fresh colours in retrospect, as an artist will discreetly touch up some cracked and fading mural. But I do not think so. Even then I had—perhaps more continually than in later years—that blinding intensity of vision in which every separate leaf, twig, pebble, dew-drop, blade of grass, the play of sunlight on water, the springing pelt of a stroked cat, thin, liquid music heard on a summer hillside— lark or shepherd's flute—the dazzling intricate miracle of a single spring flower: all impressed themselves on my senses with such intensity that often the awareness became agony rather than joy, I had to shut my eyes and stop my ears to the endless, radiant clamorous assault of the world about me.

A stone washed white and smooth by the river, a bird perched singing in a transient scatter of pink almond-blossom, the smell of wood-smoke in autumn, the winds that thunder down like great winged beasts from the mountains—each of these has a share in the divine. I remember Thales once saying that the mind of the world is god, that all things have an inner soul, that spirits are everywhere. I think I knew this before I had words to express it. Nature moves towards epiphanies: behind the pattern of honeycomb or frost-flower, revelation waits.

When Pittacus had gone, my mother's mood changed again. She was warm and affectionate towards my father for the rest of the day, touching him (a thing she never ordinarily did in public) and relaxing into a shared intimacy which I found so odd as to be a little ominous.

[31]

Looking back, it is easy—too easy, perhaps—to find an explanation for her behaviour. Pittacus can only have come to sound out my father as a possible supporter against Melanchros in Mytilene; and my father had agreed—or had been talked into agreeing, which could be regarded as the same thing.

Since the only possible way of removing Melanchros was by a carefully-planned armed attack, my father now counted, in my mother's eyes, as a man of action by anticipation, a conspirator in embryo. Perhaps this is unduly cynical of me: but it remains a fact that, a month later, my mother became pregnant for the fourth time, having previously—in her usual forthright manner—announced that she had better things to do with the rest of her active life than bear more useless children.

This morning, miraculously, summer returned, with clear skies and only the faintest sketching of clouds out over the Aegean. I could not bear to stay indoors, and walked up across the headland alone: in this mood I did not want even Praxinoa with me. Life is so unbearably short; we hover momentarily in its radiance like a mayfly, or the bubbles of some mountain stream. The sun lay warm on the scattered grey stones beside my path; there was a smell of thyme in the air, and on a distant hillside the rusty sheep moved with quiet contentment, jingling their bells. I wanted to stamp every detail on my memory—the white frill of foam round the rocks below me; the startled, questioning eye of a hare as it rose from its form at my approach and went scampering up into the pine-woods; the brown, bellying sail of a merchant-man, labouring south-west to Chios; the chick-peas blowing golden along the shore. For the first time in over a month I felt the small, intense excitement of a new poem shaping itself.

But the mood could not be sustained and evaporated with the writing of the poem—which proved a pale ghost only of the experience I had hoped to catch. Now I sit by lamp-light, hidden, secretive, feeding on memories, the shutters drawn to behind me. I walk by the mind's deep green pools softly, and far below the great fish stir, moving in slow gyrations surfacewards. As they rise I feel fear. I have always lived so intensely in the present, and now my yesterdays are coming back to torment me, with their evanescent heartbreaks and illusory delights. I cannot call up the past, because it has never died: it lives with me, silent, stalking unobtrusively behind my shadow, biding its moment. Which, at last, has come.

When I returned from my walk there was a sealed package waiting for me on my writing-desk. By the blobbed, botched waxing, and the deep impression of the big signet ring, I knew it must be from Charaxus. I opened it up. It contained the cancelled mortgage deed to my property, a bundle of receipts from the various merchants and shop-keepers to whom I was in debt, and a small linen bag—also sealed—neatly packed with fifty mint-new silver staters. There was also a brief covering note which read: "I hope the agreed enclosures are to your satisfaction. C." Nothing else. I looked through the receipts: he had not missed a single debt. My practical, efficient, intolerable brother. What summer madness, I wonder, suddenly blew *him*, of all people, into that exotic Egyptian harbour? Was it the same wind I knew too well, the wind from a clear sky, burning, burning, was it the same for him? Could he feel what I feel? That toad-face, that gross white body. The laughter of Aphrodite.

The messenger came on a windy morning in early spring, the blown almond-blossom scattering under his horse's hooves; and my father was up and away, grim-faced, silent, his sword and armour safely stowed on a pack-horse, gone almost before he could say good-bye. Silence descended on the house: his absence was everywhere. Charaxus and Eurygyus played quietly; even my mother, now heavily pregnant, seemed somehow less vital. It was almost as though she were afraid. The house brooded, waiting, desperate for news.

It was four days before word finally came from Mytilene. Melanchros had fallen, the Council of Nobles was restored, freedom and justice reigned once more, the messenger told my mother, gabbling the phrases off as though he had learnt them by heart, his nervous, side-slipping expression very much at odds with his words. Melanchros himself was dead. His deputy-governor, Myrsilus, together with some two dozen of his more influential supporters, had been deported to the mainland. Pittacus, by unanimous election, was now a member of the Council—

He broke off at this point: my mother's expression, in certain moods, was enough to freeze a professional speech-maker just before his grand peroration. I was standing close beside her in the court-yard, clinging in sudden fear to her skirt, and I felt her consciously steel herself as she said: "And my husband?"

The messenger blinked and cleared his throat. He had a thin, goatish beard and an over-prominent nose. "Your husband, my lady,

[33]

conducted himself with most conspicuous gallantry. It was by his hand that the tyrant was slain. Unfortunately—"

"Yes?" said my mother. The monosyllable fell into the silence like a stone.

"Unfortunately, before help could reach him, he was cut down himself. He died a hero's death, my lady."

"Yes," said my mother again, in the same flat, toneless voice.

"Is there anything I can—?"

"No. Wait. Yes, there is. You can take a message to Pittacus, son of Hyrrhas. Tell him that when his duties in Council permit, I should be grateful for a written account of how my husband met his death."

Their eyes met.

"Very well, my lady." He cleared his throat again, and added: "The body will be escorted to Eresus with full military honours for burial—"

"As soon as the situation in the city permits. Correct?"

"Yes, my lady."

My mother let out a long breath. "Go to the kitchens," she said. "They will give you a meal, and see to your horse." Then she took my hand and went inside, without a backward glance. Not then, nor at the funeral, nor ever (to my knowledge) did she give any open signs of grief.

Years afterwards, during our exile at Pyrrha, I asked Antimenidas just how my father had died. He looked at me thoughtfully, black eyes searching mine. He said, weighing his words: "Your father wanted to die."

"How can you say that? How dare you say that?"

He shrugged, his long, craggy, prematurely lined face full of weary compassion.

"Melanchros had to be killed. There was no other way. Lop off the head of a tyranny, and the body withers." He was silent for a moment, staring into the flames of the great log fire: winter in Pyrrha can be deadly cold, and that year snow lay thick on the ground. "But Melanchros was well guarded. We couldn't risk a pitched battle, there weren't enough of us. One man must do it, we decided—"

"My father."

"Yes, your father." Antimenidas looked up at me sharply. "You think it was all arranged, don't you? That Pittacus chose him for the job, long before?"

I said: "Whoever did it was certain to be killed. He had no chance. No chance at all."

"Just so."

There was another silence.

"Pittacus told me my father volunteered," I said.

"He not only volunteered; he insisted. I have never in my life seen any man so bent on glorious self-destruction."

"What do you mean?"

He smiled bitterly. "Look," he said, "there were at least two excellent reasons why your father was so anxious to put himself out of the way. One of them was no secret: he'd so mismanaged his patrimony he was virtually bankrupt."

"Yes. But—"

"Curious, wasn't it, the way your mother let things get into such a state? No one could accuse *her* of being impractical."

"No."

"The role of heroic political widowhood suits her rather well, wouldn't you say? And of course, there's the state pension."

I said, with real bitterness: "We still had to sell the house at Eresus."

"Ah. So *that's* what was bothering you. Everyone has their own private selfishness, if you look hard enough for it. But really, my dear, life in Mytilene has transformed you: you ought to be grateful. Think what a dull provincial butterfly you might have become out in the back of beyond."

He kicked at the fire with his heavy, booted foot: a glowing log tumbled sideways, and a shower of sparks fanned up from the iron basket. Outside, in the kitchen, my mother was remonstrating with our new slave-girl as though she were a fractious horse. (Normally this drove scullery-maids sulky-mad, but in the present case it worked rather well: we had got the poor creature cheap because she was a semi-imbecile and roughly on a horse's level of intelligence.) Antimenidas and I exchanged glances.

I said: "My father was a brave man, and I loved him more than I can say."

"Oh Sappho, you're so obtuse when you want to be. I'm sorry for your father. I really am. He was a decent, harmless, civilized idealist: all he asked for was to be left alone to work things out in peace. But your mother was determined he had to be a death-or-glory hero—she saw herself playing Andromache to his Hector, I fancy: there's a strong romantic streak under that tough exterior.

[35]

Don't look so shocked; you'd have been just as bad if he'd lived."

"*If?*"

"Yes indeed: you were all set to treat him as Zeus and Apollo rolled into one, a golden god on Olympus: how can any man live up to such expectations? Your father killed himself, quite literally, to be what his family wanted."

"I think this conversation has gone quite far enough, Antimenidas."

He rose to his feet and wrapped the great sheepskin about his shoulders: there was something fierce, almost alien about him, the fur cap, the leggings, the studded sword-belt.

"I never contradict a lady; much less a lady-poet." He grinned. "If it's stopped snowing I shall cut down a small tree to work up an appetite for dinner. If there is any dinner. By now my brother will have drunk what's left of the wine, let the fire go out, and written three verses of an exquisitely dismal poem on the miseries of exile."

I laughed despite myself.

"Ah," said Antimenidas, with his hand on the door, "that's more like it. This curious illusion you have that you're a delicate, sensitive creature too refined for the rough-and-tumble of ordinary life. You're tougher than any of us, really, Sappho: it's never once occurred to you that you can't, in the long run, get exactly what you want. You're a ravening harpy, and I'm sorry for any man who's fool enough to marry you."

Then he was gone, in a whirl of snow and a sudden blast of chill air. I huddled closer to the fire, hands clasped round my knees, seeing the pictures form and dissolve, red to grey ash, among the calcined logs.

But for me that first shock of aching loss was an end as well as a beginning. Something died in me, a slow glaucous mist descended and thickened over my mind's most private places. When my mother told me we would have to sell our house, and move to Mytilene, and live with Uncle Eurygyus and Aunt Helen, I accepted the news as I would have accepted any other brute convulsion of the established order: nothing was safe or solid now, the foundations could crack at any time, the world was a paper lantern, perilously alight.

The slow, sensuous beauty of that dreadful spring mocked me night and day: the nightingale pouring out its liquid passion in the great pine-tree, the late-flowering jonquils and anemones on the hillside, the rich smell of the gorse in bloom, yellow as scrambled eggs, up the gorge where the spring river tumbled seawards. I leaned over the well and saw nothing but emptiness: dank, flat water, clinging weeds. The headland at sunset crouched with its paws in the water, a mountain lion, jaws bloodied after the kill. Some part of me was physically numbed, incapable of sensation or response.

So, one bright morning, with tiny white clouds scudding away to the south over Chios, we went aboard a big coastal merchant-man and left Eresus behind us for ever. There was a choppy sea running: the vessel dipped and rolled, tackle creaking, the wind thunderous in its great patched sail. I leant over the side as we beat eastward along the coast, and looked back, beyond our wake, to the high white citadel, the red tumbled roofs, the fields of spring barley, the dusty road with its scatter of tree-grown estates—all familiar as my own body, the only map I had ever learnt. My eyes dazzled as I looked, and there was a salty taste on my lips: though whether from tears, or flying spray, or both, I never knew.

III

I SUPPOSE I have closer ties with Mytilene than with any other place known to me—closer, certainly, and more plangent than the world-out-of-time memories I preserve from my Sicilian exile, closer even than the special nostalgia which Eresus can still arouse in me when I think back to my earliest childhood. After all, it is in Mytilene that the greater part of my life has been spent: first in the great square grey house on the citadel (once my uncle's property, now occupied—though his right of tenure seems dubious, to say the least of it—by my brother Charaxus); and afterwards here, outside the city, in the old, comfortable, converted farmhouse which Cercylas bought me as a wedding-present, and where these words are being written.

I know the city's moods and seasons, its old landed families (arrogant, charming, eccentric, drunken, or merely dull), its ambitious middle-class merchants, its peacocking women, and its predatory toughs. I know its scandals, its festivals, its moments of splendid and irresponsible gaiety; its elegiac autumns, and its lyric springs, when flowers and young girls blossom with the same frail, transient, heart-wringing beauty. There is a quality of tight-knit excitement about it I have never experienced anywhere else: one finds a bright edge to one's relationships here, each day holds promise of immense discoveries. Everything is clear, new, fresh-coloured. Words explode like seed-pods, scattering life. Winter brings exhilaration and self-knowledge, summer is tremulous with unanticipated desires. Memory stirs in a pattern of sunlight.

Writing these words, I see how little the years have changed me. As I pause, pen in hand, and stare out towards the blue coastline of Ionia, I am a girl of fourteen again: very nervous and defensive (which for me means aggressive) because I have just been introduced to a young man of decidedly dubious reputation. I have known about him for several years, but this is the first time we have been allowed to meet. The room is crowded: one of my mother's social gatherings, with discreet political undertones.

The young man is, I find, a problem. He has obviously taken a little more wine than is good for him, though not enough to make him a public nuisance. He has cold, amused grey eyes which give the impression of seeing right through me. He is also quite frighteningly hairy, bearded to the points of his cheek-bones, the backs of his hands bristling like a boar's hide. He has already made an impressive reputation as a poet (which is the main reason why I am anxious to meet him), and is notorious for other less respectable pursuits, which my mother thinks I am too young to be told about. (I am not—though I remain blissfully ignorant of their implications.)

There is one story, however, which everyone knows about him, and which produces an interesting variety of reactions according to the age, sex, class and moral outlook of the individual concerned. During the campaign in the Troad, two or three years previously, the young man—his name is Alcaeus, and he comes from an old and much respected aristocratic family—ran away in battle. Not content with that, he wrote a comic quatrain about his disgraceful behaviour to a friend in Mytilene, telling how he had thrown away his shield and the Athenians had hung it up in their temple as a trophy, but, praise be, *he* was still alive and unharmed. When he came home he seemed quite unembarrassed by the whole episode.

He has a light, drawling, rather metallic voice: drink does not slur it. He looks me up and down in a subtly objectionable way, as though undressing me without desire.

"Your mother"—I hear the intonations so clearly it is almost as though he were in the room beside me as I write—"your mother has been giving me a *very* detailed account of your precocious, rare, and inimitable poetic talent."

"Oh. I'm sorry." I feel my cheeks burn, knowing what this means, hating my mother, hating myself for hating her, hating this steely and objectionable young man for being in a position to patronize me.

"Please don't apologize. It was quite fascinating."

I blush and stammer. "I've w-wanted to meet you for a very long time." Idiot platitudes. Oh, *go away.* Please. You make me so miserable.

"Well," he says, smiling, "how pleasant to be sought after. If only for one's scandal-value."

Surprising myself, I blurt out: "You don't like me, do you?"

He considers, head tilted. "No. Not much."

"Why?"

Again the hesitation. "Perhaps our temperaments are too alike."

I suspect him of teasing me, and at once move in to the attack. "Did you really run away?"

"I was waiting for you to ask that. Yes, of course I did."

"Why?"

"Very simple: I should quite certainly have been killed if I hadn't."

"Are you afraid of being killed?"

"Of course. So is every man. You must not confuse courage with lack of imagination."

"But not every man runs away."

He sighs wearily. "We only have one life to spend—or to waste. I had no intention of squandering mine in a ridiculous war about some useless stretch of land in the Troad."

"Then what *do* you think is worth fighting for?"

He grins: I fancy I detect a mild note of embarrassment as he says: "You'd better read my poems. I'll send you a copy. You'll find them very different from your own, I fear."

"How can you be so certain?"

"Because"—the grey eyes glint with gentle malice—"your mother was kind enough to show me some of them."

"*What?* Oh no—"

"My dear girl, you really *mustn't* be so ashamed of your greatest gift; that's a luxury you aren't in any position to afford."

"Greatest gift?" I repeat stupidly, not yet taking in what he means.

"Heaven give me patience. Your *poetry.* You have a quite extraordinary talent, didn't you realize?"

"Please—you don't mean it—"

"Indeed I do. What astonishes me is the way a pure talent like yours can sprout from such unlikely soil. Your mind is a really grisly mixture of stupidity, stubbornness, self-satisfaction, credulity, and plain ignorance. You thrive on noble platitudes. You're so preoccupied with your own emotions that you can't begin to understand other people; and for that matter you don't seem to understand yourself."

"I'm not interested in *people,* anyway." (No one has ever spoken to me like this in my life. I don't know whether to be flattered or insulted: as a result I merely flounder. But his final words touch a raw nerve.)

"So I observe. But when you write about rivers, or apple-trees, or the moon, you're really writing about yourself, aren't you? You see summer as the sum of your own dreams."

Intrigued despite myself, I say: "And how do *you* see it?"

"Dusty. Thirsty. Endless chirring of cicadas. Flowering artichokes. Randy women and exhausted men."

Now I see my chance. "You forgot the Dog-Star. Hesiod had a bit about the Dog-Star."

He grins cheerfully: almost, one feels, he enjoys being found out. "I see your literary education hasn't been neglected," he says. "That's something, I suppose."

"At least *my* poems are my own, not other people's." (Insufferable adolescent smugness.)

"You haven't read mine yet."

"I bet I'll find one like that, though."

"Of course."

It is really impossible to be angry with him for long.

You see summer as the sum of your own dreams. It was true, of course; and nearly forty years later it is still true. Our ability to change, to impose new patterns on our lives by will and choice, is not nearly so great as we suppose. The Fates control us from birth, we say, not really believing it; we hang by the thread of our destiny. Yet these commonplace phrases contain a literal, unlooked-for truth. For half a lifetime or more we are allowed to enjoy an illusive freedom: then comes the twitch on the thread, and we jerk like puppets, obedient, mindless.

So it is with me. Desire remains more constant than its object. I am, still, what I was, inescapably chained to the rock of my passions and beliefs. In that child, that girl, all my future was contained, infolded like the flower within the seed. Alcaeus, too, is caught in the same web of necessity, and when I see him today I am stung to pity: he, too, was foredoomed. What he has become is what he always was. Perhaps the priest, peering at heart and liver for a sign of the future, is expressing a truth more literal than we suppose.

[41]

Any mention of priests, omens, predictions, astrology, or magic at once sends my mind back to Uncle Eurygyus, who was, I think, the most superstitious man I have ever known. We shared the house on the citadel with him for six years (he died when I was twelve) and my memory of that period is littered with amulets and nasty-smelling herbs and stale incense and curious gibberish-prayers in foreign languages.

There was always some new tame prophet slinking about the place, too, an Egyptian or a Persian or a Syrian: one of them left rapidly with the silver candelabra, another after trying to rape Aunt Helen (though we only had her word for this), while a third went splendidly mad in the middle of dinner, rolling about and foaming at the mouth, much to the delight of us children, who by now were hardened to such extravagant demonstrations of religious enthusiasm, and appreciated a good fit when we saw one.

A walk with Uncle Eurygyus was something of an ordeal. Before he could so much as leave the house he had to wash, with much ritual splashing, in water specially fetched from a sacred spring two miles outside the city walls. He also kept a piece of bay-leaf in his mouth: as he was an excitable and spluttering talker, he frequently lost it, and this meant we had to go straight home again. The same thing happened, more often than not, if we met a cat; but as the town was swarming with them, my uncle would accasionally com-promise by throwing three pebbles across the street, over his left shoulder. Once or twice he hit a passer-by: if it was a stranger there might be trouble, but most local residents knew about his habits and ducked. If there were no cats in sight he would peer up into the sky (he was dreadfully short-sighted) to see what omens he could deduce from passing birds. As the house faced due east, he practically never went out during the winter migrations.

I have often wondered, looking back, just what was going on in Aunt Helen's mind when she agreed to marry him. He was a decent, kindly, amiable man, well-connected and reasonably well-off, with no apparent vices except for this fiddling excess of piety: but not, somehow, the husband one would have expected Aunt Helen to choose. As Antimenidas once said to me, it was like an eagle mating with an owl. For Aunt Helen the simile is a peculiarly apt one: those great topaz-coloured eyes, that aquiline nose, that proud, poised head all suggested some royal and predatory bird. She was tall and dark, high-breasted, with quick movements, seldom in repose: a sense of latent energy pervaded her most casual gestures, her hair sparked and crackled when a comb was drawn through it. She affected a chaste, severe style (central parting, chignon, plain linen dresses) that was at piquant variance with her sensuous personality.

Aunt Helen was twenty-nine when I first met her. In eleven years of marriage she had borne four children and still managed to retain a lithe, elegant, dancer's figure. Uncle Eurygyus was considerably older than his wife. I have worked out that he must have been forty-three at the time we left Eresus; but to a child he looked immeasurably ancient, a tall, thin, wrinkled man with sparse hair and a permanent stoop. They were both on the quayside at Mytilene to meet us, and I shall never forget the expression of sheer horror that came over my uncle's face when he saw that my mother was eight months pregnant. He hastily spat in the fold of his robe, and made a finger-and-thumb gesture which (I knew from my nurse) was designed to avert the evil eye.

Aunt Helen picked me up and kissed me. She smelt beautiful: warm, alive, with a faint aroma of some scent I could not then recognize, but later knew to be verbena. There was an unexpected impulsiveness about her physical gestures. I rubbed my cheek against hers, suddenly at peace, and felt her quick, instinctive response. Then I was on my feet again, with the crowd round me (tallymen, grain-chandlers, porters with crates of plums and dried figs, sailors, merchants' clerks, the inevitable crowd that gathers when a ship docks), trying to take my bearings in this strange new world.

Smell of tar and fish. The great stone quay of Mytilene, and green mountains behind. A canal with worn wooden bridges, tall houses, the masts and spars of countless ships. Everywhere hurry and bustle, the smell of frying food. Hawsers coiled on the cobbles, drays rattling past, rows of wine-jars and oil-jars, each with its heavy lead seal. The frenzied clatter and squawk of cooped chickens, unmilked cows lowing in their pens. Everything bigger, noisier, more intense than the world I had left behind.

Long familiarity has not dulled that first brief, vivid impression: if I shut my eyes now, I see, not the new modern harbour with its dockyards and hoists and resplendent marble-faced buildings, but the old port of forty-odd years back: vigorous enough, but patched, casual, shabby. A different world. I have lived through a revolution in more senses than one, and Alcaeus—a grizzled, drifting toper now, plotting in taverns, fumbling contemptuous boys over his wine—is not its only victim. Perhaps Aunt Helen, still, in her mid-seventies, magnificently alive, understood the truth better than any of us;

though there were other, crueller words found for what she did, what she was.

And is. Time crumbles the shell of us, scores and corrodes the outer surface; but the inner self remains intact. I see that scene on the quay: time stops for me, the figures freeze motionless, like the flies in amber hawked from house to house by Thracian pedlars. Now my mother is dead, and Aunt Helen a fiery recluse, her very name a stock joke for the lampoonists; and Uncle Eurygyus' superstitious habits are only remembered as a fast-fading family legend. Now I sit at my desk, as the afternoon light fades; memory-racked, searching, eye caught and held by the delicate convolution of veins on my free hand—and then by the smouldering golden glow of the great snake-ring, which will not change, or tarnish, or be corrupted. Now or ever.

When my mother died, she left me, among other things, a locked iron strong-box containing her personal papers. I have sometimes wondered whether she destroyed any of the more interesting or self-revelatory ones before her death: on the whole I am inclined to think not. Such posthumous reticence would have been very out of character. For instance, there is abundant evidence (from her journal in particular) that my mother was, at one period, passionately in love with Pittacus; but there is nothing which suggests that she ever revealed this passion to Pittacus himself, let alone became his mistress. Knowing her private romanticism no less than her more obvious forthrightness, I regard it as far more likely that she did, in fact, nurse an undeclared love than that she destroyed all evidence of an illicit affair when it was over.

No; the gesture was, at one and the same time, an admission of our failure to understand one another while we both lived, and a pathetic attempt to mend matters in the only way she knew. There was something so deep and instinctive about the dislike I aroused in my mother that it effectively precluded any kind of normal relationship. Every simple attempt at communication was distorted, if not destroyed, by the violence of emotion which mere contact between us aroused.

I think my mother knew this in her heart; I think she knew, too, that much of her resentment was due to the fundamental resemblance between our characters. One of the most curious discoveries I made when I went through that strong-box was a bundle of poems she had written. They were very bad poems, either over-sentimental or full of ringing political platitudes; but they revealed a side of her I had never really suspected. How she must have hated, envied, and (in some strange way) *lived through* me!

Alcaeus once said that anger is the last passion to die in a man, and it is certainly true of him. Perhaps, after so many years, the hard knot of unacknowledged hatred I felt for my mother has been finally purged. Knowing that, I can see how much of her own bitterness was due to self-reproach, for (as she believed) having borne a daughter who was not only small, dark, and unattractive, but also in some way physically malformed (though this I am not, unless tiny, delicate bones be counted a deformity). What odd, secret guilt did that conviction of hers represent?

It is strange to compare my mother's impressions of those first days in Mytilene with my own childish memories:

". . . Settled in at last, though how long I'll be able to stand this madhouse I don't know. Helen is *impossible*—a mixture of all the worst vices produced by inbreeding: selfish, arrogant, patronizing, with (if half what one hears is true) the morals of a waterfront whore. How she and Draco can be brother and sister I cannot imagine. Must have a serious talk with him about her. The way money is wasted in this house is simply *scandalous*. The whole domestic side needs thoroughly overhauling. Shall set about this as soon as possible."

The fruits of her investigation were recorded in a slightly later entry:

"Went down to the kitchens this morning to get things sorted out. Found the cook doing something quite *bestial* to one of his scullions, in broad daylight, they might have been farmyard animals. I was nearly sick. Remonstrated with Helen as coolly and as reasonably as I could. She heard me out, with that infuriatingly supercilious expression of hers and then said, 'My dear girl, so long as dinner's served on time, why should you care about what happens to little slave-boys below stairs?' When I pressed the point she said, in a most unpleasant way, 'This is my house, and I run it my own way. If you don't like what you see in the kitchen, I should keep out of it.' Obviously she intends to use my financial embarrassment as a way of imposing her own will, regardless of what is reasonable or logical behaviour."

An attempt to enlist Uncle Eurygyus on her side was no more successful:

"Have made one or two attempts to begin a private discussion with E., but find him quite unresponsive. All this superstitious nonsense must have addled his brains."

Reading those words evokes a long-forgotten picture in my mind of my mother and uncle standing together on the terrace one summer evening: I can only have been seven at the time. My cousins Megara and Telesippa and I shared a bedroom at the top of the house. We heard a noise below, opened the shutters a crack, and peeped down. Poor Uncle Eurygyus was literally in a corner, his willowy back against the balustrade, just where the ornamental flower-pot stood. My mother was in front of him, hissing sibilants like an angry goose. Though not one word was distinguishable, I instantly recognized her "confidential manner." Uncle Eurygyus, being much taller than my mother, could stare into space over her head, which he did with the most magnificently glassy aplomb, nodding at intervals whenever she paused to draw breath.

We watched, enthralled. Finally Uncle Eurygyus smiled, excused himself, half-patted, half-pushed my mother aside as though she were some importunate puppy, and vanished into the house. My mother then gave way to one of her rare fits of real temper, which were most impressive. She picked up the ornamental flower-pot in both hands (a remarkable feat for a woman: it must have been very heavy indeed) and hurled it down to the flagged courtyard below, where it disintegrated with a satisfying smash. She looked round to see if anyone had observed this performance, brushed off her hands, and quickly—but not *too* quickly—went back to her own part of the house. Presumably this is what she meant by finding Uncle Eurygyus "quite unresponsive." The problem of the broken flower-pot was never solved, but I rather think one of the kitchen-boys got whipped for it, on suspicion. Just which kitchen-boy it was, and how the suspicion arose in the first place, I cannot exactly recall: but my mother was never averse to killing two birds with one stone.

Looking back, seeing these events in some sort of perspective perhaps, I can feel a certain sympathy for all the adults in this period of my childhood. Aunt Helen and my mother were natural enemies; in the best possible circumstances they would have detested one another, and sharing a house was a form of mutual torture for them. The one quality common to them both was a pure autocratic will; and as they never wanted the same thing, some sort of battle-royal was always going on. Poor Mama: her only way of getting herself, and us, out of that house would have been to sell our remaining land at Eresus; but this, understandably enough, was a drastic final step she could never quite bring herself to take.

Nor was the situation very pleasant either for Uncle Eurygyus or

Aunt Helen (though the latter, at least, had a strong position to attack from when it came to a head-on clash). They were fairly wealthy people, and their town house a large one; but it must have imposed a great strain on them—by no means only a financial strain, either—to absorb Uncle Eurygyus' brother's widow, *and* her three (shortly afterwards four) children on top of their own brood. For a man who regarded childbirth with such superstitious terror and loathing, Uncle Eurygyus seemed surprisingly partial to the act which set this dreaded process in motion. My mother, in one of her more waspish asides—ostensibly to herself, but loud enough for the children to hear and pass on—claimed that he only did it to keep Helen out of mischief.

When I think of my childhood in Eresus, what I see, first and foremost, is a landscape, bright, shimmering, changeless, its harsher moods all forgotten. There are figures moving in this landscape, but they remain subordinate to mountains and sea, the smell of spring flowers, sunlight on still water. With the move to Mytilene there comes a change in this picture: slowly but unmistakably the figures move into the foreground until they dominate it altogether. My intensity of vision grew no less in those years, and I still remain, now as then, acutely sensible to the natural world around me. But the bright and single light of childhood was fading, little by little, and one day I would wake to the knowledge of what I had lost.

I sit here on a fine autumn morning and try to picture the house as it was then—the heavy Lydian rugs in the corridors, the odd foreign knick-knacks that Uncle Eurygyus had picked up on his travels abroad; the exotic smell that permeated every room, a mixture of scent and incense and strong spices; the old, gnarled carob-tree in the courtyard, the well where, at any hour of the day, a couple of muleteers were to be found lounging about, scratching themselves and throwing dice for the next drink; the bustle and clatter from the street beyond our high wall, the cries of hawkers and water-carriers, the early morning smell of fresh bread.

But when I attempt to evoke this scene, I cannot visualize the house without its so-well-remembered occupants: Uncle Eurygyus and Aunt Helen, my mother, the old steward (who may, as my mother alleged, have drunk to excess, but who taught us to whittle dolls with pen-knives and to make cages for grasshoppers), a bevy of much-loved nurses, gardeners, grooms, cooks, and kitchen-maids, and, above all, my four cousins—grave, adoring Megara; Hermeas, who

[47]

was so fatally pliable, so anxious to be loved at any price; pert Telesippa, her long blond hair always done up in a black ribbon; and Agenor, the eldest, emotionally diffident, as first children so often are, but always inventing games for us, sorting out our problems with a rough and Rhadamanthine private justice, adult beyond his years.

It is a strange thing, but I have always had a far closer affinity with my cousins than with my own brothers—though this, when I consider again, merely means that my dislike for Charaxus goes back a long way. Eurygyus was an ailing child who died when I was nine, during that famous hard winter which old men still recall with awe (the rivers and canals froze, and ice even formed for several yards out to sea, an unheard-of thing), so I cannot have developed any particular regard for him, one way or the other; while my youngest brother Larichus, handsome Larichus whom I love so dearly, was born here in Mytilene, after my father's death, and I have somehow always regarded him as a cousin-by-adoption.

But the most unexpected event, which took place rather less than a year after our arrival, was the establishment of our private school. Today the idea is a common-place, and many families in the city have adopted it. Then, it was quite unheard-of: perhaps only two such powerful (and powerfully antipathetic) minds as those of my mother and Aunt Helen could—as it were by intellectual friction— have contrived to produce it. One thing they found themselves (rather unwillingly) in agreement over was the education of girls. They differed violently as to *what* girls should be taught, and how the process should be accomplished; but they both maintained that the existing system, whereby boys were taught in schools but girls brought up at home, was fundamentally wrong.

It is a tribute to our society that I can think of no other place in Greece, then or now, where any woman would have thought as my mother and Aunt Helen did—let alone have had the freedom to carry their beliefs into action. Not in Athens, certainly, though Athenians are fond of telling us how enlightened they are; nor in Lydia, for all its wealth and culture, where girls of good breeding (as I know only too well) are set to earn their dowries as temple prostitutes, and none—least of all their husbands-to-be—think the worse of them for it. Perhaps the freedom of women on Lesbos has been bought at a price we cannot, as yet, fully reckon. But the freedom, the power of choice, is *there*. Freedom may be abused; that is no argument against it.

My mother, of course, was determined to treat the whole issue as a matter of principle: she saw herself petitioning the Council, perhaps even addressing the Assembly in session, and getting a municipal school for girls established by law. It took Aunt Helen a long time—and enormous self-restraint—to persuade her that what mattered in this case was not so much taking a public stand on one's convictions, as ensuring that various individual living girls were actually *taught* something. So at last (with Uncle Eurygyus's all-too-willing approval: I think he felt this was one way of keeping his turbulent womenfolk from each other's throats) it was agreed that the two of them should hold classes at home. My cousins and I would form a nucleus of pupils, and the rest would follow.

Various ladies in the town were sounded out: would they entrust their daughters to Aunt Helen and my mother (under the strictest supervision, naturally) in return for the benefits of a liberal education? The response, as might have been expected, was very tepid; though whether this was due simply to engrained conservatism (as Aunt Helen believed), or to Aunt Helen's reputation (my mother propounded this theory with some relish) is hard to decide in retrospect. Perhaps a little of both.

At any rate, in the end only four more children were added to our family classroom. My mother talked Pittacus into letting Andromeda come (I think he was finding her a problem at home, and needed little persuasion). Pittacus in turn discussed the matter with Phanias, one of his closest friends, who had a five-year-old daughter called Mnasidica. (It was some time before I found out what her full name was; it invariably got shortened to Mica.) Aunt Helen approached her brother Draco, who to begin with pooh-poohed the whole idea; but his daughter Gorgo was Andromeda's best friend, and *she* talked to her mother, Aunt Xanthe. Xanthe's attitude to Gorgo was mixed, I now realize: she may well have had her own reasons for wanting the child out of the house. But in the end she persuaded Draco (as she nearly always did), and so Gorgo, together with her younger sister Irana, also became part of our group.

I say "group" advisedly. If Aunt Helen or my mother had known how inextricably, or in what strange ways, all our lives were to be interwoven in after years, would they, I wonder, have acted differently, perhaps even have abandoned the whole project? Somehow I do not think so: such considerations never touched my mother at all, while to Aunt Helen they represented an important facet of life, to be welcomed rather than avoided.

[49]

Andromeda and I are in the carob-tree. It is a warm spring after-noon. Through the branches we can see the harbour glinting below us, the ships at anchor, a solitary one-legged beggar stumping moodily across the quay. We have scrambled up—Andromeda leading, as always—with much scratching of knees and palms, and are now sitting astride a big horizontal bough, invisible from the house. My heart is pounding. I don't really enjoy climbing trees, I hate heights anyway, and my dress is dirty. I have a raw abrasion on the inside of one knee. But I adore Andromeda.

She sits there, brown legs swinging, the greenish glint in her right eye. With her short, ragged black hair and urchin grin she looks more like a boy than a girl.

"Let's see you climb to the top of the tree." There is a mischievous note in her voice: she knows perfectly well how scared I am of heights.

"You'd do it better," I say, terrified.

"I won't like you any more."

"*Please,* Andromeda—"

"Gorgo would do it for me."

"I hate Gorgo. She's silly." Snub nose and freckles, coarse auburn hair, red hands.

"You're jealous, you're jealous." Andromeda is ten now, nearly eleven: there is something disturbing about her that I don't under-stand. But then, I am only just nine, and look less.

"Don't be silly, Drom."

"Who said you could call me that?"

"Gorgo does."

"She's my best friend."

I feel the tears very close.

"Is she? Really?"

Andromeda's wry, grown-up smile suddenly lights her face.

"Keep a secret?"

"Of course."

"I like you best really."

"Do you? *Really?*"

She leans forward awkwardly on the branch. Her lips brush my cheek, her hair is like burning wire. She says: "Darling Sappho. You're such a little silly. I don't know why I like you."

This leaves me quite speechless.

"You can call me Drom if you like. But only when there's nobody there but us."

I nod, ecstatic. Suddenly we both feel a little embarrassed.

The one-legged beggar is still standing there among the barrels and drying nets, as though waiting for someone. He leans on his crutch, and his shadow falls black beside him.

I wake suddenly in the middle of the night, to a blinding branch of lightning, the echoes of the last thunderclap still ringing in my ears. The lamp has gone out. Across the room I can see Telesippa, a curled lump under her scarlet blanket, blissfully unconscious. Nothing ever wakes her. Darkness descends, and with it terror. The thunder crashes overhead.

"Meg?"

"M'm."

"Are you asleep?"

"No."

"Are you frightened?"

"Yes." This in a very small voice.

"Can I come in with you?"

"Of course—"

I scramble quickly across to her bed and snuggle in. She puts her arms round me. Megara at eleven is nearly as tall as a full-grown woman. Her long black hair is unbraided, and I bury my face in it. My feet hardly reach below her knees, though I am only a few months younger than she is.

"Meg—why, you're trembling. You really *are* scared."

She says nothing, only holds me closer. At last she asks: "Sappho, do you like Andromeda a lot?"

The question takes me unawares. "Yes—yes, I do."

"How much?" There is a painful intensity in her voice.

"I don't know. A lot."

A pause.

"Has she ever kissed you?"

"What do you want to know for?"

Another flash of lightning. For a moment I see Meg's face: strained, hurt, yearning.

"That means she has."

We both wait tensely for the thunder.

"Do you like me?" Meg asks, in that same odd, small voice.

"Of course I do."

"In the same way?"

"I—what do you mean?"

But I do know, though I cannot, as yet, put the difference into words. I try to speak, but the words refuse to come. Suddenly something hot and wet trickles on to my cheek. Meg is crying silently, her whole body rigid.

"Meg—I'm sorry—"

She shakes her head.

"It doesn't matter."

"But it *does*—"

"I'm being silly. And selfish."

I feel curiously detached, as though what were happening had nothing to do with me.

"You're all right, Meg. It's just the thunder."

A small sniff.

"Yes, that's it."

"You'll feel better in the morning."

"I expect so." She takes her arms from round me, and turns over on her side, facing the other way. "Go to sleep now. Please."

"All right."

But I lie awake for another hour, thinking, wondering. Presently the storm dies away, and a faint grey light begins to seep through the shutters. Meg groans and mutters. Only when I slip back to my own bed does sleep at last claim me.

My mother is reading Homer with us. As usual, she has turned to the *Iliad*. We would all much rather follow the adventures of Odysseus, among the Laestrygonians, in Polyphemus' cave, shooting the wooers. But this, my mother feels, is a story which lacks moral seriousness.

"'One omen is best, to fight for your country,'" she declaims. We yawn and wriggle our bottoms. It is not a sentiment to which most small girls respond with any great enthusiasm. Only Andromeda looks remotely interested. My mother makes a little speech about Troy. There is fighting there again. The treacherous Athenians are trying to steal our outposts. But our brave soldiers will—

My attention wanders. Gorgo is picking her nose and looking out of the window at two pigeons in the courtyard. Her small sister Irana—also auburn-haired—sits with a cross little frown on her face: I don't think I have ever seen her smile. Telesippa looks bright and attentive, but I know that glazed expression: she is, to all intents and purposes, asleep. Megara, her hair braided neatly, is trying not to

[52]

look at me. A shaft of sunlight lights up Andromeda's face. My heart contracts: I am lost in a golden dazzle.

Suddenly I realize my mother is asking me a question: how did the Trojan War begin? I want to show off, do something silly, please Drom.

"Aunt Helen," I say, with an inane giggle.

My impertinence earns me a whipping: one of the worst I have ever had. I suspect my mother's motives; she would like to agree with me, I fancy, but feels that a united adult front must be preserved. I could have borne the whipping cheerfully: what agonizes me is Andromeda's angry, contemptuous expression. For several days afterwards she will not speak to me.

IV

LOOKING back, I can see—all too clearly—just how unfortunate that schoolroom gaffe of mine was. I could not know, then, one central fact which only emerged several years later: I mean, Aunt Helen's liaison with Pittacus. She had, it seems, been his mistress, on and off, for at least a year before our move to Mytilene. My mother lost no time in discovering this (to her) highly scandalous relationship. Like many strong-minded women (especially those with a hidden streak of sentimentality about them) she was apt to image copulation proceeding behind every closed door; and in one case at least her suspicions turned out to be justified. Her awareness of the situation can hardly have improved anyone's temper—least of all her own.

Aunt Helen, in turn, would have been less than her usual acute self if she had failed to diagnose my mother's own silent passion for Pittacus. Andromeda, too, obviously had some idea of what was going on, and took my joke as a pointed allusion to her father's extra-marital pursuits: she worshipped him with uncritical violence and resented the smallest real or imagined slight on his character. One of Alcaeus' early tongue-in-cheek patriotic poems, written on the outbreak of war in the Troad, contained several double-edged references to Helen and Thetis which suggested that he knew all this and a good deal more besides.

If the matter had remained a private feud merely, no great harm would have been done. But my mother was not the sort of person to let a situation rest; nor, when her own pride was involved, did she make any very clear distinction between personal and public morality. What she now did was unscrupulous to a degree, and I have never understood how she squared her actions with her declared principles —though here she could display, on occasion, the kind of casuistry that would shame a seasoned statesman.

To put it bluntly, if she could not have Pittacus, she was determined that Aunt Helen should not either; and since Uncle Eurygyus was blandly indifferent to her confidences, she decided—apparently without the least qualm—to get her way by what I suppose must be called political means. Her main point of attack was through Draco, Helen's brother and—more important for my mother's purposes—a member of the Council. She so worked on him about the trouble with Athens in the Troad that what had begun as a mild diplomatic quarrel over trading concessions was soon blown up, with much patriotic tub-thumping, into a full-scale war.

Could we, cried Draco, well-primed with my mother's fiery platitudes, let Athenians desecrate the tomb of Achilles? Could we—this was slipped in almost as an afterthought—allow them to steal trade from under our very noses? The Council decided that they could not; and so voted. After that, there merely remained the business of electing a commander-in-chief. When Draco proposed Pittacus, the result was a foregone conclusion: he was, indeed, by far the most able man for the job. My mother took much simple pleasure in telling Aunt Helen (with what I now see was a well-calculated air of innocence) that her lover—though she did not put it quite like that— had been ordered abroad on active service.

Where (as both of them knew) there was a sizable chance of his being killed.

My mother's ruthlessness—to herself no less than others—was, and remains, something quite exceptional in my experience.

The curious thing was Aunt Helen's reaction. If my mother hoped to provoke some sort of scene—tearful reproaches, blazing anger, perhaps even hysteria—she was disappointed. Aunt Helen smiled rather vaguely and said yes, well, the occasional campaign abroad was a good thing for energetic, ambitious men: city politics did tend to become cramping after a while. From then on she treated my mother with a sweet, considerate politeness that would have scared anyone else half out of their wits; but my mother took it all quite placidly and was heard to remark that Helen might, in time, become quite a reasonable person. You just had to be *firm* with her.

But Pittacus did not, in the event, get himself killed: he had a natural and instinctive talent for survival. What safeguarded him, I now see, was his indifference to aristocratic principles. He was not quite a gentleman (as his enemies never tired of reminding him) and thoroughly enjoyed exploiting noble scruples. His morals were as pliable as his wits, and his political career, examined in detail, looks downright shady.

Yet he was, I cannot help believing, a fundamentally good man. The changes he brought about, his personal conduct once he had attained supreme power, the wisdom and tolerance he displayed in dealing with opponents of any sort—all tell the same story. He believed he knew what was best for his country; and he may well have been right. If he had personal ambitions, they were not of the crude sort that most tyrants display. He wanted power simply as an effective instrument for achieving reforms; when the reforms had become established tradition, his interest in holding office evaporated.

I am sad now that I spent so much of my life as his political enemy. Not only because I was twice exiled in consequence, but also because my allegiance deprived me, for long periods, of a wise, generous, forbearing friend: one whom I could ill afford to lose. But at this time Pittacus was still on the threshold of his career. My mother, by securing his appointment as commander-in-chief, had set him firmly on the lower rungs of the political ladder—which was not, I suspect, her prime intention.

Pittacus embarked his troops on a bright, windy morning in late March, and everyone flocked down to the quayside to see them sail. He stood on the poop of his flagship and made a short speech, with no bombast or heroics, promising to conduct the campaign to the best of his ability. I think most people were a little disappointed: they wanted a rousing send-off. But he certainly looked a magnificent figure, with his glittering greaves and helmet (the great horsehair plume nodded like Hector's) and his heavy scarlet cloak snapping in the wind. Perhaps, even to a hero-worshipping eleven-year-old, he was not quite so tall and godlike as he had seemed on that now-distant summer afternoon in Eresus: the waistline under his corselet was thickening, and the first brindled flecks of grey could be seen in his beard. Yet he was still only thirty-five.

The libations were poured, and the priest offered prayers for fair sailing; then Pittacus stripped his great broad-bladed sword from its scabbard and held it aloft, and the trumpets sounded, and the hawsers were cast off. A silence fell on the crowd, broken only by barked commands from vessel to vessel as the new white sails, each with its black dolphin device, were hoisted and spread, and the fleet, in line ahead, moved slowly out of harbour. Then, as though at a signal, the cheering began, and we waved them out of sight up the blue, gull-haunted channel that would bear their ships northwards to Adramyttium and the Troad. My mother cheered as loudly as anyone. All patriotic occasions moved her to the point of tears.

Pittacus' dispatches caused a certain amount of head-shaking in Council. They were brief, factual, and very much to the point. A general who tells no more—and no less—than the bare truth, especially when it reflects against himself, can be a little disconcerting. After the disastrous battle in which Alcaeus (together with many other young men) dropped his shield and fled, Pittacus reported as follows: "Today we suffered an ignominious defeat outside Sigeum. Our comparatively light losses can be ascribed to the fact that our troops—being less encumbered—ran much faster than the enemy. The defeat was due, in about equal proportions, to incompetent generalship and indifferent discipline. Courage alone cannot win battles. Efficient training is more desirable than fine speeches. Meanwhile we—my men and I—learn, expensively, in action. Please dispatch two hundred new shields and fifty bushels of wheat by the next supply-boat."

As though to annoy my mother—how shrewdly, I wonder, had he sized up her relationship with Aunt Helen, and what had Draco told him?—Pittacus never once wrote to her, all that summer. What was more, he rubbed in the omission by sending me a note—to my great surprise—with every dispatch-boat. My mother insisted on reading the first of them, and snorted when she saw the signature. "Chiron!" she said. "*Chiron*, indeed!" She rubbed her nose with her finger, and made a vaguely disgusted noise. "Sentimental nonsense." She thrust across the room, skirts hissing, her whole big body vibrant with suppressed energy. The sunlight glinted on her lustrous black hair as she stared through the open window. I saw her clenched fist resting on the sill, each knuckle as white and hard and polished as ivory. She had, quite obviously, forgotten the little episode in our courtyard at Eresus—if, indeed, she ever noticed it.

Then she turned round, with an abrupt, constrained gesture, and it was as though I had never seen her before. Her whole face was different, contorted with loathing; an uncontrollable muscular spasm seemed to take her features and twist them down, like soft clay, into a terrible grinning rictus. She began incoherently to talk about the

[57]

act of love; a stream of words burst from her lips, a sick torrent of dammed-up hatred. I tried not to listen, to stop my senses against that red, hard, wounding physical imagery.

What had been natural was smeared in filth, the innocent leered like a satyr. Pain, suffering, humiliation, disgust, the cock strutting on its dunghill, the triumph of the barbarous, rutting male. There was no gentleness, no tenderness, no disinterested friendship or simple warmth any more. Only the ravisher, the alien invading Thing, terror, pain, blood, destruction: an obscene, thrusting, wounding act that led, in time, to gross physical ugliness, pain past all bearing, sickness, the risk of death.

At last she stopped. "You'll learn," she said, in a calmer voice. "You'll learn. I'll see that you learn." And went, with that fierce, awkward, aggressive gait of hers, which conceded nothing, yielded to no one, never compromised.

I looked at the brief note that still lay on the window sill. "Troy is a pleasant place to picnic, I should think. In armour it is *very* hot. When Achilles chased Hector three times round the walls he must have done it in winter. Or perhaps heroes were immune to heat. Do you think a hero ever sweated? There is a ladybird crawling up my arm, and I've just noticed for the first time—after having him around for four months—that my orderly has a cast in one eye. Chiron." I puzzled over this, still shaking from the impact of my mother's tirade, trying to work out what possible connection there could be between the two. It was no good. Nothing made sense any more. The bright sky seemed suddenly overcast, as though a thin grey veil had been drawn across it.

The letters continued to arrive at irregular intervals. It never occurred to me that I should answer them, and I don't suppose Pittacus expected me to, either. "I have been trying to train my men in field-manoeuvres," one began. "I am rapidly coming to the conclusion that the only sensible man in the *Iliad* was Thersites." And again: "Lizards are the most practical of creatures. When pursued or caught, they throw off their tail and grow a new one. I should like to see human beings acquire this faculty. It might prove amusing."

By the same boat as his notorious dispatch to the Council came this: "An enforced holiday is very pleasant: we lie in the sun and feel happy to be alive. Which, after all, is the sum of existence." A little later I got the following cryptic communication: "I have been watching the fishermen here. While we manoeuvre or fight, they are still busy with their nets. Who, I ask myself, shows the greater sense?

Yet no one wrote an epic about a fisherman. Man steers his life by the fixed stars: he knows his task, the prescribed words and actions that are required of him, and of others. But why should I not exchange the sword for the net? My will is free. I am the wise Chiron. You said so yourself."

A couple of weeks later extraordinary news reached us from the Troad: Pittacus had challenged the Athenian general, Phrynon, to single combat, and killed him. The whole town buzzed with rumours. When the dispatch-boat docked, there was an excited crowd to welcome it. Fortunately for us, the courier—a pleasant young man named Archaeanax, who had distinguished himself in the early stages of the campaign—also happened to be a second cousin of Aunt Helen's. After he had discharged his official duties he came up to see us: a shy, fair-haired boy, still limping on a stick from a wound in the muscles of one thigh.

Aunt Helen fussed over him, making him lie back on a comfortable couch, propping him up with cushions. He seemed to enjoy this. When he had had some wine, my mother (whose impatience must have been almost tearing her in two by now) snapped: "Well? What *happened?*"

Archaeanax smiled. "It was a joke, really," he said. "Just the sort of thing the old boy *would* think up."

Aunt Helen said: "Is it true that the old boy, as you call him, killed the Athenian commander in fair fight? Single-handed?"

Archaeanax said thoughtfully: "Well, he certainly *killed* him, yes. And single-handed." One hand rubbed half-consciously at the muscles of his wounded leg. "You know we had this defeat? Afterwards Pittacus got the veterans training us in battle-manoeuvres. But his heart didn't seem in it, somehow. He used to go for long walks by himself along the beach; he liked watching the fishermen at their nets. One day he brought a net back into camp. I met him, and asked him what on earth he wanted it for. He grinned and winked, in that way he's got, and said: "Just a little Thracian trick, my boy: it may save everyone a lot of trouble." He was always making jokes about his father being a Thracian, you know—"

"Yes," said Aunt Helen gently, "I know." My mother flashed a quick, furious glance at her.

"Anyway, the next thing we heard was that he'd issued this challenge to the Athenian commander—single combat, both armies watching, the traditional generals' duel. If Pittacus won, we were to get back Sigeum. If he lost, we were to give up our own present possessions in the Troad—Achilles' tomb and all."

[59]

My mother said, sharply: "Did he have authority from the Council to make such a proposition?"

"I presume so." Despite his youth, Archaeanax could look very bland on occasion. "But then you must remember, Lady Cleïs, I'm only a courier: I deliver dispatches, I don't read them."

All this time I had been in the corner of the room, near the hearth, bent over a piece of embroidery, and keeping very still and quiet in the hope that no one would notice me. But it was all I could do to stop myself giggling out loud at that last remark: not for a very long time had I heard anyone put my mother in her place so neatly, and with such apparent ease. From Aunt Helen's fine aquiline profile (which normally gave very little away) I could tell that she was pleased with her cousin's performance too.

Her own question was rather different. "The Athenian general must have felt very sure of himself to accept such a challenge," she said thoughtfully.

"Oh, he was tough, all right. In fact he won the Olympic Crown as a free-style boxer at the age of eighteen—*very* un-Athenian, I'd have thought, but there it was." Archaeanax applied himself to the wine-jug. "He wasn't one of those dreary ex-athletes who run to seed, either. One field punishment he used to serve out in the Troad was to make defaulters box with him before breakfast. On the whole they preferred the lash. He was a first-class swordsman too—"

"Which Pittacus certainly is not." My mother's tone was tart in the extreme.

"He's not bad," said Archaeanax loyally, "but he's no athlete, that's true enough. I don't mind saying, we all thought Phrynon would eat him, even giving away ten years and more. But what could we do? He was the general. Besides"—he grinned—"I think we all knew the old boy had something up his sleeve. He simply isn't the sort to chuck his life away in a display of useless heroics."

My mother frowned but said nothing.

"So the morning came, and the two armies settled down a hundred paces from each other, and the heralds fussed about with trumpets and proclamations—*you* know—and then Phrynon came striding out in his armour, a really impressive sight, too, over six feet tall and big with it. He had on one of those Corinthian helmets with cheek-pieces and a nose-guard, and he stood there dancing from foot to foot, and swiping at the air with his sword. Pittacus glanced at him, grinned, and went on polishing his shield. He really was getting a splendid shine out of it. Then he stood up, very leisurely, and put on his helmet, and loosened his sword in its scabbard, and made quite sure his shield was settled comfortably on his left arm. He seemed more concerned about his shield than anything else.

"The heralds were getting a little edgy by now, but eventually Pittacus stumped out to them, and we all cheered him as he went. There were a few pretty ribald jokes too. Then the two contestants, after a bit of parleying, were squared up, and we saw that Phrynon had the sun behind his shoulder, shining straight at his opponent. Remember, it was pretty early in the morning. Pittacus had lowered his shield-arm, and just stood there, waiting, like a patient bear.

"Then the heralds stepped back, and the trumpet sounded, and several things happened very quickly. Phrynon drew his sword and lunged forward: Pittacus sidestepped, flashed up that bright-polished shield into Phrynon's face, flicked out a fisherman's net from behind it, and had the poor booby trussed up like a boar in the toils before he could get the sun out of his eyes. The more Phrynon struggled and bellowed, the worse he got entangled; and then he called Pittacus the bastard son of a whore, which was silly of him, because it may very well be true, as you know, and Pittacus drew his sword and ran him through so hard that the hilt cracked his breast-bone. And that was that."

There was silence in the room for a moment.

At last my mother said: "Of course, the Athenians refused to accept such a victory." Her voice made it quite clear that she would have refused to accept it herself.

Archaeanax laughed. "Of course they did; they'd been made to look complete fools."

"That was not quite what I meant."

"I'm sorry; I don't understand."

"There are commonly accepted standards of conduct on such occasions—"

"Are there?" said Archaeanax. "I didn't know. It seems to me the main object in fighting someone is to disable your opponent, and stop him damaging you. If he happens to be more stupid and hidebound than you are, he has no one but himself to blame."

Archaeanax was a little flushed; the wine had clearly begun to take effect on him.

My mother said: "I fancy I know where you got those ideas from, young man, and they are not what I would expect to hear any person of good family profess in public. We have certain values, and we cannot afford to abandon them. It would be a betrayal of all we stand for."

When my mother became really angry, she also tended to be pompous, as though her mind was under such pressure that she could only express herself in platitudes.

"If I have offended you, Lady Cleïs," Archaeanax said, getting up, "I offer you my most humble apologies."

"You can't go yet, cousin," Aunt Helen said lightly, "we haven't heard the end of the story, and you haven't eaten."

"Oh, the story has a very dull conclusion, I'm afraid. After a day or two of bickering, both sides agreed to an armistice, pending arbitration."

"So the war is over," said Aunt Helen.

"It looks like it," said Archaeanax, sounding very cheerful. "We'll all be home in time for the vintaging, if we're lucky."

"And who," said my mother, "is to arbitrate?"

"King Periander of Corinth has been approached, and is agreeable."

"That man is no more entitled to be called a king than my sweeper. He's a common tyrant."

"He succeeded his father," Aunt Helen said. "It raises a nice problem, doesn't it? How many generations are necessary to legitimize a dynasty? Just what is the formula for producing royal blood?"

Archaeanax coughed, teetered, and said: "If you will all excuse me, I'm late for another engagement."

Aunt Helen extended her hand for Archaeanax to kiss. "It was so pleasant seeing you, cousin. When do you sail?"

"Tomorrow, I'm afraid."

"Ah. Be sure to give my regards to—your commander." Her lips twitched briefly. "And my congratulations."

Archaeanax picked up his stick and limped after the slave. Both women watched him go. It must have been a singularly uncomfortable exit.

When he had gone, my mother, still fuming, said: "Periander, indeed."

"We could do worse."

"The man's unspeakable, a tradesman—"

"In case you'd forgotten, this is very largely a trading dispute—despite the tomb of Achilles."

"Money isn't everything," said my mother.

"Indeed not, when you have it."

The two women looked at each other.

"Besides," my mother said, rallying, "you can't possibly expect justice from a person without any morals or principles—"

"Oh?" said Aunt Helen.

"You know perfectly well what I mean," my mother said, and her voice had that unpleasant hissing violence about it again. "He and his mother—"

"You were in the bed with them?" said Aunt Helen contemptuously. "Why is it that people are so willing to believe any tittle-tattle as long as it has to do with sex?"

"Perhaps they have good reason."

"Perhaps. I don't care for Periander much myself; but *my* main objection to him, if we're on the subject of morals, is his ungovernable temper. A man who can kick his wife into a miscarriage—one from which she subsequently dies—and all because of some idiotic story told him by a concubine, can hardly be called a stable character. I notice that isn't *your* first objection, though."

I gave a tiny gasp at this: Aunt Helen turned and saw me. It was extraordinary how fast her moods could change. She smiled with real warmth and said: "Oh my dear, what a bore all this nonsense must have been for you. Could you go down to the kitchen and tell them we're ready for dinner now?"

I nodded, unable to speak, thankful to get away. My mother said nothing. She never referred to the episode again in any way, and she made no objection to Aunt Helen giving me orders (something which would normally have provoked a first-class row). I began to wonder if I knew anything about her—whether I had been living all my life with a dangerous, inscrutable stranger, ready to strike at me when I was most vulnerable, nourishing my trust only to betray it.

The last letter Pittacus sent me before his return home from the Troad was somewhat longer than the others. "We have had the chance of observing a tyrant at close quarters," he wrote. "This is instructive, but a little unnerving when he happens to be sitting in judgment on you. However, our particular specimen had a painful boil on his nose, which suggested that he wasn't immune to the ills of lesser mortals. He was also a great bore, I'm afraid, like most businessmen who think they ought to talk about art to show how broadminded they are.

"You will probably have heard stories about what an ogre Periander is, but on this score he disappointed us all. He ate no children before

[63]

breakfast (in fact he has rather a weak digestion for a tyrant) and was obviously most anxious not to offend either party in the dispute. As his commercial counsellors spent most of their time negotiating profitable trade agreements with us *and* the Athenians, quite impartially, I can see his motives. Between ourselves, I rather admire them. So next year we shall see a good many more Corinthian merchant-men docking in Mytilene. This will do us much more good than playing at soldiers, which is an expensive game, and not nearly so enjoyable as people try to make out.

"At all events, Periander's verdict, when it came, was something of a joke—though few people apart from Periander himself much appreciated it. Both armies were assembled, like packs of naughty schoolboys before their master, to hear him pronounce sentence—which he did from a rather vulgar little pavilion brought along specially for the purpose, and set up midway between us and the Athenians. He spun out the proceedings as long as he could, with much introductory preamble and flourishing of trumpets: no wonder, because his decision, when he finally got to it, was that both parties should keep what they then held. Having unburdened himself of this Rhadamanthine platitude, he and his retinue took themselves off—a wise precaution, I thought—leaving us to work out the details.

"Neither side has done exactly well, though it would be hard to argue that Periander was prejudiced in his judgment. Athens is landed with an expensive outpost from which, in its divided state, she can expect little advantage. We, on the other hand, will have to establish a permanent garrison here to make sure the Athenians stay behind the new frontier line. The main beneficiary, of course, is Periander himself: he's secured some nice trade agreements, and left two troublesome rivals watching each other instead of competing with him for markets in Ionia. Arbitration is obviously a profitable business. I think I shall take it up myself one day. Chiron." Then came a characteristic scribbled postscript:

"This is the last of these letters. I hope you haven't found them too boring or incomprehensible. A girl of twelve, I know, has more important things to think about. Treat them as lessons, if you like: all lessons are dull, after all, and even Chiron can't hope to avoid prosiness on occasion. But remember, my dear, that there is a great deal in life which Homer (for whatever reason) saw fit to ignore altogether. The sooner you realize this—not that I imagine you want to at the moment—the happier, ultimately, you will be. Some people go through life without ever admitting it at all, which is not, on the whole, a good

[64]

recipe for happiness. In any case, I have enjoyed writing to you: it is pleasant to have one correspondent at least who can be relied upon never to misinterpret one's motives."

So the army sailed home, as summer's heat began to soften towards autumn; and Pittacus was cheered through the streets (looking rather sheepish, I remember) and afterwards given a splendid banquet in the City Hall, at which he got splendidly drunk. Next day the Council (whose members had not forgotten his tart dispatches) appointed him Chairman of the Board of Commerce, a job which most people considered very much beneath them, and which therefore fell, more often than not, to unpopular nonentities.

Pittacus did not seem in the least put out by the implied snub; he even, in his impulsive way, went so far as to declare that there was no post he would rather hold. At first this claim caused much superior and ill-natured amusement at his expense. But very soon, as he marched, with positively Herculean energy, into the Augean stables of public finance, the joke was dropped: it became apparent—even to the most hostile critic—that Pittacus had, indeed, meant exactly what he said.

I cannot remember a time when I was not familiar with the idea of death. Even as a child in Eresus the sounds of mourning, the smoking funeral torches, faces lined or, worse, nail-scored with grief formed a familiar element in my circumscribed world. A bloated ox lay dead in a ditch, kites and vultures flapping over it; the sick, sweetish stink of corruption turned my stomach, but I did not feel fear, much less surprise—perhaps because I was, myself, so intensely alive. I could not conceive death as having any relevance to me personally: I walked among mortals like an immortal God, immune and curious.

Perhaps this is why the deaths of those close to me—even my own father's—always moved me less deeply than I expected. At nine years old children, they say, are inconsolable: every loss is a kind of death. It was not so for me. During our third winter in Mytilene my little brother Eurygyus, who had always been a sickly child, caught a racking cough, which went to his chest and killed him, without any fuss, in less than a month. He was just over five at the time of his death: we had, in fact, celebrated his birthday at his bedside. My mother and I both won praise for the brave way in which we bore our loss; the truth is that I felt almost nothing (rather to my own bewilderment), and I very much doubt whether my mother did, either.

This is not to say that I was, or am, insensible to suffering. But I cannot, except in the most superficial way, feel loss where I have not known love. An enemy would call this yet another proof of my all-engrossing self-centredness: I regard it as simple honesty. You cannot mourn the absence of what you never knew; the most you can feel is a generalized sorrow for the transience of human life. Perhaps I should have loved my brother, but the truth is that I scarcely knew him. When I paid my last respects over that tiny, open coffin, the waxen face I kissed might have been a mask. A child's death is always inherently moving, and to that extent I experienced sorrow: personal loss there was none.

Curiously, I was more upset (for a variety of reasons, I now see) by the sudden death of Uncle Eurygyus, which happened two or three months after Pittacus returned from the Troad. I seldom thought about him; none of us did. He was a tall, shambling ghost on the periphery of our lives, remote and abstracted, a subject for easy jokes, yet—somehow—a little frightening too. Anyone who so continually meddled with divine matters was bound to have a touch of the numinous about them. I could always feel when Uncle Eurygyus was coming, however soft his tread: there would be a gentle prickling at the base of my scalp. Sometimes I tried to picture the world as he saw it: a dark, threatening, dangerous place, full of invisible pitfalls and destructive powers all the more horrific for being so arbitrary.

Yet to the casual observer his death, like his life, must have seemed a faintly comic affair. He had lately developed a great fad for magical herbs: the house was full of nasty-looking (and often nasty-smelling) roots that no one was allowed to touch, while there were always two or three villainous old crones hanging about the back-door, muttering, much to the alarm of the kitchen-boys, who were almost as superstitious as Uncle Eurygyus himself. One of these unpleasant hags persuaded him to make a midnight expedition into the hills at the time of the full moon—there was some special root which could only be dug up when various unlikely conditions had been fulfilled—but was careless enough to pick a time when the autumn rains were due. Uncle Eurygyus got a terrible soaking, failed to find his root, and died of lung-congestion five days later.

To my utter astonishment, I found myself crying my heart out at his funeral. Perhaps I felt sad on Aunt Helen's behalf; perhaps I knew, instinctively, what an unobtrusive buffer he had formed between her and my mother; perhaps I was just at that difficult, between-states age when tears come easily and often for no apparent reason. Then

I caught my mother staring at me in a very odd way, her face a mixture of disgust and lubricious speculation. This made me pull myself together with remarkable speed; but not before my cousin Agenor, who always looked so much older and more protective than his years —I think he was fourteen at the time—had put a comforting arm round my shoulders, and given me a clean handkerchief, and made a warm corner in the grey desolation that lay like a winter on my heart.

We stood in an awkward group round the bier, the tall tapers flickering behind us, not knowing what to say to each other. Uncle Draco was there, an even taller version of Aunt Helen, with a tendency to look down his nose like a broody heron. Aunt Xanthe, plump and sweet-natured, stood beside him, with little Irana, and dark eleven-year-old Ion, the brother I had never before met, and Gorgo. Gorgo was thirteen now, her red hair burnished and lustrous like her mother's, her face subtly transformed in the past year from a snub-nosed moonishness to something softer, more delicate, alive with secret warmth. I thought of her and Drom, and the coldness deepened inside me: I was so small, so dark, so plain. No spark of warmth, let alone that extraordinary glow. I shut my eyes miserably. Nothing can be the same again, I thought. And then a voice in my head, unexpectedly, said: *But do you want it to be?* Yes, I whispered. Yes. *Do you?* Yes. I think so. *Do you?* I don't know. I'm afraid—

Of death?

No. Never.

Of life, then?

Perhaps.

Of yourself?

Always.

Why?

I don't know—

Do you want to stay as you are?

Yes, yes, please yes—

For ever?

Yes.

I opened my eyes again and found that Aunt Helen was looking at me, with odd, fixed intensity. For a moment I felt, with a stab of irrational terror, that the secret voice in my head was hers, that she was a part of me, possessing me. Then the moment passed, but her eyes still held mine: I seemed to become weightless, to gyrate in a soft dazzle of candle-flame, a still, bright centre, while the words ran unbidden through my head.

The terror of the spring. Beauty hurts. Light hurts. Light after darkness. Stumbling from the cave like Persephone, to unfolding buds and green spikes in the furrows and a tide of longing in the blood. A strange face looking back from the glass, a body grown suddenly unfamiliar. The usurper, the alien. Who cannot be withstood.

Who is yourself.

V

PERHAPS the most unexpected result of Uncle Eurygyus' death was the change it brought about in Aunt Helen: a change which, directly, or indirectly, affected every member of the household. It is hard for me, having been so intimately involved in it, to explain just how, and why, it came about. My mother, with her usual common-sensical briskness, declared that Helen was suffering from temporary religious mania—and added tartly that she had at least chosen an appropriate object for her devotions. Like most of my mother's assertions, this one had just enough truth in it to mask its fundamental superficiality and wrongheadedness: it left one with the uneasy suspicion that she might, after all, be right.

At first Aunt Helen was very quiet and withdrawn; it seemed almost as though her personality had been drained away, leaving nothing but an animated husk behind. She spent much time alone in her room. She spoke seldom, and then only to arrange some necessary household matter. Her eyes had an inturned look, as though she were searching herself—for what, and why? Her brother came visiting once or twice to see if she needed help and was politely frozen out: curious to see that great heron of a man reduced with so little effort. The slaves had more or less run the house before and continued to do so now, blandly ignoring my mother's brisk attempts to re-organize them.

My mother fumed, but was powerless: she threw all her considerable energies into our lessons, which very soon reduced us to semi-hysteria—all, that is, except for Andromeda, who disconcerted my mother by treating her as a huge joke, and nice Mica, now ten years old, who wanted to please, had a good mind, and remained quite placid when shouted at.

Midwinter encircled us: snow powdered the carob-tree, darkness fell in the afternoon, ships lay harbour-bound, and we woke, late and drowsy, to the sound of last night's warm ashes being raked over in the braziers. We read Homer, and learnt to weave, and practised an hour a day on the lyre, under the guidance of a wizened little Lydian music-master who made the rounds of the big houses, and obviously enjoyed teaching young girls.

Agenor, Charaxus, Hermeas, and now Larichus too (who was just seven) went out to school every day, escorted by old Sosias, who had been born to a slave-girl in Aunt Helen's family house, and had come with her on her marriage. It was a standing joke that Sosias would, one day, learn to read. He sat through every class at school, one eye on his charges, the other peering wistfully at the blackboard. He had been doing this since Uncle Draco was a schoolboy, his enthusiasm undiminished, the alphabet as great a mystery to him as ever.

My cousin Meg and I had a close but difficult relationship, punctuated, at irregular intervals, by violent emotional storms which neither of us quite understood. We were both several years older than Telesippa, who went half-mad with boredom when left to her own devices, and spent much time and ingenuity in doing all she could to torment us. The house was loud with little-girl teasing, slaps, tears, and peevish recriminations. Sometimes my mother would step in, very high-handed, and attempt to restore order—which, of course, invariably made things much worse. Only Aunt Helen, lost in some unimaginable world of her own, seemed immune to all these domestic stresses—indeed, quite literally unaware of them.

It was a late afternoon in the turning month between winter and spring, when Pittacus called, unannounced, stumping into the house with a blast of cold wind at his back, wrapped in his heavy black Thracian cloak. The hills were a froth of early almond- and apple-blossom, dappled in delicate, wind-blown colours, so beautiful and transient I could scarcely bear to look at them. My mother, always a great walker, had marched off after lunch, dragging Meg and Telesippa with her. There had been a stormy row because I flatly refused to come.

I said I had a headache, which was true.

"Of course you have," said my mother. "Moping about indoors all day long."

"*Please*, Mama. I really do feel ill."

How could I ever explain that what I found unbearable was the thought of her striding between those almond-trees, taking over my private vision, converting it into her own prosaic terms? There were few doors that resisted my mother's pushing, few rooms, however intimate, that she did not explore and diminish. She had an instinct, which almost amounted to genius, for reducing dreams to dust; yet if anyone had seriously suggested this in her hearing, she would have been hurt past measure at such ill-founded malice. She was not a hypocrite, which made things worse: most of the time she had a quite touching faith in her own opinions.

So I became obstinate and sulky, and my mother hysterical and vituperative, and neither of us gave an inch. In the end she slammed out of the house with my two cousins, leaving me in a state of trembling exhaustion. My head throbbed, my stomach was queasy, a sour metallic taste lay at the back of my mouth. I lay down on a couch and closed my eyes. The house was very still. The boys would not be back from school for another two hours; the slaves were all dozing in their quarters on the far side of the house, and Aunt Helen was shut away upstairs. Violent-coloured patterns—gold-edged purple pansies, jagged scarlet streaks, flashes of greenish light—danced and pulsed inside my eyelids. I felt as though I might be sick at any moment.

It was then that Pittacus appeared: I jumped up in surprise as he entered.

"No," he said, reading my thoughts, "I didn't bother your porter." He spun a key round one finger by its ring. "The garden-wicket is so much less public than the front-door. Don't you agree?"

I nodded, not trusting myself to speak. His face had a high flush, and there was a curious artificial precision about his voice: it made me think, for no apparent reason, of a man picking his way across a swamp, from tussock to tussock. He had put on a good deal of weight since I saw him last; though he carried himself as well as ever on those thick, slightly bandy legs of his, he had the unmistakable beginnings of a pot-belly, while his hair and beard were rapidly turning grey.

He said: "Is your aunt upstairs?"

"Yes."

He seemed about to add something, but thought better of it. He stood there, looking at me in a fixed way that made me feel thoroughly uncomfortable, still swinging the garden-key from one finger. Then he turned and went clumping up the stairs: I heard his heavy footsteps move along to Aunt Helen's door, and the sound of the door opening and shutting again, and a faint, sharp, muffled exchange of voices. For a moment or two there was silence. I felt my heart pounding, and when I touched my forehead it was clammy with cold sweat. I stood beside the couch, waiting.

Then, suddenly, the voices exploded again, with an unmistakable angry note about them; and the door slammed, and Pittacus came back down the stairs, muttering to himself. He stopped when he saw me, and stood there, looking very ruffled and put out. A lock of hair hung over his forehead, and a vivid red weal ran across one cheek. He grinned at me, rather sheepishly. For the first time I realized he was not altogether steady on his feet.

"Well," he said, and took a step or two towards me. My throat was dry: I felt paralyzed. "Your aunt's a very stubborn woman, Sappho my dear."

He frowned and shook his head.

"Don't understand. Unkind." The slur in his voice was now unmistakable; whatever had happened upstairs had, clearly, drained his last reserves of self-control.

I said nothing, conscious always of his hot eyes on me.

"*You're* not unkind, are you?" he said, and took another step forward. I had never heard that particular tone in his voice before. He was close enought now for me to smell the stale wine on his breath. Then, with a kind of sob, he reached out and put his great brown scarred hands over my breasts.

A cold, awful thrill, half-terrified disgust, half an even more terrified excitement, ran through me. I could not move or speak: I had become a thing, an object. For an instant, an instant only, time stood still. Then those searching hands shifted from my breasts, gripped me hard, swung me off my feet and on to the couch like a limp doll. His face was over me, all tenderness gone from it now, huge, bearded, frightening past belief, eyes suffused, the weight of his body pressing down.

"*Ahh*," he said, an appalling animal snarl, and clamped those great wet hairy lips on my mouth. I gasped, sickened by the smell of him, the heat, the unspeakable slobber of saliva: and as I did so his tongue forced itself into my mouth, a monstrous polyp-like invader, while one hand groped at my thighs. I can never forget that instant, never find words to describe the degree of revulsion it aroused in me.

I must have bitten him instinctively, without knowing I did it. I heard him give a shout, and then he was standing up, wiping blood from his mouth with the back of his hand, quite sober now, a dreadful expression on his face. My stomach contracted as though squeezed by a giant fist: I rolled over and vomited on the floor, in long, agonizing spasms. When at last I looked up, my eyes starred with tears, he had gone. I heard the click of the garden-gate. Then I sank back on the couch, faint, shaking, drained, deadly cold.

All I could see was my mother's face, twisted in that near-insane rictus of loathing; all I could hear was the dreadful hissing torrent of words, the hate and pain and horror, the nightmare. *You'll learn,* she had said, and now I had learnt, my illusions and trust shattering like thin shards against the granite surface of reality. *True: all true, every word.*

At that point I fell asleep: and I had not yet woken when my mother and cousins returned from their walk. With great fuss I was put to bed and dosed with herbal infusions: my mother always enjoyed a crisis. For the next few days—encouraged, perhaps, by my unexpected docility—she was heard congratulating herself, at frequent intervals, on having had the good sense not to let me out of the house that afternoon. "The child was obviously sickening for something," she said. "After all, she's my daughter. If I don't know her, who does?"

It is easy—too easy—to say of some event: *If only this had not happened, my life would have taken a different course.* Yet I find myself tempted to make the assertion when I look back on that dreadful afternoon. If I had not become estranged, in those particular circumstances, from the one man who both understood and could help me. If I had not, in self-protective reaction, swung violently over to my mother's way of thinking—not only about human relationships, but every aspect of life. If I had not, in consequence, become—very much against my natural inclinations—deeply and actively involved in politics. If Myrsilus had not returned from exile and seized power at the precise moment he did. If my mother had been able to accept the love I offered her. If Aunt Helen had not, for the first time in her life, lost control of her emotions. If Andromeda had not been her father's daughter. *If, if, if.*

This won't do at all. I'm getting maudlin. My task is to take these broken pieces and see where they fit together, not to cry over them. I have never had any patience with self-pity in others, and I have no intention of indulging it in myself. Besides, why should I? Many people would envy me my life. Even now. I have had wealth, and the taste to enjoy it. I have been granted the maker's divine gift of song. I have loved and been loved. Sorrow is a natural condition of life:

[73]

only the child demands unbroken happiness. But the child in me, I know, is still strong.

It is getting dark. Soon Thalia will come to light the lamps, her hair braided softly round that neat, beautiful head, her body alive with love, so that every part of her seems to sing as she moves. Yet Thalia is a slave. What then is slavery? And what is freedom? Which of us can truly be called free?

For a week now I have hardly stirred from this room. Reality recedes into the past, and I follow it.

Why should I dream of Sicily?

Perhaps Pittacus' visit had shocked her, too, in some way; perhaps she had some notion of what had happened between us downstairs afterwards; but for whatever reason, Aunt Helen suddenly came out of her semi-tranced state, almost as though nothing had happened. Almost, but not quite. There was a curious inner glow about her, something quite indescribable but beyond question *there*: even my mother saw it. Aunt Helen came up to my bedroom the following day, and we smiled at each other, and sat for a little while without saying anything at all. I was still shocked, and apathetic: but I have a naturally resilient temperament, and already the first raw horror was beginning to fade.

She looked at me with those great golden eyes of hers, and put one hand on top of mine. She was tall and clean and beautiful and smelt like a spring garden. I felt a great upsurge of affection—and something more, something instinctive and physical.

She said, as though continuing a conversation begun long ago and in another place: "Growing up is so hard, my darling. For someone like you especially."

"Why me?"

"Because you can see what there is to fear."

We looked at each other. I nodded. Aunt Helen smiled, that deep, beautiful smile which seemed to irradiate her entire face. She said: "All power is divine, Sappho: and the power to create is the first essence of divinity. Those who make share, however humbly, in godhead. They fashion a world from chaos. Do you understand?"

"Yes," I said. "Not the words. But I understand."

Aunt Helen said softly: "Creation takes many forms. We should honour them all. To make, truly to make, is not an easy thing." She looked at me. "It means labour and suffering. It means a pouring out of the self. It means self-surrender and love."

[74]

"Love?" I shied at the word. Aunt Helen's hand tightened gently on mine.

"Yes, love. You are right, there is something terrible about love, and we do right to stand in awe of it. But we deny it at our peril. It is the force that binds our many-sided world together—stars, seeds, the swarming life of ocean and forest. If we reject it, we reject ourselves, we are nothing. Aphrodite is a cruel Goddess; all true deities are cruel by mortal standards, and we question their divinity if we pretend otherwise."

I shook my head, quiet, desperate. "It's no good," I whispered. "I can't. I can't."

Aunt Helen said: "Aphrodite has many moods, and many faces. Her gifts, like all gifts, can be abused." For an instant our eyes met in a kind of naked understanding. "You must have trust, Sappho. Whatever the appearances, you must have trust."

"Trust? In what?"

She hesitated a moment before replying. What she then said surprised me more than anything else.

"In divine protection. I think—how shall I put this, my dear?—that you possess, without knowing it, the precious gift which all seers, priests, and poets share to some degree: you stand a little closer to the Gods than other mortals. They speak through you, or will speak, when the time is ripe; and in return you will have their communion and protection."

I shrank a little under the bedclothes: it was as though some ghostly finger had reached out to lay its indelible mark on my forehead. "Why me?" I whispered. "Why me? Why can't they leave me alone? That's all I want, ever."

Aunt Helen said, compassionately: "You will find, in time, that this knowledge creates its own solitude."

There was a short silence. When Aunt Helen spoke again, it was in her ordinary, day-to-day voice: the alarming thought flashed across my mind that she might have been in some sort of divine trance herself.

"Well, I mustn't sit here talking all day, darling; you need rest and quiet."

"I'm feeling much better now," I heard myself say; and then realized, rather to my surprise, that it was true.

What none of us, I think, had ever realized was just how much, in his own quiet way, Uncle Eurygyus had over-shadowed Aunt Helen

[75]

during his lifetime. We would, no doubt, have ridiculed such a notion: to all appearances it was she who had the whip-hand over him. But after his death, and once she was through her mysterious period of withdrawal, Aunt Helen—there is no other word for it—blossomed out. She lost no time in erasing all traces of her husband's more curious habits: the day after our discussion upstairs she went through the house in a kind of purifactory fervour, like Odysseus after the slaying of the wooers. Despite my mother's protests (once she had someone in bed she liked to keep them there) I got up to watch the fun.

The fortune-tellers and old crones and seedy oriental priests who were always hanging about the back yard found themselves sent packing for good. Aunt Helen made a small bonfire of the withered garlands and dream-manuals, the astrological charts, the malodorous roots and herbs, the accumulated apotropaic junk of several decades. Cobwebbed bottles full of doubtful-looking liquid were smashed or poured down the drain. For several days the house was almost uninhabitable: every slave-girl was busy scrubbing, washing, and cleaning. The smell of sulphur became quite unbearable.

So far, my mother was pleased to approve; she had obviously been itching to do much the same thing herself. It did not occur to her (knowing her temperament, I should have been surprised if it had) that Aunt Helen's distaste for the hocus-pocus of superstition was based, not on rational common sense, but on a deep and genuine religious instinct. Such a notion would have struck her as paradoxical, or, worse, merely frivolous. She dealt with a lot of the world's more intractable realities in this way.

Besides, Aunt Helen led an irregular sexual life; and in my mother's view nobody who did this could possibly have a right attitude to the Gods. How she arrived at such a conclusion altogether defeats me: but (as often happens with those who proclaim their trust in pure reason) the workings of her mind were largely conditioned by her emotions.

Religious faith, and the visible pattern of ritual in which that faith is enshrined, have played so all-pervasive a part in my life that I find it hard to remember, at times, how late I came to them. As a small girl I would be dressed appropriately for festivals, but no one told me what they meant; I knew about the Gods, yet only in the sense that their names and functions were a familiar part of my childhood landscape. My father's attitude to the divine I can only guess at; my mother's was one of respectful indifference. She conformed socially (for so independent a person it was curious how sensitive she was to public opinion), but never went beyond that; the whole field of religious experience, in the personal sense, she was content to leave unexplored.

When Aunt Helen took me, without question or explanation, to the old, small tempe of Aphrodite that stood on a spur of the citadel, facing out across the Aegean, I hung back in the forecourt, heart pounding, so frightened I could scarcely stand. She waited, very easy and patient, smiling under her widow's veil. It was a fine spring day; a breeze off the mainland whipped white flecks from the ruffled cobalt water, and the sun struck down with unexpected heat, burning my cheek. Everything glittered, shone bright, was exultantly alive. I thought: *But what am I afraid of?* Before the mood could pass I said to Aunt Helen: "All right. I'm ready." We went in together.

It was cool and quiet and shady after the sunlight. Here and there light flowed down, a slanting shaft between columns. Candles flickered: I smelt incense, and the faint, sweetish aroma of fresh-dried blood. The walls were hung with pictures: I looked at the one nearest me, and saw Aphrodite rising from her foam-born shell, golden-haired, virginal, immortal. At the great central altar the sacrifice had been concluded: two girl-acolytes, in white robes, stood by, heads bowed, while the priestess chanted the final litany, her voice high and pure and remote, like a young boy's. The words were half-familiar, yet it was as though I had never heard them before: they sang through me, illuminating and transfiguring:

> *"Queen of heaven,*
> *Mother and Virgin,*
> *Star of the morning,*
> *Born from the foam,*
> *Mother of seasons,*
> *Adored and adoring.*
> *Holy of holies,*
> *Lady of light—"*

"What must I do?" I whispered.

"Listen. Pray. Wait."

I knelt there, my eyes on the great image of the enthroned Goddess. She seemed to float in air above the altar, divine, majestic, the Queen of Heaven indeed. I stared, entranced, at the thick tresses rippling down below her flowery coronal, at the white linen robe with its intricate woven hem and pattern of golden stars. The Goddess' eyes seemed to look straight into mine: a soft, amused, enigmatic smile played round her lips.

Presently the priestess began a long prayer; and again, without warning, I experienced that strange sense of weightlessness and release. I seemed to float up, up, through thin, clear, dazzling air, till at last I hung poised in immeasurable space: I looked down, and below me—many-coloured, intricate, splendid—lay the world of men. Far away, like waves on some remote dream-shore, the voice of the priestess rose and fell: "The Gods below and above the earth acknowledge your sovereign power. It is your hand, Lady, that sets the stars in their courses and gives light to sun and moon. At your bidding spring returns after winter; by your universal power winds blow, seeds quicken, buds swell and burst, the corn stands heavy in the furrow, the grape hangs full on the vine. You bring together bird and beast after their common kind; it is your potent divinity that lights the spark of passion in all living creatures the world over, that decrees where and when the spark shall fall—O Cyprus-born, Child of the Sea-foam, Lady of Beasts, Paphian, Evening Star, Daughter of Heaven, immortal Aphrodite . . ."

The voice faded: there was a strange ringing silence in my ears. The Goddess seemed to grow bright, haloed with a cold, unearthly radiance like that of the full moon. Did those lips move? My name, I heard my own name, uttered quietly, lovingly, several times over: so might some devoted mother address her favourite, wayward child. *I am here*, I whispered. *I am here*: and the tears welled up, the cold fear in my heart melted. I bowed my head in adoration: words sang through my exultant mind like swarms of bright migrant birds, winging southward in the sunlight over green capes and a blue dazzle of sea.

When, at last, I looked up, everything was quiet and still: the priestess and her acolytes had vanished. The sacred flame still curled upwards from the high altar; the Goddess still looked down on me with her quiet, enigmatic smile. But now I saw, clearly, that this was an image only, of wood and skilfully painted wax, robed, bewigged, adorned with jewels. The vision, the radiance, these were gone, as though they had never been. The candles flickered: two middle-aged women were praying quietly at a side-shrine. The old man who sold incense and sacred pictures and small votive offerings had dozed off over his stall.

I knew, then, that the Goddess had manifested herself to me; that

[78]

she had been bodied forth in the image men made to receive her, and had called me by name to her service. The words, the bright words, still ran through my head, in intoxicating patterns and rhythms. How serve her? How thank her? How but by using the gift she had released in me? The sacrament of song, the sweet agony of creation. Winged words, Homer had said, and till now the phrase had meant nothing to me: but now, now, I saw, I knew, the iridescent upsurge, the poised bird-swift beauty. Inspiration, they had told me, was a spring, a cold clear rising spring, watched over by the Muses: but now that spring rose in my own heart, a transfiguring flow. All new, all changed, the gates of my mind opening on a strange, unimaginable country.

Presently this exultation, too, died down, leaving only a deep, steady glow in the core of my being. *All things are possible,* I thought, and then, wonderingly: *I am not afraid. I need never be afraid again.* I blinked, smiling: the afternoon world, the here-and-now of my physical existence closed gently around me. Aunt Helen took my arm, and together we walked out into the sunlight.

It was several days later, and without any direct reference to what had happened in the temple, that Aunt Helen said: "The gifts of the Goddess can be dangerous, Sappho."

"What do you mean?" I was curious rather than alarmed.

"I mean"—she hesitated again—"that some part of your inner self is forfeit, now and for always. What you have surrendered you will never be able to redeem. Or only at a price you cannot pay and survive. Whether it will be worth the sacrifice, you alone can tell."

"It will be worth it," I said, glowing, confident.

"I hope so, my darling. I hope so."

It has taken me nearly forty years to understand the full force of those words.

Then I said, not quite knowing why: "Aunt Helen—what do *you* believe in?"

She turned down the corners of her mouth in that familiar, wry gesture. "Survival," she said, and then, unexpectedly: "Will you promise me one thing?"

"Of course—"

"*Whatever* may happen, don't judge me too hard. Try to understand."

"I promise," I said, bewildered. "But what—?"

"You've promised," she said. "That's enough."

I turned over lazily in bed, still half-asleep, listening to the early-morning clamour from the street outside. It seemed quite extraordinarily loud—horses clattering to and fro, studded boots scraping over the cobbles, a babble of loud, anxious voices, somewhere in the distance a trumpet-call several times repeated. Then (quite inaudible as usual) the city crier making one of his interminable proclamations. I buried my head in the pillow.

"Sappho—"

"Oh, go *away*, Meg."

"Something's happening, something important—"

"I can't stop it."

"*Listen.*"

I blinked my eyes open. Meg was bending over me, her long black hair hanging unbraided round her face, her flat, little-girl breasts with the pale nipples exposed inside her loose nightdress. I sat up quickly. Down the hill, somewhere near the market, the crier was still at it. Meg moved across to the window and unbolted the shutters.

". . . wherefore the so-called Council of Nobles is hereby dissolved, and the city of Mytilene placed under martial law until such time as all rebels and enemies of the State shall have been apprehended. And that for the duration of the said emergency the said Myrsilus, Leader of the People, shall exercise full and plenary powers, including those over life and limb, until such time as an elected Popular Council take office. And furthermore, that an amnesty is hereby declared, in favour of all who by word or deed have lent support to the usurping government during the said Myrsilus' enforced and illegal exile, provided they do make public protestation, on oath, of their allegiance to the said Myrsilus and those ministers whom he may, in the lawful discharge of his duties, appoint to hold office . . ." This final sentence put something of a strain on the herald's lungs, and he stopped at the end of it, presumably to get his breath back. I told Meg to close the shutters: there was a draught blowing right through the bedroom.

"But I want to hear the rest—"

"Haven't you heard enough already?" I snapped. The violence of my own reaction surprised me. "We're back where we were ten years ago. Government by tradesmen."

Meg giggled. "You sound just like your mother," she said.

"Well, *I* want to go and see the fun," Telesippa announced, swinging her blond plaits and looking a good deal more than twelve. "When something exciting happens, all you two can do is sit and *talk*." She swung out of bed, prinking her toes. "Praxinoa!" she yelled.

We had recently, as a special growing-up privilege, been given a slave-girl all to ourselves. Praxinoa was a solid, phlegmatic-looking eighteen-year-old, a Sicilian Greek from some village near Syracuse, born in captivity and sold by her master when he went bankrupt. We were all (though we would have died rather than admit it) just a little afraid of her. When you are fourteen, four years makes a great deal of difference. Besides, Praxinoa was so big, so muscular, so un-self-consciously physical in her response to life. She was given the tiny corner garret that had been our lumber-room: the first time I went in there—without knocking: one could not, somehow, knock on a slave's door—I found her standing, naked, in an old hip-bath, sluicing herself down with water. She held the water-pot balanced on one shoulder: her legs were slightly apart, and drops glistened on her full, heavy breasts.

Shock and embarrassment literally took my breath away: I just stood there staring. I felt my cheeks burn crimson, and was conscious, at the same time, of a secret excitement so keen it almost hurt. She looked up, smiling, shaking the thick, rather oily black ringlets out of her eyes, quite unconcerned. Then she saw my expression, and her face changed too. She stepped quickly out of the bath, turning away as she did so, so that I saw the wide white spread of her hips and buttocks. She took a towel and wrapped herself in it.

I withdrew, agonized, trembling, ashamed. Neither of us referred to the incident again. Sometimes I thought she had forgotten it. Then I would catch her dark eyes watching me, in an odd, speculative way, and my turmoil of uncertainty would begin afresh. What she was feeling, or thinking, I had no idea, and my own reaction I thrust into the back of my mind, refusing to face its implications. Looking back, I can afford to be amused by my own naïvety; but it was not in the least amusing at the time.

Now I watched her warily as she bustled in at Telesippa's summons, very neat and unobtrusive, her black hair parted severely in the middle, her face in some odd way wiped clean of personality. Telesippa was still young enough to enjoy the novelty of ordering her about. She demanded hot water, and a clean dress, and hairpins, all in one breath. She stripped off her nightgown and pirouetted in front of the mirror: I have never met anyone who took such an unself-conscious and unashamed delight in her own body. Giggling delight-edly, she flicked each nipple with thumb and first finger till they stood out hard and firm from her still half-grown breasts. Meg and I caught each other's eye, and flushed, and looked away. Both of us were prudish to a degree about exposing ourselves in anyone's presence: Telesippa worried us all the more, I now realize, because her lack of embarrassment implicitly challenged our own assumptions.

While Praxinoa was brushing out her hair, Telesippa said: "What's all this about Myrsilus? Will anyone be killed? Can we go and watch?"

"I'm sure I don't know," said Praxinoa, still keeping up a hard, steady rhythm of brush-strokes. "You'll have to ask your mother or Lady Cleïs about that sort of thing." She sounded a little put out: why, I could not imagine.

When we got downstairs we found the boys hanging around in a disconsolate group outside the lobby. The only cheerful one was Larichus, who beamed and said: "No school today, no school today—"

"Be quiet, you little beast," said Hermeas.

Agenor's eyes met mine. "Mother says we're not to go into the streets. There may still be some fighting. She's probably right."

Telesippa swung her plaits. "Why can't we have some fun for once?" she asked crossly.

"A curious notion of fun you have, sister," Agenor remarked mildly.

Telesippa put out her tongue. "You're dull and mean and I hate you," she said.

Charaxus stood silent in one corner, frowning and biting his nails.

"But what does it *mean?*" Meg said to no one in particular.

There was an angry hiss of skirts behind me. "It means," said my mother, in her best crisis voice, "that those who care for this city of ours will have to fight—*fight*, do you understand?—to restore freedom and justice and the rule of law. It may take months, even years. But we have done it once, and we can do it again."

None of us quite knew what to say to this. The noise outside had died away: all I could hear now was the long-drawn cry of some itinerant vegetable-seller trudging up the hill. Whatever was happening, life—and vegetables—had to go on.

It was odd how little difference (despite all my mother said) this change of government seemed to make. Somehow I expected everyone to go round with long faces, as though carrying an intolerable burden; but the market-place remained as busy and cheerful as ever, taverns and shops did a brisk trade, the same tanned, tarry sailors lounged about the quay, winking at girls or exchanging stories. Myrsilus did not, on the face of it, look a tyrant: he was a grey-haired, grey-faced man of medium height and unremarkable appearance, and the worst his enemies could find to say about him was that he worked too hard: such grinding hours were more appropriate to a slave or a tradesman than to a man of reasonably good family occupied by affairs of state.

A blazing summer morning: outside, in the plane-trees, the cicadas keep up their steady chirring, dancers with midget castanets. In the cool shade of the courtyard I sit, abstracted, while words gather slowly in my mind, globe themselves like resin from a cut tree-trunk, are written down. Solitude enfolds me. It is the day after my first, curiously unsettling, encounter with the young poet Alcaeus.

"Don't let me disturb you." It is my mother's voice, behind me; she can move more silently than her own shadow when she chooses. I jerk round, startled. "I'm sorry, Mama—I didn't know—" Then I think: *What am I supposed to be apologizing for?*

She says: "Another poem?"

"Yes, Mama." I shrink into myself a little: the reaction does not escape her.

"Anyone might suppose you had something to hide." The eyes are darting, curious; she glances down towards the wax tablet in my lap.

"Of course not—" But instinctively I put one hand over the tablet. My cheeks flush hot with vexation.

"If you'd rather not show me—"

"It's not finished yet."

"I see." (I never cease to be amazed at the degree of sheer incredulity my mother can inject into those two words.) "I thought perhaps it might be the kind of poem"—her eyelids snapped nervously—"you would prefer not to let me see at all."

There is no possible answer to this. I wait, stiff and silent, for her next move.

"Really, Sappho, poetry is no excuse for sulkiness."

I know better by now than to deny the charge.

"I'm sorry, Mama."

"You sit about indoors far too much. It's bound to make you peevish, especially in this weather—"

"I was out yesterday—"

"Yes. And I know very well where you went." She moves restlessly from foot to foot, as though her clothes chafe her. "Helen has no business to involve you in this—this religious mania of hers. It's quite intolerable. The atmosphere in those temples is thoroughly unhealthy. Nasty hocus-pocus, just the sort of thing calculated to impress adolescent girls. What *you* need is something to occupy your mind—"

[83]

"Yes, Mama. I'm sure you're right."

She pauses for a moment, considering. "You spent a long time talking to that ill-mannered young poet last night."

"He did most of the talking."

"You didn't discourage him, I noticed."

"He's insult-proof, I think."

"Perhaps he wasn't *attentive* enough for your liking."

"If you really want to know, Mama, he frightened me."

My mother hesitates. "Oh, Sappho, my dear, I wish I knew whether I could trust you. Sometimes you seem so hard and hostile and alien. It's a sad thing when one can't be certain of one's own daughter's loyalty."

Her gift for bringing in just a touch of pathos at a crucial moment verges on the uncanny.

"Of course you can trust me, Mama," I say impulsively; and I mean it.

She hesitates, then moves away abruptly and takes a short turn down the colonnade, her shadow fluttering beside her: she always walks close to the pillars, where the sun can reach her face. She seems to be weighing up something in her mind. At last she comes back, and stands over me, her body blocking out the light.

"I would like you to do something for me—for us," she says, in a strained, intense voice. "No. Not for any individual. For the city." She hesitates, then adds: "Before I say any more, I should warn you that it might involve you in very real danger."

This flicks a raw nerve in me. "My father died for the city," I say hotly.

There is a short silence, broken abruptly by the clatter of my writing-tablet as it drops to the ground.

My mother says, almost as though talking to herself: "No one would suspect you. Why should they? What concern has a girl of your age with plots or politics? You can pass unnoticed, almost as though you were invisible. Your world is made up of quarrels and jealousies, of picnics, new dresses, dancing, poetry, idle chatter, foolish whispering in corners about boys. You can go to any house, at any time, and no one will so much as notice you. Afternoon visiting is a pastime you enjoy, I believe."

"What is it I have to do, Mama?" I ask. Already I am regretting my generous impulse; already the hot needles of irritation are probing at my self-control.

"We need someone to carry messages between—certain houses.

Myrsilus has spies and informers everywhere. There can be no more open meetings."

"I see."

"You accept?"

"Of course," I say.

There is a pause.

My mother says: "Don't you want to know the names of those involved?"

"It's not hard to guess." Then I look at her and say: "Myrsilus must know them all as well as I do, Mama. Why does he let them remain at liberty?"

"Because if he imprisons or executes half a dozen of our most distinguished citizens, there will be nothing to choose between him and a naked tyrant like Periander."

"Perhaps," I say thoughtfully, "he's holding his hand till they commit themselves, so that he can make a show of giving them a fair trial."

My mother stares at me, surprised. "So your head isn't always in the clouds. Of course. That is one of the two major risks we must face."

"And the other?"

"Betrayal." The word hangs in the bright air for a moment, like some small, almost visible cloud. Then—as though the point were not worth further consideration—she goes on briskly to reel off a list of the expected names—Phanias, Pittacus, Draco, Deinomenes. At the end of it she hesitates again. "There is one other house, Sappho."

A pause.

"Yes, Mama?"

With apparent irrelevance she says: "A pity you feel so strongly about our young poet."

"He had me at a disadvantage. It was so embarrassing."

"What *do* you mean?"

The long-suppressed question bursts out. "Why did you show him my poems?"

My mother blinks once or twice, and laughs. "Good heavens, why shouldn't I? Is there anything terrible about that?"

"I wish you'd asked me first. After all, I wrote them, and they're private."

Nothing irritates my mother more than any suggestion that she does not have the right to manipulate her children's lives for their own supposed benefit.

"Any *normal* girl would be only too glad for a successful young

[85]

poet to consider her work. Gratitude has never been one of your stronger virtues, Sappho."

It suddenly strikes me, at this point, just what my mother is up to. The lessons would be a convenient cover: two poets were bound to adore each other. At the same time Alcaeus's reputation should prevent any awkward entanglement. My mother has probably arranged the whole thing in advance. The only possibility her plan failed to allow for was that I might be disobliging enough to detest Alcaeus on sight.

I stare, bemused, torn between laughter, tears, and angry resentment. In a way almost too ridiculous to think about I have, it seems, become a conspirator. The wax tablet, with its unfinished poem, still lies on the ground at my feet.

VI

PHANIAS' house stood—stands—a little outside the city, up in the cool foothills overlooking the sea, with mountains and pine-forests behind it and an uninterrupted view across the straits. It was built by Phanias' grandfather: a remarkable man, round whom the crust of legend had already begun to accumulate in his own lifetime. He chose a site on a shallow rise, facing south to catch the best of the winter sunlight—and perhaps, too, so that he could enjoy the constant sight of his own land. As far as the eye could reach along that flat, fertile coastal strip, to the last southern promontory, everything—olive-groves, corn-land, vineyards, pasturage—was his inalienable free-hold.

This great estate he had built up over the years, worked on with tireless energy and bequeathed intact to his son and grandson. (It was a standing joke in Mytilene that the family produced one male heir only to each generation, thus avoiding any division of the estate: a tribute, as one wag put it, to the power of wealth over desire.) But at the time I am thinking of, Phanias had two daughters only: his wife Ismene was almost thirty and after seven years' barrenness seemed unlikely to bear a male heir at all.

If I shut my eyes I can see the house in every detail: I know it as one can only know a place where one has experienced extremes of happiness or despair. I know the deep cistern where small green lizards lie, motionless except for a faint palpitation in the throat, waiting to catch those tiny flies that skim across the surface of the water. I know the trim walled kitchen-garden, with its orderly rows of cabbages and onions, its sweet-smelling herbs—thyme, rosemary, basil—its weathered bee-hives and its fishpond. I know the stables, and the old barn with the olive-press, and the paddock (there was one big oak-tree in it: I could still climb blindfold up to its central crotch), and the rose-arbour—and the apple-orchard. The house itself had the same comforting sense of tradition and permanence and simplicity: I always found myself *touching* it, running my fingers sensuously over wood or stone. It was built of fine-squared white ashlar blocks, with heavy cross-beams and iron-studded oak doors; yet the dominating impression was one of airy lightness. On the south side there was a wide, shady upper terrace paved with black and white marble. The two deep wells never ran dry, even in the height of summer.

Phanias' grandfather had called the house Three Winds. No one in the family knew why; but no one would have dreamed of changing the name.

Praxinoa and I are jolting up the paved drive of Three Winds in a mule-cart. Though autumn is in the air the sun is still high, and we both carry parasols. Our mule-driver is a sour, taciturn little man, who prefers (I suspect) animals to human beings, and sits hunched on his box, whistling through broken teeth. I am still excited by the idea of being allowed out on my own, with only a slave-girl as escort. Anyway, Praxinoa doesn't count as a slave. She is becoming, if not a friend, at least a privileged confidante.

Between us stands a basket of candied fruits, a present from my mother to Ismene. I am holding a roll of my latest poems: some are very bad indeed. But this, as my mother has been at pains to point out, does not really matter. What matters is the message on the back of the roll, which has been written with some preparation made from milk, and will become visible when held near a fire. I am going to pay a call on my friend Mica (whom I do not particularly like) and leave her my poems (which, being only twelve, she is too young to appreciate). I am a month short of my fifteenth birthday, very conscious that I have an important, grown-up job to do.

For this reason I am a little stiff with poor Mica, who is waiting for us in the stable yard and comes running out at the sound of our wheels clattering up the drive. She is short and cheerful and un-repentantly plump, with the clumsy gestures of a puppy. But her hands are exquisite, the hands of an artist. Which, surprisingly, she is.

"Sappho, you're really here, oh, it's wonderful, I've been so excited, and you look so *beautiful* in that dress, pale yellow, lovely, and Mama says we can play in the paddock—"

"*Play?*" I am practising some of my mother's more subtle intonations; this one—a rising note of gentle incredulity—I find very effective. Mica flushes, and breaks off in mid-flow. The mule-driver hawks, spits on the cobbles, looks interrogative. Praxinoa collects the fruit-basket and the parasols and stands behind me. I tell the mule-driver to come back an hour before sunset; he nods briefly and clatters off, still without saying a word.

"Mama's expecting you; come and see her."

We walk through cool, white, arched corridors to Ismene's private living-room, away from the central hall and courtyard. She is working on a big tapestry—centaurs and Lapiths—and rises, smiling, when we come in. Her hands are very like Mica's, and she is plump too; but in her the flesh has assumed different, more harmonious proportions. The room smells of sweet grass and wax: the table and presses are old, beautifully polished, smoothly warm to the touch.

"Sappho, my dear: how good of you to come." She is hardly taller than I am, but holds herself very erect. Her thick black hair is drawn back in a chignon: I notice, to my surprise, a few faint streaks of grey in it. There is a worried preoccupation at the back of her eyes that belies the welcoming smile. Mica dances to and fro beside me, irrepressible, adoring.

"Mama—doesn't she look *wonderful?*"

Ismene considers me gravely. "A most exquisite young lady," she says, and means it.

I beckon Praxinoa forward with the fruit, and make my small—carefully prepared—speech. I see Ismene's eye on the roll of poems: how much, I wonder, does she know? Then my eye strays to the wall, where there is a small, vivid, striking likeness of her, painted on wood, and hung to catch the afternoon light: again that imperceptible anxiety about the eyes, caught with extraordinary skill and unobtrusiveness.

"Do you like it, Sappho?" says Mica eagerly. "Do you think it's the way Mama looks?" I realize, amazed, that the picture is *her* work: how can this coltish, ridiculous child possess such insight? Then I catch the thought up, ashamed: who am I to question the unpredictable manner in which the Muses dispose of their gifts?

"Yes," I say, "I like it very much."

"Can I paint you too, Sappho? Can I? Can I? Please say yes—"

"Your guest must make up her own mind, Mica," Ismene smiles.

Sitting for my portrait, I decide, is a more lady-like way of passing an hour or two than playing hide-and-seek or other childish games.

"That would be very pleasant," I say graciously.

She actually claps her hands with excitement.

"Oh, *thank* you—" she cries, and is gone, in a helter-skelter of flying feet, to collect her paints and brushes.

Ismene says softly, "Poor Mica."

"But she's so happy—"

"My dear, it's not easy, being a talented child. You know things before you're old enough to understand them. Or to bear them."

Our eyes meet.

"I know," I say, and the pretensions are stripped off me like the shell from an egg; I am left exposed, vulnerable, ashamed.

"Be kind to her. Be patient."

"Yes. I promise."

"It's a difficult time. For all of us."

"Of course. Lady Ismene—"

"Yes, my dear?"

I glance quickly at Praxinoa: she is standing by the doorway, her face heavy and impassive, contemplating the half-finished tapestry.

"No—it doesn't matter."

I can hear Mica's returning footsteps on the stairs.

Ismene says: "If you ever feel you want to talk to me—"

I feel a sudden overwhelming urge to pour out all my secrets and fears to this warm, tranquil, understanding woman, who would never be shocked or angry at any confession. But there is no time, and the words will not come: they have been thrust down too long into the dark, inarticulate recesses of the mind.

Mica has tied a yellow ribbon in her hair: she is clutching easel, paints, a new square of box-wood, a bundle of brushes. A young house-slave (not much older than Mica herself, to judge from her appearance) comes panting in behind her. With Praxinoa's assistance, the artist is gradually relieved of her various burdens.

"Come on," Mica says, catching me by one hand, "I know where we'll go—" and now her mood is infectious. I find myself caught up in it, and we run giggling down the corridor (so solemn with its family portraits and yellowed busts) towards the courtyard and the stables: I glance back once over my shoulder and see Ismene turn back slowly to the big tapestry on its frame.

Outside the air is warm and murmurous with bees: down in the corn-field I can see the reapers bending to their task, the tall brown ears falling, the flash of a sickle in the afternoon light. They are singing as they work, an old, simple tune of a few phrases only, repeated again and again, its pattern shaped by the rhythm of their work, its haunting plangency distilled from a thousand harvests. Down the rose-walk Mica goes, feet flying, and through the low gate to the orchard.

Here there is a dapple of sunlight and shadow, and the workers do not sing: they are silent, absorbed, swaying on tall ladders, half-hidden among leaves, each with a deep basket over his or her arm. The trees are old, crotched and gnarly, with here and there a heavy-laden branch propped up on a fork of olive-wood. There are apples, pears, quinces. A gentle breeze rustles the leaves: the atmosphere is slow and tranquil, so tranquil that even Mica slackens her pace and walks silent beside me.

In a small open space is the biggest and oldest apple-tree I have ever seen in my life. It must be well over twenty feet high, with a scarred, massy bole as thick as three men's bodies; here and there gum has trickled and hardened on its surface, and its lowest horizontal branches are well out of my reach even when I stand on tip-toe. The pickers have not reached it yet; everywhere great clusters of red apples are visible through the leaves.

But what first catches my eye is not the tree itself. From one of the biggest branches—some time ago, to judge from the way the ropes have scored deep into the bark—a child's swing has been hung, with a simple wooden seat. As we approach, the afternoon sun is shining through the foliage in our faces, gilding each leaf with Hesperidean fire. The swing curves up and back in a smooth arc; the diminutive figure clinging to the ropes, hair flying, seems all air and spirit, a dryad's child, intangible, evanescent.

Then we are under the tree, away from the transfiguring sunlight, and the child in the swing is human after all, a small, grave, brown creature who wears a crocus-coloured dress and looks somehow awkward, a changeling, with her fringe and her great grey eyes and her delicate fingers curled about the coarse twist of the ropes. She is, perhaps, seven or eight years old: her dark auburn hair is coiled round her head in a neat plait. The swing slowly comes to rest: she surveys the stranger with cautious appraisal. I feel that a sudden gesture of any sort could send her arching away into the sun, leaving the swing empty behind her. Then, tentatively at first, she smiles, and her whole face becomes radiant, transfigured. It is as though she has captured the sun and drawn it into herself, so that all light and warmth proceed from her. She slides off the swing-seat and stands there, suddenly awkward, not knowing what to do with her hands and feet. There is a greenish smudge on one cheek.

"Hullo," she says.

"What's your name?"

"At-Atthis." She stumbles a little over the second syllable. "Is Mica going to paint you?"

"M'm."

"You'll have to sit *dreadfully* still."

"I don't mind. I like doing that."

"Do you?" She considers me, the grey eyes very serious under their incredibly dark lashes. "So do I sometimes. When I want to think."

Mica says: "What do you think about, silly?" Her voice is affectionate, warm, teasing. She is obviously very fond of Atthis, despite the difference in their ages.

"Oh, things. If I sit very still I can see right through the sky."

"And all the colours and shapes change," I say quietly.

Atthis looks at me. "Yes. You really understand, don't you?"

Mica says: "We'd better start on the painting, Sappho. There isn't all that much light left." The sudden irritation in her voice is unmistakable.

"All right."

She poses me carefully at the foot of the apple-tree, sitting with my legs folded under me and to one side. I am still holding the roll of poems.

Mica says: "You should have a pen too." Her whole tone and bearing change when she is painting, or about to paint: become confident, adult, incisive. The small slave-girl, who has been giggling quietly with Praxinoa, is sent scampering back to the house for a pen.

So I sit there, quiet and at peace, holding the pen to my lips in the stylized gesture of a poet seeking inspiration, while Mica works at her portrait. Her powers of concentration are remarkable: she only glances up at me occasionally, and, as far as I can tell, never makes a mistake. Atthis is lying in the grass, elbows spread, chin resting on her cupped hands. Sometimes she glances at Mica or me, but not often. She is more absorbed by the tiny insects scurrying to and fro around her. None of us says anything: a companionable silence enfolds us.

Presently two pickers—middle-aged men with close-cropped, greying hair and beards, their faces of the same seamed, leathery texture as their arms—come down the path to our tree, carrying ladders and baskets. They, too, catch the atmosphere: they smile, say nothing, prop up their ladders, and climb quietly into the sun-dappled green foliage overhead. Slowly the shadows lengthen across the orchard. Now and then a twig drops from a high branch, there is a crackle and a rustle, the tiny shudder as some more than usually resistant apple is prised loose. Mica's shoulders hunch with urgency: she must, she will, beat the setting sun.

More footsteps: slower this time, easy, relaxed. Phanias comes strolling down the grass path, a tall figure in light summer riding-cloak and soft white doeskin thigh-boots. He must be rising forty, but there is no trace of grey in his hair or beard. He wears his hair long, in the old-fashioned style, pinned at the nape of his neck with an ornamental gold clasp. His belt is broad, and studded with gold rosettes; a hunting-knife in a plain leather scabbard hangs from it.

At the sight of him Atthis is transformed. She springs to her feet, arms outstretched, and Phanias, laughing, swings her up on his shoulders. (There flashes into my mind a sudden memory of Pittacus and Andromeda—how many years ago? nine? ten?—in our courtyard at Eresus.) Awkwardly I get to my feet to greet him, smoothing out my pleated dress. Mica is so absorbed she has not even noticed his arrival. She glances up at me, bites her lip in vexation.

"Oh, Sappho—you've *moved!*"

Phanias stoops to kiss the top of her head. She whirls round.

"Papa—I'm so sorry—I didn't—"

"Hush, lamb. Don't fuss." He is looking at the portrait: his eyes flick up to me and back again.

"It's good, Mica. *Very* good."

Something, somewhere, is wrong: his voice has a worried edge to it.

"Really, Papa? You really like it?"

"It's very good," he repeats, and comes across to me (Atthis still perched on his shoulders) and takes both my hands in his. But he has not said he likes it.

"Sappho, my dear child, you become more charming every day. Odd how seldom talent and good looks seem to agree. The Gods are jealous creatures. You must tell me how you disarmed them."

This polite speech he has to deliver bent forward in a rather awkward posture: I am so tiny, he is so tall, and he has forgotten to let go of my hands. I reflect (but do not say so) that if I could

[93]

really disarm the Gods, I would prevail on them to make me a foot or so taller.

I smile, lower my eyelids modestly, and draw back from him in a kind of half-curtsey. Atthis gives me a quick, mischievous grin. Mica, her painting abandoned, is a nervous twelve-year-old again, and a stab of pity for her goes through me.

"Can I see it, Mica?"

"I don't know. I'm not sure if it's finished—"

"Yes," Phanias says, though whether to her or me I am not sure, "yes, it's finished."

I study the portrait for a moment in silence. It is a brilliant likeness, done with most delicate colour and line; yet the more I look at it the more uneasy I become. It is as though I can see the skull articulated beneath the painted flesh. There is an unidentifiable element there—is it in the eyes? the lips?—of coldness, hardness, a quality which makes me think of smooth marble, or the wintry sea. The smile is, at first sight, warm and amused; the lips sensitive, tender. But that alien element persists. It is as though Mica, all unknowing, had painted a ghost in my body. Suddenly I find Aunt Helen's words echoing through the emptiness of my mind: *The gifts of the Goddess can be dangerous ones. You will find that out, in time, and you must do it alone . . . Some part of your inner self is forfeit, now and for always.* No, I tell myself. *No.* This is dangerous nonsense.

"Mica, it's wonderful. I adore it."

"Oh, Sappho." She lights up with happiness. Yet her face has a white, drained look: it is as though she had gone through a serious illness.

Phanias says: "Some portraits, some of the best, are *grown into*." He is studying me thoughtfully.

My fingers curl and clench: it is only at this moment that I recall the true reason for my visit. I hold out the roll of poems to him: "I would consider it an honour if you—" The phrase is a secret sign: I have learnt it by heart, but he swiftly cuts me off half-way through it.

"Oh no, my dear: the honour will be mine." His heavy eyebrows come together: is he mocking me? "You forget how well qualified I am to assess talent in the young." No, not mocking: there is a great sadness in his eyes, the sadness of a man who sees the future and is powerless to change it.

"Well," he says, "we had better be getting back to the house.

I fear your mule-driver is a restless character, Sappho. A touch of discipline would do him no harm."

At the orchard-gate he pauses and looks back, gazing—as his grandfather must so often have done—down the slope of the hillside to the half-reaped corn-fields, to the laden fig-trees and trim rows of vines, with the sunset-crimsoned sea behind them.

"It looks so permanent, doesn't it? So unalterable."

I nod my agreement.

He says: "Nothing is permanent." His long, lean fingers have been playing with an apple-twig: abruptly, they snap it through. "We can only do what we must, knowing it may not be enough. Do you understand me?" He speaks as though no one else were there.

"I understand you, my lord."

"Then you should understand, too, that—for what it is worth—you have my gratitude." He turns from the gate and moves into the fragile perfection of the rose-walk, with its pergolas and arbours, carrying Atthis on his shoulders: once or twice she has to duck her head. Mica blinks, rubs her eyes with doubled-up fists. I see the scatter of freckles below each knuckle. "I knew it'd happen," she says.

"What?"

"A headache. A really terrible headache. It happens every time."

"Every time you paint a picture?"

"No." She struggles with her knowledge, fumbling for words. "Every time I get one *right*. But that means—oh, I can't explain—letting go, surrendering. It sounds weak. But it isn't, Sappho—it hurts more than anything—" She breaks off, yawns as though she would never stop. "So tired—Sorry. Just tired—" Then she turns, like a sleep-walker, and follows her father up the shadowed path. Praxinoa and the little slave-girl, their arms full of painting gear, look at me, hesitate. I nod, and they go on.

I am alone, for a moment, by the orchard-gate. Our big apple-tree is still visible, head and shoulders above the rest. The two pickers come by, slowly, with full baskets, their ladders over their shoulders: they grin and nod as they pass me. Suddenly I see, glowing in the last low rays of the sun, one perfect, burnished apple, hung in a cluster of dark leaves from the very highest branch. Inexplicable happiness surges up inside me.

Perhaps they forgot it? No, I tell myself, with a glance at those broad, purposeful, retreating backs; no, *they* wouldn't forget. It's the one they couldn't reach, that no one can reach—

[95]

And I turn and run, skirts flying, up the rose-walk, into the house, my heart brimming over with an exultation I cannot begin to understand.

Pittacus said, tapping his desk with big, spatulate fingers, not looking at me: "I know this must be an unwelcome visit, Sappho."

"I would rather not discuss it."

"We have to work together. We were friends once. As far as I'm concerned we still are."

I made no comment on this.

"My dear," Pittacus said patiently, "you have sooner or later to face the fact that most men in the world—let me put it delicately for your benefit—worship at the shrines of Aphrodite and Dionysus, very often in conjunction. You are a poet—and, from what I hear, a devotee of Aphrodite yourself. You need to learn the meaning of passion."

"Not like that." My voice was little more than a whisper. "Please, I don't want to talk about it." I felt horribly aware of his gross physical presence: that coarse-pored nose, the great lumpish shoulders. The room had a stale, feral smell about it, like a wild beast's den.

As though sensing my reaction, he got up and threw the shutters open, letting in a stream of fresh morning air. He sighed and stayed a moment with his elbows resting on the sill, staring down at the harbour below. A big Black Sea grain-ship was being unloaded—I had seen it on my way up—and I heard the creak of block and tackle, the *whoomph!* as a netful of sacks settled down on the quay-side, the sound of voices shouting in outlandish dialects. The fresh smell of tar drifted up to me on the breeze.

He said: "I love this house, Sappho. I love living here, at the heart of things." He made a curious shaping gesture with his hands, as though smoothing a pot on the wheel. "Can you understand that? I love to walk down in the warehouses, and see those sealed bales and jars, the merchandise from every corner of the world. I love the dry smell of chaff in the corn-chandlers' store; the mixed aroma of figs and olives and salted fish in the market. I love to sit over a cup of wine in the potters' quarter, and listen to sailors' talk. I love to watch the silversmiths at work in their booths, and the ropemakers, and smell fresh clay, and feel the heat of the fire at the forge when iron is being hammered out on the anvil."

He watched the grain-ship for a little, lost in thought: he seemed to have half-forgotten me. At last he said: "I learnt a lot in the

Troad, you know. Important things." He picked up a small jade fig-urine from a side-table, an Egyptian cat, smooth with much handling, and turned it over in his fingers as he talked. It struck me then that the whole room was littered with such objects—a reddish, rounded stone picked up from the beach and used as a paperweight; a variety of little votive images, many exquisitely carved in ivory; a globular, greenish bottle with a silver stopper—all of which were equally satis-fying to eye and hand.

Pittacus said: "Makers are important." He turned and grinned at me. "Which means, *you* are important. We do right to call a poet a maker. But we are wrong to ignore his fellow-makers." He gestured out of the window. "Grain, timber, hides, wine, oil, rope, pots—these are real, these are *made*, grown, shaped, fashioned. These are the fibre and fabric of our lives."

He began to pace to and fro, with his heavy, nervous, impatient tread.

"What happened in the Troad? What did we achieve? Nothing. A futility. We lost good men, spent hard-won money, and for what? An idiotic squabble, empty talk of honour. It took Periander half an hour to make fools of us all. That taught me a lesson I shall never forget."

"But you were a hero—" I exclaimed, stung out of my indifference, my sulks forgotten.

"Do you really believe that? I saw one possible way of saving time and expense. I took a calculated risk." He shrugged half-humorously. "Sometimes I think Hesiod has more to teach us than Homer. Was there ever a more monumental testament to man's pride and folly than the Trojan War? I ask you."

"You *can't* believe that. It's shameful, dishonourable. Tradesmen's talk—"

"There are worse things to be in this world of ours than a trades-man, my dear. You can't eat honour, and the world has changed quite a lot since they buried Achilles; I'm by no means sure we should be proud of possessing his tomb."

I said, beside myself: "I despise you." It was true; and yet his words had made me uneasier than I cared to admit.

"I'm sorry about that," he said, and sounded as though he meant it. "I would like you to trust me, my dear."

"Why?"

He paused for a moment, considering. "May I give you a piece

of advice?" he said at length. "Don't worry: I'm only too well aware
you aren't likely to follow it."

"Very well." I was uneasier than I cared to admit.

Pittacus said: "Politics—especially the kind you've got yourself involved in—is a dirty game. Nothing like Homer at all. You may
fancy you know the rules; I can assure you you don't. You're the
lamb that strayed into a forest of wolves, my dear. Go back where
you belong, before the wolves get you."

"And where *do* I belong? In the boudoir, I suppose."

He sighed. "You're very like your mother, aren't you?"

"I am *not*."

"Well, we won't argue the point. I've said all I can. Think it over."

"I don't need to." I began to get up, smoothing down my skirt;
but before the movement was well completed Pittacus picked up
the silver hand-bell on his desk, and rang it, thus suggesting that
it was he who had terminated the interview. I stamped my foot
in sheer childish vexation, realized—too late—that this was playing
straight into his hands, and had recovered some sort of dignity by
the time his understeward appeared, with Praxinoa trailing behind
him.

Pittacus said: "This—lady"—the hesitation was only fractional—"is
leaving now. Please escort her out." He watched Praxinoa with frankly
sensual appreciation as she folded the light shawl about my shoulders:
somehow that irritated me more than anything else.

I smiled sweetly and said: "I promised to see Chione before I
left." Chione was Pittacus' wife; she had brought him a very substantial dowry, and everyone said (probably with some justice) that
Pittacus had married beneath him for money. Chione, at this time,
was in her mid-thirties, an amiable, untidy, large woman with badly
bleached hair and a remarkable talent for exotic cookery. Despite
myself, I rather liked her. I sometimes wondered how two such
improbable parents had produced Andromeda. With Tyrrhaeus,
Drom's younger brother, there was no difficulty or surprise: he was
a darker, surlier copy of his father.

"Please don't bother to see me out, Theon," I said to the steward.

He inclined his head. "As you please, my lady. Was I mistaken,
or did the faintest of winks—the merest tremble in one eyelid—
change his expression for an instant? "I'll tell the mistress you're
coming through, then."

"Yes," said Pittacus good-humouredly, "do that." He seemed suddenly a mischievous schoolboy, bubbling over with secret enjoyment: only his eyes remained cool and watchful, and it struck me then just how formidable an enemy he would make if the occasion ever arose.

On my way out, feeling cross and distracted, I nearly ran into a man in the lobby: a tall, sallow, overdressed dandy with lank black curls and too many rings. He had hot black eyes and smelt of stale perfume. His name was Deinomenes, and he was a former member of the Council of Nobles, where he had not been at all popular.

"Sappho, my dear," he said, and I felt the pressure of his fingers on my shoulder, the quick slide and shift. "A fortunate meeting." The black eyes flickered in furtive lubricity. "Pittacus is a lucky fellow."

The implication infuriated me more than anything else could have done. I drew myself away sharply, inclined my head.

"Please excuse me, my lord Deinomenes. I am late already. I have no time for idle gossip."

He laughed, unruffled.

"They're always in a hurry afterwards."

"I bow to your experience, my lord," I said, and swept away down the lobby, with a crisp and satisfying rustle of skirts. I could feel those lecherous eyes following me. Then he turned, raised one hand in casual farewell, and walked through the archway towards Pittacus' private quarters. I remember thinking, in mingled irritation and amusement, what an unlikely pair of fellow-conspirators we made.

I took my troubles to Alcaeus, and got, as I might have expected, very little sympathy. The poetry lessons envisaged by my mother had by now become an established routine; except that they could not, by any stretch of the imagination, be called lessons, and more often than not had little to do with poetry. We sat together in the family library, where—as my supposed mentor put it—we had literary sling-shot available to hurl at one another's heads when the need arose. To my annoyance, Alcaeus proved quite horribly well-read; I had somehow taken it for granted that a young man with such irritating mannerisms must also be a pretentious ignoramus. Dispelling this illusion he found intensely enjoyable—so enjoyable, indeed, that he spun the process out as long as he possibly could. Praxinoa and one of the house-slaves sat in a corner during these sessions, spinning wool, whispering together, unnecessary chaperones.

The room, like most rooms in that ancient, tradition-soaked, lovingly cared for house, generated a curious atmosphere of assurance and tranquillity. It smelt of wax and dust and leather, of oiled cedar-wood and dry aromatic herbs. Heavy faded tapestries hung above the book-shelves, and yellowing busts of Alcaeus' ancestors glowered down in apparent disapproval at this eccentric—not to say degenerate—growth that had suddenly sprouted from so distinguished a family tree.

I told him the gist of my conversation with Pittacus. He listened without comment, heavy eyebrows drawn together, fingers interlaced. I found myself staring at the thick black hairs that flecked the backs of his hands, and became thicker still along his dark, meaty forearms, so that you could see the way they lay all in one direction, like an animal's pelt.

When I had finished he said nothing. The frown deepened; his eyes were on the worn black-and-white pattern of the marble floor, but he seemed to be looking clean through it.

"Well?" I asked a little sharply.

"Well what?"

"How can a man in his position think as he does. Why?"

Alcaeus leaned back in his chair. With slow deliberation he picked up the wine-jug and poured us each a cup; frowning, and as though his life depended on it, he peeled and quartered an apple from the waxed ivy-wood bowl with a small silver fruit-knife.

At last he said: "So all conspirators—please correct me if I misunderstand you—are united in a common cause?"

I flushed. Not for the first time, Alcaeus had succeeded, with one neat stroke, in knocking a flawed cornerstone from the edifice of my assumptions. The moment the words were out I saw this; and Alcaeus saw that I saw. He sighed, and went on: "Because all of us are involved in a plot to overthrow the regime, you suppose we must all be doing so for the same reason—the virtuous, noble, moral reason with which we justify our actions."

"What other reason can there be?"

He appraised me again.

"You really believe it: how strange." With unexpected gentleness he laid one hand on my arm for a moment.

"You must try to understand, Sappho," he said. "If a cause is worth fighting for, worth achieving, it makes no difference that the means employed are disreputable, that the conspirators involved are shabby, self-seeking rogues. What matters ultimately is achievement."

"You're wrong, wrong," I cried. "You can't build a fine house on rotten foundations—"

"But if there's no alternative—"

"The house will fall."

There was a moment's silence. Then, surprisingly, Alcaeus nodded. "Just so," he said. "Just so."

"So you agree with me after all," I said.

"No."

"But what Pittacus told me—"

"That," he said, "is another thing again."

"It worries you. I can see it worries you."

"Oh yes. It worries me. As you know, I've always had a lively regard for my own skin. I prefer it intact." The corners of his bearded mouth turned down: he gave a savage little smile.

"Then why—"

Alcaeus drank his wine at a single gulp and poured out some more. He suddenly looked bored past belief. "It was good advice," he said. "Take it."

"Don't treat me like a child—"

"It's appropriate, I think."

My hands clenched and shook: I wanted to claw his face to ribbons and was astonished at my own violence.

Raging, I said: "I'd rather be innocent, and a child, than what you are."

He grinned. Don't tell me; I know. A drunkard, a coward, a lecher—"

"No," I said, in a breathless voice. "A joke. A sport. Pathetic. Sterile."

Alcaeus eyed me with glinting malice.

"What an *amusing* notion," he said. "And coming from *you*, of all people."

"Oh?"

"A certain ironic inappropriateness, wouldn't you agree?"

"I don't understand."

His eyes searched me, incredulously at first, then in frank astonishment.

"I don't believe you do," he said. "I really don't believe you do." He gave an unpleasant little laugh. "If you want enlightenment on the subject, you might try asking that leggy green-eyed sweetheart of yours—does she still climb trees, by the way?—or your so-devoted cousin. Or—" and he glanced down the library to where Praxinoa stood, big-bodied, impassive, her black hair glinting in a shaft of sunlight.

I shook my head, uneasy, irritated, anxious only to get away.

[101]

"We mustn't lose touch," Alcaeus said at the door, silky malice edging his voice. "We have so much in common, you and I."

That year spring came suddenly, like the opening of a door. One day the sky was heavy with piled clouds, and cold winds blew, scattering the early blossom: the next, we walked abroad in a dazzle of sunlight, the air was all gold and bird song, the stones came warm under our fingers. The swallows returned, as though their bickering conversation had only been interrupted for a few moments, looping and diving round the familiar landmarks—carob-tree, barn, southern-facing garden wall—waking us early with their plectral trill and a black shudder of wings under the eaves. Small green lizards stalked warily up the cracked, mossy stones of the cistern, watching, blinking, as the first mayflies skimmed deliriously across the water. Butterflies scribbled their brilliant-coloured signatures in the dancing air, and the silver-skeletal winter fig-trees groped sunwards with new, quickening fingers.

Blue haze smoked the headlands, the pine-forests turned a deeper green between shadow and sunlight: when you walked there, on the dry fallen needles, you could smell resin in the air like wine. Now fishing-nets were brought out, fresh-tarred for the spring season, boats came creaking down from the slips, the first big merchantmen were warped out through the narrow channel and set sail for Egypt or the Black Sea. After that long winter, life began again, sweeter and richer than one could have dreamed, Persephone returning in triumph to her flowery meadows.

Light filters through the treetops, high above my head, a pricking, refulgent scatter of gold-dust. I am lying on my back, knees a little drawn up, head pillowed on my hands. Somewhere a wood-pigeon is calling—that soft, sentimental, endless coo—and far off in the wood I can hear girls' voices: Telesippa's, Meg's, Gorgo's, excited, full of laughter, yet remote as the voices one hears in half-waking dreams.

Andromeda is stretched out beside me, half-raised on one elbow, watching the play of sunlight across my face. Her own features are half-shadowed: I can only guess at her expression. The white linen dress she wears is smeared with tree-mould, and has rucked right up above her knee, exposing a long, brown, surprisingly muscular leg. We are lying in a natural hollow, three sides of which are surrounded by a spinney. My heart is thudding so hard against my ribs that I feel certain Andromeda must be able to hear it too. But she gives no sign; just lies there chewing a piece of grass, her eyes always on me.

"Well," she says at last, in that low-pitched, mocking voice of hers, "here we are."

"Yes."

What can I say to her? And what is it I feel when she walks into a room, with that awkward, boyish, striding gait?

Achilles on Scyros.

Her eyes search mine: I catch a glint of secret amusement in them, and something else, something very near contempt.

"Do I bore you terribly, Sappho?" she asks.

"How *can* you think that—?"

"We have so little in common."

"Do we?"

"Tell me one thing."

Silence.

"You see?"

The wood-pigeon coos and chirrs overhead. It suddenly occurs to me, with the force of a revelation, that Andromeda might be right. This idea ought to distress me: instead, unexpectedly, it makes me want to giggle. I get up, brushing twigs and dead leaves from my dress.

"Let's go and find the others, then."

"Sappho—don't be hurt."

"I'm not hurt. If you only knew—"

She hesitates a moment; lays one brown hand on my arm. The forest is suddenly very still.

"We may never get another chance," she says.

"I don't understand."

"You will. Oh, you will."

The shutters stood wide open: moonlight silvered the bay below and cast soft, chequered shadows across the sleeping city. Lamp-flames flickered in the night-breeze, and from the cistern a solitary bull-frog complained, with testy monotony, to the unlistening stars. Everything was still, familiar, folded in peace: the dimly outlined carob-tree, the rucked and angled rooftops stretching down to the harbour, the courtyard, the crumbling garden wall. It seemed impossible that in a quiet myrtle-grove, less than a mile away, men were, at this very moment, preparing to kill or be killed: for their ideals, their ambitions, or other reasons best not thought about. Well,

I thought, they have a good night for it; and my fingers pressed hard into the woodwork of the shutter, as though I needed physical proof of my own existence, in the here-and-now that embraced this still moonlight, that unimaginable silent violence.

Aunt Helen sat beside the hearth, in her favourite high-backed chair, her face half-shadowed, the fine planes of jaw and cheekbone thrown into startling high relief. She was so still she might have been carved from ivory. My mother, in contrast, was as restless as a caged beast: she paced to and fro, taut with impatience, occasionally pausing and staring out into the courtyard.

"Past midnight," she said.

Aunt Helen tapped on the arm of her chair: a tiny, impatient gesture I knew all too well. She said: "There's nothing any of us can do. Except wait."

They will all be assembled now, I thought: Pittacus, Phanias, Deinomenes, Alcaeus, Antimenidas and the rest of them, shadows moving through blacker shadows under the moon, whispering to each other in the sweet-smelling darkness. The arms are cached there for them, oiled and wrapped in linen, buried, marked, waiting. Ready to strike. Then, over the blackness of the wall beyond the carob-tree, a humped shadow rose, wavered for a moment, vanished again. I heard a soft slither and thud as someone dropped to the ground, the sound of panting breath. The watch-dog stirred in its kennel, growled, woke. There was a sharp rattle as it sprang to the end of its chain and began to bark. Then, quietly but with urgency, a familiar voice called: "For heaven's sake, somebody strangle that damned dog—" and terror gave way to near-hysterical relief.

"Antimenidas," I said.

He came swiftly across the courtyard and in through the open doorway, stepping between us and the moon, his great black cloak like a pall. Sweat glinted on his face, and his chest was heaving. Even in the reddish glow of the lamp-light he looked tallowy-pale. His hand clenched on his sword-hilt: he looked round at each of us in turn. For a moment no one spoke. Then my mother said "Well?" in a kind of nervous bark, and Antimenidas' restless eyes settled on her. There was angry compassion in his voice as he said: "It's over. Finished before it ever began. I should have known."

"What do you mean?"

"He's betrayed us, sold us. The pot-bellied old fox."

"*Pittacus?*" My mother's voice scooped up in angry incredulity. I glanced at Aunt Helen, who was nodding slowly to herself.

[104]

"Yes: Pittacus. He's gone over to Myrsilus—he and that time-server Deinomenes together."

"You're lying," said my mother, and it was as though the words were directed at me.

"No, Lady Cleïs, I'm not lying. I only wish I were."

"He might have been held up—" My mother's voice lacked conviction.

Antimenidas said, wearily: "Pittacus is never late—least of all when his life depends on punctuality."

Aunt Helen said: "Of course you're right. It's just what he'd do."

I thought of Phrynon, trussed and tangled in a fisherman's net between two armies; I remembered the words scrawled on a note from the Troad: "I am rapidly coming to the conclusion that Thersites was the only sensible person in the *Iliad*." I heard that humorous, faintly burred voice remark: "You can't eat honour, and the world has changed quite a lot since they buried Achilles."

"Yes," I said in a small voice, "yes, it's just what he'd do."

Aunt Helen looked at me sharply: for a moment there was perfect understanding between us.

Antimenidas said: "If I know Pittacus, we've got till daylight to get out of Mytilene. The last thing he wants at the moment is the embarrassment of having to deal with his—late fellow-conspirators, shall we say? Myrsilus would insist on having the lot of us executed—except for little Sappho here, perhaps"—he flashed me a cheerful grin —"and that would leave Pittacus looking very shabby indeed. But if we're still in town tomorrow, he's no alternative. I don't propose to let myself be crucified just for the pleasure of reducing his popularity."

"Most commendable of you," murmured Aunt Helen.

"My impetuous brother, I may say, wanted to attack, regardless— which was just what Myrsilus hoped might happen. He'd have had the perfect excuse for a mass execution—with Pittacus sitting by, stroking his beard and looking judicial."

"*Alcaeus?*" I exclaimed. This surprised me more than anything.

"Poets," said Antimenidas, "are not renowned for their consistency of behaviour—even when it comes to a fight."

My mother said, in a hopeless, defeated voice: "But why? *Why?*" No one answered her. There was a moment's awkward silence.

Then Antimenidas cleared his throat and said: "We have good friends at Pyrrha, Lady Cleïs. The guards at the north-west postern will let you through. A carriage and horses are waiting at the Three Mules Tavern, on the Pyrrha road. But there's no time to lose."

"No. No, I suppose not." All my mother's drive and energy seemed suddenly to have deserted her. "The children—I must wake the children—" She picked up a lamp and went out, moving like a sleep-walker.

Antimenidas said: "Lady Helen, what will *you* do?"

"I shall stay here, naturally."

"Ah. Your position is—safeguarded."

"It is also uncompromised, I would remind you." Her topaz eyes gleamed: there was anger behind the amusement.

"I see," said Antimenidas.

"I thought you would. I don't share your weakness for lost causes, I'm afraid."

An hour later I was jolting along in a crowded, uncomfortable carriage, staring at the moonlit waters of the Gulf and the mountains rising dark behind them. A solitary night-fisher, defying the moon, made a pin-point of light far out towards the further shore. The spring air was heavy with the scent of flowering gorse. I yawned, conscious always of Praxinoa's solid, reassuring presence beside me, with Larichus asleep in her arms. Opposite me my mother dozed and muttered; Charaxus blew his nose—he had one of his thick colds again—and hunched into the corner like a small, distempered owl.

This is happening to *me*, I thought, still not really believing it. I'm going into exile, running away like a thief in the night. Then suddenly, it occurred to me that, far from feeling any distress, I was really rather excited. After all, it wasn't as though we were leaving the island: you could hardly call it exile at all. It'll certainly make a change, I told myself. And there aren't many girls of fifteen who can say they're political exiles.

The carriage rattled on through the night. Presently I, too, fell asleep, my head on Praxinoa's shoulder. I was still unconscious when we reached our destination.

VII

EVERY year the sea eats a little further into Pyrrha. Its advance is slow, barely perceptible: then one day a lonely cottage crumbles into the water; masonry cracks, slides, vanishes; or the pilot, stepping ashore from his skiff, sees five steps only on the green-stained water-stairs where there were six before. The small, crisp waves of the Gulf lick inexorably at dykes and harbour-works, undermine slip-way, embankment, or black, corroded jetty. In the couch-grass above the foreshore salt glistens; scoured grey pebbles are cast up among the poppies and charlock; as the outer defences are washed away, the roots of the dwarf-pines clutch further into nothingness, bone-white, gnarled, helpless, like the hands of ancient beggars outstretched in supplication, expecting nothing but indifference or a curt refusal.

One day, perhaps, Pyrrha will go back to the sea altogether. One day the small carrion fish of the Gulf will nose among these pillared colonnades, and obscene polyps crouch, palpitating, where now I see, as I write these words, worn marble flags strewn with rough white sheepskins, an iron-bound Cretan sea-chest, a table set for chess, the big, watchful hunting-dog curled up by the hearthstone, one eye on the glow from the iron fire-basket. Or perhaps—who knows Poseidon's inscrutable mind?—the advance may be halted before then, and the Gulf's senseless appetite turn elsewhere.

I have come back here from Mytilene on a sudden impulse, not knowing what I sought, afraid what I might find. I have brought nothing with me but a bundle of old memories, two long-dead years' fast-fading hopes and regrets. Engulfing time eats at my past as inexorably—and as indifferently—as the salt tide that thrusts inch by inch into the heart of Pyrrha. The ink is illegible in places already, the edges of the paper have begun to turn brown and crumble. New faces, other houses, the stare of alien curiosity or half-recognition. The smell of seine and tar, small fish gleaming silvery-blue, like tempered steel, in their wet wicker baskets, empty shells scattered over the cobbles.

I did not even tell Ismene and Agesilaïdas that I was coming: what could I have said in a letter? Besides, to sit at home—home?—and wait for an answer would have been unbearable. Between decision and action took an hour, no more. (I paused at the shrine of Aphrodite, licked finger and thumb, firmly snuffed every candle. The last one, with a hiss and a crackle, burnt my skin: a small raised blister on the ball of my thumb presses against the pen as I write.) The carriage rattled over stone and pot-hole as it had done that moonlit night thirty-five years ago: and how much wisdom had I gathered? Every turn in the road was familiar: I felt, suddenly and for a brief moment, as though time were eclipsed and I a girl again, excited, fearful, inexperienced, riding into my unknowable future. Which is for once only and cannot be recalled.

Ismene said: "We knew you would come one day, my dear. We were waiting for you."

Time is gentle with me here. I sit for hours browsing through old letters and diaries (so fragile, so tangential these records of my kingfisher days: how recapture the colour, the sunlight?), my mind running undisturbed down those private summer paths that have for so long been closed to me. Sometimes I walk, hour after hour, among the hills, cloak snapping in a high autumn wind, past parched corn-stubble or high, wild outcrops of liver-coloured rock where kite and buzzard circle, waiting for a death. So much has changed: the town seems smaller, grey and shrunken, as though it had foreknowledge of its own ultimate destruction.

But some things have not changed, and these I experience with a transfiguring recognition, a sense of incredulous wonder and gratitude. They are my touchstones to the past, my proofs against all the demons of illusive doubt. One day—hardly knowing where I went, letting my feet guide me—I walked across the bridge and up the immemorial road that follows the coast northward to Mesa: the wide estuary with its salt-flats, the golden patchwork of corn-land beyond, the poised and meditative herons, the shy wild horses, the solitude.

No one remembers when Mesa itself was abandoned. Its houses

have crumbled and collapsed till their stones are barely distinguishable from the grey rocks on the hillside. All that remains today is the great white temple of Aphrodite, alone in that vast expanse, with its walled precinct and soft-robed priestesses. No one, again, knows how old the temple is; but its columns are of wood, black and cracked with age, bound round in many places with thick iron hoops. There is a sacred image of the Goddess which none but the high priest may see: it is kept veiled all the year round, and lamps burn before it in the sanctuary. Naturally, it gives rise to rumours. It fell from heaven. It was fashioned by Hephaestus for the illegitimate son of Orestes who supposedly colonized Lesbos.

Alcaeus had his own, highly characteristic, version of the secret: according to him, the statue was so gross, so ludicrously ugly, that to display it in public would bring the Goddess's cult into unseemly disrepute.

As I walked along the spur-road between estuary and temple, wrapped in the loud silence of wind and sky, time fled back: once more I heard—so clearly that he might, in physical truth, have been there beside me—that young, metallic, cruelly gay voice dissect my butterfly world with razorish malice. Too easy for me, wounded by his barbs—and flushed by my first public recognition and triumph—to convince myself he spoke merely out of envious pique: it was only later that I came to recognize the despair, the cankering self-hatred that fed his destructive aggressiveness.

In the temple precinct the air was warm and still: the walls seemed to hold a lingering summer heat, windless, soporific. I sat down on the old stone bench beneath the plane-tree: nothing had changed. Crystal-clear, the spring still welled up in its worn stone basin, and chattered away down the same tiled runnel through the apple-orchard. (Did the local farmers still pay tithes for irrigation-rights? It seemed unlikely that Aphrodite—or her priestesses—would forgo so easy and profitable a source of income.) In the pines and cypresses of the sacred grove innumerable doves called: the pomegranates were noisily alive with sparrows. Outside, scarcely a hint of green on the hillsides: the ground was parched, brown, barren. But here, in this holy enclosure, the traveller or worshipper would find soft green turf, watered daily, protected from the sun's fiercest rays, a quiet oasis of peace.

I sat there meditating for several hours. No one disturbed me. Yet now I felt, in some indefinable fashion, alien, an intruder. A faint breeze stirred the branches overhead: the rustling leaves had a soothing, hypnotic quality about them. On a small altar by the spring incensed oil burnt in one flickering lamp: its smell—so evocative so pervasive—permeated the heavy autumn air. The doves, Aphrodite's doves, cooed as senselessly as any stupid woman brought face to face with the man she adores; the water chattered down its runnel with the dreadful insistence of a village gossip.

I slept there for a little; then, slowly, I made my way back to the coast road. I went down into the rippling shallows of the estuary, and bathed my face and arms and feet in salt water. The afternoon sun was still bright, and presently I could feel a thin, delicate rime of salt on my cheeks. Two wild black stallions fled as I approached; far out in the Gulf I could see the triangular brown snippet of a fishing-boat's sail. I was alone, utterly alone; and now, for the first time, I began to perceive the true depth and extent of my solitude.

How long had it been since I drove up to Three Winds, that blue and never-to-be-forgotten day? The shady orchard, Mica bent over her brushes and colours, Atthis a child swinging high among the apple-boughs—Oh, Atthis, I would have stopped time for you if I could. For you; for me. *I loved you once, Atthis, long ago: you seemed to me a small, awkward child.*

Ismene is over sixty now, and Agesilaïdas in his mid-seventies. Both have the same coarse, plentiful white hair, springing away from the forehead in a high crescent; both are walnut-brown from the outdoor life of garden and field and orchard. They might well be brother and sister. When Phanias died—so soon after the birth of their late, much-longed-for son—it seemed as though Ismene would be a widow for ever, struggling soberly against odds to preserve Three Winds intact. But five years later, to everyone's amazement, she married Agesilaïdas.

It seemed, at the time, a most improbable choice. Agesilaïdas was a bachelor of forty-seven, a pleasant, cultured dilettante with an adequate—but by no means large—private income. He had a small town house in Mytilene and owned property in and around Pyrrha, where his family had lived for generations. Like many aristocratic lovers of the arts, he had a marked predilection for good-looking or talented boys. He was more unusual, perhaps, in always treating his favourites with intelligence, kindness, and unswerving generosity, so that they remained his friends long after any physical liaison between them had ended. His interest in their welfare extended to their wives and children; he was always ready to hear their problems, lend them money (which he could ill afford to spare) or put in a word on their behalf with some influential friend.

He did not, on the whole, frequent the same circles as Phanias, which made his subsequent marriage to Ismene all the more puzzling. From time to time—like most reasonably well-connected citizens—he would be a guest at Three Winds, but his true social interests, as one might expect, lay elsewhere. He cultivated the brilliant—writers, artists, rising politicians—or the merely beautiful. He was not ambitious for power himself, but every successful or aspiring statesman seemed to be his friend. (He had, for instance, an unexpectedly close relationship with Pittacus.) Of course, he knew Alcaeus very well indeed. It was he who, with characteristic generosity, put a house at our disposal in Pyrrha when we were banished from Mytilene and in countless unobtrusive ways helped to make those years of exile more tolerable. Agesilaïdas was the centre, the knot binding us all together; so much so, indeed, that when I heard the news of his marriage to Ismene (I was still in Sicily at the time) I felt, oddly, that I knew him much better than she did.

What impelled her to marry him? I am still not certain. Perhaps she craved security, kindness, comfort, but felt incapable of ever again giving herself emotionally to a man. Perhaps she knew that Agesilaïdas would never make demands upon her that she was unable or unwilling to fulfil. I could think of no other reason, at the time; and yet I have to admit that, as marriages go, this one must be counted a notable success. It may be that Agesilaïdas, too, had his reasons—and these not merely, as gossip said, a desire to lay hands upon Three Winds. He was, after all, nearly fifty: he must have been beginning, like many people in his position, to feel the wintry nip of age and loneliness.

Now, twenty-five years afterwards, he and Ismene are in perfect accord: they sense each other's moods almost before their own, and the love between them is warm, enduring, tangible. They make a room brighter simply by being there.

So we watch each other in the evening lamp-light, sitting late, the three of us, over a bowl of good Samian wine, treading cautiously through our tangled memories. There is so much that cannot be spoken, even today.

Agesilaïdas picks a fig from the dish in front of him, peels it reflectively. "I remember the morning you and your mother first got here, Sappho. You were all tousled with sleep, like a very small bird. And rather cross."

"I must have been a terrible nuisance."

He smiles. "Do you know, my dear, you still haven't quite lost that habit of apologizing for yourself? How strange. And rather touching."

Ismene says: "It might have been yesterday. You've changed so little."

She means it. Ismene, you're so good, so generous. *Why can't you hate me a little?* You should hate me.

I laugh. "Lamp-light has always been kind to me."

She says: "Do you still have Mica's portrait?"

"Of course. Phanias was right: I did grow into it."

There is a tiny, edged silence.

Agesilaïdas says: "When did you last see Mica?"

"I don't know—two, three months ago, perhaps."

Ismene says: "How is she, Sappho?"

"She's very well."

Rich, popular, successful: a fashionable society hostess, the Lady Mnasidica. Whose name is never abbreviated. Who has given up portrait-painting.

Ismene says: "She must be so busy these days—"

"Yes."

"Of course, marrying Melanippus made a great difference."

Agesilaïdas says quickly (as though knowing how impossible I find it to answer this question—it *is* a question, of course—with any degree of honesty): "I don't suppose, from all one hears, that Melanippus sees quite as much of Alcaeus as he did once."

Dangerous ground here. I say, picking my words, making a half-joke of it: "Alcaeus has become—something of a recluse. But then, so have I."

They exchange quick glances. What do they know? What are they thinking?

"Melanippus, Alcaeus—they were so close once." Agesilaïdas shakes his head sadly. It is hard, even now, for him to admit that personal relationships, once established, can ever reach a final breaking-point.

"Yes. I know."

"That old scandal, that poem about throwing away his shield—he wrote it for Melanippus. He thought it might—amuse him. And you see, he loved Melanippus. Melanippus could make his cowardice—bearable."

"What—?"

"Does that surprise you? Did you never realize how bitterly ashamed Alcaeus was of his action? So much so that he had to crucify himself publicly with a bad joke?"

Agesilaïdas' voice falters. To my astonishment, I see his eyes are bright with tears. Ismene quietly takes his hand.

Something—guilt, perhaps—impels me to say: "I'm sorry. I wish I could help Alcaeus myself. The Gods know he needs friends now, if ever. But there are—" the words stick in my throat.

"Personal reasons?"

"Yes." I take a deep breath. "Personal reasons." Those cruel, unforgettable words, like an incantation, drum through my brain: Alcaeus must be laughing to hear them sung in the waterfront taverns, they are his last and best revenge on me. *I a woman ripe for pity, I whom every ill has seized on*—They have sung my songs, too, before now; I can expect no mercy. I know—who better?—just how cruel men can be. *Grievous trouble comes upon me, in my fearful heart the belling*—cruel, too cruel—*of the stag brings lust and madness.* Charges all the more excoriating because true. I have lost my sense of humour and my dignity together. *By the wiles of Aphrodite came my ruin*—

Ismene says: "Were you always enemies? I can't remember a time when the two of you weren't bickering and slandering each other. And yet I once thought—"

"We enjoyed quarrelling, in some curious way," I say quickly. "But we *were* close, you know. I can't explain this very well—"

(A fragment of long-forgotten conversation floats into my mind: "You don't like me, do you?" "No, not much." "Why?" "Perhaps our temperaments are too alike.")

"It doesn't matter, my dear," Ismene says. "We understand."

The intolerable weight of her compassion. The careful way they both avoid asking me questions that might probe or hurt—what has happened between me and Cleïs, what my immediate plans are, how much truth there is in all the rumours they have heard. The future stretches away in front of me, bleak, grey, purposeless. Sleep is the one panacea.

But sleep will not come. I lie and toss restlessly, my mind gnawing at the past like a caged rat. The close air stifles me, the bedclothes chafe my limbs, though autumn is well advanced. I get up and fling the shutters wide. Moonlight streams in, the scent of basil, the cry of a hunting owl. Why did I throw away the nepenthe Alcaeus brought me from Egypt? Fear? Pride? It would be more than welcome now. What was it bound the two of us together in that endless, half-mocking enmity? How deep was the mask?

Was: I am thinking of him in the past, as though he were already dead. What Agesilaïdas told me shocks me more than I care to admit. Perhaps, if I am honest, what I find most disconcerting is my own lack of insight. If I failed to discern that crippling shame, if I took the irony and sophistication at their face-value, then how deeply mistaken, in essentials, may my judgment of him have been? And if I am to revise my judgment of him, must I not thereby also condemn myself?

When I think of that bitter, grizzled old man, so pathetic in his drunkenness and his defeat, I am afraid for myself. Some of his guilt lies on my shoulders; I must share the responsibility for what he has become. He cried out to me in his distress, and I was too young, too cruel, too self-centred to understand or care. Condemnation is so easy—and so satisfying. To watch Agesilaïdas with Ismene is a hard lesson to my pride, even now.

Must I always destroy—or be destroyed? Was the long spring and summer of my happiness an illusion? Dare I look back across the years?

In the sunken garden there is a pleasant ornamental pool, with two shallow basins at its centre: water spouts sluggishly from the mouth of a cheerful little bronze fawn, who bears his verdigris patches and general air of neglect with apparent equanimity. Under waving weeds, through a dim green translucency, fish flicker and dart like flashes of fire. The garden is generally a little unkempt: hedges need clipping, weeds sprout between the stones, the cabbages have rocketed, and in the orchard plum- and apple-trees riot unpruned. The last of the roses scatter blown, waxy petals on the grass. I can see my mother itching to be at it all: to sweep, clean, burn, set in order. *Bachelors,* her expression says, all too clearly, *can never be trusted to look after anything.* Not even exile can diminish her passion for organizing the world's universal incompetence.

Agesilaïdas says apologetically: "I'm afraid things have got a little out of hand, Lady Cleïs. It was the best I could manage at short notice." He runs one hand through his shock of dark, wavy, greying hair, and gives my mother a most disarming smile. Alcaeus has accompanied us on our tour of inspection: his obvious intimacy with

Agesilaïdas is a little embarrassing. Now, from behind my mother, he flashes me the ghost of a wink, as though in complicity.

My mother says: "On the contrary, it's enchanting. We're really most grateful to you." This is her polite social voice, accentuated now by the sense of being under an obligation: it has, in the past, frozen lesser men, but Agesilaïdas merely raises one eyebrow a fraction, and continues to smile.

"My dear, we couldn't possibly have let you stay in that poky little place—"

"Especially," says my mother, "when we have a local celebrity in the family." Her skirts hiss, Medusa-like, over the flags.

Agesilaïdas clearly thinks this is a remark best ignored. He takes her arm. "Perhaps you'd like to come and go over the domestic quarters with me—and you'd better be introduced to the steward, he's a crotchety creature, but he does cheer up wonderfully when there's a tenant in occupation—" Skilfully he walks her back to the house; Alcaeus and I are left staring into the deep green pool, watching the fishes come and go.

He cocks his head on one side, appraises me. "Violet-tressed, holy, honey-smiling—Sappho," he drawls: he has chosen three traditional epithets for Aphrodite. "You have a very goddesslike look in your eye, my dear. It terrifies me sometimes."

Then, in a different voice, looking away from me into the pool, he goes on: "There's something I would like to tell you about. I don't know how." He spreads out his hands: there is a subtly defeated quality about the gesture. "You could help, if you wanted to. There's no one else—"

Silence. At last I say: "Tell me, then."

There is naked agony in his eyes.

"I am ashamed to. I can't—"

My entire being shrinks from him: fear, contempt, embarrassment flood through me, make me cruel in self-defence.

I hear myself say, in a cold, priggish voice: "If it were something decent, something honourable you wanted to tell me, you wouldn't feel ashamed, you'd talk openly. But your eyes are like a sick dog's, full of nastiness—"

He gets up, with an abrupt, jerky gesture: his face is wiped clean, a cold expressionless mask.

"Bitch," he says, and the word is all the uglier for being pronounced without heat, with an air of tired indifference. "Cold, cruel bitch. You're all the same. All of you." Then he turns and walks swiftly back to the house. For so broad and solidly built a man the delicacy of his tread is astonishing: he might be a trained dancer.

I stoop down beside the pool, and my reflection greets me: sunlight glints behind those dark eyes, fish move through the chambered greenness of that tremulous skull. I shiver faintly; but it is a warm day, a new poem has begun to take shape in my head, and under the pressure of that engrossing excitement all else is soon over-ridden and—for the time being at least—forgotten.

Meg's handwriting is like her personality: neat, well-controlled, but from time to time bursting out in wild emotional loops and flourishes. It is odd, still, to get a letter from her, a tangible reminder of her absence, to break the seals knowing that though Mytilene is no more than twenty miles away I cannot return there. Odd, and a little unreal. I have not yet, emotionally, accepted the fact of my exile.

"Darling Sappho," she writes, "it was wonderful seeing you, if only for a short time. We should be grateful to the Goddess, it was her festival after all. I wanted to stay longer—I mean, there's no law against our coming to Pyrrha, is there?—but Mama said no, it would be most inadvisable, and when Mama talks like that there's no arguing with her."

This is most interesting. The last thing one could call Aunt Helen, in the general way, is cautious. But she was, if not exactly cool with me during her visit, at least a little restrained: her natural warm spontaneity was damped down, she seemed to be giving some kind of public performance. Just what, I wonder, is she up to now?

"The most extraordinary news—I forgot all about it when I was in Pyrrha, I was so excited at seeing you—is that Ismene, after all these years, has—guess what—had a son! Can you believe it? Phanias, of course, is in a seventh heaven of delight, and has quite a new look in his eye, they tell me, when he rides round the estate."

(So he was luckier than the rest of us. Or did he, too, fail to keep the rendezvous that night? No, not Phanias. An anonymous warning, then? From whom? And for what ulterior motive? This is something I don't want to think about.)

"They have called the child Hippias, after Phanias' father. All Mytilene came out to Three Winds for the name-day ceremony. I've never seen so many members of the government in one place at the same time. Myrsilus was there himself, and really, he seemed a nice enough man—a bit grey and negative, perhaps, but nothing worse."

[116]

(I remember, with ironic relish, what Pittacus once wrote me about Periander of Corinth: that he ate no children before breakfast.)

"I tried to hate him for your sake, darling—you know?—but it was difficult: there simply wasn't anything to get hold of. Just like those small hard round nuts—you try and bite on him, and he's gone. That smooth impenetrable surface—perhaps it's the reason for his success, I don't know."

There are times when I find Meg so irritating I could scream.

"The only person who put him out of countenance at all was that rich young man who's a friend of Alcaeus—Melanippus. Have you ever met him? *Terribly* aristocratic and in-bred, generations of first-cousin marriages there by the look of him, long nose, long hands, and that flat, straw-coloured hair. Myrsilus was talking to him about art, and saying how important it was for any government to encourage talent—something about the State taking over the responsibilities of noble patrons in a democracy, which was a little tactless when you think who he was talking to. "In that case," Melanippus murmured, looking down his nose, "isn't it a little perverse to exile your best artists?" I missed what Myrsilus said then, but he looked quite annoyed, for him.

"Pittacus was there, of course, looking *most* impressive in his new robes of office, and hardly drinking at all—I suppose he feels he's got to set a good example now. No, of course, you won't have heard the news—he's been elected joint-president with Myrsilus! This came as a *great* surprise—I mean, when you think about his past career it's barely credible, is it?—but I gather the vote in Council was almost unanimous, and all the guests at Three Winds were delighted, or said they were, and we had a lot of toasts and congratulatory speeches, and really, by the end you'd have thought it was Pittacus's name-day —the poor little baby was very much left out of things. Still, Ismene could hardly take her eyes off it, even to be polite to important guests, so I don't suppose it worried.

"Mica was a *great* success—she's suddenly grown up a lot (extraordinary what a difference a year can make) and she spent *hours* in a corner talking painting with Melanippus, while all the mamas who had eligible daughters on hand sat and glowered—except *our* mama, of course, who was much too busy to notice where Telesippa and I were, she seems to have given up religion for politics (that *does* sound unkind!) and spent most of her time charming Myrsilus, of all people. She's in a funny mood at the moment, I'm a bit worried about her.

[117]

"There's no other real news from here. Hermeas and Agenor and Telesippa send their love. We all miss you very much, Sappho darling. Mama says if you behave yourself, and keep out of bad company (what does she mean by that?) you may be allowed home quite soon. When I asked her how she knew, she just smiled and said: "Private information." So please, darling, do be careful—I can't wait for you to come back, it's so lonely and empty here without you. All my love—Meg."

I find it hard, looking back over thirty years later, re-reading this letter with all the hindsight experience brings, to recapture the precise mood of black and angry misery into which it threw me. I cannot, I think, do better than set down, word for word, the entry I made in my journal at the time, adolescent hyperbole and all. It may at least help to explain some of my subsequent actions.

"Despair clouds my mind: colour drains away from the world around me, grey houses lean in over my head as I walk. Numb tongue, a ringing in the ears, nausea. Will there be no end to these betrayals? Pittacus I can at least understand—a Thracian tradesman, clever, unprincipled, coarse, ambitious, a sensual man of vulgar appetites, selling what ideals he had for power. But Aunt Helen (I try to read some other meaning into Meg's letter; it's no good, the truth is *there*, inescapable), Aunt Helen whom I have adored and idolized and loved as I could never love my own mother—how could *she* do such a thing? Brightness and faith are tarnished, lost in a shabby morass of expedience, compromise, vanity, greed. Whatever happens, however hopeless the goal may seem, those of us who are left must, *must* hold fast to the truth. And truth, ultimately, is meaningless without action. For the first time, I am proud to be an exile."

All this I poured out—hurt, confused, angry, proud—to Antimenidas: there was no other person (my mother least of all) in whom I dared confide, yet exile made such a sharing doubly imperative. Antimenidas heard me out with great patience, and then said: "So now you're beginning to understand."

"I think so." The fish flickered mindlessly in their pool: the sunken garden was an admirable place for privacy without scandal.

"You can't help admiring Pittacus, in a way. That's the worst part of it." Antimenidas flicked a pebble into the water and was silent for a moment as concentric rings spread out from the point of impact. "Did you hear about his dealings with King Alyattes of Lydia?"

I shook my head. Antimenidas gave me his hard, craggy smile.

"Well, Pittacus managed to extract two thousand gold pieces from him, no less; quite an achievement."

"In return for what?"

"Oh, come, Sappho: Alyattes doesn't like the idea of Myrsilus any more than we do. That money was to finance the revolution in Mytilene. I don't doubt Pittacus promised Alyattes some profitable trade monopolies when the Council of Nobles was restored."

"And where is the money now?"

"Why, in the treasury at Mytilene: where else? It provided Pittacus with what you might call his entrance fee to Myrsilus' government."

Despite myself, I giggled.

"I know," said Antimenidas, "I know: that's what I mean. You can't resist the old fox: he's so outrageous."

I said: "But Alyattes won't be quite as easily amused."

"Indeed not. His ambassador has already delivered a very stiff little note to Pittacus. Mark you, it had to be couched in rather general terms: no one likes to admit bribing the wrong party. But the upshot was plain enough to anyone with inside knowledge; Alyattes wanted his two thousand gold pieces back and hinted at all sorts of un-mentionable consequences if he didn't get them."

"What did Pittacus do?"

"Told Alyattes, through his outraged ambassador, to go and eat onions and new bread."

"Onions—?"

Antimenidas made a rude and expressive noise with his pursed lips.

"Oh. I see."

"A nicely stage-managed incident, don't you think? Pittacus badly needs to build up his popularity just now. This was a heaven-sent way of doing it on the cheap."

"But he took a frightful risk, surely?"

"Risk? There was no risk at all, and he knew it. Alyattes isn't going to war over a mere insult, he's got more sense. Besides, in a month or two some well-briefed envoy will travel very unobtrusively from Mytilene to Sardis and do his best to persuade Alyattes that Myrsilus is as good a source of trade as the Council of Nobles. Alyattes would grab at any straw that looked like recovering those two thousand gold pieces; so I fancy the process of persuasion should be quite easy."

"And Pittacus had all this worked out in advance?"

"Not a doubt of it."

"But—"

"Oh, I know what you're going to say, Sappho. It's shameful and vulgar and dishonest. It's the end of virtue and good government. I agree. And because of that I shall go on fighting."

He fell silent for a moment: the lines and shadows in his prematurely aged face seemed to deepen. He said sombrely: "Perhaps to die fighting is all that remains for us."

"You can't believe that. You mustn't."

"Do you think I want to? Do you think it's easy to face the possibility that our traditions and beliefs, our whole way of life are on the brink of destruction?" He stood up, fists hard-clenched. "When I look at Pittacus, I see"—he swallowed—"our world as it may be very soon: a world ruled by profit, not honour; a world where gold has more power than the sword, and oaths are made to be broken; a world of greasy bankers and base-born tradesmen and sordid, ignoble ambitions. If that is what the Gods have in store for us, I want no part of it."

I said: "Do you believe we have a chance? Honestly?"

Our eyes held for a moment.

"Yes," Antimenidas said, "we have a chance."

"Then that is enough."

He nodded. He said: "Your world is threatened, too: you are right."

"My world is yours, Antimenidas."

"Perhaps. My brother's, too, would you say?" His voice was tinged with irony. I flushed. "You mustn't be so unkind to Alcaeus, you know. Especially now. He's too—vulnerable."

"I'd really rather not discuss the subject."

"How hard you can sound at times: it's a warning to the unwary. I told you last winter you were a ravening harpy, and I was right." He smiled to draw the sting of that last remark. "But Alcaeus is desperately unhappy. He needs city life—public life—more than most of us. He's drinking very heavily. His work is—well, he's written almost nothing, and that—I know I'm not a judge, but—"

"What are you asking me to do?"

Antimenidas said: "He *is* my brother. I have some kind of—responsibility for him. His emotional problems are his own affair, I know. All the same—" He broke off, took a quick breath, and said: "I want you to stop hurting him. Just that. You hurt people more than you know, Sappho. You have a kind of hard, innocent cruelty that's all the more frightening for being, so often, quite unconscious. I'm not asking you to *help* him—though you could, and at the moment I don't think anyone else could. Just to leave him alone."

"Please. I don't want to talk about it. I'll do what I can."

"That's all I ask."

"And we have a chance? You mean that?"

"Yes."

"Then we must live in hope."

"It is our last chance," Antimenidas said, and spat hard, on the marble pavement.

So, one moonlit summer night, a group of aristocratic rebels stormed and captured the citadel of Mytilene. But they did not lay hands on Myrsilus or Pittacus, and they did not long hold what they had won. The townsfolk who should have flocked in thousands to their liberating banner were apathetic or actively hostile. By noon next day the attackers were besieged in the citadel, with little water and less food. At sunset Myrsilus offered them terms of conditional surrender. They could, at least, make the gesture of refusal. Myrsilus left them to their own thoughts for the night, and attacked with his toughest troops just before dawn.

Cicis, Alcaeus' brother, was impaled on the door of the council chamber with a javelin, and hung there for several hours, coughing away his life in slow agony. And Phanias died fighting beside the best swordsmen of Pyrrha, cut down at last and hacked to pieces by a blood-crazed guardsman, against Myrsilus' orders. They stuck his head on the city-gate and sent the battered trunk back to Three Winds for burial. But Alcaeus and Antimenidas and a dozen more surrendered; and presently, away in Pyrrha, we saw a detachment of Mytilenean troops come riding up to our house and knew they had come for us. The Council of Pyrrha made no protest: they dared not. Too many of their citizens lay dead among the defeated rebels.

We had had our last chance.

VIII

NOTHING has changed in the house: it is as though I had never left Mytilene. When I stepped through the front-door to the lobby, wrapped in my dark blue travelling-cloak, still hooded against the sharp autumn winds, Scylax gave me the same brief nod, the same monosyllabic greeting, as he does after my regular afternoon walk. Apollo twitched, gargled perfunctorily in his throat, and composed himself for sleep again. (As porter and watch-dog they make a ludicrous pair. But then, what have they to guard?) I hesitated at the end of the lobby, as though searching for something. The house was warm and well-aired; I could hear voices in the kitchen-quarters, and my nose caught—above the more immediate scents of beeswax, lime-wash, and dried lavender—the faint, delicate aroma of a slow-simmering, herb-filled stew.

What, then? What was missing, what intangible absence nagged at my mind with that dull, persistent ache? My eyes took in one familiar object after another, from the two tall Athenian jars to my old, much-polished hall-chair, its wood seamed and patterned with dark cracks: I wanted to touch them for reassurance, they were amulets. (Yet I had never really *liked* the jars: the pattern on them might have been designed by a mad child with a precocious talent for geometry, and I only kept them—or so I told myself—because they were a present from Periander. Which, if one cared to think about it, would form an equally valid reason, to my mother and others like her, for refusing to have such tainted objects in the house at all.) But now the amulets failed me: my defences were down. Emptiness: not-being. Tears gathered behind my eyes, I felt a simple, nameless grief. And then, suddenly, I put a name to it: there was no sense of home-coming.

I paused on the upper gallery, then flung open the door to Cleïs' room. The shutters still stood half-open, and late afternoon sunlight streamed in, illuminating the same miscellaneous clutter of objects. And then I saw an addition: a sweeping-brush laid beside the bed, a small heap of greyish dust. Again, irrationally, I felt on the point of weeping. I went out quickly, down the corridor, fingers clenched over thumbs in the hopeless, reflexive gesture of a miserable child.

When they brought us into the big public ante-room outside the council chamber, the first thing I saw was that stained and splintered hole in the great metal-studded door, an ugly irregularity among the gilded dolphins. It was as though Myrsilus had deliberately left it there: a silent reminder, a grim piece of reality for sensitive and impractical revolutionaries. There, I thought, there where the sunlight swarms with dust, there beside the marble pillars, only a few days ago, a man died horribly, a man I knew well, a living, breathing individual. There he hung, like a fish on a spit, in what agony I cannot begin to imagine, till death loosened his bowels and laid dust on his blind eyes. Yet I, seeing the marks of that bloody ordeal, can only feel wonder, joy, thankfulness for the life that still sings so turbulently through my own veins.

They were there waiting for us, a small, defiant group hedged in by Myrsilus' guardsmen: Alcaeus, Antimenidas, and the others—not more than a dozen in all—who had, for whatever motives, chosen in their extremity to surrender rather than die. Looking at them, I felt a stab of guilt: my mother and I had been kept under nothing worse than house arrest, whereas they—it was only too plain—were fresh from the cells of the city prison, dirty, unkempt, still in the clothes they had been wearing at the time of their arrest, still showing rust-coloured bloodstains on cloak or tunic. Antimenidas had his head swathed in a grubby bandage; another man leant heavily on an improvised crutch. They were not an impressive sight. I suspect that Myrsilus deliberately prevented their having access to clean clothes, barbers, or even washing-water: the more repugnant and ridiculous these aristocratic rebels could be made to look, the better.

I felt my mother stiffen beside me, sensed her instinctive disgust and the expression—too familiar—of frozen scorn with which she would at once conceal it. Alcaeus gave me a strained, rueful smile: Antimenidas, white-faced, was staring away from us towards the doors of the council chamber. That black, ragged scar in the wood gaped like an open wound. None of us said anything to each other, even by way of greeting: what words could have been adequate? Then the doors swung open, creaking a little on their ponderous bronze hinges, and we moved forward into the council chamber, over mosaics of fishes and birds and dancing boys, the guards iron-shod footsteps echoing beside us, to face the justice of Myrsilus.

Today, miraculously, warmth and light have returned. Beneath the sun's relentless glare colour drains from vineyard and pasture, air shimmers, the sky is hazed with heat. Here in Mytilene peasants call this the "little summer": now, between vintage and olive-harvest, they have a brief respite from their labours. A few late cicadas chirr uncertainly in the plane-tree. My shutters are flung wide open: as I lean out, breathing the morning air, my eye is caught by two swallows' nests under the eaves, soft cones of pleached mud, empty now, abandoned till the spring. Why should this commonplace sight disturb me so?

Perhaps I envy these birds their freedom, this mysterious migrant urge that carries them over seas and frontiers, their poised sense of destination, their light indifference to human laws and restraints. Yet the thought of them leaves me restless, anxious, full of fearful premonitions. They are a reminder of my mortality; how many more times will I see them return with the spring? I can make poetry from this freedom, this indifference: yet always at the back of my mind I see, not a bird, but the raped and tongueless Philomela, twittering madly as she recalls the monstrous feast, the axe, the blood, the mindless metamorphosis.

In the spring she returns, Pandion's daughter: her freedom an illusion, her indifference bred of despair, her eloquence rooted in archaic guilt and hysteria. Am I—can I be—wiser or happier than Philomela? Should I envy the tongueless swallow?

Myrsilus and Pittacus sat side by side in high-backed, gilded chairs —you could not quite call them thrones—which stood on a daïs at the far end of the chamber. Above the chairs hung a scarlet canopy, and over the canopy were two crossed banners: the standard Pittacus had carried during his campaign in the Troad, its black dolphin threadbare now, its colours faded; and a new, resplendent device, quartered with bee-rosettes and corn-sheaves as well as dolphins, and bright-woven in scarlet, black, and gold. This, presumably, was the city's new official flag: I remember thinking—even in that moment of high drama—how vulgar it looked. Perhaps Myrsilus, in an excess of civic zeal, had designed it himself.

The council chamber was little more than half-full. I detected some embarrassment in the air as we advanced between those curving tiers of benches: was it, I wondered, on our behalf or theirs? Out of the corner of my eye I recognized Draco: he half-smiled, then quickly looked away. I could not blame him. The sooner we were disposed of, and the whole unpleasant episode forgotten, the happier everyone would be. I could see it in their faces. They stared at the floor, coughed, conversed in whispers, fidgeted uncomfortably as they waited for the hearing to begin. I found myself feeling rather sorry for them.

The only people present who seemed quite immune to this atmosphere—indeed, unaware of it—were our self-appointed judges. Myrsilus remained, as ever, a grey, expressionless, impenetrable enigma. His hands were folded together in his lap, while his eyes explored some remote prospect that he alone could see. Pittacus, on the other hand, seemed positively to be enjoying himself. He sat there beaming at us all, prisoners and councillors alike, with the same benign interest: from time to time he would complacently stroke his now sizable paunch, as though it were a piece of sculpture which he took especial pride in having produced.

When we were all standing—still guarded—on the floor of the chamber just below the daïs, a hush fell. Then Pittacus leaned over and whispered to Myrsilus, who nodded.

"The ladies," he said, in his clipped, neutral voice, "may be seated." Two ushers hastily produced chairs for us.

"Thank you," my mother said, "but we prefer to stand."

"Ah," Myrsilus observed, with dangerous mildness. "Let me rephrase my last remark: the ladies *will* be seated."

"We still prefer to stand. We do not recognize discriminative treatment as between—"

"*Sit down,*" said Myrsilus, and it was as though, in that confined space, a whip had been cracked.

My mother sat down.

I began to revise my opinion of Myrsilus.

Then I realized I was still standing myself, and flopped quickly into my chair. I felt a sudden dreadful urge to giggle.

Myrsilus nodded to the guards, who came thunderously to attention

[125]

and marched out. One sentry only was left on either side of the great double doors.

"Now," said Myrsilus, "we might as well begin."

His clerk rose, unrolling a lengthy document, and began to read the charges: first those against Alcaeus and his fellow-rebels, then (which took rather less time) our own indictment as aiders and abettors of conspiracy. We were not, I noticed in a curious, detached way, accused of being accessories after murder. Well: that was something. The clerk droned on: ". . . and conspiring to subvert the democracy." Then he stopped abruptly, as though he had run out of ideas, and in a brisk, fussy way began to roll the charge-sheet up again.

Myrsilus surveyed us all in turn, as though to observe what effect this catalogue of our enormities had had on us.

"I don't suppose," he enquired in his blandest voice, "that any of you intend to plead not guilty to these charges?"

There was a moment's silence: then Antimenidas said: "No more, my lord President, than you intend to administer justice in respect of them."

"Take care what you say, Antimenidas. I am warning you in your own interests."

Antimenidas shrugged. "I can scarcely prejudice my position further," he remarked. "At least let me have the satisfaction of a little plain speaking." He glanced out towards the ill-at-ease groups huddled on the council chamber benches. "Some people here may even take my words to heart. For the future."

Myrsilus said: "You really still believe that? How remarkable."

"If things had gone otherwise, you might well be standing where I am standing now, my lord President."

Myrsilus nodded: he seemed, in some private way, amused. "I concede that," he said, as though humouring a precocious child. "But I am not."

Antimenidas stared at Myrsilus: then his eyes glanced up to the banners hung crosswise above the daïs. He was soiled, grimy, even—with that filthy piratical bandage tied round his head—a little ridiculous. But no one could deny him dignity.

He said: "No: you are not. And that, my lord President, is the whole sum of the matter. Let us have no creeping cant about law or justice or democracy. What is going on here has no part in them. It is the triumph of the stronger: it is the victor purging his conscience in the sight of men. This is war, my lord President, and we are your prisoners. You shame the name of justice if you pretend otherwise."

Myrsilus seemed quite unmoved by this outburst; he might have been debating a philosophical point after dinner.

"Twelve years ago," he said, "you and several others conspired to murder the elected, democratic President of this city. Can you justify that?"

"We did nothing of the sort."

"You deny an act that is public knowledge?"

"We executed a usurping tradesman, a common revolutionary tyrant."

"By what authority?"

"By the authority invested in the hereditary Council of Nobles, now illegally dissolved."

Myrsilus said, his voice rising: "And you deny the right of this court, this government, to pass similar justice on yourself?"

"Naturally."

"You are a man, Antimenidas. As Melanchros was. As I am."

Antimenidas shook his head. "A man, yes. But not as Melanchros was. Not as you are, Myrsilus. My family is the third oldest in this island; my ancestors were kings and warriors in golden Mycenae. Six of our line have been President of the Council. Ten died leading the city's forces on the field of battle. I have rights here, ancient and inalienable rights. You have nothing but the rule of force and your glib lawyer's tongue. *Nothing,* do you hear? And neither force nor glibness will make you anything but a murderer if you kill me."

Myrsilus was silent for a moment. At last he said bleakly: "But if *you* were to kill *me,* you would be justified in so doing? Legally? Morally? Politically? Let me be quite clear on this point."

"Yes. I would be justified."

There was another silence.

"Thank you," said Myrsilus, "for being so explicit. I am grateful to you. There is, I think, little point in debating this matter further. I would only remark—a platitude with which you will doubtless be acquainted—that as time creates a tradition, or a dynasty, so, in due course, it is liable to destroy it. Ultimately a man must be judged by what he does, not what he is—and less still by what his forebears have been. You, and those like you, are living on borrowed credit from the past. No doubt you think that a vulgar image: a tradesman's image. That is your weakness. You are still asserting your rights in a world which has less and less use for you. Did the common people

[127]

of this city greet you and your friends as deliverers, Antimenidas? Would you have been standing here now if they had?"

Antimenidas said nothing; he was staring at a shaft of sunlight that slanted down on to the mosaic floor, and seemed, suddenly, to have lost all interest in the proceedings. Myrsilus hesitated a moment; then he leaned across to Pittacus, who had sat silent throughout this exchange, bearded chin jutting out, eyes fixed expressionlessly on the ceiling. They conferred in whispers: Pittacus nodded his agreement.

Myrsilus rose to his feet, and the clerk waited, pen in hand, for the verdict.

"Antimenidas, son of Ariston, this tribunal finds you guilty, before Gods and men, of sedition, conspiracy, armed rebellion against the State, and unlawful trespass, while a proscribed exile, upon the territories of Mytilene."

The final count came as a mild anti-climax: Antimenidas' mouth twitched momentarily in something very like a smile, and Pittacus did not bother to conceal his amusement.

Myrsilus said: "By your acts, and the testimony you have given before this tribunal, you make it clear that you refuse to acknowledge the laws, ordinances, and elected authorities of this city. Have you anything to say before judgment is passed upon you?"

Antimenidas spat on the floor with disdainful vigour: I remembered the sunken garden in our house at Pyrrha, the darting fish, the stillness. *We shall not have another chance.*

"You bore me," he said. "Get this farce over with. Take me out and kill me. I am tired of words."

Myrsilus smiled, very much the master of the situation again: it was, I realized, part of his strategy to make his opponents or victims lose their tempers.

He said slowly, almost reflectively: "As you surmise, the maximum penalty for the offences of which you have been convicted is death: that you should be taken from this tribunal to prison, and thence, within three days, to the place of execution."

There was a purring note in his voice: he reminded me, at that moment, of an old grey cat, crouched by the fire, watching a disabled mouse. Involuntarily, I shivered. I knew the place of execution; so did everyone in the chamber. It lay a little way outside the city-walls to the north-west, a barren hillside within sight of the Methymna road. There was one tree on this hillside, a great dead plane, silver and skeletal now, scoured by wind and sun over many years. Here sat the kites and vultures, wings folded, like shrunken old women in black rags, waiting; and below were the crosses with their rusty shackles and neck-collars. Sometimes a strong man took a week to die, and travellers would hear his hoarse, inhuman shouts, and spur their horses on faster into the hills. Death came more quickly in winter, with freezing north winds and merciful oblivion. But all through the summer the vultures waited, knowing their due—black, flapping furies with beaks that blinded and tore, obscene in the sunlight.

Myrsilus paused a moment, smiling that grey and dreadful smile of his. Then he said: "However, this tribunal is merciful. Despite what we have heard here today, we believe in tempering the people's justice with mercy, even for the most incorrigible offender."

From the expression on Antimenidas' face, it seemed plain that mercy was the last thing he had expected, or, indeed, desired: he had prepared himself for a hero's death, and now this, too, was to be denied him.

"Furthermore," Myrsilus continued, "we cannot, in all seriousness, regard you or the obsolete faction you represent as a real danger to the State. The folly of your speech and behaviour precludes such a belief; it also raises a legitimate doubt as to how far you may be held responsible for your own actions. In such cases, as you know, the law prescribes clemency."

Again, a faint ripple of laughter ran round the chamber. Antimenidas stared at Myrsilus, face burning, eyes bright with incredulous rage.

"We therefore condemn you to a renewal of exile, until such time as this tribunal may decide that your offences have been adequately purged. You are hereby granted ten days to set your affairs in order. During that period you will have reasonable liberty of movement. Your property is declared forfeit to the government and will be sold at public auction. If, after ten days have passed, you are still within the boundaries of this city, you may be slain at sight with impunity."

Antimenidas said softly: "I am going to kill you, Myrsilus. By my head I swear it."

"I should perhaps explain," Myrsilus went on, as though there had been no interruption, "that exile from this city means, now, effectual exile from the island of Lesbos."

I gave a tiny gasp: it was as though a cold hand had closed over my heart. The idea of leaving Lesbos was unthinkable: my whole life had been spent here; uproot me and I would die.

"As a result of our recent disorders, we have taken counsel with the rulers of Eresus, Methymna, Pyrrha, and Antissa. Agreement has been reached between us that a person exiled from any one of the

Five Cities shall not be granted asylum by the rest. You are therefore required to take ship from Mytilene within the period of grace prescribed. Let the tribunal's verdict be set down in the records of this chamber."

The clerk said: "It is so set down, my lord President."

Myrsilus nodded, as though he had achieved something.

A sudden wave of blind indiscriminate fury surged through me. I hated them all, without distinction of party or position: Myrsilus, wrapped up in his grey self-importance, with his idiotic banners and lawyer's sophistries; Pittacus, so grossly opportunistic, so hungry for the trappings of public office; Antimenidas, the failed idealist, the master of the useless gesture; my mother, with her false male heroics and her sentimentality; Alcaeus, so irritatingly sensitive behind those masks of irony, so futile in action, so aggressive with words. I hated them as a child hates, and—let me be honest—for much the same reason: they had, between them, destroyed my bright, secret, cherished world, the world that was—is—so much more real, more meaningful than these shabby political posturings. That was all I could see; all, in the last resort, that I cared about. To know this—clearly, without any doubts or hesitations—brought me relief as intense as it was unlooked for.

I remembered my mother's hard, contemptuous voice saying: *What concern has a girl of your age with plots or politics? Your world is made up of quarrels and jealousies, of picnics, new dresses, dancing, poetry, idle chatter.* How furiously I had resented those words at the time; yet they were true, true, true, and my real betrayal had been to deny that truth, to act out my small, contemptible part in the public farce that was now drawing to its conclusion.

I love all beautiful, delicate, sensuously pleasing objects, I thought, I love spring flowers and moonlight on water and the wind moving over a field of ripe corn. I love rich, exquisitely woven materials, to look at and touch: the soft rasp of gaily-striped Milesian wool, the crisp white matte folds of fine Egyptian linen. I love the smoothly swelling curves of a master-potter's jar, so irresistible to the fingers as one moves past it. I love all things worked in gold; I love the hard brilliance of precious stones. I love all fragile, swift-fading physical beauty. But my first and greatest love is for the singing words, intangible, immortal, by which all these things can be given living substance for ever. Winged words: Homer was right. Winged like the eagle, circling and gliding in sunlight, high among crags. Winged like the arrow, swift and terrible to its mark. Winged like those great beasts, Sphinxes, Griffons, Chimaeras, that guard the holy places of Egypt and Babylon and the Land of the Two Rivers.

Once he had dealt with Antimenidas, Myrsilus wasted little time on the other prisoners. The joke had gone stale on him: he was bored, and showed it. Very quickly he pronounced identical sentence upon Alcaeus and the other survivors of that ill-fated assault on the citadel: the only exceptions were two men from Pyrrha, whom he sent back, under armed escort, to appear before their own civic tribunal. Then he turned to us.

"Lady Cleïs," he said, "it appears to me that you have suffered unduly from the mistaken convictions held by your late husband and his friends." His tone was quite different now: warm, animated, sympathetic. I had never been quite so surprised in my life; nor—to judge from her expression—had my mother. She flushed like a schoolgirl, frowned, blinked, began to protest, changed her mind at the last moment, and covered her indecision with a fit of nervous coughing.

"Therefore," Myrsilus continued—none of this, clearly, had been lost on him: the smirk was back again—"therefore, it is the decree of this tribunal, taking into consideration your widowed state and the children for whose welfare you are responsible, that you be dismissed with a reprimand."

My mother half-rose. She said, in an odd, breathy voice: "I protest, my lord President. I refuse to accept this verdict—"

"I fear you have no option, Lady Cleïs," said Myrsilus: he sounded very cheerful about it. My mother sat hunched forward, hands grasping the arms of her chair. Looking at her then, seeing her deep bosom and fine, queenly profile, I thought in astonishment: Why, she is an attractive woman, a woman men might die for. Then, instinctively, I glanced up at Myrsilus, and knew—though nothing tangible showed on his face—that the same thought had occurred to him.

"Lady Sappho," Myrsilus said, and, as though in a dream, I rose to my feet. "Lady Sappho, this tribunal finds that you have been deeply implicated in seditious and revolutionary activities—"

A faint, but quite audible, intake of breath could be heard round the council chamber as he pronounced these words.

"—by association, consent, and the carrying of treasonable messages on many occasions. This tribunal is conscious that, in your case, extreme youth and inexperience may palliate what would otherwise be most grave offences. We emphasize this, since the sentence we will impose

[131]

upon you is designed, in part, to protect you against undesirable influences till you are of an age to judge rightly for yourself."

I stood very straight, schooling my expression, hands folded in front of me, head high: if I did nothing else, I would put Aunt Helen's deportment lessons to good use.

"This tribunal decrees, therefore, that you suffer the penalty of exile, to such a place and for such a period as the tribunal may hereafter determine and communicate to you. Until that time you will remain within the city boundaries. Let the verdict of the tribunal be recorded."

"It is so recorded," the clerk said.

There was a brief, awkward pause. Some sort of official acknowledgment seemed to be called for, so I dropped Myrsilus a stiff little curtsey. It was not, perhaps, quite appropriate to the occasion (I caught the swift glint of amusement in Pittacus' eye), but it was better than nothing.

The next few days were, one way and another, a considerable strain. My mother prowled the house like an angry wildcat: Meg retreated to bed, pleading a sick headache, and I felt strongly tempted to follow her example. But there was so much to be done—clothes and books and knick-knacks to sort, pack, or put in storage; the endless, exhausting round of farewell visits—that I simply could not afford the luxury. In any case, darling Aunt Helen protected me from Mama's worst tantrums—which perhaps was only fair, since she provoked several of them herself. ("Some people are *so* hard to please," she remarked at dinner on the day of the verdict. "Antimenidas appears to be furious because he wasn't executed, and here are you black-guarding Myrsilus for the unspeakable crime of not sending you into exile.")

But this was not, I fancy, my mother's main cause of annoyance. It soon became apparent that someone had been working very hard on my behalf in high places. A bare two days after, the tribunal (which meant, in effect, Myrsilus) had laid down Sicily as my place of exile, Aunt Helen had all the arrangements made. I would stay with her younger brother Lycurgus, one of the biggest landowners in Syracuse. ("He may be dull, darling, but he's a *most* enthusiastic patron of the arts.") She had also—even more improbably—caught a visiting celebrity on the wing, as it were, and talked him into acting as my escort on the journey. This was the distinguished poet and musician, Arion, now here on a brief visit to Lesbos, his birthplace, from Periander's court at Corinth. The moment Aunt Helen had met him, and found out he was planning a trip to Sicily, the poor man never stood a chance—or so she told us.

All this fell too suspiciously pat for words, to my way of thinking; and I have no doubt my mother felt so too. I had to remind myself at intervals that I was being sent into exile, and not on a cultural tour. I began to wonder just what had been happening behind the scenes, especially when my mother (having decided it was her parental duty to accompany me) was informed, through offical channels, that she would not be granted a permit for foreign travel.

It was easy enough to guess at the motives involved. Aunt Helen was determined to prise me loose from my mother's control (a task most people would have dismissed as impossible) and give me a chance to enjoy a change of scene abroad. Pittacus found me a personal embarrassment for several reasons and would be only too glad to get me out of the way for a while. But Myrsilus: what was there in it for Myrsilus? Then, abruptly, I remembered the curious charged exchange between him and my mother in the council chamber. So *that* was it. I nearly burst out laughing. How, I wondered, had Aunt Helen convinced him he stood a chance? Perhaps by presenting me as the too-clever, unmarriageable, devoted daughter, always ready to poison any threatening intimacy with jealous innuendoes: it was just the sort of fabrication which would appeal to her.

So my mother fumed, and I puzzled, till at last curiosity got the better of me, and I asked Aunt Helen straight out whether she had arranged the whole thing.

"Darling Sappho, you really *must* learn not to ask questions like that."

"Yes, Aunt Helen," I said as demurely as I could.

"And don't put on those kittenish airs with me."

"No, Aunt Helen."

"I think you'll like Syracuse, you know. It's a good place for young people. New. Exciting. A sense of discovery in the air. Besides"—she put her head on one side and studied me thoughtfully—"you'll benefit from a little constructive spoiling."

"Spoiling?"

"Indeed. You show every sign of possessing naturally luxurious tastes. With any luck, Lycurgus and Chloe will indulge them to a point where you refuse, thereafter, to put up with anything less. That should be extremely useful to you in later life. When you think of getting married, for instance."

I said fiercely: "I shall never marry—" and then paused, taken aback by the vehemence of my own reaction.

"Ah," said Aunt Helen, and there was a compassion in her eyes that robbed the words of any hurting quality, "you are in love with your own virginity. It's not as rare a complaint as you might suppose; and it seldom proves fatal." Then, unexpectedly, in her fine, light voice, she sang the opening line of an old folk-song I had first heard as a child in Eresus: "*Maidenhead, maidenhead, where are you gone from me?*" And without thinking I gave her the response: "*Never again shall I come to you, bride, never again—*" and my eyes filled with tears.

"You see?" Aunt Helen said gently.

I shook my head.

"You will, darling. You will." She took me in her arms, and cradled my head against her breast, and rocked me gently, like the small child that in so many ways I still was.

Antimenidas came to say good-bye. The bandage was gone now: a brown, ropy scab ran slantwise across his cheek, and the flesh round it was pulled together in a series of angry, puckered folds. Neither of us made any direct reference to what had taken place before the tribunal. He sat in the colonnade with me and drank wine: his dark eyes were wary.

"What will you do?" I asked. "Where will you go?"

He shrugged. "I have little choice. My property is confiscated. I know only one trade: war. The King of Babylonia needs mercenaries for his campaign in Judaea. I shall try my luck there."

Something in his expression, the way he emphasized those last words, made me say: "Don't try your luck too hard, Antimenidas. Let it bring you safely home."

"Let it bring me a good sword first," he said, with a glance at his empty belt. "They took that too." Then he smiled that singularly sweet smile which always looked so odd on his hard, grained, craggy features. "If I *do* come home, Sappho, I promise you—"

"What?"

"No. Wait and see."

I said: "Is your brother going with you?"

He shook his head, frowning.

So they had quarrelled again.

"Then where—?"

"Egypt, my dear. The pursuit of wisdom." He drew down his mouth, as though in contempt: the scar twisted, stretched. He finished his wine and stood up, hesitated, then—as though in answer to my unspoken question—said: "Alcaeus has never found it too difficult to finance his—adventures."

"It must be pleasant to have such generous friends."

"Yes." Antimenidas stared at me ironically. "You, I gather, should appreciate that better than most. Well. Enjoy yourself in Sicily—though I fancy that's unneccessary advice."

He picked up his light summer cloak and flung it over his shoulders. He looked very tall, standing there in the colonnade with the afternoon sun behind him.

"Good-bye," he said, and turned away without waiting for an answer, his long, uneven stride echoing across the court.

"Wait—" I called, breathless, not knowing what I meant, only what I had to do, fingers reaching for the clasp of the thin chain that held the amulet at my throat, the golden amulet I had worn since I was a baby. "Wait—" And then, as he looked back, I threw the amulet towards him, with a quick, awkward gesture, so that it skidded along the polished stones and came to rest in a patch of sunlight. As his hand closed over it I felt the touch on my throat and breast, a wrench, a pang. He will go safely now, I thought. He will come home unharmed. I smiled as I watched his long shadow out of sight. Then I remembered my own coming journey, and despite the heat a quick shiver ran through me.

There were weeds sprouting between the stone blocks of the drive up to Three Winds; not many, but enough to catch the eye. Already Phanias' death had, in a hundred tiny ways, affected things that seemed stable, permanent, part of the natural order. Mica, too, at seventeen was very different from the bubbling, excited twelve-year-old who had sat painting me under the apple-tree. Her plumpness had dropped away, her freckles were fading: only her hands, those fine, strong, sensitive hands, remained what they had been, in a world where they no longer had any true home.

Yet Three Winds itself still looked reassuringly the same, with its high, white rooms, its seasoned beams, its all-pervading scent of sweet grass, beeswax, jasmine. Down the familiar arched corridors we walked, Mica and I, past the central courtyard towards Ismene's private chamber. As we crossed the lobby I found myself staring, memory-haunted, at the great tapestry of centaurs and Lapiths on which Ismene had been working that summer afternoon five years ago.

Time looped out and away: there was nothing between then and now, all lost, strange, alien. *Hold on,* I told myself. *Have faith.*

"Mica—how is she? How has she taken it?"

Mica's eyes were lonely, sad with the knowledge that would always be a little more than she could bear, that was the price of her talent.

"She's—different. It's not just Papa's death. I wish it were."

"No—don't—"

Sometimes the truth is too hard to put into words.

But she burst out: "It's all finished, Sappho. Everything's finished—" There were tears on her cheeks. "I can't explain. I'm sorry."

Ismene, in black, rose as we came in, took both my hands in hers. It was not her appearance that shocked me most. That outgoing stream of warmth and reassurance had dried up. She was a husk, a ghost: she had no more to give.

I offered formal condolences on the loss of her husband: I did not trust my own spontaneous words.

She said: "Some losses are—supportable. Given time and courage, we shall learn to live again, to reshape the pattern—do you see?— without his presence."

"Yes. I understand."

"But something else is lost, Sappho. Surely you, of all people, must realize that? An atmosphere, a unifying force, the power that made Three Winds more, much more, than a house and so many acres of land, that gave it meaning and joy—"

At least Three Winds has an heir now, Lady Ismene. That should bring you comfort."

"Should it? What will become of his heritage in the years ahead? Can I turn back time for him? Can anyone?"

I remembered Phanias at the orchard gate: *It looks so permanent, doesn't it? So unalterable.* And then: *Nothing is permanent. We can only do what we must, knowing it may not be enough.* So he, too, foreknew, foresuffered: the irony of Hippias' birth could not have been lost on him. My heart turned suddenly cold: what unspeakable thread of despair linked the two images that flashed and merged in my mind—Phanias, skewered on the swords of Myrsilus' guardsmen; my father, red with Melanchros' blood, going down under a rain of dagger-thrusts, the butchered tyrannicide? What was it Antimenidas said, that winter day in Pyrrha? *Your father killed himself, quite literally, to be what his family wanted.* No, I thought, there is more to it than that: more, and worse.

I spoke the easy, conventional words of reassurance: "Have no fear, Lady Ismene. Hippias will rule Three Winds when he comes of age."

Strange and ironic prophecy.

"Thank you," she said, with a white little smile. "But it is you who need our prayers now, Sappho." Then, with a formality that matched my own: "May the Gods grant you a calm passage, safe landfall, a speedy return: all that your heart most desires."

On a sudden impulse I asked: "Where is Atthis? I must say good-bye to Atthis—" And suddenly this became all-important, it was the one thread back to that lost, still, sunlit perfection, the timeless moment in the apple-orchard.

"I'm here, Sappho." The voice from the doorway behind me was clear, sweet, a little sad. "I'm always here."

"Don't forget me when I'm gone," I said, turning. She stood there in her black mourning robe, sharp-outlined against the white of the corridor: a slight, enchanted creature, neither child nor woman, with budding breasts now, but the same enormous grey eyes, the same neat-coiled hair, like dark burnished copper, the same brown skin and heartrending awkwardness of movement I remembered from that first meeting long ago.

"I shall never forget you," she said; and there was something about her that brought all three of us up short, lifted the moment out of its half-teasing casualness onto quite a different plane.

All that your heart most desires.

I caught my breath, recovered myself, and said, laughing: "You will, you know." But I had seen the sudden flash of prophetic sadness in Ismene's eyes: so must Cassandra have looked during those early years in Troy, the years of bright unknowing.

IX

SUNLIGHT glittered on the calm waters of the Saronic Gulf:
there was scarcely enough breeze to fill the great patched sail overhead. Down below decks, on their thwarts above the bilge-washed
ballast, the rowers heaved and sweated. Oar-blades dipped, thrashed
whitely, rose wet and glinting, wavered like the legs of an upturned
beetle. The air was alive with sharp interdependent noises: the leathery creak of oar-tholes, the higher-pitched stress and play between
rope and timber, the timekeeper's hoarse, rhythmic bark, the slow
froth and slap of water, close-penned goats and sheep complaining
loudly from their unwanted vantage-point in the bows.

I stretched myself like a cat, glad, as always, to come up from the
women's quarters—that cramped, sour-smelling pit of loud unprivacy—
and breathe fresh air again. I was also enjoying a sense of stolen
privilege. Arion, being the most distinguished passenger aboard (and,
what was more important on a Corinthian ship, in high favour with
Periander) had the freedom of the captain's poop-deck: this meant
canvas chairs, cushions, decent seclusion, and a comparative immunity
from the smell of goat—or goatish fellow-travellers. Since (as he said)
he enjoyed sunning himself, and had, in a weak-minded moment,
agreed to act as my escort, it was only fair that I should be allowed
to accompany him.

He was, I think, one of the oddest men I have ever met in my
life: a small, bald, brown, wrinkled creature, with wicked black eyes
and the beginnings of a hunchback. Despite his shortness (he was
only an inch or two taller than I was), the casual physical strength
he displayed on occasion impressed everyone—and was meant to. I

have seen him lift a full amphora or a pig of lead with one hand, putting some brawny sailor to shame. He had probably decided early in life that strength, talent, and eccentricity would, between them, more than compensate for his physical shortcomings: I found myself, unexpectedly, envying him that rocklike self-assurance, the huge and mischievous delight he took in his own outrageousness.

He did the most extraordinary things: he seemed determined to defeat not only human conventions but natural law too. He would remove every stitch of clothing (except for an exiguous white loin-cloth, such as a field-slave might wear) and lie for hours at a time grilling himself in the sun, till his hairy, crab-like body was burnt as brown as the ship's timbers. Yet far from incurring serious illness as a result of such exposure, he seemed actually to thrive on it. When I asked him why, he said, with the ghost of a wink, that because of his brilliant musicianship Apollo had made a special exception in his case. "Of course," he added, "one day I'll lose my touch; and then he'll probably flay me like Marsyas, out of pure spite."

The first time he dived overboard he caused a good deal of panic (except among the crew, who knew all about his little peculiarities); but after a while we got used to him frolicking round in the water like a dolphin—he was a superb swimmer, as so many physically handicapped people tend to be—and a special rope ladder was rigged from the counter to let him scramble aboard after his dip. He could shin up the rigging faster than any sailor; and he was capable, it seemed, of out-drinking everyone on board. When he was full of wine he told endless exotic travellers' stories, in which fact and fancy seemed to mingle like the coloured warp and woof on a loom. One man unwisely called him a liar, and was hit so hard that he remained unconscious for two days.

Now Arion squatted cross-legged on a cushion in the sun, flexing his strong musician's fingers after an hour's work with me on the lyre. He was a magnificent teacher: patient, ruthless, dedicated. He made no allowances whatsoever for feminine weakness. At the end of one particularly testing exercise he suddenly grabbed my right hand as though it were a horse's hoof and he a farrier, and said: "No wonder girls can't get any real tone out of a lyre. Too busy keeping their fingers pretty."

He thrust his own index-finger under my nose. The nail was grotesque, long and claw-thickened, the flesh of the top joint calloused to a hard yellow pad.

"D'you see that? Thirty years' work. Thirty years' slavery, if you like."

"I can believe it."

He snorted at my tone. "Ugly, isn't it?"

"Yes. And unnecessary." But I regretted the words almost as soon as they were uttered: for him, I saw, this repulsive physical distortion was a proof of endurance, a source of pride.

He said: "Have you ever *used* an Egyptian plectrum?"

"No, but—"

"Then you're in no position to argue, are you? Damned little sliver of ivory. No feeling in it. Not part of you."

Stung, I said: "What do you do when you want to write a letter? Slit up your finger-nail with a penknife? Trim it to a point? Dip it in the—"

He cut me off with an abrupt bark of laughter. "All right, all right: never labour an obvious point. Bad habit you've got there, my girl. Comes of living on that extraordinary island of ours, h'm? H'm?" The eyes twinkled beneath their fierce tufted brows. "No one to contradict you. Parochial outlook. Stultifying."

I flushed, hurt. "That's not fair—"

"Is it not? Don't forget I was brought up on the island myself. The people who sent you into exile were doing you a favour."

As this was what I privately felt, too, I found it hard to disagree. I said with some diffidence: "But an island has some positive advantages—"

"Indeed it does." Arion sounded pleased. "And most of them are its disadvantages turned inside out. To take one obvious example. When we reach Corinth, everyone will know where you come from the moment you open your mouth. Vocabulary, idiom, that very charming brogue of yours: unmistakable. But with me it's different: my accent is international, all the edges have been rubbed off it. My vocabulary's been patched together from a dozen countries. I belong everywhere and nowhere. Which of us is better off?"

"Well—" I hesitated; and the more I thought, the harder I found it to answer.

Arion's black eyes twinkled. "Just so. There is a price to pay for the individual voice, is there not?"

"But the price is worth it."

"Ah, Sappho, how that remark places you! Ask them in Sparta or Crete, even in Athens, what value they put on the individual voice: you will get a very short answer. There all men speak, or strive to speak, with one voice—that of the State. Talk to them of private passions, of the heart's supremacy, of the still, significant moment—all these things that your island has enabled you to perceive and cherish—and they will either laugh you to scorn or treat you as a subversive anarchist."

"You seem to forget," I said, "that I am, at this very moment, in exile for my political activities."

"Oh, Sappho—" He shook his brown, bald head, momentarily at a loss for words. "You know, when I came back on this visit, I could hardly believe my eyes and ears—such grotesque little intrigues, such outdated Homeric sentiments! Do you realize that even the armour your soldiers wear is nearly a century obsolete by mainland standards?"

"Are the alternatives you propose so very attractive? Is the voice of the State silent in Corinth?"

"Corinth," said Arion, "is like myself: international. It stands, in every sense, at the crossroads. All art should, ultimately, be cosmopolitan: and most artists know it. That is why you will find so many of them there."

"Indeed? I thought it was because Periander paid them well."

Arion grinned. He looked more like a monkey than ever. "You see?" he said. "This voyage is broadening your mind already. Of course artists will go where they are well paid; so will any skilled craftsman. The notion of the unpaid bard singing as his Muse dictates was all very well when he belonged to a nobleman's manor. But even in Mytilene—as you know to your cost—life isn't like that any more."

He nodded down towards the central well of the ship, where a fat merchant was checking the seals on a lashed-down cargo of wine-jars.

"There goes our future, Sappho," he said. "Yours and mine."

"An ignoble future."

"Is it so ignoble? I wonder. Men like Periander and Pittacus have a vision, too. They see a world of peace, prosperity, open frontiers: a world which traffics as freely in ideas as it does in wine or olives, a world where war and narrow national prejudices have no place, a cosmopolitan world in which the artist, the maker, is honoured above the mere ranting general—" He broke off, perhaps a little embarrassed by his own fervour, and chuckled: "It's not only cash that keeps me in Corinth, you know."

[141]

"I'm sure it's not."

We both fell silent for a moment, staring out across the bay towards the green folded mountains of Salamis and Megara. Behind us, on the port bow, lay Aegina, and beyond Aegina the hazed mountains of the Argolid. There, under our horizon, stood Mycenae, Agamemnon's Mycenae, rich in gold and blood, where men had known honour and upheld that honour with the sword.

I thought: And what will he be like, this faceless, stateless artist, hawking his talent from one patron to the next, talking of visions when there is nothing in his heart but flattery, greed, fear? He will be like Arion, the great, much-courted, eccentric Arion, who has done no original work for years, who is empty and twisted and has nothing left to him but technique—that clubbed nail, that badge of his existence!—who belongs nowhere, who believes nothing.

I looked at him squatting there, armoured in his deformity, and for the first time felt nothing but pity: pity and slight contempt. Why is he coming to Sicily? I wondered. Not just to compete in some international musical festival. Perhaps the wind of favour at Corinth is veering into another quarter. Perhaps he wants to see if the obsolete, decadent, aristocratic Sicilian landowners can, after all, offer him a better sinecure than Periander. And what fresh shape will his vision take then?

I said: "From all I've heard, Periander isn't exactly a pleasant person."

"You mustn't believe all you hear. Besides, he's old now. Old, and embittered. His personal life"—Arion shrugged—"has been—unfortunate. His wife's death, his quarrel with his son. You know the stories."

"Yes," I said, "I know the stories." Aunt Helen's voice, cutting and contemptuous, came back to me: *A man who can kick his wife into a miscarriage—one from which she subsequently dies—and all because of some idiotic story told him by a concubine, can hardly be called a stable character.*

"By the way," Arion said, with careful casualness, "it might be tactful *not* to mention the reason for your exile, or indeed that you're in exile at all: he's a little touchy on that subject."

"It all sounds quite alarming. Do you really think I ought to meet him?"

The twinkle was back in Arion's eye as he said: "Periander doesn't eat the nobility nowadays; they're too busy working for him. Besides" —and the twinkle broadened into a grin—"he was only told to lop off the *tallest* corn-ears: you remember?" He looked me up and down, with bland malice, and said: "You're *quite* safe, I should think." Then he lay back, arranged a yellow silk scarf over his eyes, and went to sleep.

When I remember Corinth, it is always with a sense of vivid, terrifying unreality, as though my recollections had been superimposed on some mad dream-landscape of the mind. But then there *is* something nightmarish about the whole Corinthian Isthmus, that ass-backed rope of rocks stretched between two encroaching gulfs below the mountains, that shingled, sand-blown wilderness which has, through a geographical accident, become Greece's supreme monument to human ambition and lust.

In these narrow passes, under the shadow of that towering rocky citadel, whole armies have been fought and held. Here, astride the same narrow neck where once Sciron dispatched unwary travellers, there runs the great stone-blocked slipway which Periander built from shore to shore. Day in, day out, teams of oxen strain at their safety ropes, while on wet wooden cradles a queue of black ships—like so many Egyptian gods, or Trojan horses—edge overland, barnacle-naked, trailing garlands of green slime, to their innumerable destinations. Iron-bound wheels grind harshly against the sides of those deep marble runnels, dung lies steaming in the salt Isthmus air, all along the slipway there is wordless shouting, the crack of drovers' whips.

Poised on his black wet rock beyond the curving arms of the eastern harbour, Poseidon stands, dolphin and trident aloft, stony eyes alert for all weathers, a landmark, used with familiarity by sailors and circling gulls. Up behind a thicket of masts houses fan out—white, grey, lemon—across the hillside. Wet quays are clamorous, customs-hall and fish market echo with tramping feet, trolleys, auctioneers' harsh parrot-cries. Clash and hammer of bronze-workers in spark-bright alleys, the goose-hiss of hot plunged metal. Red, blue, green, black, the rough dyed wools of the rugmakers; tang of salted fish in creels; sweating, goatish cheeses.

Here the goldsmiths are tapping with their minuscule hammers: one looks up, grey-faced, secretive, eyes caught by the pomegranate necklace at my throat. I pause, two booths on, pick up an exquisite brooch of rock-crystal: inside the crystal, a marvel of art, is a tiny gold figurine, no longer than my finger-joint, Thetis bearing the arms of Achilles to Troy. But I am an exile: I put down the brooch and move on, Praxinoa a black shadow behind me.

Round the brick-kilns air is dancing, there are roof-tiles packed flat in the yards between layers of straw, my fingers drag over the matte surface of an unfired terra-cotta bowl. Smell of wet clay, wheels spinning in sunlight, pots surging up, bellying, finger-shaped at a touch, their bright mud-glister soon gone. Then the painters, bird-faced with absorption, jars of coloured pigments at their elbow, peck-ing and swooping and dabbing over rows of buff-plain vases—too many vases, unending labour, mere repetition—sketching in friezes (the usual themes: chariots, warriors, wild-beast hunts) red and pur-ple, leaving no spaces (value for money), cramming each corner with rosettes, acanthus-leaves: skimping their work, too, tricks of the trade —smudging an outline, stretching a leopard's spring further and fur-ther: four, not six, will encircle the vase now, no one will argue, the market is rising, Corinth can make art, export it, destroy it.

All too large, too loud, too violent: in false perspective, and smudged, like the leopards; built on shingle, a mirage of gold, a whore of a city, pimping its culture for quick returns, buying esteem with a show of wisdom, buying poets, musicians, artists, cankered, corrupting, sick at the heart. The blood that was spilt can never be dry, the lopped corn-ears gush red in the furrow. Old men sit by the fountain under the shade of the plane-tree, playing draughts, their eyes wary and hooded. The public statues look down, too bored or cautious to make any public pronouncement; better to watch, wait, survive.

Two thousand feet up, on the summit of the great black rock that lowers over Corinth with the air of a sleeping Titan, I stood, godlike, the wind in my hair, all Greece spread out below me. There to the north, remote and snow-bright peaks, rose Helicon and Parnassus. Beside those high, singing waters, in that clear air, the Muses had their home; there, over Delphi, eagles circled towards the prophetic navel-stone that marks the world's centre. In the east lay the islands of the Saronic Gulf, and beyond them, a blue shadow, the mountains of Attica. Southward were Argos and Mycenae; to the west, range on dark folded range, rose the forest stronghold of Arcadia. I turned from quarter to quarter, and the world hummed under me, soft, deep, a great spinning top for my delight. Horizons fled, the sky expanded, brighter than white steel in the forge. The city at my feet shrank into nothingness, a small festered chancre, forgotten, insignificant.

So Arion found me a little later, leaning on the stone parapet, oblivious and content. He had sent me on ahead by mule: he said he needed exercise. When he reached the summit of the rock there was not a drop of sweat visible anywhere on his baked, brown, matte skin. His black eyes blinked lizardlike; there was something very saurian about him that morning. I felt Praxinoa stiffen, reflexively, at his approach.

"Well, now," he said. "As I might have guessed. Always prefer your landscapes *without* figures, h'm?" The tufted eyebrows jerked and twitched. "Let me restore the balance. A rare sight, a *very* rare sight." Lizard-tongue flickered, licked lips. "Aphrodite has many strange devotees, h'm? But this—"

He beckoned imperiously: I fell into step beside him. Our feet kept easy time: he was perhaps half a head the taller, no more. Up the wide, worn steps we plodded, our shadows falling short in front of us, up past the flower-sellers with their garlands, past the hawkers of incense, past the candlemakers' workshops, past the booths where men with tired, cynical eyes display trinkets, scarves, and cheap, gaudily painted statuettes of the Goddess whose great temple towers above them, on the rock's highest spur, tall-columned, bright with gilding and murals. Here, in the precinct itself, were moneychangers and booksellers; the one-legged huckster (what childhood memory stirred at sight of him?) sitting by his wicker cages full of white, bickering, sacrificial doves; the stalled lambs (white also: reputed blemishless) in their cramped pens; the fortune-tellers, the blind beggar, a crudely limned picture of shipwreck hung from his neck.

Here you could smell cooking meat skewered over charcoal; here the dust was splashed with wine where men had drunk, and wiped their mouths, and emptied the cup for luck; and here were other men, many of them, foreign travellers and merchants by their dress, who all showed the same sick, hot, furtive eyes, who hesitated, joked with a stall-keeper, fingered a sacred picture, then, abrupt and determined, strode up the steps into the temple.

Arion said: "Do you know what they are here for, h'm?" His dark, lubricious eye moved over me and away.

"No." And then, before he could speak again, I knew: how could I not have known? Colour flooded to my cheeks as I recalled the knowing jokes about this temple that I had heard, or overheard, in Mytilene—in particular, about its band of so-called "sacred slaves," a thousand strong, women dedicated to the Goddess, who must, in Aphrodite's name, prostitute themselves with any stranger willing to pay gold for the privilege.

"Ah," murmured Arion, "I see you remember." He was watching me avidly, eager to savour my every reaction. "A notable custom of the city. And profitable, of course; *very* profitable. Not everyone"—he brought out the old saying as though it were his own—"can afford to visit Corinth, h'm?"

"Not everyone would choose to."

"You're young, of course. And—inexperienced." There was something about the way he said this that made me feel, almost literally, slimy. "But as a devotee of Aphrodite yourself—"

"I find the spectacle—revealing." Was my voice cool and distasteful enough? Whatever happened, I must not, would not give this twisted creature the pleasure of seeing me behave like a shocked virgin.

Our eyes met: in his I saw the same dreadful sidelong desire, they were the eyes of a rutting dog. He laughed; his lips curled away from his teeth. I knew, now, why he had brought me here. He said: "Fortunately, I can afford to—visit Corinth."

I put my hand up to my mouth, stifled a yawn. "How pleasant for you."

"You will, I am sure, excuse me if I—pay my respects to Aphrodite, h'm? H'm? It won't take too long—"

"No; I expect not. But please don't shorten your devotions on my account."

He hesitated, as though about to say something more; then turned abruptly, and moved towards the temple. I watched his diminutive figure scuttle up those broad white marble steps in the sunlight, a lustful crab: saw Praxinoa's dark Sicilian features freeze with silent contempt. Yet, unexpectedly, I felt not loathing, but a sudden flood of pity and compassion.

Once, long ago perhaps, in a simpler age—so my thoughts ran—this ritual act had possessed meaning, virtue, power: was a celebration of godhead, a passionate striving towards some ultimate union with the divine. But here I could see nothing except cold lust, mean and solitary concupiscence, defilement under the sun. I thought: Each man who spills his seed so wantonly in that sacred place commits a pollution. Here, if anywhere, is the sick, corrupt heart of Corinth.

Then I recalled a curious story—one of the many—told about Periander: how (among other acts of violence committed on seizing power) he had hunted down all the city's procuresses, tied them in weighted sacks, and drowned them. Some regarded this as a sign of stern morality: but standing there in the temple precinct I knew better. Like any ruthless businessman, Periander was, quite simply, eliminating competition: he had murdered those wretched women in order to monopolize their trade. Not content with that, he had become bawdmaster to the Goddess herself, making her temple a common whorehouse, and—I had no doubt—diverting the profits into his own coffers.

I have tried, at a distance of some thirty years, to be as objective as I can over this faintly unpleasant little episode. I know, now, that I *did* behave more like a shocked virgin (which, after all, I was) than I felt disposed to admit at the time. My censoriousness was not, in itself, admirable: it amused Arion (that harmless, pathetic old lecher); and I suspect the Goddess herself—knowing all, foreseeing all—must have laughed at the misplaced rectitude of her twenty-year-old votary. There are many kinds of desire, many roads to adoration and worship: who was I to condemn these men in my ignorance? How could I be so sure that their act was a pollution, or the motives which inspired it displeasing to the Goddess?

Worst of all, may I not have read into their eyes (for whatever reasons of my own, reasons perhaps best left unexplored) emotions which they did not feel, an attitude of which they were wholly innocent? To you, the unknown and unknowable strangers, in this fiftieth year of my life I offer my humble contrition. The divine punishment which I now suffer—so agonizingly appropriate to my offence—should give you ample satisfaction.

But I was right about Periander: time has not changed my judgment on his character, or lessened my contempt for all he did. Arion duly arranged a meeting between us, rather against my will—indeed, he was so insistent about it that I suspect Periander had commanded him to produce me—and I found myself, one evening, being escorted by two armed guards through a labyrinth of corridors, where every sound rang harsh and metallic, clash of iron-studded boots on stone, rasp of keys in innumerable locked doors, clinking armour, clang of shot bolts, till at last I reached a small, plainly furnished chamber, with heavy grilles over its deep stone windows, and lamps everywhere—on tables, in wall-niches, and, as centre-piece, a great, winking bronze chandelier hung from the ceiling.

The man who sat there, an untouched cup of wine in front of him, a peeled grape half-way to his lips, was so different from what I had expected that, forgetting my manners, I stood and stared at him, openly incredulous. He was thin and stooped, balding, clean-shaven, with a muddy, blotched complexion and a red-veined, oddly pendulous nose. His lower jaw was weak, retreating in creases and folds of slack flesh. Despite the heat, he sat huddled in a heavy woollen cloak. He never once, during the interview, looked directly at me: his eyes flickered round the room, as though expecting an assassin in every corner. From time to time he caught himself dribbling and dabbed at his mouth with the sleeve of his cloak.

We exchanged polite commonplaces for a little: he clearly knew all about me, had read some of my poems, seemed anxious that I should be comfortable. Had Arion arranged suitable accommodation for me? Did I need anything? I must not be shy: Corinth—he wiped away a glistening thread of spittle—was an enlightened city, he had made it a centre of art and learning, wise men came from all over the Greek world to enjoy his patronage. A young poetess should be treated with respect. I was not, he had gathered, making a lengthy stay. Just passing through. A pity, a great pity. Next time. I need only write to him. Personally. The rheumy, suspicious tortoise-eyes came up in a dreadful attempt at gallantry: he gave a high, cracking laugh. The guards at the door stirred uneasily. Periander's thin voice rambled on: after a little it became obvious that he could not hear me, or had forgotten I was there. I sat, frozen, as the dreadful words spilled out.

"Never trust them, never. All trust is betrayed. Mildness destroys itself. Cut them down. Walking in the corn-field. But the blood is expiated, the Furies no longer walk, they are sleeping. Yes, sleeping. Gold repays. I have brought this city to greatness. Build on sand, she said. Melissa, ah, Melissa, do you remember that first day? You were bringing wine for your father's labourers, Melissa, in a light white dress with a red border. Harvest-time. Cicadas in the plane-trees. Dust and sweat. So beautiful, Melissa. So beautiful—"

He sat hunched at the table, fists clenched, staring at nothing. There was a faint tremor in his right cheek.

"A whore, I believed a whore, Melissa, a jealous whore. Can you forgive me? I did what I could to make amends. The oracle of the dead, the whispering old women, the wood-doves." His voice suddenly rose in an agonized shout. "They said you were cold, Melissa— cold, naked, shivering. Your clothes were not burnt in the funeral pyre, you said. Naked, a naked ghost, naked and unforgiving. So cold, Melissa. Why were you cold? My own words back to me from beyond the grave. *The oven is cold when I bake my bread in it.* I gave you dresses, Melissa, a goddess' ransom. All Corinth's finery burnt to warm you. Cold, Melissa, still cold. Why do you still turn

[148]

your face away, Melissa? You and your son both? He will never come back. I have nothing. Nothing. Why do you torture me? Why?"

His face changed, crumpled. He stared past me, horror in his eyes. "No. No, *you* are sleeping, I know it. I cannot see you. Ah, accursed still! Unclean. Defiled. I cannot. There is no peace from you. No cleansing. Melissa too. Polluted, unforgiving. Black wings, blood. In dreams the terror, the memory. But the guilt was yours, yours—" and then, in a high, terrible scream: *"Mother, forgive me!"* His head fell forward: his teeth were clenched, froth showed at the corners of his mouth.

As though a spell had been broken, one guard ran forward, propped him up in his chair like some broken-backed dummy, while the other tugged at a heavy bell-rope. Footsteps, lights, a physician in his long blue robe, a glass of some blackish cordial. Jaws forced apart, choking, swallowing. Then, an age later it seemed, the eyes blinked open. He coughed, sat up, instantly in possession of his faculties, like a wild forest animal that sleeps on a hair-edge of alertness, ready for any danger that may approach. He took in the scene at a glance: it must have been tolerably familiar to him, since he showed no surprise, only grim recognition.

"I owe you an apology, young lady," he said, and his voice was now surprisingly strong: for the first time I appreciated the quality in this man that could, still, command absolute obedience. "Please forgive me if I alarmed you." He shot me a sharp glance: I smiled, shook my head. "I am, I fear, subject—without warning—to these unfortunate attacks." The physician, a tall, impassive, bearded man—a Coan, by the look of him—nodded professional agreement. "And please, if you will"—steel crept into his voice: this was a command, not a request—"forget any—nonsense I may have talked. One symptom of this disease, this fit, is a temporary delirium."

"I quite understand, my lord."

"Yes: I thought you would." He smiled, briefly, and held out his thin, blotched, old man's hand.

"Good-bye, my dear. I hope to meet you again."

"Thank you, my lord. I am honoured."

"Don't let Arion bully you: the man's a fool."

"No, my lord."

"And have a good trip to Sicily."

He sat back, sweat glistening on his high forehead, and dabbed at his mouth with the sleeve of his gown. I curtseyed, as I had curtseyed to Myrsilus, and walked out into the high, echoing corridor. Behind me I heard a key grate in its wards, the slam of heavy bolts. Every lock in this fortress seemed to be rusty. Perhaps, I thought, he forbids the guards to oil them: perhaps those dreadful metallic sounds, like the dead ring of gold, offer him the only comfort he can understand.

Two days later we took ship again, from sand-blown Lechaeum on the Gulf, aboard a smaller, faster vessel, bound for Syracuse with a cargo of decorated roof-tiles. Arion became his old, relaxed, caustic self the moment we left harbour: I think he must have been as relieved to see Corinth drop away over the horizon as I was. He showed neither embarrassment nor (what would have been worse) suggestive over-familiarity: indeed, he behaved towards me just as though nothing in the least untoward had happened, which I found a great relief. For an hour each morning I practised on the lyre with him, as we had done throughout our previous voyage together. He told me, unexpectedly, that I "showed signs of improvement." This, from him, was high praise.

One change in his disposition, though, I could not help but notice, almost as soon as he came aboard. He was now very flush with money and enjoyed letting the fact be known. Presumably he had persuaded Periander to advance him travelling-expenses to Sicily—and a substantial retainer, by the look of it—as Corinth's official representative at the festival. I found myself wondering, in a spirit of youthful cynicism, just how much he would be expected to refund if he came back without the first prize. But this was hardly the sort of question one could put to an international figure, so instead I asked him where the festival was to be held.

"Himera," he said briskly. "Odd place: up on the north coast, right away from all the other Greek settlements, h'm? Plenty of Sicels around there still—"

"Sicels?"

"The old people. There from the beginning—before the Gods, they say. Well. Small, dark, secretive folk, live up in the mountains now, mostly. What's left of them. Like wild goats. Wild tempers, too. Fire in their bellies. Gods themselves once, h'm?"

I stared down over the bulwark at the cobalt water creaming past and said without thinking: "Hephaestus under Etna. It sounds—appropriate."

He nodded. "They're great metal-workers: I've seen work done in Sicily you'd never get a Greek smith to match. But they guard their trade secrets. All they have left, h'm? And a reputation as magicians, of course. More witches in that island than anywhere except Thessaly."

An involuntary shiver ran through me: somehow Arion's matter-of-fact tone made it sound much worse.

"I've seen them at night on the hills, grubbing roots, h'm? Twenty years ago. Things may have changed—"

My mind went back, suddenly, to poor Uncle Eurygyus, and the dreadful old women who came clustering round our courtyard, obscene bundles of black rags, bats in daylight. They did not seem at all amusing now.

I said with sudden determination: "Do *you* believe in it? Magic, I mean?"

His black eyes blinked at this direct frontal assault. "I don't know. Perhaps there's no simple answer to that question. We've all seen so much superstitious rubbish, h'm? Love-potions, spells for a fever, that sort of stuff. But there's something about Sicily"—he spread his hands —"I can't explain. You'll see. The women—they have a dark, sidelong way of looking at you. Like a snake. You feel the power. You say to yourself, perhaps they *can* bewitch you. Or call down the moon. Or change themselves into screech-owls after dark." He frowned. "I've never been so conscious of screech-owls as I was in Sicily. Swooping and shrieking at night: they keep you awake. Once one got into my bedroom, I thought I was dreaming still, that hellish screeching and flapping, h'm? No light, the lamp had gone out—" He scratched his bald pate, blinked. "Snakes too," he said. "Everywhere. Black. Golden brown. Those dark holes into the hot earth. Burning. There's a violence, you'll see: something held down, secret, dangerous. Like the molten fires under Etna. Or Hephaestus, h'm? Sometimes the giant lies still, and you can forget him. Then, one spring day, when you're walking among the poppies, he heaves and groans in his sleep, and the hot mid-day fear grips you—"

I managed a laugh. "You make it sound the most enchanting place." My heart was a small, hard, cold, thudding lump, a separate entity over which I had no control.

"Dear me," Arion said, apologetically, "how I do run on: you should have stopped me if you were—bored." The shaggy eyebrows twitched upwards in amusement. "It *is* an enchanting place—so rich, so fertile you'll not credit your senses. Great forests alive with every sort of bird and beast, rich grazing-land, corn-fields that stretch beyond the horizon, vast estates, fine houses. Fine painting and music, too; art

[151]

takes root and sprouts there like every other living thing. Rich, rich —why, you can almost see the gold glint in that black soil."

The ship drove steadily westward, sail bellying, towards the still-hidden mouth of the Gulf. We were, as before, sitting on the after-deck. The steersman stood close behind us, leaning on his great rudder-oar: so brown and lined was his face, so impassive, it might have been a carved figurehead. Only his eyes were watchful: and sometimes—was it my imagination?—they seemed to settle on Arion with a kind of derisive, anticipatory relish.

X

"BUT, *darling*," said Chloe, spinning round, eardrops aglint, in a swirl of lime-green skirts, "isn't she the most exquisite creature you ever saw? Like an ivory figurine—" She caught my hand in hers, almost dancing with delight and excitement. "Helen must be mad—why on earth didn't she *tell* us? Lycurgus, she's your sister, can *you* explain?"

Lycurgus, who was obviously used to his wife's enthusiasms, smiled and said: "Perhaps she wanted to give you a pleasant surprise, Chloe. You know how you adore surprises." Then, turning to me, tolerant, amused (as though, I thought, Chloe were a high-spirited puppy): "You mustn't let my wife overwhelm you, Sappho. Especially after a long journey."

I said, with unpremeditated candour: "I think she's wonderful." And meant it. If Chloe had been surprised, so, beyond my wildest dreams, was I. Whatever I had been expecting (someone staid and middle-aged, certainly: faintly disapproving if not downright contemptuous) this exotic Sicilian beauty was not it. I gazed at her with open and rapturous fascination: that unbelievable skin, like thick, smooth-poured cream, the chignon of gleaming black hair, the barbaric gold bracelets, the matching emerald ear-drops and pendant necklace that so unobtrusively picked up and intensified the pure green of her eyes. She's like a cat, I thought, a beautiful, pampered cat: exquisitely alive in all her senses. I had a sudden urge to stroke her, to make her purr.

"But those *eyes*, darling, that wonderful secret smile—" Her clasp on my hand tightened: I felt the sharp pressure of her long, almond-shaped nails. So the cat had claws too.

"Stop it, Chloe: you'll embarrass the poor child." But I felt that if anyone was embarrassed, it was Lycurgus himself.

To tell the truth, I could have danced over the moon. For the first time in my life someone had told me I was beautiful and meant it: the passionate appreciation in Chloe's eyes was as exhilarating and incontrovertible as sunlight after a storm.

My whole body glowed with sensuous awareness: I could feel each separate part of me catch fire. The secret, scarce-acknowledged shame and disgust I had nursed against my physical imperfections (as my mother had taught me to regard them) suddenly melted, flowed, vanished: it was as though Chloe, by that simple contact of fingers, had drawn my misery into herself, a beautiful enchantress whose magic worked to generous, life-enhancing ends. Then, over her shoulder, I caught sight of Arion, watching every move, each least change of expression, with those black, snakelike eyes, and remembered his words: *More witches in that island than anywhere except Thessaly.* Our hands drew apart: I got the uncanny feeling that she, too, knew just where Arion was, could have described his every gesture.

Lycurgus said to Arion: "We're most grateful to you for escorting my niece on so long a journey, sir. I hope"—this with a slow, consciously charming smile—"she was no trouble to you?"

"Indeed not, my lord. It was a privilege to have so attractive and, I may say, *talented* a fellow-traveller."

For an enlightened artist who dismissed the aristocracy as an obsolescent anachronism, I thought, Arion wasn't doing badly. His whole voice and bearing had changed: if not exactly unctuous, he was something more than deferential. I wondered if he adopted the same approach while extracting money from Periander.

"The privilege is all ours," Lycurgus said. "We are honoured to have so famous an artist under our roof." His intonation had that over-sweet, over-solicitous quality about it which well-bred people often tend to assume when dealing with their inferiors on terms of social equality. But Arion, I was amused to see, took the words at their face value.

Chloe said: "The steward's looking after your baggage. Come up on the roof for a little and enjoy the view."

Lycurgus led the way up a broad wooden staircase: Chloe slipped her arm through mine as we followed. Behind me I could hear Arion's neat, finicky footsteps on every tread: if Chloe looks like a cat, I

[154]

thought, *he* walks like one. When we reached the top I paused, astonished by the breadth and splendour of the panorama spread out below us: this must be very nearly the highest point of the entire city. The roof itself was flat, with mosaic tiling and an ornate marble balustrade: it ran round three sides of the courtyard, and resembled nothing that I had ever seen on Mytilene. Even Three Winds seemed staid by comparison.

There were pots and tubs everywhere: a sweet, heavy scent of stock and basil hung in the late afternoon air. A low table was set out with silver wine-server, bowls of fresh fruit—apples, figs, grapes, pears— and plates of honey-cakes. On either side of the table stood a cushion-strewn couch, with carved ivory facings: and at the head of each couch, like guardian statues, waited two male house-slaves, who stared through us and past us, immaculate in their white robes, so still they scarcely seemed to breathe. I caught my breath: I had never seen Nubians before, and the carved black planes of their alien features, the faint raised cicatrice on each cheek, came as an almost physical shock.

Lycurgus beckoned to me, and I stood beside him, leaning over the balustrade. He took an obvious, and to me rather endearing, pleasure in talking about his city: a trait, I was to discover, which most colonial Greeks shared.

"This hill we're on forms part of the quarter of Achradina," he said. "Down there in front of us is the Little Harbour—mostly for fishing-vessels, as you can see. The island with the causeway is called Ortygia—"

"What wonderful old houses it has."

Behind me I heard Chloe laugh. "Indeed yes, darling. That's rather a sore point. But we mustn't be envious. Not everyone can live on The Island." Somehow the way she pronounced those two words made it clear that they were a title rather than a mere description. "You have to be directly descended from one of the original colonists, and even then there's a strict order of precedence."

"How extraordinary," said Arion, looking as though he found it most impressive. It occurred to me then, for the first time, that there might be Syracusans who could patronize Lycurgus and Chloe in much the same way as they themselves could—and did—patronize Arion.

Lycurgus ran one hand through his thick, bleached hair. How old was he? Thirty-eight? Forty? Odd to think that he was Aunt Helen's brother. "Of course," he said smoothly, "Syracuse probably comes as something of a change after Corinth."

"You must," added Chloe, "find us terribly dull and provincial." She bent mischievously over Arion: the little man's nose was level with her full, creamy bosom, and his emphatic denial a trifle incoherent. All the same, I thought, there was just enough truth in what they both said to provoke reflection. Syracuse was no less rich and resplendent than its parent city: yet in a hundred and fifty years it had acquired a wholly different atmosphere, leisured, elegant, self-confident. Perhaps a hustling Corinthian businessman *would* be irked by the slow, formal rhythm of living, the way such rich material was subdued to brilliant yet essentially severe patterns, the traditional, almost hierarchic atmosphere. Yet this pattern was, I sensed, by no means so stable as it appeared on the surface: Lycurgus and Chloe, to look no further, had an outlook in some subtle way at variance with it.

Lycurgus went on with oblivious enthusiasm, pointing out the Great Harbour, and the fortified headland of Plemmyrium opposite Ortygia, and the low, reedy marshes that stretched inland towards New City and the heights of Epipolae, with the Anapus River an invisible tree-dotted line running through them. There were the stone-quarries, yes, *there,* down on my right beyond the Achradina wall. Eighty feet deep in places. Only slave-labour, of course, and mostly condemned criminals, they couldn't last long in that appalling place, roasted by day and frozen at night and worked for twelve-hour shifts—

"Darling," said Chloe, sharply, "come and sit *down:* your guests don't want to hear about quarry-slaves, they're *starving.*" There was a sudden, momentary edge of irritation in her voice, and something more, something that eluded me.

"What? Oh, yes. I'm so sorry." He turned reluctantly from the balustrade: his smile was boyish, disarming. I came to know that smile very well after a time. We all sat down: Arion and Lycurgus on one couch, Chloe beside me on the other. I was intensely aware of every movement she made, of the way her hand held the cup as she drank from it (she wore no rings except for a plain gold wedding-band), of the way chin and throat tilted, the pout of her lips against the cup's rim, the embossed silver bright behind wrist and fingers. Her bitter-sweet perfume, a little acrid, filled my nostrils: I drew it in hungrily, as though it were a physical extension of her, glancing sidelong at the swell of her breasts, the way her thigh beside me, shadowy under the lime-green summer dress, spread a little where it rested on the edge of the couch, amazed at myself, but not afraid, not afraid at all, exulting in the violence of feeling that coursed through me, wondering at life's sudden diamond-bright simplicity.

Lycurgus was saying to Arion: "Of course, Himera is much less out of touch today than when you were last in Sicily. This festival now: it would have been impossible to hold it there twenty years ago."

Arion nodded, his eyes on the silverware: he looked as though he were mentally pricing it.

"So I gather from my prospective host."

The Nubian slaves, dark as their own lengthening shadows, filled cups, carried round dishes of fruit, always alert, anticipating every command, mute, expressionless.

Curiosity and reticence battled for an instant in Lycurgus's eyes. "And that would be—?" he murmured.

"Teisias, son of Euphorbus." Arion was carefully off-hand: a celebrity himself, he could not afford to sound over-impressed by rival claims to fame, and thus went about his name-dropping with some circumspection.

"Ah: of course. A foregathering of lyric eagles." The way Lycurgus said this did not make it sound an unqualified compliment.

"Teisias," said Arion, weighing his words as though he expected, or at least hoped, that they would be passed on to the person under discussion, "is a very great artist: his fame and influence are international. His technical innovations—"

"Ah yes," said Lycurgus quickly: he had no intention, it was clear, of letting Arion get launched into so perilous a subject, sensing, with some justice, that once the little musician was under way, nothing short of physical violence would stop him. "Technical innovations, yes, well, so you admit that? We too, you see, can nurture genius. Sicily is not so backward as they would like to think in Athens or Ionia."

"I am honoured to be his guest," said Arion, bridling.

"Of course," Chloe put in, "you'll be his fellow-competitor, too, won't you? It sets a nice problem in etiquette. Should the perfect host allow his guest to defeat him, or does artistic ambition outweigh mere good manners? Not," she added, a shade too artlessly, "that the situation need arise in your case, of course." I could have hugged her.

"The Muses," Arion pronounced, getting quite appallingly pompous as he was forced on to the defensive, "do not appreciate such mun-

[157]

dane considerations. The true artist offers them the tribute of integrity, devotion, craftsmanship: they reward him with the divine gift of inspiration."

"Sometimes," Chloe said, "they appear a little slow in recognizing his virtue. Perhaps, being ladies, they become bored by repetition: what would you say?"

Arion popped a ripe fig into his mouth, and chewed it with lingering relish. "I would not," he said at last, black eyes twinkling, "presume to judge the motives of any ladies—least of all those with divine connections."

"And valuable patronage to bestow: of course not. How prudent of you. Teisias is not, I believe, married?"

Arion glanced, with swift comprehension—and scarcely veiled malice—from Chloe to myself and back again. "Only to his art, Lady Chloe: only to his art. Like our charming and brilliant young friend here."

I felt the hot flush rise to my cheeks: there was nothing I could say.

"Sappho is young still, Arion." The voice remained cool, amused; but I could sense the anger under it. "You mustn't try to marry her off prematurely—even to so chaste and impeccable a suitor."

"I bow before your experience, Lady Chloe. In the field of matchmaking I would not venture to argue with you."

The sun was sinking beyond the western mountains: a chill breeze suddenly sprang up, and the streets below us lay grey and shadowed. Lycurgus said: "I think we should go in: it gets cold at nightfall," and we all moved towards the stairs. Far away on the northernmost horizon, Etna lay, snow-capped above her subterranean fires. Chloe smiled and ran her hand lightly down my bare arm. I began to tremble: Arion's eyes contracted till they seemed mere black pinpoints. But he said nothing.

Later, towards midnight, I sat up in bed, unable to sleep, pleasantly warm from the wine I had drunk at dinner, chasing fugitive scraps and phrases of a poem which obstinately remained just out of reach. (A child again, vainly pursuing the bright crimson-and-black butterfly that looped and fluttered above me in the spring sunshine, plunging shoulder-high through tall green barley all dabbled with crimson and yellow and white: poppies, kingcups, giant daisies.) My senses were taut, expectant: I was intensely conscious of textures, shapes, colours, smells—the smooth white wax of the writing-tablet, its wooden back pressing flat against my raised knee through the coarse woollen coverlet; the bumbling insect that fluttered, bent on self-immolation, round a cluster of six steady lamp-flames (the lamps were grouped on a little inlaid table where I could easily reach them); the faint scent of rosemary and lavender from the sheets, the oval mirror in its scroll-gilt frame. All sharp, intricate, distinct: all now pressed indelibly on my memory.

She came, as I knew she would come: still in that lime-green dress, smiling her secret smile, green-eyed as an Egyptian cat, broad gold bracelets aglint in the lamp-light, thick smooth black hair drawn back above her ears, bitter-sweet scent in the air where she walked, a dark enchantress whose every movement had power. She sat on the bed and took both my hands in hers: the pendant necklace lay heavy between her swelling breasts, deep green emerald resplendent on that pale, cream-smooth skin.

"Well, my darling?" she said very gently, and her dark eyebrows lifted in a gesture that was at once interrogative and ironic. I nodded, lips parted, scarcely knowing what I did; and then Chloe's warm arms were round me, and her soft, open mouth on mine.

"Are you happy, my love?"
"Happier than I've ever been, than I dreamed I could be."
"You're so young, so sweetly young."
"Oh, Chloe—I never knew—"
"Hush, my sweet."
"It's so new, so strange."
"Are you afraid?"
"Of you? How could I be? And yet—"
"I know: I know."
"It's so violent and sudden, like an autumn storm, when you're walking in the forest and then, before you know it, a great gale is thundering down through the oaks—"
The finger on my lips, the warm hair lying loose across my breast.
"There are no words for this. Hush—"
"There must be words, words give shape, life—"
"Ah, no: words are the shadows fluttering behind life. Life *is*, life exists: enjoy the bright moment, be grateful."
"How else can I express my gratitude? Words are the gift the Goddess has bestowed on me: I can offer you no other tribute."
The slow turn of warm flesh, the scented drowsiness: memory's golden net.

"Sappho, my darling, it's *you* I want, here, now, alive: your love, not your tribute. Keep tribute for queens and Goddesses, I am neither."

"Call words a spell, then, an enchantment to catch sunshine, call down the moon of your beauty."

"My beauty must fade: you cannot stop time for me with your enchantments."

"What, then? What can I give you?"

"This. And this—"

"Yes. Yes. Oh, love—"

"Hush, my sweet: hush."

Moonlight filtering through half-open shutters, a twist and a flicker of bats in the starlit air. Round the full moon the stars lose their brightness, fade in that cold unearthly refulgence which now, incredibly, silvers Chloe's warm, smooth body, her generous breasts, the long curve of one thigh. Barred and patched with shadow she lies, a Circe of darkness with strong enchantments at her command.

I fled to you as a child to its mother, Chloe, with the same warm instinctive trustfulness, the same unrestrained physical response. How shocked I would have been had anyone—even you—told me that at the time!

You were my first lover, Chloe: you taught me to accept, joyfully, the passions in myself which you aroused. But what sprang up between us, like some long-dammed fountain from the living rocks was also that gush of pure tenderness which unites mother and child, the tenderness I knew afterwards for my own daughter: no less intense, no less physical, yet wholly alien from the passion of desire. You were the mother I never had, warm, soft, spontaneous: you drove out my daemons, destroyed my fear, gave me back myself.

Those first months in Sicily were dreamlike, unreal. I seemed to move, a bright dancer, through some glittering, enchanted masque: Syracuse was a rare jewel I held in my hand for my delight, a mirror where I saw reflected all the passionate awareness of life that Chloe's love had given me. Chloe herself did everything she could to encourage this delightful state of mind. (What was it Aunt Helen had said? *You show every sign of possessing naturally luxurious tastes. With any luck, Lycurgus and Chloe will indulge them to a point where you refuse, thereafter, to put up with anything less.* Like most of Aunt Helen's predictions, this one proved remarkably accurate—though I have often wondered if she also foresaw, knowing Chloe as she did, what other tastes I would develop in the process.) I was showered, dazzled, by new dresses, rare jewellery, exotic perfumes. My room seems, in memory, always to have been littered with unrolled bales of material—rose-pink Syrian damask, saffron muslin from Cos, heavy Egyptian linen embroidered with stars and strange, stiff, heraldic beasts; woollen fabrics from the wide looms of Italy, woven in soft green checks or black and scarlet stripes, delightful to handle, smelling faintly of herbs and wood-smoke.

Always Chloe was there, laughing, elegant, full of enthusiasms that bubbled and flowed like a hillside waterfall, snatching up a length of silk and draping it round me, arguing with harassed dressmakers, iridescent as a dragonfly, the centre round which all our lives revolved. She introduced me to a whole range of cosmetics I had never known in Mytilene: soon my dressing-table was crowded with a bewildering assortment of flasks and pots and bottles, with lipstick, rouge, eyebrow-brushes, nail-enamel, scents, lotions, subtly tinted powders.

Here, on the third finger of my left hand, above my wedding-ring, are the entwined gold snakes that were Chloe's first gift to me, symbol and pledge and commemoration, untarnishing, chthonic. I moved in the bright burning circle of our love, and time flowed past softly, leaving the bubble for a while intact.

Close to the sea, so close that only a narrow causeway separates them, rises the spring of Arethusa. I often used to linger there, drawn by some obscure fascination, standing for an hour or more with my elbows propped on the old stone parapet above the pool. Deep and still it lay, its surface a dark green mirror to my thoughts, ringed by a selvedge of feathery Egyptian papyrus, guarding its secret and its legend: the nymph surprised naked, while bathing, by that great Arcadian hunter Alpheius, and changed by chaste Artemis into pure, eternal water, a deep stream flowing under the Ionian sea to far Ortygia. (Some say that Alpheius, too, was metamorphosed into a subterranean river, and thus, at last, consummated his love.) Chloe told me that a cup dropped as an offering in the waters of Alpheius had been found, months later, in Arethusa's spring.

If I watched that green, mysterious surface long enough, its depths would come alive: between still fronds a thin, barely visible thread of bubbles ran surfacewards, forced up from unimaginable stone caverns where no light ever shone and where, they say, strange blind white fish live out their sunless days. Sometimes, at such moments, I seemed to be myself the secret spring in which that delicate thread rose to break and shape itself in patterns of singing words.

During those months poem after poem flowed, fully formed, from my fermenting mind: I was possessed, in every sense, bound by enchantments I had never dreamed of, and the pure crystal waters of creation ran bright through my green veins. Still in a dream, I moved across the chequered chessboard of Syracusan society, an ex-iled pawn among peacock queens and swarthy, side-stepping knights: there were receptions, dinner-parties, and, at last, a recital, my recital, alone in front of invited guests, the famous, the wealthy, the influential, all gathered to hear the dark, tiny poetess from Lesbos—and perhaps to take a closer look at Chloe's latest lover. I sang and played for her alone; hers was the magic and the tribute of words, the dancing music that caught and held them, close as the twined gold snakes bright on my finger, my gift for hers, my heart in her body.

They applauded and wept: I saw only her green eyes, alight with tender laughter, her warm lips, the dark, smooth hair drawn back above that lovely face. When, at last, the dream ended, I found I had, without knowing it, become a famous artist, a figure to inspire the passions—admiration, envy, even awe. The poet's mythical aura had descended on me unawares: I wore it awkwardly at first, like some late inheritor of a throne who steps out in crown and royal purple to face the crowds after his anointing.

Lycurgus and I are standing together on the roof-terrace, looking out across the crowded white houses of Ortygia towards the Great Harbour. I have never broken through his smooth, smiling outer de-fences, the mannered mask he presents to the world: my relationship with Chloe makes it doubly difficult for me to be at ease with him. What is he thinking, what does he know? What do he and Chloe talk about when they are alone together? The questions swarm in my mind, clamouring for an answer. It is characteristic of me, of Chloe too—though for very different reasons, I suspect—that we have never discussed Lycurgus, never plotted his true position in the complex pattern of our love. Daemons of fear and jealousy prowl in my mind, guarding a gate I dare not enter; and meanwhile Lycurgus is easy, polite, charming, an amused husband (one would say) encouraging his wife in her efforts to bring out and launch this small, shy, adoring chrysalis as a resplendent butterfly.

Under one fear another, deeper one: what does Chloe's love mean to *her*, how much is it worth, how deep does it run? Sometimes she seems the gay, casual dragonfly and nothing more, accepting devotion as her due, skimming over the bright surface of reality, as elusive and untouchable as Aphrodite herself, the Goddess of a thousand lovers. I can only trust, accept, take the moment of happiness and enjoy it to the full. Then I look at Lycurgus, bent over the balustrade beside me, fingers interlocked (fingers that know Chloe's body as I know it), thick bleached hair falling across his forehead, and I think: This man is my lover's husband; I am his guest, I enjoy his hospitality, and in return I sleep with his wife like any common adulterer. Why should my sex protect me from that name?

Breaking a long silence he says, with slow deliberation: "I love my wife. Because I love her, I desire her happiness with my whole heart. The fulfilment you find in each other is a source of joy to me too. You may think that strange. If you do, you should reflect that love can take many forms, not all of them easy or familiar."

"Other passions can ape the name of love: isn't that just as true?"

"Indeed it is." His eyes search mine. "There are many masks, and many false gods. But Love you can recognize, even when he wears a mask: his hands are outstretched, bearing gifts, seeking nothing. The empty hands that clutch at pleasure, the voice crying, 'Give!'—these have no part in him."

I nod, bemused: where have I heard such words before? Of course: from Aunt Helen, who is Lycurgus' sister (the binding ties of blood, the whole world linked like a web) as she sat on my bed and offered me comfort: *Aphrodite has many moods and many faces.* Chloe's bright features dissolve, are overlaid by the brutal, drunken, suffused mask of Pittacus, in his weakness and his lust.

"I understand, my lord." Are his words aimed at me, then? Is the strength and purity of *my* love, rather than Chloe's, being called in question? Startled, I realize that this possibility is something I have never, till now, so much as considered.

He scrutinizes me with odd fixity.

"Yes: I think perhaps you do." He draws a deep breath. "Let me make one thing clear, and then we need never refer to the subject again. You are welcome in my—in our house for as long as you may

[163]

wish. I bear you no ill-will or reproach. You are not"—he blinks quickly—"imposing on me in any way. I regard you only with affection and love. I believe in your love for Chloe: because I believe in it, I accept it."

His words are so formal, so stilted, that they can be nothing but a shield held out to cover his naked, too-vulnerable emotions. I nod in gratitude, eyes brimming, unable to speak. It is only later, alone, that I begin to think about Lycurgus himself, to wonder what complex motivation could bring a man, any man, to declare himself in such terms.

On the twilight edge of sleep a question poses itself, unbidden and unexpected: *Why have they never had children?* But the question goes unanswered, slips over the smooth, black edge of the chasm, plummets, echoing, down to where nightmare and fantasy wait to rack the unconscious mind.

Ceremony, of one sort or another, governs our lives to a greater extent than we suppose. It is strange how my Sicilian memories constantly return to the formal, the ritual occasion: perhaps then, more than at any period of my life till now, I needed that sustaining framework which men build to contain and shape and enrich the random pattern of their individual existence. Without the hallowed and hallowing acts, words, observances which mark the year's passing, enshrine the great facts of birth and renewal and dissolution, we would be no more than leaves blown down a grey, limitless valley, a whisper of rain-washed bones.

There were the small, private rituals: the pinch of incense dropped in the flame of Aphrodite's house-shrine, the gesture with finger and thumb to avert the evil eye. There were the odd and often pathetic commissions which began to come my way: would I compose an epitaph for a child who died at three months of a fever? would I find comforting words to sustain an inconsolable widow in her bereavement? I never refused such a request; I knew—who better?—that a healing balm lies in such formal verses, they draw out and delimit the unresolved pain.

But many requests were of a happier nature. Looking through the yellowing papers on my desk I see the rough draft of a thank-offering to Artemis by Aristo, daughter of Hermocleitus. For a moment memory fails me: who was Aristo? What was her thank-offering? Then I see a long, beautiful, ivory-pale face, the robes of a priestess: she was dedicating her still unnamed baby daughter to Artemis' service. *I am a child who cannot speak*—Where, I wonder, is the statue now? What has become of Aristo's daughter?

But, ironically enough, what I found myself asked to do most frequently—so often, in fact, that it became a fashionable craze among Syracusan high society—was to write and compose wedding-songs: processional chant, bridal farewell, ribald catches for the feast, formal epithalamion. There is only a limited number of things one can say on such occasions, and I said them all: night after night, as an honoured guest, I played and sang amid the raucous laughter and the rose-petals and the thump of the drums, till some sweating, frightened, half-drunk young couple would be thrust into their bridal-chamber, like haltered oxen ready for the sacrificial axe.

There, in pain and darkness, while the revelry went on outside, a girl would be deflowered on the great herb-strewn bed, and the proof of her defloration triumphantly displayed at the window by its grinning accomplisher, in the light of countless waving, smoky torches, to an approving roar from the crowd below.

One day, as I walked in the hills above the city the spring air cool on my face, the tall planes riotous with bird-song, my eye was caught by a splash of purple against the fresh-turned soil: a hyacinth, trodden into the furrow by some careless labourer's boot, yet still retaining an echo of its lost, fragile beauty. The image haunted my mind for days afterwards: what could more aptly express the invasion of maidenhood, the shattering of transient innocence?

My wedding-hymns were, as I said, much sought-after: everyone agreed that no marriage ceremony was complete without the charming and delicate accompaniment I provided for it.

A short, characteristic note from Arion: "You will be pleased—at least, I presume you will—to hear that the judges awarded me first prize in the Himera festival. One cannot, alas, eat a wreath (unless one happens to be a donkey, and even then it would be somewhat short commons), so I have been persuaded to give a series of public performances on the mainland, in Rhegium and Sybaris and such-like places, where gold is plentiful, but artistic discrimination, shall we say, a little to seek? The experience should prove nauseating, but profitable: a commonplace which (if all I hear from Syracuse is true) you are now discovering for yourself." The letter concluded with a self-caricature in lieu of signature: a frolicking dolphin, its features unmistakable, a lyre tucked under one fin, moneybags dangling from its jaws, and a garland—slightly askew—perched above them.

[165]

In the streets black-clad women bow and sway, hair streaming loose and grey with ashes: their wailing rises in harsh, discordant waves throughout the city, from Ortygia to the distant heights of Epipolae, mourning for the dead Adonis, done to death by the boar's tusks far away in the Syrian hills, the lost lover of Aphrodite. From his spilt blood springs the scarlet anemone, her thorn-flayed flesh dyes the white rose crimson.

Down the street comes the slow procession, shaven heads, a dead skirl of flutes, the bier borne aloft with the young dead God on it, who yesterday lay in his marriage-couch, many-garlanded, decked in flowers, fruits and honey-cakes piled about him, a bridegroom for one day only. *Adonis is dead*, keen the women, *Adonis is dead*, and the words sigh skyward, darkening heaven, *The tender Adonis is dead. Cytherea: what can we do? ah, what can we do?* Then the antiphonal answer, loud, despairing: *Beat your breasts, maidens, rend your garments.* Blood-dabbled cheeks, the slow thud of the drums, down to the sea by Arethusa's spring now, the image cast on the waves: *Woe for Adonis, the four months' sojourner!* But tomorrow is joy, is resurrection, Adonis will rise again, deathless, ageless, like Aphrodite reborn from the foam, the year in his godhead, the tree of life branching out of him.

Soon after the festival of Adonis I caught a fever: nothing serious, but enough to keep me in bed, sweating and shivering, prey to fantastic dreams, my mind moving a little above and beyond reality. Chloe sat with me for hours, silent now, watchful, but—did I imagine it?—a little restless and impatient, as though fretting to be away. Then, on the third day, she broke the news to me: she and Lycurgus were travelling out to visit their estate near Enna. A pity, but the trip had been planned: they couldn't put it off now. They would be away for at least ten days. "But you'll be well looked after, darling. I've given them strict orders."

The pressure of her hand, a quick smile, that heavy, acrid scent: the crisp rustle of a new, kingfisher-blue dress. Something was gone, withdrawn, a spark, something powerful but intangible: she hates illness, I thought, yes, of course, how could she not hate it, with her vitality, her unquenchable zest for life? Excuses were easy to make, left a shadow behind. But Chloe's shadow went with her, through the door, into the bright Sicilian sunlight.

I dozed and dreamed, woke, slept again. Always the same dream: I was in the temple, standing before the great image of the Goddess, the smell of incense and dried blood in my nostrils. There were the golden stars on the white robe, the flowered coronal, the eyes that looked into mine. The lips moved, but I could not catch the words they framed: wave-like chanting rose to drown the message, grew louder, louder, till suddenly a voice cried: "This is the Queen of Heaven," and it was Chloe I saw, Chloe crowned and robed, green eyes bright in the half-light, a cold effulgence round her.

A priestess stepped forward, white, anonymous, bearing a black veil, and draped the Goddess like a mourner: the chanting changed its note, took on that terrible harsh plangency I knew too well: *Adonis is dead,* the thin voices called, *Adonis is dead.* Then, in a blinding flash of light, the veil was split apart, to reveal the passionate, hate-filled, distorted features of my mother; and I woke, screaming incoherently, to the startled faces of two maids keeping vigil by my bedside.

On the tenth day her letter reached me: a tiny note, hastily sealed, the bold, looping handwriting for once shaky and indecisive. All it said was: "I can't go on. I can't explain. Try to forgive me, darling. C." The fever left me an hour after I had read it: I sat up in bed, numb, unfeeling, all my facial muscles stiff, as though I had just recovered from a stroke. It was thus that the courier from Enna found me, late that same afternoon.

He came into my bedroom unannounced, sweat-stained, covered with dust from his long ride, and told me, in a few blunt, brutal phrases, that Lycurgus and Chloe were both dead, murdered by bandits in the wild hill-country beyond Agyrium. "Yes," I whispered, "yes. I understand. Thank you." He hesitated a moment, cleared his throat, and said awkwardly: "I'm sorry, my lady." A long pause. "Well—" and he backed towards the door, tangle-footed, desperate to get away.

Long after he had gone I still sat there, staring at the wall, unable to move, nightmare and truth mingling inextricably in my mind, so that the crowned Queen of Heaven merged into that other figure my imagination saw so clearly—a torn, naked body abandoned among wayside rocks, its lily flesh carrion now, raped and bloody, those bright green eyes mere gristle for vultures' beaks to tear, the last, desperate message an enigma no one would ever solve.

XI

NOW the year moves on towards winter, and still the weather holds. The days are cooler, but still bright: the sea remains calm. Here from my hillside window outside Mytilene I can watch the heavy-laden ships labouring down the straits, bound for Chios or Athens. Or, perhaps, Syracuse. I follow their progress against that pale, cloudless sky. For the first time I find myself, against all expectation, thinking: *it is not too late.*

I sit, face cupped in my hands, conscious of the blood's slow pulsing behind my temples, through my whole frame, conscious of it, today, as a woman, having had the reminder that my creative strength—in its most potent, physical manifestation—remains undimmed. I am fifty years old; and I could still bear another child. His child. The yearning desire came on me unawares, pierced me with a terrible sweet agony, so that the very muscles of my womb seemed to contract, and my breasts to engorge like those of a nursing mother.

But I thrust the desire down, fought and conquered it: the Moon cannot follow Endymion, no enchantments are powerful enough to call back the migrant, vagrant heart. Let him squander his beauty and his strength on Sicilian whores, let him die—as he is sure to die one day—in some dark alley with a cuckold's knife between his ribs, or as Chloe died, under a cruel, indifferent sky, broken, violated, a bare carcass robbed of all humanity, all power to bind or to enthral. Let him die, and let me find peace.

If I had not been in so deep a state of emotional shock after Chloe's death, I might have derived much quiet, malicious pleasure from its immediate consequences. No one could decide whether I was to be treated as Chloe's ex-lover (in which case they could patronize me with impunity, and get me out of the house in the minimum decent time), or as an honoured family guest, virtually Lycurgus' adopted daughter (which meant, since the will had not yet been read, that I had to be treated civilly, at the very least), or as a distinguished resident foreign artist who might well add to the city's cultural prestige.

The result, in terms both of hypocrisy and embarrassment, was memorable. Slaves veered between veiled insubordination and oily obsequiousness, while the visiting deputation from Syracuse's Council of Nobles confined themselves almost entirely to official condolences and platitudes: they might have been hedging their bets on a doubtful starter at the races.

When the Notary-Public revealed the contents of Lycurgus' will, however, this saving uncertainty was abruptly removed; and I began to realize, for the first time, just how precarious my position could become when I stood alone, an exile and a woman, in this alien city.

It was an odd group which gathered to learn Lycurgus' last wishes and bequests: the President and Treasurer from the Council of Nobles, attended by three rather scrubby-looking clerks; a dark, jowly, middle-aged man, with a close-shaven skull and a large signet-ring, who turned out to be Lycurgus' banker; the manager of his Enna estates, a short bearded Sicilian Greek who spoke in so broad an accent that I could barely understand him; myself, feeling both an intruder and an unwelcome embarrassment to everyone (yet Lycurgus had, after all, been my uncle by marriage); and a stranger who said very little to anyone, a lean man of something over middle height, with pensive grey eyes, fair hair, and an abstracted manner.

Of course, the most curious thing about this assembly was the absence of relatives—that chattering horde of aunts, cousins, spinster sisters, half-brothers and the like, who descend on the dutifully mourning family like hungry crows in winter, ready to peck up any crumb that may be thrown to them. For that matter, where was the family itself? There were no children of Lycurgus' marriage; and all his family connections lay in Mytilene. Chloe herself had been an orphan, with (as far as I knew) no living blood-relatives. I sometimes thought it was as though they had both, in a curious way, tried to cut themselves altogether adrift from the normal network of human relationships.

So we sat there, in that white, high-ceilinged room which Chloe had done so much to make beautiful—the thick Milesian rugs, the honey-yellow sheepskins, the wine-and-blue tapestry, Amazons embattled against Theseus, which ran the whole length of one wall, the strange, haunting Egyptian statuettes—and drank sweet wine, and ate small honey-cakes, and watched the Notary-Public fuss over his sealed and beribboned documents.

Then I became aware that the taciturn stranger had come out of his revery, and was watching me. I looked up: those extraordinarily clear grey eyes met mine without any embarrassment or dissimulation. He raised his eyebrows fractionally, as though to say: What are *we* doing here? And I felt my lips twitch in the ghost of a grin.

I studied him carefully for the first time, matching his own frank scrutiny. He had thick, crisp fair hair, worn rather longer than the fashion, and sun-bleached in places till it was almost white. By contrast, his face was tanned—the metaphor is just—to the colour and consistency of leather. He wore a short beard; his hands were unexpectedly delicate—not weak, rather the opposite, a wire-drawn elegance, tension concealing strength.

The Notary-Public cleared his throat gently to attract my attention: he was ready at last, and wanted a perfect anticipatory tableau. The will, yes, that was the will he had there, a single sheet of parchment with Lycurgus' seal dangling from it: and despite myself I craned forward a little, curious, expectant.

It was one of the briefest wills I have ever heard; and also one of the most unexpected. Lycurgus left his entire estate to Chloe: there were no other bequests whatsoever. "Since under Syracusan law," the Notary-Public read, in his thin, precise voice, "women are deemed beings incapable of reason, and therefore debarred from inheriting property in their own name, I appoint my friend and financial adviser, Callias, son of Sotades"—the shaven banker smiled, and rubbed one finger across his nose—"as administrator of the estate on my wife's behalf, her decision in all matters being final."

This little joke did not, I noticed, amuse the President. But then came a clause which rapidly changed his expression, while the Treasurer sat up in open delight. (He may not actually have rubbed his hands, but he gave a strong impression of doing so.) "In the event of my wife's death, the above-mentioned estate, with all goods, chattels, livestock and other property whatsoever pertaining thereto, shall be made over, unencumbered and in perpetuity, to the City of Syracuse, for such public use as the Council may determine." There followed a few details on the granting of freedom to certain household slaves: and that was all. Neither Draco, nor Aunt Helen, nor my mother, nor myself, nor Charaxus and Larichus, nor any of my cousins, were so much as mentioned. In death as in life, Lycurgus had effectively cut himself off from ties of family. Yet he had accepted me as a guest; he seemed on friendly enough terms with Aunt Helen. What had prompted such obscurely paradoxical behaviour?

There was a moment's dead silence. Then the President said: "Is that all?"

The Notary-Public nodded and rolled up the will with a snap that had the air of finality about it. "Yes: that is all."

"Ah." The President eased himself quickly to his feet. "Then we may as well adjourn."

"One moment." The voice was lazy, but had an edge to it. We all looked round in surprise: the brown-faced stranger seemed rather pleased with the effect he had produced. "I don't think that *is* all, you know," he said mildly, and stretched out one hand towards the Notary-Public. "May I see the will, please?"

The President blinked, coughed, and recovered himself. "On what authority?" he asked. "Who *are* you, sir?" It was only now I realized that the stranger must have simply walked in uninvited, exuding such calm self-confidence that no one had questioned his right to be there.

"My name is Cercylas, son of Lygdamus: you might call me a very distant cousin of the deceased. Now: the will, if you please."

He stepped forward and, before the Notary-Public could stop him, had twitched the document off the table and was examining it closely. He held it to the light; he turned it upside down; he scrutinized the seal with particular care. Finally he handed it back. All the time the Treasurer watched his every movement with sharp, wary eyes, as though expecting some sleight-of-hand substitution.

"Well, sir," the President said, "if you have no further questions—"

"I think you are forgetting"—Cercylas looked from face to face—"the problem of this unfortunate young lady's future."

"Her future can hardly be considered our official concern." The President's voice was icy, remote.

"Oh?" I had seldom heard such a wealth of polite contempt injected into one syllable. "Lady Sappho is now, I would remind you, *your* guest, my lord President, the city's guest, and you are bound to treat her according to the laws of hospitality."

I gasped; so did the Treasurer. He said: "This is the merest effrontery, sir."

"Not at all. You have heard the will read. This house"—he extended his arm—"has become your property; and Lady Sappho is resident in it."

[171]

The President and the Treasurer looked at each other: the President muttered something which sounded like "shyster quibbling." I found myself scrutinizing one particular Amazon in the tapestry with almost insane concentration.

Cercylas said: "Lady Sappho has achieved a considerable reputation here in the last year or two—a well-earned reputation, if I may say so." He threw me a quick smile, with the same faint hint of complicity in it. "Any scandal"—he stroked his short beard—"would be most regrettable. I'm sure you agree."

The Treasurer said quickly: "We shall, of course, make every possible allowance for Lady Sappho's unfortunate position. That was always envisaged." He looked to the President for support: the President nodded. "There is no question of immediate, ah, removal. Lady Sappho will have ample time to make other arrangements."

"How long?"

"Well, now: a matter of months—"

"How many months?"

The Treasurer's eyes snapped hesitantly. "Perhaps three—"

"Three. Very well." Cercylas' grey eyes glanced round the room. "We have witnesses, my lord President."

There was an awkward pause: Callias scuffed his foot across the floor. Then the Treasurer said, a thin sneer in his voice: "Might one ask, sir, just why you are so preoccupied with this lady's welfare?"

"One might." Cercylas turned and faced me. His eyes were warm, amused, affectionate. He said: "A conventional reason, I'm afraid, but none the less adequate for that: because I am going to marry her."

The strange thing was (as I said in a letter to Meg a month later) that the moment he spoke the words, I knew they were true: and not only true but inevitable, as inevitable as tomorrow's sunrise. The knowledge had nothing, then, to do with love or desire. It was rooted in recognition: if ever I have believed in the thread of the Fates, it was at that moment. Here was my destiny, prepared for me before time, no more to be refused than the breath in my lungs, and, inexplicably, as familiar. I sat there bemused, while they all looked at each other, uncertain how to deal with this preposterous situation, searching for adequate social phrases to mask their embarrassment, anxious only to be gone. Of course, I was in mourning: that made everything much more difficult.

But at last, with some semblance of dignity, they filed out: the President nodding briefly, his eyes hooded, withdrawn; the Treasurer cold and glittering, a snake disturbed—and, snakelike, running the tip of his tongue in and out, nervously, between hard, thin lips; the three clerks with heads averted, saying nothing at all. But Callias the banker (whom I had met once or twice before) smiled, and gave me his hand, and said that I should let him know if he could be of service to me; and Lycurgus' little estate-manager shook his head sadly, as though unable to believe the things he had seen and heard that morning, and wished me happier days, his thick Sicilian accent distorted still further by emotion, tears starring his eyes.

So I was left alone with Cercylas, in that great, white, sunlit room that had been Chloe's creation, the room where her personality was omnipresent still, as though independent of the physical self it survived; where her vivid smile, like her scent, still hung invisibly in the air.

He stood by the open window, head a little bent, so that the sunlight struck gold from his thick hair, hands clasped behind his back. How old was he? Thirty? Forty? I could not tell. There was something unchangeable about him, something that defied the ordinary ravages of time. (How tragically ironic that sounds in retrospect!) He was a man clearly accustomed to wealth; yet the hard, spare lines of his face betrayed no weakness, no self-indulgence. If privilege had left any mark on him, it was in that quality of leisured irony with which he confronted men or situations, and which can only spring from unquestioning self-assurance.

I said: "I must thank you for your help. It was—most opportune."

He smiled gravely. "And I must apologize for an intolerable impertinence."

I gave a quick glance round the empty room. "At least," I said, "the impertinence would appear to have served its immediate purpose."

"Well, yes: you might put it that way." He moved slowly into the middle of the room, as though feeling out its atmosphere and character. By a small occasional table he paused, apparently to examine the bric-a-brac littering it. He ran one finger over an Egyptian cat, carved in lapis lazuli; then his eye fell on a small, exquisite scent-bottle. I felt my heart contract.

"Lydian," he said, picking it up. There was a quick, iridescent gleam as he held it to the light. He unstoppered it, sniffed delicately. Our eyes met.

He said: "She would have wanted you to have a remembrance of her, Sappho."

I nodded, and stretched out my hand, past all surprise now, accepting. The twined gold snake-ring glinted on the third finger, the marriage-finger; and he touched it once, quickly, as he put the bottle into my hand. Then we stood quite still for a moment, facing each other: the floor was paved in great squares of alternating black and white marble, like a chessboard, with us the two last remaining pieces.

He said, following my glance: "At the court of the Great King in Babylon there is a terrace, chequered with squares such as these, where Nebuchadnezzar and his nobles play at chess after dinner. Each piece is a slave, who moves as the player bids him."

I gave a tiny gasp: it was like having another mind inside one's own skull, I felt transparent as air.

"And what is the forfeit?" I asked.

"Ah." He sounded pleased, as though I were a pupil who had passed some unspoken test. "The loser's slaves are forfeit to the winner."

"But here, now, there are no slaves."

He said: "No, indeed. Here we must make our own moves—"

"And suffer for our own mistakes."

"Just so," he said, and as though by common instinct we both moved together, away from open ground, and sat down one on either side of the table where wine, fruit, and cakes had been set out. I struck a hand-bell, and the door-slave came, a little slow at first, a little surly, to fill our cups.

"Your health," Cercylas said.

"Long life, my lord."

He paused a moment, the cup half-way to his lips, as though considering. Then—"Long Life," he said, drained the cup at one draught, and tossed the dregs on the floor.

I said: "Are you really a distant cousin of my uncle's?"

He gave me a level look. "All men are distant cousins," he said. "Shall we say that between some the distance is considerable?"

"Then—why did you come here this morning?"

"To do exactly what you saw me do." He nodded at the slave, who sprang forward and refilled his cup with quite remarkable promptness. "You see, your position here is not only embarrassing: it might also become dangerous."

"Dangerous?"

He sipped at his wine. "Oh yes. Because, you see, that will is, beyond any reasonable doubt, a forgery. No doubt certain—omissions surprised you. You did right to be surprised."

"But who—why—?"

"Very simple," Cercylas said. "Lycurgus was a wealthy immigrant with no immediate relatives except his wife. He was not, as you may have gathered, over-popular among the more conservative members of Syracusan society. I fancy the gentlemen who have just left found the opportunity too tempting to resist."

"But that's impossible—they're—"

"Gentlemen, as I said." The ironic note was back in Cercylas' voice. "A second copy of your uncle's real will *may* be hidden somewhere in this house still, but it would do you very little good to produce it."

"I see." I laid my hands flat on the table in front of me, palms down, and studied them. "Then what am I to do?"

Cercylas leaned back, considering. "There are several possibilities. You could try, for the time being, to continue your life here in Syracuse—the commissions you receive might help you to a certain independence. But that has obvious drawbacks."

I nodded.

"You could make a formal plea to Myrsilus to have your term of exile curtailed; but—for various reasons—I doubt whether he would prove agreeable. You could try your luck with Periander in Corinth, though I gather the old man is not exactly *reliable* these days."

"I found that out for myself."

"Yes. I know."

"You seem to know a great deal about me, my lord Cercylas."

"Indeed I do: I have made it my business." The tone was warm, amused, ironic: I could not tell just how seriously he meant what he said. But again there came over me that strange sense of inevitability, of recognition.

I said: "Have you any further suggestions?" The palms of my hands were damp against the table's inlaid surface.

"Only one. Which you know."

"That was not a suggestion; it was a statement of fact."

He smiled charmingly. "I have apologized for what I said then."

"But you still believe it."

He made no direct answer to this. Instead he said, after a moment: "Do you want to go back to Mytilene?"

"Yes. But—"

"It could be done, Sappho: if you were willing."

We looked at each other.

"Why me?" I whispered. "What can I give you? What can I ever give you?"

"Have I asked for gifts?" He laid his own hands briefly over mine. He said: "I remember once, as a child in Andros, seeing a man buy a caged bird, a rare, exotic creature, in the market. When he had paid for it—and he paid a very great deal—he stood there, within full sight óf the stall-keeper, and opened the cage, so that the bird flew free."

I said: "I take your point, my lord Cercylas. Did the man wait to see whether the bird had been trained to return to its keeper?"

For the first time, Cercylas looked momentarily disconcerted. Then he laughed. "How old are you?" he asked.

"If you know so much about me, you should know that too."

"Perhaps I do. Shall we say, old enough to face emotions without the shield of wit?"

"If you like." We both smiled.

"Well," he said, rising to his feet, "you have three months' respite, at least."

"I'm grateful for that: more than grateful."

His eyebrows rose a fraction. "Are you? I wonder." He smoothed down the folds of his summer cloak. "Do you always enjoy postponing inevitable decisions?"

I said: "Only Fate, my lord, is inevitable."

"Just so." He smiled. Then he put one hand inside his cloak and drew out a sealed package. "I nearly forgot," he said. "I promised I would deliver this to you in person."

"Promised? Promised whom?"

He was half-way across the room to the door as he turned and said: "Oh, your cousin Megara. And her mother."

"*You mean you have just come from Mytilene?*"

He nodded; springing surprises seemed to be one of his favourite pastimes. "A month ago," he said, and then, as though the fact required some explanation: "You see, I travel a good deal." An instant later he was gone: firm footsteps echoed across the lobby, the watch-dog barked twice, a door slammed, and I heard chains and bolts rattle. I stood there, the package in my hand, staring at the empty doorway.

I know nothing about him, I told myself helplessly. Nothing at all. Nothing: everything. I felt as though all individualism, all ability to make decisions, to control my own life, had been suddenly paralyzed in me. With slow, leaden steps, my limbs moving like those of a sleep-walker, I went back to the table, sat down, broke the seals on the package, and began to read.

There were three separate letters enclosed, each very different in appearance and character. The smallest also looked the most intriguing: battered and dog-eared by much travel, annotated in several unfamiliar scripts, smelling faintly of musk. On the back, just under the seal, my mother had made her own characteristic contribution. "Forwarded unopened," her jagged, unformed handwriting proclaimed—which I took instantly to mean that she had prised the seal loose with a hot knife and knew every word of the contents by heart. I unfolded this letter carefully: words that had travelled across so many seas and frontiers deserved respectful treatment.

It was from Antimenidas and had been composed three months previously.

"Greetings," he wrote, "wherever you may be, from a humble mercenary captain—now discharged—in the City of Earth and Heaven, the Abode of the Gods, the—oh, I forget the rest of Babylon's honorific titles, and she can very well do without them. She is vast and splendid and terrifying, and means to be: a desert mirage come true. The Great Whore, our Jewish captives call her, and it is an apt description. Magnificence touched with vulgarity, lush abundance concealing a cold, savage heart.

"When we trudged down the last long road from Judaea, and passed under the great Ishtar Gate, with its bulls and dragons and lions golden-bright in the sun, with its towering lapis-blue crenellations, out to the Sacred Way, I felt fear for man's presumption and pride. How long, I wondered, before the walls of Babylon fall, as the walls of Jerusalem fell to us, when we stormed that last redoubt and fought our way, street by street, to the Holy of Holies itself? Will the priests of Babylon die as these old men died, their thin bodies arched over the sacred scrolls they could no longer protect, their blood on our careless swords? Will the King of Babylon be borne into captivity as, then, the King of Judaea rode chained behind us through the Ishtar Gate?

"As you see, I am not the stuff of which true professional mercenaries are made: squeamish, homesick, superstitious, I prefer the risks and heartbreaks endured by Odysseus to an ignominious death which lacks even the smallest touch of honour. Odysseus, at least, came back to Ithaca in the end. So, the Gods willing, shall I. I am nearly forty years old; it is time to make an end of wandering.

"How prosy and sententious all this sounds! And how remote from the gossip, the exciting details of heroic feats-at-arms you will want to hear about! Well, two tit-bits for your entertainment. By luck

[177]

rather than judgment I unhorsed a most elegant Jewish cavalry officer, and took his sword: this splendid weapon was forged in Damascus, and has an ivory hilt inlaid with gold. The sword so went to my head that I killed a regular giant with it, a great creature five royal cubits tall (well, perhaps a hand's breadth short of five) and now they are making up ballads about me in Babylon. This is rather embarrassing, because the giant was a shambling ass, and (I suspect) feeble-minded: I found killing him no more trouble than spitting a kid.

"I still wear your amulet: as you see, it has brought me safely through all dangers so far. I hope that very soon I shall be able to return it to you personally, on the soil of our native land. (Why does exile produce such worn, emotional platitudes? They must satisfy some dreadful need in our starved minds, I suppose.) Meanwhile, to tip the scales of fate, I have a gift for you in my baggage: it is bulky, and of a most awkward shape to pack (you should feel flattered), but so appropriate that I could not resist it. The Gods grant us both a speedy homecoming, and happier days."

The Gods answered the first part of your prayer, Antimenidas: but who shall vouch for the second? Every night, when I sit at my dressing-table between the star-pointed flames of those great seven-branched candlesticks, with their legacy of unexpiated bloodshed and horror, I remember your words. The curse is coming home now, Antimenidas: the Gods have waited too long, their cold eternal passions must be satisfied. Blustering Ares brought you back like Agamemnon, took your life with casual spite, wastefully, to no purpose. Now I am left, watched by malevolent Aphrodite: her laughter haunts my sleep, the clear, thin mirth of a mad child. But it is when the laughter ceases, when the Goddess tires of her sport, that my true hour of reckoning will have come.

The second letter was from Aunt Helen. Like many women with a strong, vivid, colourful personality, she had less than no gift for correspondence. What filtered through on paper was a pale reflection only of that eagle-bright individualism: she needed to touch, to see, to hear. Physical actuality was as vital to her as the spilt blood to those squeaking wraiths who gathered about Odysseus in Hades. Like Chloe, she found words a thin, disappointing substitute for life; and as a result they would not, somehow, work for her.

But now, reading these four pages of trite, conventional phrases, I sensed a constraint, an embarrassment, as though she were covering up her real thoughts. This was so utterly unlike Aunt Helen that at first I refused to believe it. Yet, obstinately, the nagging instinct persisted. Half-way down the final page, with careful casualness, she wrote: "I had hoped to give you better news, the news you have been waiting for too long now. But the authorities, because of various complications, are proving obdurate." This was the only reference she made to my exile, and the second sentence seemed evasive in the extreme. Under her signature she had scribbled, as an afterthought: "The bearer of this letter may prove useful to you in Syracuse. Extreme charm, I have found, should always be handled with caution: but Cercylas of Andros has done more than most men to convince me that it does not invariably denote a rogue. I smiled at the postscript: in its own way, I thought, *that* sentence was singularly evasive, too.

The third letter was from my mother. She wrote at long, irregular intervals: spiky notes, often half-illegible, full of unexpected wit and scathingly malicious anecdotes. Rather to my surprise, I found myself enjoying them a good deal: they revealed a side of my mother I had never appreciated when we were living together. Our abrasive contacts, unhappily, blinded both of us to much we would have found congenial in the other; and when our eyes began to be opened it was already—though I at least did not know it—too late. *Too late, too late:* those hopeless, fatal words recur again and again in my life.

"From what one can gather," she wrote, "you seem to be all the rage in Syracuse: don't let it go to your head. Or, for that matter, your heart. Sicilian Greeks have a certain reputation, as you will doubtless have discovered for yourself: so I hope Lycurgus displays more responsibility over your welfare than his sister did."

(Letters are so unreal: voices from the past, unknowing comments on a flux of moods and actions that renders them, often, obsolete before they reach their destination, an ironic gloss on the now-accomplished future.)

"Helen is really becoming an open scandal: I suppose, to be charitable, we should blame it on her time of life, though when you look at her past record—! And in any case, a woman of forty-six who suffers from sexual infatuation is repellent enough, without incurring public ridicule by making no attempt to conceal, let alone restrain, her desires."

[Voices from the past: voices from the grave. The cruel words stung me then: now they have a deeper, more personal application. Reading them again, I ask myself: Is this, perhaps, my only motive,

[179]

an act of defiance against her intolerable, ineluctable domination? Am I a puppet, whose strings are twitched by dead hands?]

"When young Archaeanax—you remember him?—came courting Telesippa, Helen simply made a dead set for the boy, I've never seen anything like it; and when I asked her what she thought she was doing, she had the effrontery to say that a girl like Telesippa deserved something better than a well-mannered male virgin with one lame leg: those were her *exact words*.

"He was Helen's lover for months, the whole city knew about it. Then the affair cooled off, and can you imagine what happened next? *He married Telesippa after all.* The scene at the wedding-banquet was quite grotesque, have *you* ever been to a reception where the bride's mother was the bridegroom's ex-mistress, and most of the guests knew it? But all three seemed the best of friends, it was quite unnatural, *I* thought. In fact Telesippa's fonder of Helen now than she's been for years, she's always in and out of the house these days, though being pregnant may have something to do with it."

(That, too, makes uncomfortable reading for me now. How old was Hippias then? Five? Six? And Cleïs, my daughter Cleïs, was not yet born. How the Gods must laugh as they look down on us from their eternity of foreknowledge, and see our pitiful delusions of freedom, self-mastery, individual choice!)

"But then, Helen can get away with anything. Do you know what the latest rumour is? They say she is going to *marry Myrsilus,* and when I told her the stories that were going round she merely laughed —but she made no serious attempt to deny them.

"There is one quite repulsively vulgar song being sung in the taverns at the moment—it's supposed to be a sea-shanty, but no one could mistake its real subject—all about an old ship with rotten, leprous timbers, worn out by endless voyages, stem sprung, seams forced apart, barnacle-ridden: you see the kind of thing I mean. Now, the song says, they're going to get a few lusty shipwrights to go over her, put a lick of paint on her bottom, and send her to sea again: this time she'll hit a reef and go down for good. Just the kind of scurrilous nastiness your friend Alcaeus might have composed—in fact, some people say he *did* compose it, but as no one, to my knowledge, has had a word from him since he vanished into Egypt, this seems unlikely."

As I read my mother's words over now, I remember the promise I gave Aunt Helen after our visit to the temple of Aphrodite: *Whatever may happen,* she said, *don't judge me too hard. Try to under-*

stand. Well, I have kept my word. Experience has brought me understanding; it has also robbed me of the right and the desire to judge. But then, so soon after Chloe's death, alone in her white, silent house, with that warm ghostly presence all about me, it was hard to remember the promise I had given; harder still to keep it. But I tried. Bitterly I thought: *Well, at least I know what was wrong with that letter of hers.* And then: What she does makes no difference to what she *is,* to the relationship between us. We are, inescapably, what we always were, and will be.

"But if Helen *does* marry Myrsilus," my mother went on, "I can only say that they'll be a well-matched couple. That vulgar old satyr had the effrontery to pester *me* with his attentions—considering the official position he holds I could hardly hope to avoid him all the time—and then, when he had me alone, he would begin pawing me, like some lecherous pot-boy. Still, I flatter myself that I discouraged him in the end. Public opinion of the better sort does count for something in Mytilene, even today. But when I think of all our futures being determined by that contemptible creature, I almost envy you your Sicilian exile."

I found this very strange indeed, and in its own way almost as devious as Aunt Helen's more patent evasions. My mother obviously knew that her behaviour had been, at least in part, the direct cause of my continued exile, and this was as near to an apology as she could get. But the whole account of her relationship with Myrsilus sounded fundamentally false; and if it *was* false, what had really happened? The more I read, the less certain I became: truth, once so bright and clear-cut a concept in my mind, now began to recede through a mist of ambiguities, suppressions, and special pleading. Nothing was what it seemed: below the surface of appearances, horrors crawled.

"If I sound—as I suspect I must—somewhat moody and querulous, put it down to ill-health. I won't go into unpleasant physical details, but I am suffering, in a fairly acute form, from the same irksome condition of late middle-age as Helen."

This, too, was most uncharacteristic. Apart from the candour, it showed my mother attempting, if not to apologize for herself, at least to offer some explanation of her conduct. Normally she was hardly aware that other people existed, let alone that they had feelings which one should take into account. Was she, perhaps, more seriously ill than she suspected—or would admit? At the thought I found myself, much to my surprise, swept with a kind of childish panic. However much I had resented my mother, she had always been *there,* a symbol of stability amid change, the embodiment of home. *No, I whispered, no, not that.*

As though catching my mood and adapting herself to it, my mother now, with her usual brisk dispatch, set about giving me the latest domestic news.

"Marriages seem to be in the air at the moment: poor Ismene is very much taken up with some middle-aged bachelor dilettante, and looks like abandoning her role as the inconsolable widow of Three Winds. (There are rumours that she means to sell up the estate piecemeal: what would Phanias have said, I wonder?) Mica is still busy painting—like you, she has begun to attract fashionable commissions —and little Atthis has grown into a very presentable sixteen-year-old: quite out of the gawky stage now, but not, I'm glad to say, liable to blush or giggle when addressed by a member of the opposite sex. What they both make of their prospective step-father I can't imagine: such a change after Phanias, and in any case they're bound to be horribly jealous, all stepfathers are monsters by definition where children are concerned."

I paused a moment, the letter in my hand: how long had it been since I thought about Atthis? And was my sudden melancholy now due to missing her, or to the thought of Three Winds being sold— another landmark gone, another childhood stronghold stormed and destroyed? Like Phanias' grandfather, I had always assumed unquestioningly that Three Winds would go on for ever.

"Your cousins Megara and Agenor send their love: they, at least, seem to have resisted the current passion for plunging headlong into matrimony. Hermeas has been very moody and sullen—quite unlike himself—but they are pleased with his work in the Treasury, which relieves me: it took a good deal of backstairs persuasion to get him the appointment. Larichus is too young for marriage, but not, alas for the role of Ganymede: he has been appointed an honorary cupbearer at official banquets in the City Hall—which means, as far as I can gather from Helen, that slightly tipsy councillors and visiting ambassadors will have the privilege of pinching his nice little bottom as he serves them wine. He has turned out an almost embarrassingly beautiful boy, a kind of adolescent Apollo.

"This, I fear, is more than can be said for Charaxus—but I mustn't be uncharitable: he *is* my own son, after all, a fact I often need to remind myself of when I look at him these days. (For his age he has put on a really astonishing amount of weight.) I know you and he never hit it off, either: he *does* have an unsympathetic personality,

I fear. But he has matured in the most surprising way since he attained his majority and took over control of what's left of the family estate: his natural flair appears to be for business, which doesn't make him more attractive, but is undeniably useful.

"Now *he* intends to take a wife, too: his chosen bride is none other than Gorgo's little sister Irana, whose freckled insipidity has changed not a whit since she left the schoolroom. At first I thought —unjustly as it turned out—that they'd picked on each other because no one else would ever look at either of them. But then I discovered, what Charaxus had somehow wormed out of the girl long before, that her grandfather in an eccentric moment had entailed three-quarters of his estate to her—on the condition that she married before she was twenty-five. Otherwise the bequest would revert to her parents. No wonder Draco and Xanthe kept *that* a dead secret for years! And how typical of Charaxus to have sniffed it out: for his nose for money is as unerring as a pig's for truffles. Oh dear: there I go again.

"A pity we can't talk. We would have more to say to each other now, I think. Good-bye, Sappho." After my name she had written something else, then scratched it out: despite all my efforts I have never managed to decipher those last words. What spontaneous phrase had her iron self-control instantly checked? Sometimes, even now, I pore over that small, rusty, thicket of heavy pen-strokes, struggling to wrest its secret from it, to tease out the one bright word which, in so many years, my mother never used to me. Perhaps it is as well the phrase remains illegible: at least I can cherish, always, one small and constant spark of hope.

I was still brooding over these letters when, three days later, Meg's brief, awkward note reached me (forwarded express, at vast expense, by the official dispatch-boats) and I learnt that my mother had died suddenly, of a haemorrhage, only ten days after Cercylas sailed from Mytilene.

If that had been all, I could, perhaps, have borne it. But, for the only time in her life, Meg showed a flicker of the thwarted passion and jealousy that lay deep under that selfless, devoted heart: she enclosed, without comment, the report of the surgeon who had attended my mother in her last illness. That, surely, was an act of gratuitous cruelty. She could have destroyed the evidence, buried the truth with my mother's body, left me that one shred of illusion.

But the report was there, and I read it: it still lies among my papers. In that cold, curiously brutal jargon so beloved of the medical fraternity, the surgeon—an Egyptian, with a passion, it seemed, as strong as any diviner's for probing among dead entrails—informed me that for some years my mother had suffered from progressive, incurable cancer of the womb: a disease, he added (with the cheerful insensitivity of his kind) which in its final stages was liable to produce, among other effects, a violent and irresistible sexual frenzy.

There. I have got the words out, exposed the horror in daylight. My hands are trembling: when I touch my forehead it is cold and clammy. The shadow hangs between me and the sun. I am my mother's daughter. So many recurrent patterns spring from our inescapably shared flesh: why should this one, too, not be what in my darkest hours I name it? It is a jest the Goddess would relish: the illusion of passion, the fearful claws ready to close.

I have said already that I do not believe my mother permitted herself any sexual irregularities. I still believe that. There is nothing in her papers which suggests otherwise: not a word, not a hint. It is easy—too easy—to put these disjointed pieces of evidence together and draw them into a persuasive pattern. *I will not, must not, do this.*

Why did Thalia look at me so strangely today? I have no visitors: my friends—even Meg and Agenor—avoid me as though I had some contagious disease. Perhaps (take it which way one likes) I have. I sit in the silent house and write: memories whisper, down the reaches of the lamp-lit night fear circles my self-imposed solitude, a wild beast prowling ever nearer the fires I have lit to hold it at bay.

Cercylas said very gently: "Sappho: what do you want?"

I sat there in the garments I had first put on to mourn Chloe: the same black silk robe, the same heavy veil. The fingers of my right hand kept on at the snake-ring, twisting it over and over. I said, in the flat, dulled voice of a small child, who half-recalls some magic formula taught him by his nurse: "I want to go home. I want to go home."

He looked at me, the lines of his face deepening with compassion. He said: "There may be a way. I can't promise."

"You mean it?"

"Oh yes. But it will take time, and it will—demand something of you. A sacrifice, if you like."

"A sacrifice?"

He said, picking his words: "I can only guess what personal motives were involved at the time of your original exile. But some people, I

[184]

suspect, have made serious errors of judgment; and others have changed their attitude in the time you have been away. To put it bluntly: while Myrsilus lives, I doubt whether you, or any of your fellow-exiles, will be allowed back to Mytilene in your own right as citizens."

I stared at him hopelessly.

"I can't tell," he went on, "whether your mother's death will make any difference. I rather think not."

Our eyes met for a quick moment: then he looked away again, staring out at the cloudless summer sky framed in the pillars of the colonnade. He said: "On the other hand, I happen to have a certain amount of personal influence, both at Corinth and at Mytilene. If I were"—he hesitated only fractionally—"in a position to stand surety for your conduct, to be your guarantor in every sense, I think the thing could be done."

There was a long silence. Why do I argue and hesitate? I asked myself weakly. This is inevitable. It has been inevitable from the first moment we met. I do not know if I love this man, if I am capable of loving him. But I trust him. That is something. And now, here, I need him. He may be able to give me what is as precious to me as living breath: the safe homecoming I have prayed for so often, and so despairingly.

Perhaps I hesitate because I am taking so much: what have I to offer in return? Perhaps I still, even in my extremity, baulk at marrying a man for what may well be wholly selfish reasons. Perhaps I resent his putting me in the position where I am forced to weigh such a choice, between my heart's most private and conflicting intimacies.

The last bridge, the final hesitation.

"I am still in mourning, my lord."

"A formal betrothal would suffice, I think."

"Betrothals have been broken."

"With unhappy consequences."

"Marriages are not always happy."

Cercylas smiled. "Life is not always happy; would you deny life?"

"The temptation exists."

"To be conquered. By patience and understanding. There are no demands, no rights. Only what is freely given."

"Is that, too, a pledge?"

He nodded. Against the light behind him the edged outline of his thick hair glowed, suddenly, like burning gold.

I stood up, numb, as though in a dream. My lips framed the words I must say, yet I scarcely heard them: only his swift change of expression, the sudden tightening of his clasped fingers, told me that he had understood that brief whispered sentence.

XII

THIS is ridiculous. I really *am* losing my sense of proportion. No one could guess, from what I have written, that Cercylas was, without exception, the most intelligent, sympathetic, and amusing man it has ever been my good fortune to meet. As for my account of how I came to marry him, it makes me sound like Iphigeneia being led to the sacrificial slab at Aulis. Nothing could have been further than the truth.

Indeed, when I re-read all I have written, I am astonished by the amount of sheer dishonesty that has found its way into nearly every episode. What an innocent, priggish, hard-done-by little genius I am making myself out for posterity! When I consider this self I have created, so laudable in all her motives, so dedicated to her art, so fundamentally pure even where the physical passions are concerned, I scarcely recognize her.

Well, today I propose, while this mood of cheerful self-criticism is on me, to correct the picture a little. No one, certainly no poet, ever tells the whole truth; but at least I can do my best to fill in my more glaring omissions, and admit a few of my less palatable faults. (Once the words are actually written down, not even my admitted talent for self-deception will, I hope, allow me to suppress them. But one never can tell.) Besides—a preliminary exercise in candour—I am by no means sure, now, that my self-portrait is as flattering as I hoped. It does not satisfy *me* (at any rate not in my present mood) and after a couple of generations may well fail to impress anyone. By then, in all likelihood, the stylized mask we insist on our poets wearing will have changed beyond recognition.

There is, too, a more immediate problem facing me. I must, soon, give some account—to satisfy myself no less than curious future generations—of the group, circle, salon, artistic centre (what *should* one call it?) which came to be known, half-ironically, as the "House of the Muses," and which, for almost two decades enjoyed, under my direction, a remarkable—indeed an international—reputation. But by its very nature it always generated controversy; and already, only three years after its dissolution, it is fast becoming a myth.

Or rather, as one might expect, two conflicting myths.

On the one hand there is the establishment described by my more ardent admirers, jealous of what they regard as any slur on my character, eager to idealise the past. *Their* House of the Muses is something between a philosophy salon and a young ladies' finishing school, and I the brilliant, fastidious teacher at whose feet girls from as far afield as Salamis or Pamphylia sat to be instructed in poetry and elegant deportment, perhaps even, like Erinna and Damophila, to catch the spark of my inspiration and become poets themselves. Some have even ventured to describe me as a priestess of Aphrodite: the aim, no doubt, was to emphasize my chastity and my devotion to religious matters, but—as might have been expected—less charitable people picked on the phrase and gave it a very different interpretation.

According to them, my House of the Muses was little more than a high-class brothel, in which the only arts taught were those of the courtesan; and I myself a sexually insatiable monster, seducing most of my girl-followers, conniving at—or even myself procuring—their male lovers (whose attentions I afterwards shared), and flinging unseemly public abuse at members of a similar rival group when they contrived to entice away one of my own favourites. From this traffic I was, further, supposed to derive a very substantial cash profit.

It hardly needs saying that these two myths (like the rival factions which propagated them) reflect, in unmistakable fashion, the social and political rivalries by which our unhappy city has been torn throughout my lifetime. The House of the Muses was, essentially, created both by and for the old aristocracy, whose ideals it upheld with steadfast devotion, and whose support it therefore commanded. In a sense I succeeded where Antimenidas and his friends failed so lamentably: perhaps this accounts for the almost insane violence of those who attacked me—all, one may note, in some way connected with the new regime.

There: once again I have to pull myself up on the brink of specious and flattering self-exculpation. I was not conscious, at any time, of being a political figure in the true sense of the word: the House of the Muses existed simply and solely because it gave me pleasure and, latterly, provided me with a much-needed source of income. As for the way of life I expounded, that was no more than my natural heritage: I spoke for myself, and in so doing became an unwitting public symbol of the class that had bred me.

How much truth, then, was there in each of these two myths? It would be tempting to accept the version put about by my friends: after all, I have tacitly accepted it already in most of what I have written. But such shabby subterfuges are for the living, who are vulnerable still. There is not, I fancy, much embarrassment in Hades.

I composed that strange final sentence late last night, when the lamp was beginning to flicker, and the wine I had drunk to detach my mind from its surroundings. What did I mean? Why should I allude, in so casual a fashion, to my own death—and as though it were close upon me? Yet it is true that the *idea* of death has long obsessed me. When, at certain moments of deep emotional stress and despair, I experienced the desire to pinch out the flame of life within me, it was with a strange yearning pleasure, a dreamy sensuousness. Even as a child the map of Hades, put together in my imagination from the old myths, held an extraordinary allure for me: I saw myself lying on the dewy lotus-grown banks of Acheron, peaceful among the quiet dead. It was an escape from life, in the most literal sense.

Why should I think of death *now*? I am unaccountably more relaxed and cheerful than I have been for months. I do not for one moment believe that I am suffering from cancer of the womb, as I hinted so dramatically a little while ago: it would be an ironic and appropriate twist of fate, but the physicians assure me I have nothing to fear. There will be no recurrence of the dreadful illness I endured five years ago, with its nightmare sweats and haemorrhages, its deep black drowning pits of despair, its apathy and flat exhaustion.

I remember a cheerful Coan doctor reassuring me, as I lay on my day-bed under an awning, too weak even to move: "You mustn't worry, Lady Sappho: it's a natural symptom of your age, nothing more." The tears rolled down my cheeks: perhaps I was laughing, who can tell? That smiling, jolly face: those devastating words, a judge's sentence. The world seemed to recede from me, down an endless dark tunnel.

But now, five years later, I feel intensely alive, in every fibre: fire scalds through my veins, I am consumed, exultant. Now, today, at this moment, I can still hope.

There is a kind of knowing-and-not-knowing, an elusive and specious attitude to uncomfortable facts or emotions which enables one to deceive oneself no less effectively than other people. My childhood was not quite so innocent, nor my adult life by any means so fastidious, as I have hitherto contrived to suggest. Yet which of us does not—and with good reason—conceal some at least of our private actions and thoughts from the world? No. Let there be an end of excuses now.

It is true, in the strictly physical sense, that Chloe was my first lover. Yet for years before we met I had experienced (with Andromeda above all but with other girls too, who mostly remained quite unaware of my feelings) a burning intensity of passion that was—I cannot emphasize this too strongly—something quite apart and distinct from ordinary, physical desire. I see, now, that I was deeply in love with Andromeda over a long period; but I never, at the time, acknowledged a physical dimension to my feelings—which perhaps was why I found some of Alcaeus' hints and innuendoes so disturbing.

It is easy to forget, also, how large a part of any poet's emotional life is conducted in the mind and the imagination—so much more real, for him, than the world of physical appearances, so tangible that he will slide at will from the real to the imaginary until, in the end, there is no clear frontier between them. The passions which stirred me were embodied in this secret world, this dream-dominion of pure, silver-clear, crystalline adoration, so that my creative imagination could dwell on some loved face or body and, in fantasy, find fulfilment there without disturbing the delicate balance of unknowing which governed my conscious thoughts. I burned, yet the fire was contained, transmuted. As I grew older, inevitably, the perilous frontier between desire and knowledge became less distinct: this was the time of nightmare, of knowing-and-not-knowing, when, waking, I closed my eyes deliberately to what my mind understood, but refused to accept. It is not hard to understand, now, that state of latent, unexplored desire which had so instantaneous and devastating an effect on Chloe.

For my behaviour to Pittacus, though, I can find no such excuse: it was done knowingly, and from plain prurient curiosity. I refer, of course, to my description of his drunken attempt at rape, which, in one vital respect, does the old ruffian something less than justice. It is true that he made the attempt; it is also true that I panicked in sheer revulsion before he had got well started. What, for obvious reasons, I refrained from mentioning is the fact that I quite deliberately provoked him into it.

I was bored; I had had a violent quarrel with my mother; and my imagination—never slow in this respect—had not been idle while he was upstairs in Aunt Helen's room. By the time he came down I had convinced myself, quite wrongly, that I was ready for anything. If it was not a demure little sensualist who stood waiting by the couch on that spring afternoon (how self-flattering one's imagination can be!) it was not a mere innocent, frightened child, either; and I think, looking back, that I thoroughly deserved the sharp lesson I got. At least it convinced me I was not quite so grown-up as I supposed. As for Pittacus, he showed what, in the circumstances, I can only call great forbearance. If I had tried my little tricks on Myrsilus, or even on Deinomenes (*he* made no mistake about me, even after one chance encounter) the story might have had a very different ending.

How much *did* that afternoon, in fact, change the whole course of my life? My extravagant assertion was, naturally, designed to make me out an innocent victim—just as, I now see, I have been trying to excuse my present embarrassing passion by a broad hint that it is a mere symptom of disease, for which I cannot be held responsible. But until I reached middle-age—indeed, till the aftermath of my illness—only girls ever engaged my full passions. I did not have a violent aversion to men; I was, quite simply, not aroused by them.

On the other hand, I do not believe my passionate regard for the condition of virginity, or the sadness which the thought of its loss invariably engenders in me, has much to do with distaste for the sexual act. I suspect it is, rather, a legacy from the private, exquisite, intense world of my adolescent imagination: here, moving through the shadow-play of reality, I mourn that lost perfection still.

My main objection to marriage was far more practical: I saw it as a permanent threat to my independence of mind and action. When Cercylas made it clear that he would respect me *as an individual human being*, I was prepared to accept his proposal. I must not give the impression (I suspect I may have done) that one condition of that acceptance was an agreement, on my husband's part, to forgo his marital rights. The prospect of this experience did not much excite me; but I was not repelled by it, either.

On the other hand (oddly when one considers my own nature), I find that men such as Alcaeus, whose passions are centred exclusively on boys, arouse a strong and instinctive antipathy in me. When I see the lovers he keeps—Lycus especially, with his long curled hair and shadowed eyes, his powder, his lipstick, his mincing, affected walk—I feel not only repulsion, but also a sense of personal outrage: by usurping a false femininity, these creatures somehow diminish my own womanhood.

What I really dread, I suspect, is revealing, not excess of feeling, but rather a fundamental lack of it. Cold emotional self-centredness is not a comfortable characteristic to face in oneself: there is something inhuman about it, something crippling. Only, perhaps, through the sexual act have I ever been able to give myself completely and selflessly: devotion, of the kind which my cousin Meg has in such abundance, has always brought out my hardest, most ruthless side. That is not a pleasant admission, either.

I have always thought Meg designed by nature for a life of passionate celibacy, deriving sexless, vicarious satisfaction from ministering to those emotions in others which she is afraid to confront in herself—or which, quite simply, she does not possess at all. As a result I have used her, without compunction or gratitude. I am quite sure that when she sent me the Egyptian doctor's report on my mother's death she was not being in the least malicious. The situation defeated her, that was all. She could not think what to say and so took the easy way out.

Similarly, the most terrible thing about Chloe's death, for me, was my own lukewarm reaction to it. After a day or so I simply felt *nothing*—no grief, at any rate, though I was intensely angry, on the practical level, at being left in so embarrassing a position. How many people, I wonder, after the death of someone they have loved feel, in their heart of hearts, as I did—yet shrink from the admission, even to themselves? Grief must be feigned, the social myths preserved.

Indeed, my entire Sicilian exile, as I describe it, sounds like a beautiful, bedazzled dream. This it most certainly was not. I spent those years abroad working extremely hard at my art: I attended lectures, researched, wrote, studied choreography and musical technique, and in general laid the foundations of those varied skills, as teacher and creative artist, which I used to such good effect on my return to Mytilene. But hard work—particularly in a poet or a lady—is regarded as boring and undignified by well-bred people, who would much prefer to hear about the Muse's inspiration, or the spring of Helicon—which, as Alcaeus once told me, has strong aperient qualities, not perhaps the best symbol for divine afflatus.

How, I wonder, would *they* react to the knowledge that, two days after Chloe's death, far from languishing in heartbroken bereavement like any properly-brought-up lady poet, I spent the morning studying with my music-teacher (a mild stimulant after Arion's slave-driving), wrote a cheerful, not to say near-bawdy, commissioned wedding-song in the afternoon, did my regular two hours' daily practice at the dancing-school, ate a large dinner after it, drank enough wine (but not too much) and spent half the night making love to Chloe's exotic Spanish maid, long desired and now, at last, available?

Yet how much of this, too—what I so presumptuously dare to call the truth—is self-mockery and self-deception? Tomorrow, in another mood, I may deny what I have said today, the glass may show me another, equally plausible face. The mask peels away to reveal a second mask behind it, and where shall the truth be found? Can anyone, can I, see Sappho as she really is?

Nevertheless, I shall let what I have written stand, with all its ambiguities and contradictions. That, at least, is a kind of honesty.

It isn't true, Chloe's death broke me up so completely I thought I would never recover from it. The account I wrote yesterday shows how completely one can distort the truth without ever straying from external facts. All I set down are the physical details—but how much implication there is behind them!

I remember that day very well, the cold, bleak horror of it, the colour drained out of everything, the absurd little creature that was myself moving through it like a mechanical doll. No, I did not languish in bereavement as professional mourners or indifferent widows do, making the expected show of grief, playing a conventional part. My sorrow was too deep for such calculated dishonesty: I was literally stunned, and all I could do was cling to my day's routine, some framework round my inner chaos.

I suggest (do I not?) that because the wedding-song was cheerful and bawdy, I must have been feeling cheerful myself. But other poets, if not the public at large, will know, as I do, that wit often springs from the deepest depression. When I say I was cold, that I felt nothing, this was true in the most literal sense: *I felt nothing,* my senses were anaesthetized by shock, as doctors can numb a limb by the administration of certain drugs.

As for Chloe's maid—again, convention will say this shows callous indifference. But in his heart of hearts, even the conventional moralist will know how closely linked are the mysteries of death and creation.

After a funeral the sexual desire is strongest. We do not care to admit this, but it is true. And Chloe's Spanish slave-girl was a part of Chloe; our love-making was, in one sense, an act of mourning and farewell. We poured libations to her spirit, the tears were streaming down our faces as we kissed.

Why, *now*, should I have the temptation to destroy myself in the eyes of posterity, to blacken my motives, emphasize all my least likeable faults? Is it in fact the truth I seek? *Know yourself*, the oracular precept runs; was there ever a simpler, or a harder injunction?

I wonder, now I come to think of it, why I have never, except in the most oblique and allusive way, mentioned my frequent private dream-visions of the Goddess? Perhaps because they no longer take place, and the Goddess herself has turned away from me—hard, in retrospect, to think of that smiling, affectionate countenance, so familiar for all its divinity, as a mask for cold capricious malevolence; harder to accept those cherished manifestations as something worse than mockery.

But another, more commonplace reason may be that they, the visions, are—were—so comfortingly matter-of-fact: when a poet is honoured with divine epiphanies they should, one feels, have a fine revelatory frenzy about them. But I somehow established the same sort of personal relationship with the Goddess as I had done during my later childhood with Aunt Helen. Whenever there was a crisis in my private life—and when was there not?—I would pray for the Goddess to appear to me; and either that night or the next, she invariably did.

I once discussed these visions with Alcaeus, after his return from Egypt. He was full of newly acquired esoteric lore that he had picked up from the priests at Memphis, and a little inclined to self-importance; but he knew enough—I now see—to be properly suspicious of my story.

He said: "What does the Goddess *look* like when she appears to you?"

"Very much the same as the cult-image here in her temple."

"Just so. How is she attired?"

"In the same embroidered robe."

"And her, ah, mode of transport?"

I said: "She flies down through the air in a chariot drawn by birds —sparrows, doves, I'm not sure."

"Where does the dream take place? What is its setting?"

"A temple precinct. There are trees, and a stream, and sunlight overhead, and somewhere smoke from an altar."

"And what *happens?*" Alcaeus asked, sounding genuinely fascinated: he had developed a keen if irreverent passion for obscure cult-practices during his exile. "I mean, is there any formal ritual? Do you fall on your face in adoration? Are there other petitioners?"

"No, nothing like that. I'm always alone. We just—talk. But—but it's impossible to get too close to her, there's a radiance, a power, I can't explain—"

He nodded, as though he took this part of it for granted. "She talks informally, then? Like a human being?"

I gave an involuntary giggle. "Well, yes, very much so—I mean, I do summon her rather *often*, and generally for the same thing, you know how I am when I fall in love."

"No," Alcaeus said with faint malice, "I fear I don't; but I'll take your word for it."

"Well, she makes some sort of comment like: What's the matter with you *now*, Sappho? Why are you calling on me again? What girl have I got to win over for you *this* time?"

"She has all my sympathy, if a mere mortal may presume to offer it to a Goddess."

"Then she asks me who it is that's wronging me, and I tell her."

"And then?"

"Then she generally says something like: Well, I hope you know what you're doing: the girl may be very coy *now*, and avoid you, and not accept your presents; but in no time *she* will be the one chasing *you*, and showering you with gifts, and besotted with helpless love, and then you'll appeal to me to get rid of her again—is it worth it?"

Alcaeus said: "What remarkably sensible advice: why don't you try following it once in a while?"

I flushed. "Would *you?*"

"Perhaps not."

How much older he looked: yet he was—what?—still only thirty-six.

I said: "Well, what do you make of it all?"

He considered. "I'm not sure. At first I thought it was all nonsense, you dreaming what you wanted to hear—the visual details are so trite, there are no other worshippers, it's a private dialogue between you and the Goddess, rather as though she were your mother."

"*What?*"

[195]

"But that last thing you told me: I don't know. I just don't know."
He frowned, then gave me his famous cool, ironic smile. He said:
"Perhaps it would be better for you if it *was* all nonsense, don't you
think?"

"Why?"

"Well, think of the alternative: you spend a good deal of time
calling down the Queen of Heaven to sort out your piddling emotional problems—and I don't suppose that's all, either; you've probably
got her finding lost brooches by now, and healing warts, and procuring fine weather for picnics—and then, after all the trouble she's
taken, you consistently ignore her advice! Sooner or later, Sappho,
the Goddess is going to stop finding you an amusing little plaything,
and decide that you're just a bore, a tiresome, self-centred, imperti-
nent bore. When that day comes, my dear, I wouldn't like to be in
your shoes at all."

It was never easy to decide when Alcaeus was serious and when
he was joking. Sometimes his most flippant remarks had an unexpected edge to them.

I said, laughing: "Oh, you're impossible."

"So you often tell me. But I exist. The same two statements might
be made apropos the Gods, don't you think?"

"The Gods move in a different sphere: they do not resemble human
beings."

"I grant you the different sphere. But if we can trust Homer, the
Gods are rather like malicious children, with unlimited power and
an irresponsible taste for exercising it on us poor mortals. So I should
watch out."

"I'm grateful for your advice."

"Are you? I wonder."

It was then that he made me a present of the little glass phial he
had procured in Egypt, the phial which contained nepenthe, the
poppy of oblivion.

I have been looking through the desultory, intermittent journal I
began to keep at the time of my marriage. (Odd, that of all self-
regarding habits it should be this one which I have always found it
impossible to maintain with any regularity.) Because of their gaps
and omissions, re-reading these entries has a strange, almost halluci-
natory effect on me: some long-forgotten incident is vividly illumi-
nated, as lightning will branch through the darkness during a storm
at night, and then, abruptly, all becomes black once more. I feel,

incongruously, an eavesdropper, an intruder upon the private thoughts of this twenty-five-year-old woman who is not myself but an alien stranger. I don't think we would much care for each other if we met.

"Seagulls overhead in the spring sunlight, swooping and yapping round the mast-head. Cercylas knows each different type, name, habits, breeding-grounds. To me they are just gulls. He says I should observe more closely, that a poet should understand the world around him. His range of knowledge is vast and unpredictable. Stars, mathematics, medicine—whatever can be named and ordered. He has a passion for tidiness.

"A few moments ago we sighted the citadel of Corinth. Strange, to be coming back now, nearly five years later—*five years!*—with nothing changed, the blue waters of the Gulf, the long rocky coast-line; it might even be the same thick-waisted merchantman, dipping gently along with its great patched sail spread to catch every last breath of wind. I sit on the after-decks and write, as I once sat with Arion. Cercylas is somewhere forward, he always leaves me to myself when he sees me get my tablets out.

"How little I know of him, really. Even in the six months that passed before I could come out of full mourning, and get married, he remained tangential, enigmatic. He never speaks of his family. There has been no suggestion that we should visit Andros. He has been travelling constantly for years. If he ever was a merchant, he has long since abandoned his calling: perhaps he made a lucky early fortune. He is knowledgeable about jewellery, pictures, rare luxuries such as silk and amber. Sometimes I wonder if he has been married before. Absurdly, I can never bring myself to ask him. Even his age remains a mystery."

[Of course, the air of mystery, the elusiveness, was deliberately cultivated: Cercylas knew very well it would please me. I found out later, through various friends, that he was forty-four at the time of our marriage; that his parents had died during the great plague on Andros when he was ten, leaving him a large fortune; that he had trebled this fortune by the age of thirty, through clever speculation and trading ventures; and that he had never been married. Nor, so far as anyone could tell, did he care for boys. The aloofness was only half a pose. But he knew influential people everywhere, and the speed with which he persuaded Myrsilus to revoke my decree of exile was astonishing. I have sometimes wondered if he was not, in some very discreet capacity, a political agent for Periander.]

[197]

"Corinth now a bright, colourful, exciting city, no sense of cruelty or oppression. Stroll down street of the goldsmiths, this time can buy what I like. Cercylas inveterate *bargainer,* which embarrasses me. Haggled over lapis ring till I begged him to come away, said I didn't want it. Cercylas just smiled that infuriating lazy smile of his, went on arguing. Got ring in end. Am wearing it now, with what Cercylas calls 'a nice air of grievance.'

"At dinner this evening heard *extraordinary* tale about Arion, who, it seems, recently turned up in Corinth out of the blue, and to all appearances penniless. Last heard of making fabulous profit from much publicized Italian concert-tour, no reply to sharp letter from Periander saying it was high time he came back to his official duties; so Periander naturally suspicious. Arion's explanation not calculated to make him less so. Arion said he sailed at once from Tarentum on receipt of letter, but crew plotted to rob him of his earnings. Let him sing one last song before being thrown overboard. Touching scene. While in water, miraculous school of dolphins appears, largest dolphin takes him on its back, lets him ride in comfort till they reach land. Arion deposited on beach at Cape Taenarum in southern Peloponnese, recognized, makes way home overland to Corinth.

"Periander receives this nonsense with polite incredulity, keeps Arion under house arrest, waits for ship to dock. Crew brought in for interrogation, captain explains that Arion booked passage at Tarentum, but changed mind at last moment and stayed in Italy. Yes, he was in good health then. Sudden appearance of Arion, crew flabbergasted when he tells his story, more so when Arion's loot, or part of it, later found hidden in ballast of ship. Arion vindicated, crew executed, Arion becomes hero overnight, beloved of Gods, recipient of divine aid and so on. Large statue of Arion on dolphin's back commissioned for public square.

"Our host claims to know true story, but warns that this cannot now be revealed, since it would make Periander look a fool. According to him, Arion was determined to stay in Italy and enjoy his enormous success: the last thing he wanted was to come back to Corinth and surrender bulk of Italian windfall to Periander's treasury officials. Besides, Periander now very moody and unpredictable after his son's death: court retainer's position no longer quite attractive. Arion, understandably, determined to vanish and start new life. Goes aboard ship at Tarentum secretly, after dark, stays below throughout voyage. Bribes crew to put him off on island of Zacynthus, and to inform Periander that he is still in Italy. From Zacynthus takes another boat, sailing for Ionia by the long haul round the Peloponnese, well out of Periander's way.

"Boat unfortunately wrecked off Cape Taenarum by sudden storm. Arion washed ashore still clutching strong-box, but meets agent of Periander's travelling to Gythium. Recognition, panic, dolphin-story invented on spur of moment. Arion returns to Corinth—what else could he do?—bribes friend to secrete half his Italian gold in ship's ballast when it docks. Thus cuts losses, saves head, keeps reasonable proportion of loot, gains useful publicity. (After all, Periander bound to die soon, well over seventy now.) Just the kind of thing the old fraud *would* do."

[I thought this second version of the story true when I heard it; on the whole I still do. Arion's own explanation bristled with improbabilities, and came much too symbolically pat: after all, the dolphin is the emblem of Lesbos. This kind of thing was a habit with him. His birthplace, I happen to know, was not Antissa—as he always used to claim—but Methymna: he made the change, of course, because Antissa was where the severed head of Orpheus was washed up. Arion put it about that he was Orpheus' descendant, and had inherited the divine gift of song from his illustrious ancestor's buried skull. This got him enormous respect everywhere—except, of course, in Methymna. Yes, the unpublished version *must* be true.

But I have always been a little puzzled as to *how* he found anyone who would plant that vital evidence for him at such short notice; and since then I have heard some most remarkable (and far better authenticated) tales concerning dolphins. So a lingering doubt remains in my mind. Does it matter, after all? Arion is dead now: it is his work that lives and by which ultimately he will be judged. If posterity chooses to make a legend of him, that should at least preserve his art from oblivion.

Why, then, do I so stubbornly, and at such cost, still labour to discover the truth concerning myself?]

"The shocks and disillusions of home-coming. Fixed pictures to be eradicated from the mind, the acceptance—so damaging to one's self-conceit—that *life can go on while one is somewhere else.* Ridiculous, but at the back of one's mind—my mind—there lurks the unformulated notion that a place, people, need *my* presence to exist at all, that when I go, time stops, and the puppets stand motionless till set going by my return. But the harbour has been rebuilt, there are new houses and shops, everywhere the eye receives an unfamiliar image. Odd how strong my attachment to this dream of timeless,

[199]

unchanging peace. If it came true I would be bored to death inside a month.

"But I still can't face, emotionally, the facts that my rational mind had known and prepared for long ago. I feel that everyone is conspiring to play an elaborate practical joke on me, that sooner or later they will wipe the skilful lines from their faces, brush the white powder from their hair, and put everything back as it was before. I can't really *believe* that Aunt Helen is nearly fifty and has, despite everything, married Myrsilus; or that my brother Charaxus, by some legalistic juggling, is now master of the square grey house on the citadel, or—worst admission of all—that *I am married*, a young matron (disgusting phrase) whose life, however sensitive and generous my husband may be, is now totally *different*, metamorphosed, part of a new, unfamiliar pattern.

"Charaxus very wary with me, Irana simpering but hostile. Obviously afraid I intend to make trouble over the house. Full of talk about trading investments, profits, improving the estate. So *boring*. Charaxus at twenty-two a horrible little prematurely middle-aged tub of a man. Repulsive: couldn't bear to touch him. What does Irana feel when he makes love to her? *If* he makes love to her. And now he has poor Agenor working for him: *he* hasn't changed, still dark, shy, devoted, with that terrible air of responsibility which always makes me feel so *obliged*, even after spending half an hour in his company chatting about trivialities. Charaxus has kept Meg on, too, as unpaid housekeeper and—I suspect—handy permanent scapegoat for his poisonous temper. She kept hinting broadly that life would be so much more bearable with me and Cercylas. I have no doubt it would be—for her.

"Pittacus' wife died a month or two before my—our—return. I'm sorry. I was fond of Chione, though I seldom saw her. She had no pretensions at all, and very little breeding, but she was warm, generous, spontaneous: a real person. Their boy Tyrrhaeus has grown into a weak, surly lout with a taste for the bottle: he seems to have inherited all his father's worst qualities. Friends tell me he goes round a good deal with Larichus now. Must try, tactfully, to stop this. Larichus too innocent (and beautiful) to be true, very easily influenced *and* anxious for popularity, a disastrous mixture. What *can* I tell him without making myself look the bossy, interfering, married elder sister I'm so desperately anxious he *shouldn't* see me as?

"This morning, in the market, I suddenly came face to face with

Andromeda and Gorgo. They were standing together at a stall beside the fountain, where caged birds and other pets are on sale daily. Andromeda had a gaudy red-and-green parrot perched on her shoulder and was arguing with the stall-keeper, a thin, hunchbacked little Syrian who looked extraordinarily like some rather unpleasant bird of prey himself, with his balding head, coarse black hair, and the red, loose folds of skin under his jaw. (Can people come to resemble the creatures they keep?) Our eyes met: we quickly looked away again, like strangers. Or enemies. There was nothing to say, no possible point of contact between us.

"She has not changed at all: still the same short, rough-cut black curls, still the awkward movements, the rather large, clumsy hands, the brown, tomboyish face. What was appealing in a schoolgirl has become incongruous past belief in a grown woman of nearly thirty. As we stared, embarrassed, first at each other, then anywhere else, the parrot screeched harshly: *"Do you love me, then? Do you love me? Do you love me?"* after which, tickled, I suppose, by its own brilliance, it burst into paroxysms of mindless laughter. Startled, I turned my head back, and saw the open expression of derision on Andromeda's face. She whispered something to Gorgo, who grinned and nodded. The parrot went on laughing till I was out of earshot."

[Dishonest again: the one thing I leave out of this account is the fact that I found Andromeda as overpoweringly attractive, in the purely physical sense, as I had ever done. While that wretched parrot was having its fun (I found out, afterwards, that Andromeda had bought it months before, and now—the joke having worn a little thin, even for her—was attempting to sell it back again) I stood there in so violent and humiliating a state of excitement that I could only just control my features. She knew that, too: she always did. It was dreadful: I didn't even *like* her any more, she was coarse and inartistic and (as I soon learnt) afflicted with absurd social pretensions, which her father's position let her gratify to the full.

Aphrodite must have been in a splendid joking mood that day: perhaps it was then that her capricious divine mind formulated the notion of using Andromeda, when the time came, as one of the instruments for my destruction.]

"Today we found the house. We both knew it was right the moment we saw it, yet it was wildly different from anything I had planned for in advance. An abandoned farmstead on the hillside above the straits, a mile or so south of the city. Pear-trees in the

[201]

garden, lizards flickering in and out of the ancient, crumbling stone walls. We had only come out to see the place on impulse—it was a fine day, the carriage was harnessed up. Why not? This is the sort of thing that makes Cercylas so endearing. No hesitation, no argument, an instant picking up of one's mood.

"The owner's agent struggled with locks and bars and nailed-up shutters, helped by a *most* inefficient slave who only succeeded in making things worse, but one couldn't, somehow, be cross with him, the day was so perfect: doves cooing from the roof-top, that wonderful scent of thyme and marjoram, the excitement as room after room was opened up, light flooding in on bare floors and walls, the certainty that this was *right*, that it was where we belonged. We tried to look critical and unenthusiastic, but I don't think we convinced the agent for one moment. His slave was grinning like a split melon when we left.

"Afterwards we sat up till nearly midnight discussing alterations and improvements. Cercylas says that if I really want to we can move in the moment the place is bought and have the work done—literally —about our ears. I think he, being a tidy creature, would much prefer to wait: but somehow the idea of watching our dream take shape makes the house, for me at least, a living organism, into which we will—I hope—be slowly absorbed till we form an integral element of its atmosphere.

"I tried to explain this to Cercylas. I *think* he understood. But he knew it was what I wanted, what would make me truly happy, and that, he said, was enough for him. (He is adept, too, at sidetracking those fancies which I *think* will make me happy, but in fact won't.) I told him what Aunt Helen had said about my infinite capacity for being spoilt, and he nodded: that, he said, was the main reason why he had married me. Then, with his most disarming grin, he added: *Which leaves me little time for other activities.* The trouble with Cercylas is that I am always in danger of taking him for granted. Such constant love and devotion become a little unnerving if thought about too often: so I don't."

Again, I have omitted the most crucial part of that late-night discussion. (Sometimes I think the reason most people keep a journal at all is not to preserve the truth—far from it—so much as to reshape the past for their own peace of mind.) I had never spoken openly to Cercylas of my relationship with Chloe, though I felt certain he knew about it—and what it implied. But that night, suddenly, I had a violent impulse to drag the subject into the open, to confess, to humiliate myself. Cercylas's understanding and warmth and generosity were more than I could bear: I made use of his love, I gave nothing back. I was hateful, cold, predatory. All this I poured out, suddenly, in a confused and tearful torrent of words.

Cercylas heard me through without interruption. When I had sobbed and sniffed myself into comparative silence he said: "What a curious notion of love you have: rather like an Egyptian trade agreement, so much corn in exchange for so much wine, and special clauses to prevent bilking. Hadn't it occurred to you that one of the many reasons why I married you was because making you happy gives me active pleasure?"

I wiped my eyes and stared at him.

"Why should I dictate what form your emotional or sexual pleasures take? I don't *own* you. Why should that make any difference to what I feel for you?"

"But if I really fall in love, if I'm emotionally involved—"

"You *are* being stupid tonight, darling. Why shouldn't you become emotionally involved with anyone you like?" He shook his head and smiled. "So many rhetorical questions: I apologize. But try to understand that nothing you could feel for another woman would impinge on *our* relationship. The two spheres are distinct, they complement each other, enhance each other. There's no competition, nothing to stop you loving a woman *and* loving me. Love takes many forms: you're a poet, you should know that. So please forget this absurd idea of your having married me under false pretences: apart from anything else, it doesn't exactly flatter my intelligence."

"I'm sorry."

"*Don't* be sorry." He spoke with sudden vehemence. "It isn't in character—at least, I very much hope it isn't. One of the most attractive things about you, my love, in case you hadn't realized it, is your absolute determination to get your own way. You're ruthless as only a good artist can be. You're so implacably self-centred that you're not even conscious of the fact. I find you quite fascinating."

It was the oddest complimentary speech anyone had ever made to me. And then my mind flashed back to that winter day in Pyrrha, to a tall figure in a fur cap and sheepskins: *This curious illusion you have that you're a delicate, sensitive creature too refined for the rough-and-tumble of ordinary life. You're tougher than any of us, really, Sappho: it's never once occurred to you that you can't, in the long run, get exactly what you want.*

[203]

I laughed despite myself. "Antimenidas once told me almost the same thing, word for word."

"Antimenidas?" His eyebrows lifted a little, his voice had an ironic inflection as he said: "But of course, Antimenidas was—is—in love with you too: surely you realized that?"

My astonishment must have been obvious: Cercylas could not have asked for a better illustration of his remarks on my character. I said, rallying: "That's absurd. He called me a ravening harpy—"

"So you are, darling."

"—and he said he was sorry for any man fool enough to marry me."

Cercylas took both my hands in his: the lamp-light flickered over his brown, lined face. "I wouldn't argue with him, Sappho. In fact, I might well have said the same thing in his place. But—had you noticed?—*I* happen to love you, so why shouldn't he—perhaps even for the same reasons? One of which, without a doubt, is your quite splendid naïvety."

For the second time in as many minutes he had taken me off-balance. I said: "Ruthless *and* naïve? It sounds an unlikely combination."

"Not at all. Most of the time you don't notice people as individuals; and when you do you have a touching faith in what they *say* rather than what they do or are. Please don't ever change: it's a delightful trait."

We both burst out laughing. Then, on a sudden impulse, my hands still clasped in his, I said: "Do you get pleasure from making love to me?" I was surprised by my own candour: I think Cercylas was, too, because, for the first time, he hesitated before replying, and then merely said: "Sometimes, it depends."

"On what?"

He shook his head. "We've talked enough for one night."

Much later, in the darkness of our bedroom, he said: "Are you in love?" His hands moved gently over my bare body.

"No. Yes. I don't know—"

"Tell me about it."

"There's nothing to tell."

He was silent for a moment. Then—"There will be," he said.

"Are you so sure of the future?"

His fingertips traced the contours of my body, delicately outlined lips, cheek-bones, nose, brow.

"I know you," he said. Then, with an ambiguous touch of irony, he added: "You mustn't disappoint me, darling."

[204]

Next day Agesilaïdas and Ismene, who had been married less than a month before my return, came back to Three Winds from Pyrrha, bringing Ismene's children with them: Mica, Atthis, little Hippias, each nearly five years older than on that bright morning—so long ago, so fresh still in the memory—when I had stood at the side of the great black ship that was bearing me into exile and watched, through a dazzle of tears, Atthis' grave, sunlit face dwindle, merge with the waving anonymous crowd, vanish out of sight. Partings and reunions: what a significant element, now I come to think of it, they have always formed in the pattern of my existence.

XIII

O L D wounds ache under the scar: even now I find it hard to write about Atthis and the love we had for each other. Sometimes I am tempted to formulate that last despairing prayer for blessed oblivion. Let memory fade, let my yesterdays return to the anonymous dust that made them. But I cannot escape her, she is everywhere, in the small tree-climber vines I can see from this window, in the homeward-gathering evening star that we so often watched together, in the moonlit sea and the smell of a wood-fire and the autumn wind.

She changed the world for me, its shape and brightness and texture: because of her I could never see anything in quite the same way again, never be what I had been, for I was a part of the world and so changed with it. The filaments of our love ran out to the ends of the earth, they embraced all creation. No other love I have known possessed this universal dimension: it transcended passion. I remember once thinking: If I reach out my hand, I can scoop the stars from the firmament, night will brush like a mole's soft fur across my fingers.

When I look back, I seem to see a clear, sunlit sky, tranquil, radiant, charged with splendor: the brief time of blossom, the pink-and-white glory shed over Lesbos in springtime. Yet the pure halcyon days, the days of untroubled happiness, were transient enough: our eternity lasted two years, no more, and then the storm-clouds gathered, rain lashed the fallen petals, the spring was gone for ever.

There were bright days still to come—a burning, febrile high summer, moments of autumnal nostalgia; but never again were we to recapture that first morning freshness, that miraculous unfolding of passion from a love as pure and perfect as the crimson bud of a rose. The rose is blown now, winter waits over the mountains. Why do I still sit here, among these ghosts and shadows? So little time remains to me, the sun will soon be down.

It was the first warm day of the year when I came back from Three Winds, shaken, dazzled, walking in a sweet agony of all the senses—blinded by blossom and sunlight, bird-song exploding in my heart like some divine revelation, all the flowers of the world shedding their odour about me. Cercylas was out in the southern portico, stretched on a day-bed, reading: he glanced up at my approach, and for a moment half-closed his eyes, as though dazzled by what he saw. (A flattering fancy, of course: the sun was behind me, high still, and struck straight into his face. I am pretty sure, too, that whatever my inner feelings may have been, I *looked* like any love-sick ninny the world over.) He rolled up the book he had been studying and said: "Well, darling, how did you find the bride? Suitably—what shall we say?—*epithalamial?* Or did all those strapping children spoil the effect a little?"

I scarcely heard him. I was staring at the fig-tree that stood in the corner of the garden below the terrace: old—just how old, no one knew—with a thick, split trunk and innumerable grey branches latticed against the light. Its ancient roots reached down into the earth like knotted chthonian serpents: its branches were gnarled arthritic fingers that blossomed miraculously into buds of greenness. The whole tree seemed to writhe and move: it glowed with argent fire, it was Adonis resurgent in the skeletal corpse of winter. Today only a weathered stump marks where it once stood: the gardener's officious axe has brought down my vision of light.

Cercylas said curiously: "What is it, Sappho? That fig-tree—you're looking at it as though you'd never seen it before."

His voice came to me from some other world: remote, insubstantial. I nodded. "Yes," I said, "you're right. I have never seen it before. Never till this moment."

The pupils of his eyes contracted like a cat's: was it the sunlight again? I blinked, shook my head, and then, abruptly, the vision faded, colour and light ebbed back to normal. But the exaltation was still there, in my head and heart, transfiguring, a river of bright fire.

"I see," Cercylas said very softly; and then, with one of those disconcerting flashes of insight he so often displayed: "I don't envy poets their gift, you know; for me it would be like—staring into the sun. To see with such intensity demands a special strength."

"Yes: to see, to feel—" I hesitated; he did not.

"To love, yes. Love, after all, is a kind of seeing. That is why poets are so susceptible to it—"

"And so ruthless to those they love: isn't that what you mean?"

He smiled affectionately: there was a cool twinkle in his eye. "Perhaps. Now tell me about Ismene: I'm curious." He tossed the roll aside, and I sat down on the day-bed beside him. As I smoothed out my skirts it struck me, for the first time, that they were the same vivid lime-green as Chloe had been wearing that first day in Syracuse. An age and an exile ago.

I said: "Well, she certainly *looks* different: she's put on weight, for one thing, and lost that dreadful drawn white look, you remember? Agesilaïdas fusses round her like an old hen—"

"How old is she, for heaven's sake? Thirty-six? Thirty-seven?"

I said demurely: "Perhaps she needs a little—mothering." We both laughed. There was a pause in the conversation then, not long, but enough to hint at the different ground ahead. Cercylas said in almost too casual a voice: "How are the girls taking it all?"

I drew a light breath. "Very well, I think. They like Agesilaïdas, that's the most important thing. He's made them his allies in a kind of conspiracy to look after Ismene, and they adore it."

"So does she, I should imagine."

I giggled. "Poor Ismene; she *did* make rather heavy weather of widowhood, didn't she? But Agesilaïdas, is such fun, too: witty, civilised, well-read—"

"Darling Sappho, you make him sound the most dreadful bore."

"The girls don't think so."

"He probably flatters them into adoring him for his apt quotations," my husband said, amiably. "They're sensible enough to see he doesn't relish the interloper's role—not, I fancy, that the old thing could ever be considered a rival to Phanias."

"No: he and Phanias don't have much in common, do they? Except Ismene." I giggled again: I was more nervous than I allowed myself to admit.

"Even that might be, in a sense, debatable."

Our eyes met: his were friendly, encouraging. I said: "Do you know who else was there? Melanippus—"

"Oh? I thought *he* might have taken a trip to Egypt." For a non-Mytilenean, Cercylas was astonishingly well up in local gossip: he enjoyed nothing better than observing, with engrossed fascination, every twitch in the complex web of personal relationships throughout the city. (There is a tradition that only women possess this trait: personally I have always thought men put it about in order to take women off their guard. All the greatest gossips and scandal-mongers of my acquaintance have been men.)

I said: "Well, if he does, it looks like being for his honeymoon."

"Mica? Yes, I'd heard something of the sort. How he'll enjoy having a real artist all to himself: the fashionable portrait-painter and her husband, holding court."

"Poor Mica." She alone had looked wary and ill-at-ease that afternoon, her childish high spirits very much under control, dark smudges beneath those hurt, Cassandra eyes. But she had talked with bright, almost brittle animation, matching Melanippus' mood, playing the part he had envisaged for her. What was her reward to be? Social prestige, financial security, a tolerant, understanding husband. Only the eyes hinted at the sacrifice which these advantages would demand.

Seeing Melanippus and Agesilaïdas together—so carefully polite, such demonstrative paragons of marital and near-marital virtue—I found myself wondering how close their relationship had been in the old days, what unspoken conspiracy linked them now. Did they, as I, realize the fresh and subtle light which Mica's betrothal cast on her mother's remarriage? Imitation, especially between children and parents, is by no means always the sincerest form of flattery.

"Why poor Mica?" Cercylas asked. "She knows what she wants: she's going to have it."

"Does she?"

"Do you?" His eyes were faintly mocking, but I could sense how he hung on my answer.

"Yes: I know what I want."

"And are *you* going to have it?"

I sat very still, hands folded in my lap. The two rings on my marriage-finger glinted as the afternoon sunlight struck them: the heavy signet, the entwined and pursuing snakes.

"The Gods know," I said at last.

He nodded. "The Gods know indeed." The moment was over: we understood one another now. When Cercylas spoke again, his voice had recovered its old casual, bantering, ironic note.

"And what about Atthis? She looks a delightful creature, but it's so hard to tell what's going on in her head: that grave expression gives nothing away. Do you suppose she's brewing up some choice poison for her step-father on the quiet?"

I laughed. "Is Atthis *really* so inscrutable? Odd—no, I can see what you mean, it's just that—" However hard I tried, I could not prevent my voice changing when I spoke of her: there was a queer thickening in my throat, a breathlessness. "No, I mean, I think she likes Agesilaïdas very much."

"Well, that's lucky, isn't it?" Cercylas looked at me pensively, his grey eyes giving nothing away, his expression—it struck me, with sudden surprise—an unconscious parody of the grave, inscrutable mask which he attributed to Atthis. "She's so young. It would be so easy to hurt her."

I nodded. "I know," I said, "I know." The afternoon was warm still, but my clasped fingers felt, suddenly, as cold as ice. Cercylas got up, swinging the rolled-up book in one hand. He said: "I shall be dining in the City Hall tonight. A special invitation from Myrsilus. Now, what should *that* mean, do you think?" His eyebrows lifted in half-humorous resignation: it struck me then—not for the first time—that he knew a great deal which he never passed on to me, that there were whole areas of his life in which I had no part.

I said as demurely as I could: "It's no use asking me: try Aunt Helen."

"Heaven forbid." He grinned. "How did you acquire such formidable relatives, Sappho? There must be an art to it." I said nothing: this rhetorical question, I decided, was one that did not require an answer—luckily, since I would have been hard-pressed to supply it.

Cercylas hesitated a moment longer, then said: "Well, I must look at the accounts"—a remarkably lame excuse for him, I thought—and walked away down the colonnade, head bent as though in meditation.

I sat there a little longer, alone now yet not alone, remembering each minuscule detail of that momentous afternoon. When I arrived at Three Winds she was nowhere to be seen. Like a sleep-walker I embraced Ismene and Mica, curtseyed to Agesilaïdas, offered the gifts I had brought, conscious all the while of Melanippus' cool eye appraising me. There were drinks of sweet cordial and little sesame cakes and endless questions. It was only after an hour that I dared to say, as casually as I could: "Where's Atthis?"

Ismene smiled: "Oh, down in the orchard. She's been so strange lately, Sappho. I can't explain—remote, withdrawn, as though she weren't there at all, yet not unhappy—"

Mica said, with a touch of impatience: "Oh, nonsense, Mama, she's just at the age to go mooning about by herself: why do you pay so much attention to it?"

"Well, *you* didn't, my dear," Ismene said: I could well believe it. Mica's emotions were always kept alarmingly well under control. Agesilaïdas smiled reassuringly at his wife, as though to say: These girls' problems are now *my* responsibility. He was about the same age as Cercylas, and had, like him, a curiously ageless appearance: there was hardly a touch of grey in his thick-springing black hair.

Mica said, flouncing: "I'll go and fetch her, she's only trying to attract attention—"

I said breathlessly: "No, I'll go, Mica—I've got a bit of a headache, the fresh air will do it good—" which was, I suppose, an even more transparent excuse than Cercylas'. Mica looked surprised and a little cross; Ismene smiled in gratitude; Agesilaïdas gave me one quick, penetrating glance, then turned back to Melanippus. I slipped out of the house, picking up my skirts as I ran lightly down the garden to the orchard-gate, heart pounding, a dazzle of sunlight in my eyes, the air alive with murmurous bees and the heavy scent of roses and jasmine and honeysuckle. I knew where I would find her.

The swing still hung from the apple-tree, its ropes green with age: she sat there, almost motionless, except for a tiny to-and-fro pivoting on one down-pointed foot. Her hands were folded in her lap, and she seemed to be staring at the grass immediately in front of her: the coiled plait of deep auburn hair shone like burnished copper where the light struck it.

I stood there, trembling, throat dry, unable to say a word. Then she looked up, and her grave face broke into that glorious, transfiguring smile I remembered so well. She rose, arms outstretched, and came to me. Her every movement was simple, beautiful, certain. "My love," she whispered, "oh, my love: at last." As our lips met I saw, over her shoulder, a petal of apple-blossom, caught by some gentle spring breeze, circle slowly down to join the white drift in the grass below.

Something had died in Aunt Helen: that was the first thing I realized about her when we met again, and it gave me a far greater shock than I was prepared, at the time, to admit. The fact that she *looked* older had little to do with this impression. Aunt Helen today, in her mid-seventies, is still more striking, physically, than almost any other woman I know. But there was this strange absence, a sense of darkness, as though some inner light had gone out. The only other person who affected me in the same way (when I met him I did not know his past history) was an ex-priest who had broken his vows. Perhaps this was no coincidence.

The effect, I found, was to reduce our once-intimate relationship to something much more careful and distanced. Five years before I would have told her all about Atthis, for example: now the very idea of doing so filled me with acute distaste. As time went on I was forced to admit that on occasion I not only actively disliked Aunt Helen but was also a little afraid of her.

I find it hard to believe that her chequered sexual career was responsible for this change in my feelings: perhaps I underestimate my own prudishness, but I doubt it. I think, rather, that in my later childhood I had come to regard Aunt Helen as the embodiment of all aristocratic virtues, a person endowed with faith in much more than a circumscribed religious sense: and to find her following a course of increasingly shabby expediency during and after Pittacus' rise to power shook the foundations of my own world more than I knew. We had become almost literally strangers to one another.

So when she came round to see me, a few days after Cercylas had dined with Myrsilus, I was polite, deferential, friendly; but very much on my guard. There were too many unsolved mysteries between us, somewhere the truth had lost itself in a quagmire of private jealousies, political lies, and that lust for power which is so much stronger and more corrosive than any physical passion.

We made rather awkward social conversation for a while, and all the time Aunt Helen watched me, her great topaz eyes opaque now and heavy-lidded, her mouth set in those sharp, determined lines that are the signature, on a woman, of ruthless ambition and pride. There was a silver bowl of roses on the low table between us, I remember: one or two crimson petals lay scattered across the polished surface, like tiny shallops becalmed.

Aunt Helen said: "You know, I miss your mother. We never agreed about anything, but I respected her integrity."

"I miss her too, Aunt Helen. I think towards the end we were beginning to—understand one another."

Aunt Helen's eyes narrowed a little: I could see her trying to work out just how much I knew. She said: "Perhaps we only ever appreciate our parents when they're dead and can't annoy us any more."

"That's true." I smiled. "I don't think Mama *wanted* to be appreciated; at least, not by me. It was always when I felt most affectionate —and I did, you know, quite often—that she would, without fail, produce her most outrageously irritating tricks."

Aunt Helen picked up a rose-petal and sniffed it thoughtfully. "You're so like her, Sappho: do you mind my saying that?"

"Of course I don't mind: I know it myself now."

"Yes." She nodded. "Your exile taught you a good deal, didn't it?"

I smiled again: my fingers moved sensuously over the heavy linen folds of the new dress I had put on, for the first time, that afternoon. I said: "Should I be grateful?"

"Perhaps. You've come back a rather formidable person—distinguished poet, lady of fashion, political unknown quantity, married to a man who's just as charming and an even greater enigma."

I said: "Do I have Sphinx-like qualities? How delightful." Privately I was wondering just what Myrsilus had asked Aunt Helen to get out of me and when she would come to the point. There were one or two questions I felt like asking myself too.

Aunt Helen said abruptly: "When did you last hear from Antimenidas?"

"I had a letter just before we left Sicily. He was in Babylon then."

"And Alcaeus?"

I shrugged. "You probably know more than I do. He never writes."

"Perhaps not *letters*." Amused, I recalled the scandalous poem about Aunt Helen's sexual adventures which my mother had passed on to me. Alcaeus was rumoured to be the author, and the memory obviously still rankled.

"Oh?" I looked as blank as I could.

Aunt Helen said: "Supposing they were recalled from exile, granted an amnesty—do you think they could be relied on to behave themselves?"

So that was it. "But surely," I said, prevaricating, "the Council are responsible for such decisions. Why come to me?"

Aunt Helen shrugged. "In the last resort, of course, the Council must decide. But it's a difficult problem. You knew them both—perhaps better than anyone. You were in their confidence, you've heard from Antimenidas recently—you must have *some* idea of how they feel."

"Even if I do," I said, "I'm by no means sure it would be right for me to answer such questions."

"The Council would treat your opinions as confidential."

"I see," I said; and the pattern was, indeed, only too clear.

"Your own position is still a little anomalous," Aunt Helen said. "You're here on probation, as it were. This would be an excellent moment for you to show where your true loyalties lie."

I sat staring at the rose-bowl, considering the double-edged implications of that last remark. Since my return from Sicily I had carefully avoided any situation which might force me to declare myself.
I had cultivated a pose of individualism, emphasized my absorption
in purely personal relationships—and of course, to a great extent, the
pose was scarcely more than the truth. Now, abruptly, I had to
decide where I stood, to whom, if anyone, I owed allegiance.

By compounding with Myrsilus' regime, had I not forfeited the right
to oppose it? And did I, in the last resort, want to? Had I not moved
nearly as far from the aristocratic ideal as Aunt Helen herself?
No one, least of all myself, any longer believed in their heart of
hearts that the old days would ever return. Antimenidas had said
as much, on the day before that last, disastrous assault on the citadel.
To judge from his behaviour in exile at Pyrrha, Alcaeus had known
it too.

But would that knowledge alter their sense of irrevocable com-
mittal? I could not believe it then, and events proved me right. I
remembered Antimenidas' letter, his last, flat words in the council
chamber: *I am going to kill you, Myrsilus. By my head I swear it.*
The Gods, and his own pride, had condemned Antimenidas to a life
that could only end in tragic failure: there was no other way for him.

But Alcaeus, with his agonizing blend of political certitude and
physical cowardice, faced a still more nightmarish future—grumbling,
resentful, impotent submission to the regime he detested, and which
found him, not dangerous, but mildly ridiculous: a pathetic anachronism, a seedy, sodden, decadent aristocrat only tolerated because he
had once written a handful of good poems about flowers, and birds,
and the changing seasons, and similarly harmless topics.

Would it not, I asked myself, be wiser, and more merciful, to
deny these men the home-coming that must surely kill them? All I
had to do was express my honest opinion: that from the moment
those two landed on Lesbos, Myrsilus, if no one else, would be in mortal danger.

Yet Alcaeus and Antimenidas were my friends: could I, by a word,
condemn them—perhaps for ever this time—to the living death of
exile?

Aunt Helen's eyes were fixed on me, scrutinizing my least change
of expression. I think she thoroughly relished the dilemma she had
placed me in, the moral responsibility she was forcing me to face.
She judged my reaction shrewdly—just how shrewdly, I only found
out when it was too late. She was aware—more clearly perhaps,

than I was—of the complex, half-realized hatred I felt for Myrsilus: it seemed to amuse her. I only wonder, knowing what I do now, just why she felt so anxious to get my opinion: not for one moment do I believe that it can have carried any real weight with the Council.

No; I think that, for personal reasons I can only guess at, she was determined to implicate me in the chain of events which led from the Council's decision, and which—by answering her as I did, as she knew I would—I morally condoned.

I said: "The past is done with. Let them come home."

"If you were Myrsilus, would you say the same?" Her voice held a faint edge of mockery and something else, something I could not identify.

"I can only speak for myself, Aunt Helen."

She nodded. "So be it," she said.

The Council proclaimed an amnesty three days later. Cercylas happened to be outside the City Hall while the notice was being nailed up. He heard one labourer say to another: "Myrsilus getting cocky, eh? Thinks he'll live for ever." To which his mate replied: "I don't blame the old swine: never had a day's illness in his life. I give him a good thirty years yet." "Thirty more years of Myrsilus. Hades." That crude comment, had I but known it at the time, held the key to the entire mystery.

I cannot point to any precise moment in time when it could be said our group was formally established. On my return from Sicily I found myself much involved with the practical, artistic side of the city's religious festivals: I trained choirs and led them; I taught young girls the musical techniques I had learnt from Arion, I composed hymns and odes and the inevitable wedding-songs. A good many of these last were ready to hand: Syracuse is a long way from Mytilene, and I fear some of the citizens who commissioned an original composition as a mark of prestige were fobbed off, all unawares, with second-hand goods.

My reputation as a poet had preceded me, and it was then—with Cercylas' encouragement and support—that I put my first volume of verse, *Winged Words*, into circulation. One of the original copies lies before me as I write. There are a good many pieces in it I would like to suppress now (what writer does not regret his juvenilia?) but, I suspect, more through embarrassment at their naïvety than because of their technical deficiencies. At the time they were immensely successful, and I became a social catch as a result: though I suspect what intrigued most people was guessing the identity of my presumed lover from hints in the text.

Thus I became, almost without realizing it, the unquestioned leader of a group of friends, all girls, all with strong artistic interests. (For some reason Mytilene, unlike most cities, has few male artists: Arion, Alcaeus, one or two dull antiquarians. Antimenidas would have said, if asked, that this was due to our Cretan ancestry.) Atthis, Mica, and my cousin Meg formed the original nucleus. Telesippa would make occasional appearances, obviously not quite certain whether it was smarter to be seen with us or with the rival group under Andromeda's leadership, the most prominent members of which were Gorgo and her sister Irana.

Thus, already, conflicting tensions had been set up, cross-loyalties between group and family. Charaxus was my brother, but he was also Irana's husband and tended, rather surprisingly, to take on her prejudices or affectations. While Gorgo and Irana were enthusiastic supporters of Andromeda's so-called New Art group (which was, in effect, no more than a social off-shoot of the Myrsilus regime) their brother Ion, like his father—my uncle Draco, that is—remained staunch aristocratic conservatives. But Draco was also, through Aunt Helen, in the curious position of having Myrsilus as a brother-in-law. Social life in Mytilene could be very difficult at this period. Things have improved during the last decade or so, but every family still keeps its private list of people who must never, on any account, be invited to dinner at the same time.

So our group tended to attract like-minded followers, and thus to develop its own characteristic atmosphere. Friends introduced other friends, visiting guests from Miletus or Colophon or Lydian Sardis. Soon we found ourselves keeping more or less open house: every day there would be discussions, picnics, concerts, poetry-readings. Shy beginners would ask my advice, beg me to criticize their work. The movement was launched before we knew, in so many words, that a movement existed at all.

It was Cercylas who found the name for it: one day he came home to find nine of us sitting over nuts and fruit and twice-diluted wine arguing about Homer, counted the heads, and said: "I seem to have strayed into the house of the Muses. Ladies—goddesses, I should say—please forgive a mere mortal for intruding on your deliberations." We laughed and made him stay: the evening was a great success.

After that we developed the habit of inviting one, sometimes two, male guests to our formal discussions; and the title "House of the Muses" stuck.

When, much later, I came to be regarded as the talented, famous director of a highly exclusive finishing-school for girls of good family—an uncomfortable role, which I myself never completely accepted—it was at least as much to imbibe a way of life, a philosophy, that parents sent their daughters to me from all over the Aegean world, as to acquire mere practical or technical instruction in literature and the arts. Indeed, to begin with we had no plans for formal teaching at all. But it naturally happened that those with musical or poetic problems consulted me, and would-be painters took their difficulties to Mica: very soon the pattern of our relationships was established and went on, almost without change, to the end.

Of course, that pattern contained—as our enemies were not slow to point out—a strong erotic element. But then the same could be said for every profitable pupil-teacher relationship, where love, no less than pure reason, can enlarge the dimensions of human understanding. In particular, when I look back I see that the very foundation-stone of the House of the Muses was the love which Atthis and I bore one another—that bright, transfiguring passion that irradiated our whole world, the generous sun from whose light and warmth all who wished could draw sustenance. We were inseparable, happy in each other and our shared life, needing no other fulfilment.

Yet, oddly, we were not lovers as the world understands that much-debased phrase: not then. Those were the halcyon months of innocence. At any time, I knew, I could have taken the final step to complete and seal our intimacy; but always I held back, unable to explain this reticence even to myself, only knowing instinctively, without words, that such perfection was fragile and transient, a fine crystal globe ready to shiver into glittering dust at the first touch of— and there I pause, pen in hand, not wishing to stand self-condemned by setting down that hard word "reality."

Charaxus meanwhile had other ideas about what constituted the good life and highly individual methods of pursuing it. By dipping heavily into his (or, more accurately, Irana's) capital, he bought and fitted out one of the largest merchant-vessels ever seen in Mytilene harbour. He hired a crew, a good one, and paid them top rates. He then, without consulting either Larichus or myself, and by exercising his titular authority as head of the family, put aboard every last jar of top-quality oil and wine he could scrape together, stripping our personal reserves as well as his own for the purpose.

By the time we found out what he was at, the ship lay hull-down on the horizon, bound for Egypt: and Charaxus had gone with it. Everyone in the city said he was out of his mind: kind friends cheered Irana up with tales of pirates and storms and sea-monsters. To be quite honest, I don't think the death of her husband would have made much impression on that resilient little heart, but the prospect of losing her inheritance was almost more than she could bear.

So when, in due course, the look-outs reported Charaxus' merchant-man beating northward against the wind from Chios, most of Mytilene came crowding down to the quayside to see her dock. It was a bright morning in late autumn—too late, the pessimistic had said, for the long haul to Crete and the islands. But Charaxus' luck had held; and as the great bow-anchors went rattling down, and the heavy-laden, broad-beamed hulk swung slowly in to her moorings, I found myself more than a little envious of my brother's achievement, of the gamble that had succeeded against odds.

He came down the gang-plank, rubbing pudgy hands together, smiling, self-satisfied, and—unless I was much mistaken—even fatter than when he had left. His complexion, above that great black bush of a beard, still had the same unhealthy, lard-like pallor; he seemed mysteriously immune to sunlight, it was as though he had spent all his life underground. My envy, which had contained a streak of unwilling admiration, now turned in a flash to sharply hostile resentment. I have never known anyone with such a gift for getting himself disliked as my brother. He caught sight of me (I was in a group that included Larichus, Atthis, Ismene, and my cousins Agenor and Hermeas), waved, grinned, and vanished—clutching sheafs of what I took to be lading-bills—behind innumerable excited harbour-officials.

Presently he made his way across to us, sweating with exertion, triumphant, belly bulging through the folds of his new Egyptian-style linen robe. He was soused in some extremely powerful, over-sweet scent: Charaxus, I reflected, could make even prosperity seem offensive. His opaque black eyes flickered from face to face as he nodded his greetings to us.

"Well, sister," he said, "I presume you've rehearsed one of your less obliging speeches for the occasion."

"You had no right—"

"Right? I had every right. We'll talk about that later." He snapped dismissive fingers. "Anyway"—his face broke into a self-satisfied smirk that made me want to hit him—"hadn't you better wait to hear what your share of the profits comes to? Gold, I've found, sweetens feminine bad temper in the most remarkable way."

I said: "That's lucky for you, isn't it? I'm sure Irana will have a few interesting comments to make on the subject."

"I don't doubt it," Charaxus said equably. "But then, I know Irana. When she finds I've not only not lost her precious dowry, but nearly doubled it, she'll get down and lick the dust off the floor if I tell her to."

No one could think of an adequate comment on this remark, especially since we all had a nasty suspicion it might be no more than the literal truth.

Charaxus stared us out with brazen self-assurance. He had found a simple key to power and was now busily trying it on every lock in sight. His eye rested pensively for a moment on Larichus' blond beauty: it seemed unbelievable that these two could be brothers. From Charaxus' expression—a curious blend of the speculative and the lubricious—I began to wonder whether he might not be sizing Larichus up as a potentially profitable export for his next voyage. To judge by what I had heard of the Greek community in the delta—let alone of the Egyptians themselves—the profit-margin might well have been more than enough to overcome mere family scruples.

But all he said was: "I shall send you both a statement of accounts as soon as possible." Larichus and I looked at each other. Charaxus chuckled. "Don't worry; I can promise you a pleasant surprise." Then, brusquely, he turned to my cousin Agenor, and said: "Where's your sister?" Agenor's face was a dark, expressionless mask. "At home. Supervising the preparations for your arrival." "Good," Charaxus said, and rubbed his hands again. "Come on: we've work to do."

The two men walked off together: stride and waddle, long shadow against short, one of the most improbable working partnerships (if you could call it that) which I had ever seen. Hermeas stared after Charaxus' broad retreating back and spat noisily in the dust. No one else moved.

"Yes," said a light, drawling, familiar voice behind us: "I see what you mean, dear boy."

We all turned round simultaneously, like so many puppets. For a moment I did not recognize this tall, deeply bronzed traveller with the close-cropped hair and neat beard, the supercilious grey eyes. He leaned on a tall wooden staff that was carved with strange figures of beasts and Gods; at his heels, tongue lolling, crouched a huge black hunting-dog. He lifted one eyebrow fractionally at my hesitation, gave a brief ironic smile.

"*Alcaeus!*" I exclaimed, and impulsively held out both my hands. "Welcome home, old friend." The odd thing was that I meant it: we came closer in that unpremeditated moment than we had ever done before—or, alas, were ever to do again. "I'm sorry—I wasn't expecting to see you—and you look so different—"

"Let me return the compliment," he said. "At least, I hope it's a compliment." His five years in Egypt had left him, I noticed, with a slight but unmistakable foreign accent. His eye travelled over my striped silk dress, my jewellery, the ivory comb in my hair, the rings, the cosmetics. "The little island chrysalis has become a splendid dragonfly: a famous one, too. Do you realize I've heard Greek soldiers singing your poems above the First Cataract?"

I smiled. "How could I? You never wrote."

"No one writes letters from Egypt. It's another world. Nothing exists outside it."

"Perhaps you haven't changed so much after all: you still make the same plausible excuses."

"Well, now—" he said, and let go of my hands. I suddenly remembered that we were not, in fact, alone. Alcaeus moved forward to exchange formal greetings. "Lady Ismene," he said, and bent over her outstretched hand. "My congratulations on your marriage: your husband was a good friend to me in the old days."

Ismene nodded placidly. "Yes," she said, "I know." Just what did she know, I wondered: and did it matter?

Alcaeus turned to Larichus: "I would like to shake hands with you," he said, twinkling, "but I have a feeling you might strike me blind for presumption: I'm only mortal, after all."

Larichus was by no means averse to this sort of compliment: he lowered demure eyes and extended his hand palm downwards, as though inviting Alcaeus to kiss it. I began to see why he was so popular as a cupbearer at City Hall banquets. Not for the first time, I decided I must, even at the risk of a breach between us, have a really serious talk with my all-too-beautiful younger brother.

But Alcaeus, like the old campaigner he was, refused the bait: he shook hands briskly, and at once turned to Hermeas. Larichus scowled: a rather attractive sight.

Alcaeus said: "You don't seem to approve of your energetic cousin, Hermeas."

Hermeas said: "*Approve?*" His mouth twisted up as though he had eaten a bitter olive. "Could *you* approve of him?"

Alcaeus shrugged. "He's not my cousin. But you have my sympathy." Their eyes met. "I hope we'll see each other again."

Hermeas said slowly: "So do I. There are many things I'd like to discuss with you."

A faint, uneasy premonition stirred the surface of my mind and was gone.

"Of course." Alcaeus was amused, benevolent: had he sensed my mood? "The mysteries of Egypt. I shall obviously have to prepare a lecture on them. Private consultations for ardent young women in search of love-potions—closely followed by their mothers, enquiring about the secret of eternal life."

Atthis said quietly: "Is it true that the Egyptian priests know that secret?"

He turned, instantly responsive to her mood, his face serious and attentive. "Men believe so," he said. "Their belief is what matters."

But she would not be put off. "Do *you* believe so?"

Alcaeus hesitated. He said: "The priests die. Or appear to die."

Atthis stared past him at the bustling, noisy, colourful crowd that thronged the quayside: porters stooping under their heavy bales, water-carriers, talleymen, merchants, dark-skinned foreign sailors, laughing children, the old one-legged sausage-seller frying his wares over a charcoal brazier, crutch propped against the nearest bollard, both hands busy; waterfront whores, as bright as parrots, a thin-lipped market-inspector with his scales, the inevitable beggars and hard-luck men, their saurian eyes alert for some likely victim; the old blind woman with her basket of flowers.

She said hesitantly: "Don't you believe that if they *did* know the secret, you could tell it from their faces?"

"Perhaps." Alcaeus considered. "How would they look, do you suppose? What sort of expression does a man wear when he has seen into eternity?"

Atthis said: "I see his face as a living skull, eaten away by sadness, sadness past all bearing. I cannot envy him that intolerable weight of knowledge. Only the Gods are strong enough—and callous enough—to possess it with impunity." Then she blinked, as though waking up, ran one hand across her forehead, and burst out: "Good heavens, what a ridiculous way to talk. I'm so sorry. I can't think what got into me—" Her face broke into that radiant, heart-melting smile. With sudden tenderness I thought: She is only seventeen still.

"Please don't apologize," Alcaeus said gently. "For you, then, eternity is well lost?"

She nodded, eyes bright. Alcaeus glanced quickly from her to me, and back again.

"But you fear foreknowledge?"

"Yes."

He nodded. "Perhaps you are wise," he said, and then, with apparent irrelevance: "They say that the Helen who stood on the walls of Troy was only a phantom, fashioned from clouds, and sent there for the express purpose of provoking strife."

I said: "Where was the true Helen all this while?"

"Why, in Egypt. Or so the priests maintain. Their records, they say, go back to the beginning of time."

Again that uneasy premonition, like the first whisper of distant thunder, ran through me and was gone.

"Well," Alcaeus said, "there will be plenty of time to talk later." He smiled and inclined his head, formally polite. "I must see to my baggage. Please excuse me." He strode away through the crowd, a solitary, enigmatic figure. We saw him stop and speak briefly to a scarred, squat, weatherbeaten man, a mercenary by the look of him: then he was lost to view. The whole episode had been strangely dreamlike: I think all of us wondered, for a moment, whether he—like this new, disturbing Helen he spoke of—had really been there at all.

The picture remains undimmed by time, isolated in my capricious memory: their two heads, fair and coppery, bent together under a trellis of trailing roses, voices too soft for me to hear, Atthis' quick, warm, spontaneous laughter. She is dressed in white, there is a dark crimson ribbon in her hair. Larichus' skin gleams biscuit-brown, I can see the muscles slide in his arm as he gesticulates. Behind them is the orchard, a flight of swallows bickering overhead, blue sky ribbed with tiny clouds of carded wool.

They are so beautiful together that tears come to my eyes; the ecstasy is keen as a razor's edge, slicing through flesh and muscle, loosening all my limbs. I stand there on the last step above the rose-walk, speechless, paralyzed. Larichus is showing her something: a tiny bird, held in his cupped hands. My whole body begins to tremble uncontrollably, I can feel the cold sweat running down, my eyes darken, there is that hard, metallic ringing in my head as though I were about to faint.

Yet what I feel has no touch of envy or jealousy in it: only a yearning passion almost too intense to support, the knowledge that this moment is, for all its perfection, as transitory as those light summer clouds that have already changed their shape, are shredding out into wisps of vapour, merging with the milk-pale haze on the horizon—and an upsurging joy that my brother should share it, be part of its wholeness, should, now if now only, walk like an immortal. My love is boundless, it can contain the whole world, here, now, at this place and time—

But not eternity.

When the corn had all been gathered in, and heat danced over the stubble, when streams failed and flocks huddled for comfort under the cicada-shrill plane-trees at noon, Antimenidas came home from the ends of the earth, a Babylonian sword in his belt, his face burnt black by the desert suns of Judaea, an uneasy hero to walk our narrow streets, with a king's ransom at his command and the jagged scar down one cheek. Alcaeus wrote a triumphal ode to welcome him, and there was a good deal of cheering and flower-throwing down at the harbour when his ship put in. Presumably Myrsilus took due note of this popular demonstration, but—sensible as always—he did nothing about it. The amnesty had been granted, and that was the end of the matter.

"In any case," Alcaeus said, lounging elegantly on my day-bed, and cracking almonds with his strong white teeth between sentences, "soldiers back from the wars deserve a few flowers—not to mention the girls who throw them. And when did Mytilene last turn out for a hero's homecoming?"

I knew the answer to that as well as he did: after Pittacus' mildly comic campaign in the Troad. Our island is too rich, our climate too mild to produce a race of warriors—an accident which I, for one, have always regarded with extreme gratitude.

I said: "What do you suppose he'll *do* now?"

Alcaeus looked at me sharply. "Do? Nothing, unless he wants to. He brought back some quite fabulous loot from Babylon, you know. We're still sorting it out. Enough to keep him in comfort for the rest of his life, and—"

He broke off abruptly: I knew what he had been about to say—*his sons after him.* Neither he nor Antimenidas, though for widely differing reasons, had ever married. Now it looked as though the family, one of the oldest and most distinguished on Lesbos, might well die out for lack of an heir. I glimpsed an unlooked-for conflict in Alcaeus' mind, a guilty sense of failure, family piety set in the balance against deep natural repugnance and failing to tilt the scales.

As though reading my thoughts Alcaeus said: "Perhaps this is the better way. When the will to live is gone, let the good seed die out. What is left for us now or for those who come after us? Will our sons thank us for having brought them into a world where they live on sufferance, deprived of their birthright?"

"Who can tell? Have we the right to put words in the mouths of the unborn? Might they not cry out, despite everything, *Give us the light?*"

"*Have you never wanted to die?*" Alcaeus spoke with a sudden dreadful intensity, all the more startling by contrast with his normal cool, ironic manner. "Can you swear that you have never, *never* been tempted to kill yourself? Never known despair so great that death seemed a blessed release, the one true happiness?"

I stared at him, amazed. Then I said: "Of course I have known such despair. So have you, so have we all. But I am alive still, and you, and Antimenidas, and many others who have suffered as we have. That is an answer of a sort."

"Is it?" He dropped a nut and ground it under his heel with sudden violence. "How long do you suppose my brother will live? I can smell death on him like a lover's perfume. You've seen him, he has the sickness in his blood. He must go on to the end, do what he has to do, pray for a quick release."

I remembered the great seven-branched candlesticks in our bed-chamber, the legacy in blood and sacrilege which they bore. Then another thought struck me: my hand went to my throat.

"He gave me back the amulet," I whispered.

Alcaeus nodded. He said: "Can you still, here, now, maintain that you are truly happy?"

I said steadily, with conviction: "Happier than I have ever been in my life. Happier than I dreamed was possible." Then a tiny shiver ran through me: I remembered where, and to whom, I had spoken those words before.

Alcaeus said: "You sound as though you believe it. How odd. Were you happy when you married that poor devil Cercylas rather than stay in Sicily? Were you happy when you were deciding our future with that whorish aunt of yours?"

Stung and surprised—how on earth had he found out about so private a discussion?—I snapped: "Neither you nor your brother were above accepting the amnesty, I notice."

"Perhaps your motives and ours differed somewhat."

"That," I said, "is a matter of opinion."

"Just so. And in my opinion, my dear, your motives are very simple. You want to queen it in Mytilene; you want a rich husband, devoted admirers, a life of leisure, poetry, and private emotions. You want scope to indulge your luxurious tastes and your—interesting passions. I can admire that in a way: it's so single-minded. What irritates me is that on top of everything else you insist on presenting yourself as a sensitive idealist, a paragon of all the virtues. You're selfish and opportunistic to the core, and the most dreadful thing about it is that you honestly believe in your own innocence."

"Innocence of *what*? Even if all you said were true—which I don't admit—there are worse ambitions in life. What are you trying to tell me? That I've betrayed my friends, or the aristocratic ideal, or my father's memory? Is it so noble or virtuous to be a failed rebel, eternally mourning dead causes? We can't live in the past for ever. The old days are gone. Your brother knows that if you don't."

"But his reaction isn't quite the same." Alcaeus got up and began to pace to and fro in the colonnade. A pair of swifts swooped chattering down from their nest, and he watched them out of sight: he was passionately interested in all wild things, I recalled—another unexpected facet of his character—and on occasion spent days walking the hills, alone except for a favourite dog.

He said: "Sometimes, you know, I begin to think you're a little simple-minded. Or is it just that stubborn pride of yours? Or pure childishness? Or the fact that you're so obviously in love?"

I said nothing: there was nothing to say. Alcaeus stared at me with that passionate but detached absorption he displayed when watching a flight of widgeon or a nesting hawk. "Yes," he said, "love creates its own special obsessions and indifferences. To that extent it is, as tradition tells us, blind. But this blindness does not last. When I look at you and your demure little lover—"

"She is *not* my lover."

"How prim that sounds, Sappho! And how characteristic of you to make such fastidious, meaningless distinctions!" He shook his head. "Of course she's your lover. Whether you happen to have slept with her or not is completely irrelevant—and you know it. No, what concerns me is that you're living in a bubble, the pair of you, a self-deluding dream, and sooner or later you'll have to wake up. When

[225]

that day comes, as it must, there'll be a heavy price to pay—for both of you. But the responsibility will be yours alone. Think it over."

With slow deliberation he took one more nut, cracked it, spat the fragments of shell on the floor, nodded briefly, and was gone.

For two days I tried to put this meeting out of my mind, argue away the insidious accusations Alcaeus had brought against me. I told myself he was eaten up by jealousy and spite, a sentimental reactionary who lacked even the courage to uphold his own convictions. I raged and fretted; there was a wary look in my house-slaves' eyes when I came anywhere near them, the expression of a dog that expects to be kicked. Cercylas, with his usual consideration (or was it, I wonder, a form of emotional cowardice?) carefully avoided any reference to my mood, though I could feel it spreading through the entire house, as a cuttlefish will squirt out black ink in some clear pool, and for the same reason—to protect itself.

XIV

THE publicly known facts are simple enough and soon told. On a clear morning of late summer—records show that it was the second day following the great festival of Demeter—an escorted party, with horses, mules, and baggage-waggons, set out from Mytilene on the journey through the hills to Pyrrha. Since the travellers included the President and Joint-President of the Council, the escort was a full cavalry squadron, their armour specially polished, with banners flying, and much blowing of trumpets to clear lackadaisical cattle or country folk off the road ahead.

Myrsilus and Pittacus rode side by side near the front of the column, deep in some inaudible discussion: Myrsilus on his favourite black stallion, Pittacus astride a huge bay gelding that still seemed inadequate to support that massively dignified frame. Behind them came two mounted archers, and then what was euphemistically known as the Ladies' Waggon—a large, hard, uncomfortable cart in which Aunt Helen, Aunt Xanthe, Andromeda, Gorgo, Irana, and myself (not ideally suited travelling-companions, to say the least of it) sat on inadequate cushions and tried to make polite conversation while being jolted by an endless succession of ruts, rocks, and pot-holes. The gay, purple-fringed canopy overhead was some consolation but not much. I felt furious with Aunt Helen, who had firmly vetoed the idea of travelling by mule as "unladylike," and seemed quite impervious to the resultant discomfort. She chattered; Andromeda sulked; Irana, who was pregnant, showed signs of feeling unwell. The heat and tension and silent ill-will were quite unspeakable.

Behind our waggon—and suffering somewhat from the dust it kicked up—rode Ion and Pittacus' surly son Tyrrhaeus, who, I was glad to see, seemed to like each other's company as little as we did. Beyond them, again, were Cercylas and my uncle Draco, both of whom sounded irritatingly cheerful. My uncle's high, whinnying laugh kept ringing out at regular intervals, till at last Aunt Helen remarked that if her brother wanted to be a mare, he ought to sleep with his back-side facing the west wind—an unexpectedly coarse allusion, even for Aunt Helen, and no one quite knew whether to laugh or not. It struck me, with sudden surprise, that she was in a curious state of nervous excitement: but why?

The rest of the column consisted of grooms, cooks, stewards, valets, bakers (Myrsilus was fussy about his bread), and all the other hangers-on who attend upon travelling notabilities. We moved at the speed of the baggage-train, which was not remarkable.

Gorgo said to Andromeda: "Why in heaven's name should anyone—least of all Agesilaïdas—*invite* an official visit of this sort? I mean, he's not the ambitious type, is he, and even if he was, most people avoid it as long as they can and then try to look cheerful when the great man starts dropping heavy hints—" She broke off, conscious of Aunt Helen's predatory, hooded eye on her: she had spoken quietly, but not quietly enough. "Oh—I'm sorry, Lady Helen—"

"My dear child," Aunt Helen said, her voice full of sardonic amusement, "you haven't shattered any girlish illusions in me, you know: the phenomenon you describe is familiar and, I'm afraid, from my end of it, rather entertaining."

Irana, whose mulish taciturnity was punctuated, at irregular intervals, by indiscretions so breathtaking that no one could really believe them an accident (this, I imagine, was how Charaxus discovered about her legacy) now blurted out: "I suppose he wants a job for one of his old boy-friends: seems an expensive way of going about it, though."

Aunt Helen raised her eyebrows a fraction at this, and said, very sweetly: "My dear, you must be worried by the heat: it's bound to make you feel irritable in your condition."

The waggon gave a particularly violent lurch, and Irana turned an interesting greenish-white. Aunt Helen surveyed her with bland relish. "Your husband's away on another of his trading-ventures, isn't he? Of course you're anxious: it's only natural, especially with a first child—"

Irana leant over the side of the cart and vomited noisily. We all looked away and tried not to listen. I saw the road winding up ahead of us to the crest of the hill, white and dusty between woodlands, with patches of burnt brown scrub here and there, and one huge boulder tilted above an outcrop like a giant's gravestone. There were pines along the skyline, and beyond the road ran easily down to Pyrrha and the Gulf. A small hawk hovered, wings spread against the blue.

I saw Pittacus bend forward and put one gloved hand to his horse's snaffle, as though disentangling it: in doing so he dropped back a yard or two behind Myrsilus. We were just passing the first of the trees, in an eye-blinking dazzle of shadow and broken sunlight. A jay screamed: and then I heard something else, something like a sharp, hissing breath, abruptly cut off. Myrsilus jerked and twisted, arms out-flung, the purple cloak falling away from his right shoulder: in the instant before he fell I saw the long, black-feathered Cretan arrow standing out just below his left breast.

As the column plunged to a noisy, chaotic halt, Pittacus gathered up his reins short in his left hand, drew his sword, and swung the big bay gelding hard across the track to the right, the direction from which the arrow had come. At the same moment Cercylas spurred forward, as though to protect Pittacus, his horse's hooves crashing through brushwood, one hand lifted; and then that sharp, deadly sound came again, and I saw my husband clutch at his throat, blood pumping between a spread of fingers, and fall as Myrsilus had fallen.

No, I whispered, *no, please no,* as a child might do when some precious, irreplaceable toy lies shattered into fragments at its feet.

There was a great deal of shouting from the cavalry officers, but the words blurred in my ears. Half the troop crashed off through the trees, in useless pursuit of an enemy they had never even sighted. Mounted archers milled round our waggon, yelling at us to get down. Gorgo and Aunt Xanthe were flat on the floor already; Andromeda crouched with her head in her hands; Aunt Helen sat quite still, face frozen, eyes staring straight in front of her. It was impossible to tell, from that dead, expressionless mask, what—if anything—she was feeling.

Irana had not moved, either: she still stood hunched miserably over the handrail, retching in long spasms, indifferent to danger, conscious only of her intolerable nausea. The sight started a bubble of hysterical laughter inside me. Then, as this forced its way up, knifing into my half-paralyzed senses, I began unexpectedly to feel queasy myself. I lurched forward, bells swarming in my head, and my eyes closed on whirling, light-shot blackness. By the time I had recovered conscious-ness the column was clear of the trees and in full retreat towards Mytilene.

Pittacus, everyone afterwards agreed, had handled the situation with exemplary promptness and courage. The column suffered no further losses, though one arrow was found afterwards protruding from a tree, and another imbedded deep in the side of our waggon. It was a pity, people said, that the murderers escaped through the woods, but there was no doubt who they were, of course, despite their elusiveness. As Cercylas' widow I came in for a great deal of public sympathy—which increased still further when the fact of my pregnancy became common knowledge.

That same day, the moment news of the ambush reached Mytilene—or, according to some accounts, even earlier—a new drinking-song was heard in several waterfront taverns, which began:

> *Time to get drunk now, time for debauchery,*
> *Women and wine, since death's laid claim to Myrsilus—*

and, once again, rumour had it that Alcaeus was the author. But within twenty-four hours Pittacus had convened the Council in emergency session, and persuaded them to vote him special powers for dealing with an armed rebellion, of which Antimenidas and Alcaeus were mentioned, by name, as the ringleaders.

Afterwards he walked out of the chamber, wearing full armour, and made a short speech to the nervous, excited crowd that had gathered at news of the debate. Everything was under control, he told them. They need have no fear. Steps had been taken to prevent any lawlessness or anarchy. The crowd cheered him to the echo. It was only later that people began to realize just how far-reaching those special powers were.

Pittacus had been appointed first civil magistrate and military commander-in-chief, with right of veto over the Council and the authority to rescind any judicial verdict. Though his special office had been created to deal with a particular emergency, there was no time-limit set on it; in all but name he was tyrant of Mytilene, as absolute a ruler as Periander, with a special commission, moreover, to revise the city's laws and constitution. Now, at last, thirty years of concentrated, unswerving determination were to have their reward.

Three days later Antimenidas was trapped, at night, in the wild hill-country south of Pyrrha. He might have escaped, we heard, but for one of the Cretan archers who had come back with him from Babylon, and who—in a desperate effort to save his own skin—shot the rebel leader as he ran for the cover of the trees. So Antimenidas died at last, sprawled on a moonlit mountainside with a traitor's arrow between his shoulder-blades, his manhood and honour all wasted, the dream he fought for still unfulfilled.

Pittacus had the archer's head struck from his shoulders and impaled over the city-gate, as a warning to any others who might hope to win favour by betraying those to whom they had sworn friendship or allegiance. A gesture of this sort was just what was needed to restore public confidence: there had been ugly predictions of purges and mass-arrests, due, probably, to someone recalling Periander's behaviour when *he* won supreme power.

Pittacus also made himself a good deal more popular by the clever way in which he dealt with Alcaeus. The poet was tried in open court (the public benches had seldom been so crammed), and a poker-faced captain of mercenaries gave evidence about his arrest. The accused, he said, had been at home in bed. The arrest took place late on the night of Myrsilus' death—

Pittacus, stroking his beard in a lofty, Olympian manner, asked (what he must have known quite well) whether the accused was alone at the time.

"No, sir," the captain said, in his loud, flat, military voice. "There was a young boy, and a drunk soldier asleep on the floor."

"The boy was on the floor too?" Pittacus enquired.

"No, sir."

"Then where was he?"

"In bed with the accused."

There was some laughter at this from the public benches. Its tone seemed sympathetic rather than hostile.

"What," Pittacus went on, "did the accused say when told he was under arrest?"

The captain intoned, more poker-faced than ever: "He said, 'Just give me time to do this little passion-flower first, you great peasant.'" There was a loud guffaw from the back of the courtroom. "Sir," the captain added, vaguely aware of some implied deficiency in his presentation. The laughter redoubled.

Having skilfully reduced Alcaeus to a lecherous figure of fun, Pittacus, as presiding judge, made a short speech. The accused, he said, was not a man of action. Losing his shield once had been enough, and even that, some might infer, was a mere literary conceit borrowed from an earlier poet. (Everyone caught the reference: this was the tough poet-soldier Archilochus, whom several old men still remembered, and whose character formed a piquant contrast with that of

Alcaeus.) *His* weapons were words—and a bottle. The songs were more pot-valiant than their author. He, Pittacus, believed in suiting the punishment to the criminal. The brother of the accused had died, as he had lived, by violence. The accused himself merited a somewhat different fate. Since, alone, he had no strength to harm the city, he would be released with a reprimand—no execution, no renewal of exile—and abandoned to the scorn, obloquy, and contempt of his fellow-citizens. There was a good deal more in the same vein—absolute power tended to make Pittacus regrettably verbose—but this was his main point. Even at the time I wondered what lay behind it all.

After the prescribed mourning period and countless scandalous rumours, Aunt Helen actually did what the tavern wits had predicted: she married Pittacus. It was only then, I think, that the true pattern of these events became visible to me. Or was that, too, a mirage? When we peel the last layer from the onion, truth, what remains? Factitious tears; an emotional illusion.

But I must take the thread into the labyrinth.

I believe, now, that the death of Myrsilus was coldly planned by Pittacus and Aunt Helen in collusion. I believe they had never, in any real sense, ceased to be lovers; and that Aunt Helen married Myrsilus out of ambition indeed, but not quite in the way people assumed. She wanted, needed, to have his ear constantly, to worm all his secrets out of him. I believe the one false assumption she and Pittacus made was that Myrsilus would die in a reasonably short time of natural causes; and it seems very likely that Myrsilus himself spread this rumour by way of his personal physician, as a safeguard against political assassination. But somehow Aunt Helen found out the truth; and from that moment, I am convinced, Myrsilus' death became a foregone conclusion.

I believe that the exiles, Antimenidas in particular, were granted an amnesty in the express hope that they would themselves—from very different motives—do what Aunt Helen and Pittacus desired. I strongly suspect that Pittacus had at least one secret meeting with Antimenidas, and somehow managed to convince him that once Myrsilus had been removed, he, Pittacus, would work to restore the old regime—had, in fact, been secretly doing so since his apparent defection. It sounds flimsy; but Pittacus was a persuasive man, and idealists such as Antimenidas are always fatally prone to believe what they most desire.

I am convinced that—to make assurance doubly sure—Pittacus sub-orned Antimenidas' Cretan mercenaries. Even so, he must have had a bad moment on the road to Pyrrha, wondering whether the Cretans, with an easy target before them, might not decide to play for yet higher stakes, whether Antimenidas had not seen one further move ahead. I have no doubts, either, that the Cretan who shot Myrsilus down was privately offered a rich reward beforehand. Pittacus would not be the first ruler in Mytilene to gain virtuous credit by suppressing an awkward witness.

I wondered once whether Alcaeus did not betray his brother to Pittacus' patrols in return for a promise of immunity; today I doubt it. Of all the participants in that small, momentous drama he did the least—and thus, perhaps, had the most to hide. Antimenidas knew him all too well, and never, I suspect, gave him any real information about the plot against Myrsilus. Among the revolutionaries Alcaeus' role was that of the mere hired lampoonist: Pittacus' court verdict, in fact, came humiliatingly near the truth.

It is easy—too easy—to reduce human actions to an illusive appearance of simplicity. We are all, poets especially, incurable pattern-makers. Reading over what I have just written I am astonished at my own arrogance of judgment. I have drawn Pittacus as a devouringly ambitious tyrant *and nothing else,* as though man and function were identical. My strange interview with Periander should have taught me better—and of course, as every schoolboy knows, once Pittacus had attained supreme power he proceeded to defy all known copy-book maxims about "the typical tyrant"—all a mythical being whom I have yet to meet in the flesh.

Despite the way in which he acquired his authority, Pittacus was not corrupted by it. Nor did he become inordinately ambitious or cruel. He was not afflicted by delusions of grandeur. The worst that could be said about him was that in his old age he turned into the most terrible prosy bore, with an endless stock of Nestorian platitudes for the unwary.

He could be disconcerting too. One of his favourite aphorisms was "Know your opportunity." What, people asked each other plaintively, did one say in reply to *that?* But he never minded poking fun at himself. He passed a law doubling the penalty for crimes committed under the influence of drink: the story went that he signed the decree in so wine-flown a state himself that he was incapable of reading it.

For ten years he ruled Mytilene wisely and well, with a single-minded devotion to justice that no one could have foreseen. At the end of that time, with the city's laws and finances completely over-hauled, he surprised everyone yet again by resigning from office and handing over the government to a democratically elected Council. The rest of his life he spent pottering about the estate which was presented to him, on his retirement, by the grateful citizens over whom he had in theory "tyrannized." They even pretended to like the dread-ful didactic poems he composed for their benefit—a severe strain on anyone's benevolence, especially since he insisted on reading them aloud.

Yet he was not, I think, a happy man. About a year before his retirement his son Tyrrhaeus was murdered by a blacksmith in Cyme; the fellow marched into the barber's shop where Tyrrhaeus was being shaved and split his skull open with an axe. The public account of the affair claimed that this was a political assassination, committed by someone with the mistaken idea that Pittacus intended to found a family dynasty.

But no one really believed this. Tyrrhaeus, at least, lived up to the copy-book maxims; he was a typical tyrant's son—vain, weak, surly, lecherous—and the story which came back from Cyme was, quite simply, that he had been making love to the blacksmith's wife. Pit-tacus must have felt some deep sense of personal guilt over his son, because when the blacksmith was sent to him for punishment, he mumbled something about present forgiveness being better than fu-ture repentance, and turned his prisoner free.

Nor—and this, again, came as a surprise—did he have a happy re-lationship, ultimately, with Aunt Helen. Though she had been his mistress for so many years, her attitude to him was completely trans-formed after their marriage. She treated him with the sort of cold, haughty contempt that only an aristocrat can assume. She nagged, bullied, and scolded her husband till his only refuge was the wine-bottle. She made it quite clear that she had married beneath her. She encouraged Alcaeus privately to make rude lampoons about him, with vulgar allusions to his flat feet, his pot-belly, his untidiness, his dis-inclination to wash, his domestic cheeseparing (in later years he even grudged the oil for a lamp at dinner), and his swaggering conceit. Perhaps she had some cause for reasonable complaint; but what was it turned her into a mean, shrill, resentful virago? Poor Pittacus: in ways he paid dearly for his ambitions.

So the picture blurs and changes, shifts its proportions, reveals new, unsuspected facets. I still cannot be sure of anything, the search in the labyrinth leaves me twitching a broken thread. As with Pittacus and Aunt Helen, so with the rest. Did Antimenidas die for his beliefs, or—as he once, long ago, said of my father—because he no longer had any wish to live? Was Alcaeus a dedicated poet who became the pitiable wreck he is today through setting loyalty above expediency—or a shabby, posturing hedonist, using political defeat as an excuse for his sodden decline, a man without principles or self-respect, left clinging to two wholly sterile emotions: angry resentment and the continual nagging urge for sensual gratification?

Once I believed I knew the answers to such questions, even that— in accordance with the Delphic precept—I knew myself. Now my certainties are dissolving into air: the void engulfs me, all familiar landmarks have vanished, or taken on new, disturbing, ambiguous shapes.

So Alcaeus was released by the man who had once, long before, been his fellow-conspirator in adversity, and went home to young Lycus and a crapulous veteran called Bycchis he had picked up in Egypt and the wine-bowl's illusive consolations. On the whole his fellow-citizens treated him politely enough but left him alone. He still went for long walks over the hills. His lampoons became steadily more scurrilous and personal, crammed with obscene, spluttering invective. No one took any notice till after Pittacus' abdication, when he was warned several times about tiresome behaviour in public taverns and suddenly decided to go on his travels again. He wrote me several long, rambling letters from the Peloponnese, full of local mythology, queer legends picked up in mountain villages or lonely fishing-ports.

"Did you ever hear that Love was the child of the Rainbow and the West Wind?" one tattered, half-illegible letter proclaims. (I have to handle it carefully, or it will crumble into brittle fragments. Alcaeus always hated spending money on good writing materials—an unusual trait in a poet. Or perhaps I am justifying my own natural extravagance?) "A curious notion for horny Peloponnesian peasants to have got hold of, don't you think? In Boeotia, by the way, I found two new tales concerning your beloved Endymion. They know nothing there about his strange interlude in the Latmian cave (what sort of lover *was* the Moon, I wonder? As cold as she looks?) but claim that Zeus invited him up to Olympus, where he promptly made advances to Hera, or she to him—more likely the latter, I should think, it's strange the number of would-be seducers she collects for so staid and matronly a Goddess—and by way of punishment was hurled down to Hades, where, I don't doubt, he met quite a few fellow-victims.

"The other story is that Zeus let him choose the hour of his own death. How can one reconcile these two traditions? I sometimes have a vision of Endymion on Olympus, casting wistful glances at Hera through the bars of his cell, and telling Zeus, every day or two, 'Not yet, *you promised.*'"

The riddling Sphinx: the jester with a bundle of masks and a wounding word in season.

So many are dead now, my world cracks and slides like an old house when the first earth-tremors strike it. I think of my uncle Eurygyus, grubbing roots at midnight on the hills; of Phanias and my father, gentle men who died by the sword; of Chloe, white bones now under the burning soil of Sicily; of Irana, her young body so cruelly torn by childbirth; of Hermeas and little Timas, fever-racked in windy autumn; of Pittacus and Periander, who survived on their wits and died in their beds, revered as sages, praised by all men; of Antimenidas, who lived for honour and died so shamefully. These past months I have dwelt too much with ghosts: it is time to come up from Hades again, to breathe the living air.

I am small and neat in my movements, slender-waisted, elegant as a cat, bird-quick, a dancer still. He covered me with his hard male body, my breasts were burning flowers. I was Aphrodite, foam-born, immortal, and he my son, my lover, young as the returning spring, Adonis laid among the spears of green standing corn.

I must go, I must leave this place of death, so musty-yearning with old memories. I must follow the sun while I still may. Westward the bird flies, high and white over the barren mountains: there is, after all, a chance of freedom.

I began to lose Atthis on the day Cercylas died. In some strange way he was the shield of her innocence; our crystal sphere, so delicate and transient, remained inviolate only while he kept unobtrusive guard over it. When Atthis heard the news, she stood quite still for a moment, grey eyes wide with shock, hands at her breast. She was fighting, innocent and terrified, to control an emotion that I saw too clearly in her face: the primitive, almost feral joy of a jealous woman who sees her rival—against all hope or expectation—suddenly destroyed.

She did control it; for the next month or so I tried to pretend nothing had happened, that my imagination was playing tricks on me. But her love had become more openly sensuous, the grey eyes were suffused and dark with passion. She exulted now in her possession of me. I was hers alone: she would hold my love against the world.

But all the time I knew that this, too, was illusion. Half-waking, I still clutched at our dream, still sought (and found because I sought) the tokens of innocence in Atthis that had—like strong enchantments —held the daemons at bay. It was useless, useless. The crystal had cracked across, and in my own body lay the seed, the truth, that would leave nothing of it but a handful of glittering dust.

Yet even then I obstinately refused to admit that Atthis was so much less than the innocent dream-lover my mind had created—not only human, and a woman, but a jealous, solitary creature basked in the sunlight of my adoration, and matched my fantasy with her own, weaving a private world which we alone shared, intolerant of all in-truders, engrossed and engrossing. We were always alone together; never, except on formal occasions, with other friends. And looking back I realize how little, even in our shared solitude, we spoke to one another. Words were dangerous, could destroy, reveal.

Afterwards, it was different.

On a warm summer night, then, while the candle-flames shone soft and steady above the glow of the branching gold, and through the open shutters we could hear the sea's long murmur below us, I told Atthis that I was bearing Cercylas' child. For a moment she said nothing at all. We were lying on the great bed, a little apart, in thin shifts because of the heat: Atthis had her chin cupped in her hands—a favourite posture—and was staring out at the night, at the soft, blue-black, star-pricked sky where gods and heroes took their ease, where Orion and the Bear hung in splendour, a guiding sign for the ships that sailed their lonely ways by darkness, for all lost travellers on land or sea. Her face was in shadow: I could not tell what she was thinking.

She said at last: "It doesn't change anything," but her voice was flatly desolate. "It doesn't change anything," she repeated, as though to convince herself. I could feel her withdrawing from me, hurt, con-fused, and, yes, a little resentful: *how could I do this to her?* The candle-flames winked and dazzled: as I sat up a vertiginous dizziness spun my mind like a top, the walls tilted sideways. I pressed both hands hard into the bed, breathing deeply. No, I told myself, no, not now, I must be strong now, I must hold her. Somehow, whatever the cost, I must hold her—

[237]

Aphrodite, great Goddess, grant me this prayer. Grant me this prayer only, and I will be your servant for ever, till death loosen my limbs. Let her love me, let her love be undying, now, always. Grant this, and I swear I will honour you above all gods and goddesses, while I have breath. Aphrodite, great Goddess, Daughter of Heaven, I beseech you, give me a sign. Now, quickly—

And in the silence of my heart I heard the divine voice that was everywhere and nowhere say: *It is granted. She will love you, now, always, according to your prayer. According to my will and my decree. Let the Moon be the sign of it.* Then my head cleared, and I looked up, those unhoped-for words still echoing down the corridors of my mind. Atthis had not changed her position: she lay quite still, hands under her chin, gazing out at the night-sky. The darkness had a soft, hidden radiance about it: and as I watched, over the invisible rim of the Ionian hills, effulgent, haloed with glory, the moon swung up, so swiftly I seemed to trace its silent passage between one breath and the next. In that pale, unearthly glow, Atthis' features were suddenly revealed: a mask of white wax, mourning, pensive, with one glittering tear frozen on her cheek.

Aphrodite moved in me, a yearning, violent passion. I stretched out my arms. Atthis turned, and seemed, for a moment, to shake her head—a tiny, hesitant gesture, checked instantly. Her lips parted, and I saw the quickening rise and fall of her bosom. With slow, trembling intensity, her hands came out and clasped mine.

So, in that silvered darkness, I at last possessed Atthis: her narrow hips were mine, and her high white breasts, and the glory of her unbraided hair. We made love with a hard sensual violence of which I would never, in my long dream, have believed her capable. Then, at last, we lay still and naked in the moonlight, and looked at each other with new eyes: two grown women, sensuous, passionate, bound now by subtler chains than those of innocence, by the cataclysmic desire which is Aphrodite's coveted and deadly gift to mortals. *According to my will and my decree.* As, much later, I drifted into sleep—the moon was down now, the candle-flames guttering—I seemed to hear the Goddess' voice whisper: *Remember what you have sworn,* and then, faint and far away, a peal of thin, clear, cruel, childish laughter.

XV

O N O N E of those bright midwinter days that come just before the year's turning, I sat with Ismene, in her private chamber at Three Winds, physically uncomfortable—I was over five months pregnant—and emotionally, for several obvious reasons, more than a little uneasy. Ismene, sensing my mood, had given me some embroidery to do while we talked: it was an occupation which I had never much liked (I still don't), but for once I found it distracting. Besides, it kept my hands occupied.

Ismene said cheerfully: "Well, you're through the worst of it now, darling."

"So they tell me." I tried hard not to think of Irana. Her child had been born dead two months before, after a horribly protracted labour, and she herself had died in an hour or so, from loss of blood and heart-failure. "My brother wants me to live with him," I said carefully. "He doesn't think I should be left alone in my condition."

"That's only natural." Ismene was so apt to see the best in everyone that I sometimes wanted to kick her. "You've both had a cruel loss—"

"Oh, for heaven's sake. Charaxus didn't care a fig about Irana, and you know it. He got the inheritance: that was all he wanted. Now he's busy looking round for another heiress. Presumably to give him an heir."

Ismene said: "Why do you dislike your brother so?"

I shrugged. "I'm not sure. I've always found him mildly repulsive, and he seems to take a pride in cultivating all his nastiest natural qualities."

"But that's very unkind, Sappho, don't you feel?" Ismene's guileless blue eyes were full of cloudy concern. How, I wondered, had Agesilaïdas managed to domesticate her emotions in this odd, rather distasteful way? She was not sad, or anxious, or under any sort of obvious stress: indeed, her face was as placid, and almost as unlined, as a child's. But her hair had turned white between spring and autumn, and she gave the impression—I find it hard to explain exactly what I mean here—of having deliberately *relinquished her sex*. The result was a strange kind of neutral innocence, childlike again, so that there were numerous topics which, all at once, it became quite impossible to discuss with her.

I said: "I'm sorry. I suppose I *am* unkind. But I couldn't bear the thought of living in that house again. Especially now."

"We're all rather worried about you, my dear. You've been so moody and strange."

I bent my head over my embroidery and thought: I wonder what *you* felt when you were pregnant? Nothing, I suppose. Except what tradition told you you could feel. Did you ever wake up and realize that you'd been invaded by an alien personality, that you'd lost your will, become nothing but a seed-pod, a cockpit for explosive natural forces? Of course not. You wouldn't understand a word of it if I told you, either. Why am I here? Why am I talking to you, of all people?

"I'm sorry, Ismene," I said, and reflected that I spent a good deal of time, just then, apologizing to thick-headed people for words or actions that needed no excuse. Then, changing the subject: "When are Mica and Melanippus getting married?"

"Late spring, we thought. There's so much to do over the estate—"

"You really *are* going to sell, then?" I still somehow couldn't accept the idea of any change at Three Winds. Sitting in this familiar room, so charged with memories, so tranquil and reassuring—the same scent of herbs, the same old, heavy, well-waxed table—I felt as though one of my life's foundation-stones was about to be knocked away.

"Not the house, of course. Or the gardens, Hippias will have them when he comes of age." Hippias was eleven years old then, a fair, slender, grey-eyed boy, with an uncanny resemblance to both Phanias and Atthis: I liked him very much.

"What about the orchard?" I asked.

Ismene said: "Well, we had a very good offer, you see—" She broke off, blinking with mild embarrassment. "A big fruit-farmer. I doubt if you know him—"

"So do I."

"And the capital would be so—I mean, we do need it, and the

orchard won't be any real use to us, we're planning to live in Pyrrha after Hippias—" Her voice trailed away. After a moment she said: "Are you feeling all right?"

"Yes. Yes, of course." I blinked, and just managed to stop myself saying "I'm sorry" again.

"You do understand, don't you? I know the orchard had sentimental associations for you—"

I stared at those guileless blue eyes, that smooth, uncomplicated face, and thought—irritation and guilt curdling in my mind—that innocence, or ignorance, of this magnitude ought to be treated as a criminal offence. How could I ever, ever hope to talk to Ismene about Atthis?

"Yes," I said, "I understand."

"You've been so kind to Atthis. We're really grateful. Sometimes I feel"—she gave a tiny tinkle of nervous laughter—"that she needs more than I, her own mother, can give her. She's a strange child. I've never understood—" Ismene broke off again; her thought-processes tended to have this random, truncated, wandering pattern, which in the end, however, generally added up to some sort of coherent statement. I waited, with as much patience as I could. "Yes?" I said.

Ismene patted her hair. "Well, it's so difficult for you now. We wouldn't want you to have the extra bother." The seeming irrelevance hung in the air between us.

"I don't understand." In fact, I understood now all too well.

"Atthis told us you'd been"—she made a little hesitant gesture with one hand—"upset. Please don't suppose we want to pry, my dear. But we have Atthis' welfare very much at heart. We couldn't help noticing that you'd, well"—again the slight hesitation—"seen a good deal less of each other recently—"

"Yes." I made no comment.

"She said she thought you were under a great strain. She was very understanding, Sappho." Ismene looked straight at me, the mildest hint of reproach in her eyes. "You must realize how attached she is to you, how much she has come to depend on your love and support and example—"

"Of course I appreciate that," I said. Just what, I wondered, had Atthis told her? And what could I tell her now? To put the blame on immortal Aphrodite? *She will love you, now, always, according to your prayer*—oh yes, that was true, and more than true: her devotion remained constant and uncomplaining, her passion grew from day to day, became deeper, more violent. But my prayer, characteristi-

[241]

cally, had made no reference to my own affections: *their* constancy had been taken for granted, and the Goddess was now administering a sharp, salutary lesson to me.

The plain truth was that, at this period, I could hardly bear to have Atthis anywhere near me. Partly because my own swollen body filled me with such repulsion that I shrank from letting her see, let alone touch it, and partly because (in my semi-hysterical state) I found her childish, self-centred, and quite unbearably demanding, I began to treat the poor girl in the most unforgivable fashion. I was by turns abrupt, cold, imperious, and irritable. I lost my temper with her, rejected her tentative advances, snubbed her intellectual pretensions, took her many kindnesses for granted, and attacked her furiously whenever she gave me the slightest opening. She bored me so much at times that I found myself wondering what on earth I could ever have seen in her. Finally, after a flaring, hysterical quarrel, I told her to get out and stay out, to leave me alone. With sad, bewildered reluctance she said: "If that's what you really want—" and went away like a beaten child, weeping, unable to understand how love could suffer such humiliation.

I know too well now that it was self-hatred which drove me to this cruel, meaningless, despicable behaviour. Atthis was the living embodiment of my destructive egotism: it was myself I could not bear to face. *This blindness does not last,* Alcaeus had said, and now, in her chosen time, the Goddess had opened my eyes. Atthis was right to fear foreknowledge. Bitterly I recalled Alcaeus' parting words: *The responsibility will be yours alone.* My prayer had been answered, and one human life given an irrevocable twist by it. Now I was left with the consequences of that fulfilment.

I said to Ismene: "I think we got on each other's nerves a little— it was all my fault, I haven't been myself for the last few months—"

"Of course. That's very understandable."

"I'm quite sure it'll be all right again—later."

"Can I tell her that?"

I smiled. "By all means."

"I'm so glad. I thought—I don't know—" Her mind trod delicately round the approaches to some dark emotional forest, took fright, and hurried back to the open, sunlit plain. "But if it's just your feeling upset and ill and wanting to be alone—well. That's good. I'll tell her."

"When are you going to Pyrrha?" I asked.

"Oh, in two or three days. I do so hope she's enjoying it there. They say a change of air can work wonders, don't they?"

I nodded.

Ismene said: "What she needs most is some fresh interest, don't you agree? Young faces, new friends."

"A very sound idea."

"You know—you will forgive me saying this, won't you, my dear? —at times I did feel there was something a little, well, *morbid* about the degree of her attachment to you. Perhaps this separation may be for the best in the end, help to give her, I don't know, a sense of proportion, would you say?"

At this point I began to wonder uneasily whether Ismene was quite the simpleton she appeared. But all I said was: "Perhaps; I do hope so. It would make me feel a little less bad." And that was no more than the plain truth.

She picked a loose thread out of her embroidery, and said, without looking up: "You remember my cousin in Lydia? I think you met her here once—"

"Polyxena?" I had a blurred recollection of a tall, dark, rather striking woman, married to a well-connected Sardis merchant whose beard, rings, dress, and scent had all been a little too exotic for Mytilenean taste.

"Yes, that's right. Well, I thought it would be pleasant for her two daughters to come and stay for a while—Atthis does so need friends of her own age, and somehow she's never got on very well with the other girls here, I don't know why—" Ismene's voice trailed vaguely away again.

"I'm sure," I said, "that you've acted for the best."

"I think so too," Ismene said placidly. "Well: I mustn't keep you here chattering. You need as much rest as you can get." She put down her embroidery, and so did I. We looked at each other for a long moment.

I was still wondering just how much she knew, or guessed, when —furred and gloved against the winter wind—I stepped into my waiting carriage and rattled away down the drive. To this day I have not made up my mind. But one thing I do know: by bringing Anactoria and Cydro to Three Winds, Ismene, all unwittingly, did more than any other single person to turn an amorphous group of likeminded friends into what is remembered today as the House of the Muses.

Anactoria's portrait has the red rose in her hair, as it was on that first day we met. Mica caught all her most elusive characteristics— the secret, glinting smile, the near-transparency of skin, the oddly elongated features and hands that might, in another girl, have looked awkward, ugly even, but in her merely served to enhance a rare and delicate beauty. She was tall and looked taller because of the black tresses she wore piled on top of her exquisitely shaped head. Cydro, by contrast, was short, plump, excitable: a generous, outgoing character whose passions and enthusiasms sometimes seemed to be compensating for her sister's all-too-perfect self-containment. It was strange to see that luminous, alabaster-like complexion—the one feature they both shared—on so wildly inappropriate a face.

My daughter Cleïs was born with the first spring flowers: out on the hills, as I lay in labour, I could hear the thin crying of lambs, and under the eaves—earlier than for many years—a pair of swallows bickered and preened, old friends that I had come to know, in a way, better than many human acquaintances. (But then, swallows are mysterious creatures, oddly human themselves, with their absurd family quarrels, their speechlike chirruping, their inexplicable tameness, and the uncanny ability they display, on occasion, to penetrate one's moods—even, I sometimes think, one's thoughts.)

It was, against everyone's predictions, a quick, easy, and surprisingly painless birth. When Praxinoa placed the child in my arms— this miraculous creation of flesh, this no-longer-part of my most intimate self—I felt a physical upsurge as total and as overwhelming as that experienced during the act of passion, with something more, a tenderness that reached out to embrace the world, that transcended the prison of my inturned mind.

This was my daughter, my love, my immortality. Gently I stroked the damp wisps of fair hair, and sensed, under my fingers, that soft, throbbing centre where the skull's bird-thin bones had not yet drawn together, where beneath one stretched membrane the vital spark flickered so precariously. When those tiny lips closed, with instinctive knowledge, about my nipple, when the warm milk flowed, I experienced an indescribable agony of pleasure: I was all mothers, I was life itself, rich, inexhaustible, the force that moves corn-ear and rutting beast, the slow tides and the circling summer stars, the poet's song, the dance of creation.

Too many ghosts, too many aching memories. I sit in this empty, mourning house, while the shadows lengthen, and fear, like some faceless beast, lurks behind a closed door.

The pains have begun again. Now, yes, and now, and now again,

[244]

the squeeze of giant claws. Cleïs, ah Cleïs, I loved you more than life, my golden daughter—no, not more than life, because it was life, my life, my own vanished youth that I fought for with such blind frenzy, all other considerations cast aside—even your love. I wanted to defy time, prove myself immortal. But all I can see now are your eyes when you knew what I had done to you: the hatred, the half-incredulous contempt. *Hippias?* you whispered, and suddenly I felt old, wrinkled, dirty, full of shameful lust, without dignity, ridiculous.

But he wanted to marry me; he pleaded, he wept, Cleïs; did he weep at your feet, Cleïs, did he clasp your knees? Did he praise your body as he praised mine?

Hippias was yours; he loved you, and I took him as I had, years before, taken his sister: when we were together it was Atthis' eyes that looked into mine. I made him my slave, I thrust him down into the lime-pits of desire. I was Circe, Medea, Calypso, a strong enchant-ress, with a wand to break the years.

Can you forgive me, Cleïs?

Can I forgive myself?

Too late, too late, too late.

Too many ghosts, the running feet, the laughter, the pleasure-filled days and years, moments of shared tranquillity in the garden, sunlight under trees, a saffron-yellow robe, roasted nuts for breakfast in au-tumn, a moonlit altar and the rapt face, never forgotten, of some nameless girl leading the dance; warm lips in darkness, flower-scented hair against my cheek. Ghosts, lovers, all gone now—Gongyla who was like a wild rose, quick-moving Hero, Gyrinna beloved of the Muses, Timas who died so young, Eunica of the soft, adoring eyes, dark Anactoria, laughing Cydro—beyond the wash of the sea, down the quicklime years that scar and erode, gone, all gone, brittle leaves blow-ing in drifts under the great chestnuts, the waved handkerchief, the ship sliding out and away from the quayside, prayers for safe land-fall on journeys long forgotten, crumbling, time-worn letters, withered coronals.

When summer turned to autumn—do you remember?—I came back to you, Atthis, to your soft arms that I had shunned for so long, to your yearning tenderness and your passion. If this night could be twice as long, we prayed, if our love could endure for ever—But before the year's turning it was over again, this brief and agonizing reunion, leaving behind it bitterness, misery, broken promises and perhaps a broken heart. Who was to blame? Why did it happen this way?

Did I come back because I loved you, Atthis? Or was it from mere pique and hurt pride, the need to be irresistible, a Goddess, Aphrodite in mortal guise? *Violet-tressed, holy, honey-smiling—Sappho:* again, it is Alcaeus' voice that returns to mock me, words spoken by a pool in a sunken garden, a life ago. Goddesses—as I know, now, to my own cost—can brook no rivals. But the whispers, the sidelong glances, the snickering laughter among Andromeda's followers: Anactoria, Atthis, and Anactoria. Anactoria, Anactoria—

"Do you love her?" I asked, that first momentous night. "Do you love her?" And Atthis sadly, her passion spent, knowing me perhaps better than I knew myself: "It's you I love, Sappho. Always you." *Look,* I seemed to hear the Goddess say in cold amusement, *how scrupulously I have kept my word.* "I'm no good to you," I said. "You should stay with Anactoria. I can only bring you unhappiness, my darling." And she said: "If you want me to be her lover, Sappho, if that will give you happiness, then I will. But only for your sake." "And to satisfy desire," I said cruelly.

"Yes," she said, "to satisfy desire: empty, meaningless, torturing desire. Have you seen them slake lime, Sappho? Do you know the barrenness, the burning of it, the bone-consuming death by water and fire?"

"Hush, my sweet," I whispered, fearful suddenly, thrusting this dreadful image away, "don't talk like that, you don't know what you're saying—" and I took her in my arms again and felt her respond with a violence that had something desperate about it: it was as though she had consciously abandoned all hope of happiness.

"I love you," I said over and over again, "I love you, I love you—" as though mere repetition could, spell-like, exorcise the daemons of doubt and terror in my mind. Strange, that it was then the bright years began, the long summer of happiness and fame.

How easy it is to forget the summer storms!

There were further reconciliations, further quarrels: our relationship seemed set for ever in this soul-destroying, inconclusive pattern. Never, I think, did I seriously consider the possibility that it might change, let alone be ended. But one autumn day, five years ago, during yet another racking, hysterical exchange of insults and bitter recriminations, Atthis suddenly broke off, put her head in her hands, and sat there quite still and silent for a moment. Then she looked up, her face as expressionless as I had ever seen it, and said, with quiet finality: "I'm leaving you, Sappho."

I heard the words, but my mind refused to accept their meaning: how much, while pursuing my own inconstancies, had I taken *her* faithfulness for granted over the years?

I said stupidly: "Do you mean you no longer love me?"

She shook her head. "I still love you," she said. "I shall always love you." Her eyes suddenly were bright with tears.

"Then why this? Now?" My anger had evaporated, leaving only bewilderment behind.

Atthis said dully: "Because I can't stand any more. I've reached the limit of my endurance. Just that. Didn't it ever occur to you that I was human, that I had a breaking-point?"

I shook my head, shocked into unthinking frankness: it was true, I had never treated Atthis as a free, individual being, she was part of my self-created universe, just as I—bitter irony—was part of hers.

"No," she said, with a sad little smile, "of course it didn't, how could it have done?" Then the tears welled up, and for a moment she wept, silently, hopelessly. "Do you think I *want* to leave you?" she whispered, after a moment. "Do you suppose it's easy for me, now? In two months, less than two months, I shall be forty. I look into my mirror and see the future written there: darkness, waste, decay. What I am, you made me. Without you—" She spread her hands in a tiny, hopeless gesture. "But I have no choice, my love. This is my only chance."

I stared at her as though I were seeing her for the first time, jolted into a fresh awareness, torn with pity by the signs of age which for so long I had, somehow, managed to ignore: the almost imperceptible change in the texture of skin and hair, the dulled brightness, the deepening lines round eyes and mouth and throat. I thought: I am still the child who ran through the green corn-fields of Eresus, nothing must change for me, the world is poised timelessly in that bright dream, the shadows stand still for ever. Until I awake. Until we both awake.

What I am, you made me.

We looked at each other for a long moment in silence. Then I heard my own voice say, very gently: "Go then, my love. Go freely, and with my blessing, in friendship."

She smiled through her still flowing tears. "You mean it, don't you? You really mean it. Thank you. I must. I don't want to, I—oh, Sappho, I can't find words—" She bent her head and sobbed openly now, without restraint.

I said: "I only ask one thing of you. Don't wipe the past from your mind. Don't blacken our love with hatred. Whatever you say, whatever has happened, despite the anger and the bitterness, I did love you, Atthis. I love you still."

She looked up, anguish in her eyes.

I said: "Our love was good: never forget that. It was precious and beautiful, it enhanced life. Remember all we did together over the years, all we talked of—" and then suddenly, in an agony of nostalgia, I began to recall this incident and that, moments of laughter, the happy memories, garlands woven in springtime meadows, expeditions, home-comings, private shared intimacies—"Do you remeber when—?" till at last she said: "Please—don't make it more difficult for me—" and, filled with remorse, I fell silent.

At last I said: "Where will you go? What will you do?"

"I don't know," she said.

"You have Three Winds still. That's comfort of a sort."

"Is it? Now?" The sudden bitterness in her voice took me aback. She gathered herself together with a conscious, visible effort and said: "I may as well tell you now. You'll hear about it soon enough, I don't doubt. I'm—going to Andromeda."

The ground seemed to slide and lurch under my feet: for a moment I thought in a wild way that this was the onset of an earthquake, that we would both be killed—supreme irony—at the very instant we had chosen to part. Then, as I steadied myself, I heard Atthis saying: "I'm sorry. I know how it must seem to you. Please, *please* try to understand—"

"Yes," I said, "I understand."

What I am, you made me.

It was as though something solid and physical had broken inside my body. I thought senselessly: *Andromeda has driven a fine bargain, a fine bargain, a fine bargain—*

Atthis walked to the door, with that quick, springy step of hers, paused, turned, whispered, "Good-bye, my love," and was gone.

I felt my thumbs curl inside my clenched fists, like a small, miserable child's; and it was a schoolgirl phrase, almost comic in its inadequacy, which had to bear the full burden of my grief.

"Honestly," I told myself, "honestly, I wish I was dead—" So might Cleïs, now sixteen, have greeted the end of another minor flirtation.

I do not know how long I sat there, numb, mindless, before the first pain knifed through me, with such sudden violence that I screamed aloud, and I became aware, in agony and horror, of the warm blood flowing, as though it would never stop, as though it were my life that lay spilt across the marble flags.

I must have fainted, because I woke to my daughter's horrified scream, saw her face bent over me, framed in a cascade of golden hair, saw the terror, the instinctive physical repulsion, the mouth strained in an ugly rictus as she screamed again, and the scream broke, changed into loud hysterical sobs.

I whispered, smiling: "It's all right, darling. It's all right." I think I must have been wandering a little, because I suddenly said: "Oh, please, Cleïs, do stop making that dreadful noise, it's so out of place here, my darling. Never forget, this *is* the House of the Muses." Then Praxinoa's face was there too, black hair against gold, and I heard the sound of shouts and hurrying feet just before my eyes darkened and I fainted for the second time.

My mind is made up. I must go, now, quickly, alone: leave Mytilene, take ship to Corinth and thence once more to Sicily. It is a forlorn hope, but there is no other way for me. I ache for his hard, faithless body: that is all of life that remains, the rest is dust, despair, broken dreams.

XVI

NOTHING has changed in Corinth to the outward eye: old men still sit playing draughts and drinking under the plane-trees, ships are still hauled, black and cumbersome, over Periander's great slipway to the Gulf. In these crowded, clamorous streets, down by the docks or beyond, at the throbbing heart of the city, where armourers and potters and goldsmiths ply their trade, you can still hear the tongues of every land spoken, still brush shoulders in a dozen yards with Moor and Numidian, Greek and Arab, Egyptian merchant or dark-bearded Phoenician sailor. Periander is dead now and his seemingly impregnable dynasty fallen; but Corinth remains what it was, the city of ambition, opportunism, and anonymity, where a tide of faceless, soon-forgotten travellers daily ebbs and flows across the Isthmus. For the anonymity at least I have nothing but gratitude.

These words are being written in a dark, uncomfortable waterfront inn, which bears above its main door the sign: Accommodation available for unescorted women." I know very well what this means —in Corinth, of all places. But I have no choice: I cannot afford to be recognized. In any case it is for two nights, no more, and then I sail at dawn on a fast Sicilian galley, Syracuse-bound with mails and packages from the East. We have one scheduled stop only, at Leucas, just outside the Gulf, to pick up fresh water and provisions. I am in luck: the weather may break before the end of the month, and this will be one of the last runs to Sicily until next spring.

When I first approached him the captain looked at me curiously, recognizing my accent, impressed by my manner: why was this strange, small, middle-aged lady from the islands so desperately anxious for a passage to Sicily? Why was she travelling alone, without so much as a maid in attendance on her? His doubts translated themselves into a price which even he seemed half-ashamed to mention. But I paid it without argument and in gold pieces. Knowing my own spend-thrift nature too well, I had, soon after becoming a widow, hidden away a secret reserve: not even Charaxus, for all his financial nose, had suspected its existence. Only Phaon, all unknowing, could turn the key in that rusty lock.

So I sit here in Corinth and write, by the flame of one smoking, ill-trimmed lamp, while, outside, the tavern next door is loud with drunken singing—a crew has just been paid off—and prowling cats scream in angry passion among the refuse. The shutters are barred, but there seeps through them the smell of tar and decaying fish and meat being grilled over charcoal. I can hear a woman's shrill, drunken laugh, the thrum of a lyre, water slapping and knocking against the quayside.

Footsteps go past in the passage, there is whispering, the chink of money, the creak of stair-joists. A moment or so later I realize that someone is making love with noisy abandon immediately overhead. Detached, remote, I listen: how grotesque the rhythms and utterances of passion seem to the onlooker! Yet it is for this that I, too, am here. I find myself smiling at the thought.

Soon the invisible lovers—lovers?—reach their climax: a silence falls, and then those slow, dragging footsteps come back down the stairs. A door opens and shuts. Boots ring on the cobbles. A pause, the sound of heavy breathing. Then, abruptly, a loud belch, a tearing, torrential flow of vomit, a groan, a muttered curse. The footsteps lurch away into the night.

The innkeeper's wife has just opened my door without knocking: to see if I want anything, she says, but in reality to make sure I have not, somehow, smuggled a man in behind her back, without paying for the privilege. She is a fat, hideous slattern of fifty or so, with a wart on one cheek and a cold, lubricious eye. She stares at my writing materials suspiciously. "Making up your accounts, then?" she asks. I nod in agreement: a very fair description of what I am doing, I feel. I send her out for a better lamp: she goes reluctantly, still not sure whether there may not be a man hidden under the bed. Besides, I intrigue her: such guests must be rare on the Corinth waterfront.

As she shuts the door it strikes me that we are about the same age: yet she clearly expects me to have a lover. A compliment, of a sort: no one could imagine *her* attracting any man's attention. Or—sudden and unpleasant thought—does she take me for one of those elderly matrons who will pay well to get the perfunctory embraces of some supercilious, hatchet-faced youth? And could she, I ask myself, be right? Hitherto I have always pitied and despised such women, sad mortal nymphs in whom beauty has faded, yet desire remains strong: yet are not they, too, victims of Aphrodite's cruel caprice? Am I not ready, if all else fails, to offer what they offer, to buy the passion I cannot command?

But Phaon never took money from me, never, never, though the Gods know he was poor enough. What he did was done out of passion and desire: I know that, I must hold fast to the certainty. Or did the Goddess touch him, too, with her cold enchantment? I asked him once, laughing, as we lay together in the cave above Mytilene, how he had acquired the secret of eternal youth. He was older than he looked, well into his thirties despite that hard, brown, unlined face and the thickly waving chestnut hair: perhaps more, if gossip was to be believed.

He stirred, and sat up away from me, big hands clasped round his knees: the moonlight, streaming straight into the cave, shed a pale radiance on his broad, naked shoulders and breast. It was impossible, listening to that deep, burred voice of his, to tell whether he was joking or in earnest.

He said: "Now there's a thing, darling: and it's a queer tale too. This is how it happened. One evening a filthy old crone came aboard my boat in harbour, a real bundle of black rags, and said, would I ferry her across to the mainland? Well, I hadn't much to do that night, no trade and the shoals weren't running; and besides, there was something about the old creature, the eyes in that walnut face of hers, so black and bright, every time she looked at me I felt a shiver go through me, and the short of it was I said I'd ferry her over for nothing."

I lay quite still, listening: behind his words I caught the gentle drip-drip of the spring, and far below a donkey suddenly brayed in darkness, a long, yearning, agonized note.

"When we landed she thanked me, and then she said she wanted to give me a present, and I said I needed no present, she should keep it and buy herself bread. The gift was hers to bestow, she said, and I should have it, and the way she spoke made the hair rise on my neck, it was the command of a queen, or a Goddess. Then she put a smooth stone jar into my hand, a small thing, beautifully curved, fitting the palm so that it was a pleasure to feel and hold it, and she said, You will be grateful for this, and I stroked it with my fingertips and it seemed like alabaster to the touch. I said, What's in it, then?—expecting honey, maybe, or wintergreen for a sore bruise —and she said—it was dark now, by the bye, and I couldn't see her face too clear inside that black hood—she said, A salve to bring you your heart's desire, Phaon, youth and beauty, the love of women. What must I do? I asked, and she said, Smear it on your lips and your breast and your manhood, speaking the woman's name, and this secret prayer—which she taught me, and made me swear never to reveal. Who are you? I asked her then, and for the first time I felt fear as I looked at her. You have spoken my name many times, Phaon, she said. You have honoured me in the flesh. Take my gift, be thankful. And use it sparingly. When the jar is empty, you will be at the end of your chosen road. Then she left me, like a ghost, but I caught a glimpse of her face as she turned away into the shadows, and I would swear it was the face of a young and beautiful woman."

I found myself trembling violently, though it was a warm night. I said: "Is that a true story?"

"Now, would I ever lie to you, darling?"

"More often than I care to think," I said bitterly.

"This happened," he said. "On my father's head I swear it."

I said: "Your father has sorrows enough already."

"Aye: he lost the better of us, that's true. Pelagon was the dutiful son always, a hard worker, a sober man for the night-fishing, right." He spat on the ground. "And where's my fine brother now? Dry bones under, with a salt-white oar and creel on his grave."

We sat silent for a moment, apart, brooding.

"Your story," I said at last.

"Yes?" He sounded suddenly bored: with me, with himself, with life.

"How do you explain it? What's the truth?" My voice was taut, urgent, anxious.

He shrugged. "How should I know? Does it matter?"

"Don't you *care?*"

"It makes no difference to me," he said, and stretched his muscular arms, and yawned, for all the world like a giant cat. "Perhaps it was the Goddess, I don't know. I sacrifice a lamb once a month just to be on the safe side. Perhaps it was nothing but some cracked old witch with a pot of scented goose-grease. Your guess is as good as mine." He gave a quick, complacent snort of laughter. "I look young. I get the women I want. That's what matters."

I said, schooling my voice to calmness: "Tell me one thing—*did you use the salve on me?*"

There was a tiny pause. Then he said: "Ah now, sweet, would I need to do that? You're not the shy sort, you've passion enough and to spare. Besides, it's old wives' nonsense, I'd never have told you if I'd known you'd take it seriously—"

"*Did you?*"

"I did not, indeed—"

"You're lying," I said, "I know you're lying—" but the truth was worse: I did not know. Whatever he might say now, I would never be certain. In my heart there would always remain a nagging fear that this passion of mine, for all its violence, all its seeming reality, had been engendered by some cold aphrodisiac trick of the Goddess, and was—like so much else in my life—mere illusion.

"If you don't care to believe me—" he said, and shrugged again, safe, indifferent.

"I'm sorry. I believe you."

"That's better now." He gave his easy, too easy, laugh.

With a quick, desperate movement I thrust myself against him. "Now," I whispered. "Please. Take me now—" But he shook me loose, good-humouredly, as he might have put away a troublesome puppy.

"Not again," he said. "It's getting late. We've not the time."

That was the last time we met in the cave. He must already have seen Charaxus, already have agreed to leave Lesbos for Sicily. But he said nothing—unless those final words were a kind of valediction.

For two months after my haemorrhage—five years ago: the day that Atthis left me—no one was sure whether I would live or die. I had lost too much blood, the Coan surgeon told Megara, I lacked the strength to fight my sickness. To me it meant being trapped in a long and dreadful nightmare between sleeping and waking, from which there was no way out, an iron circle. The dead and the living walked together through my mind's barren, rocky landscapes. Then, one day, without warning, the nightmare shredded away, and I came back—a weak, skeletal-thin traveller—to the world I knew, my skin like old parchment, my hands pitiful bird-claws, yet alive, alive, moved to tears by sunlight, by all minuscule living things, by the greenness of leaves and the glint of water, by the whole miraculous pageant of existence. I willed myself to eat, I endured medicines and purges. Day by slow day the flesh crept back to my bones, my thin blood pulsed stronger, till at last, with huge effort, I stood, and tottered a few steps, and then I knew that the danger was gone, that I would recover.

I awoke, too, to the realization—never before wholly accepted—that I had become a living legend, that my nearness to death (as I learnt from many letters) could personally affect people in distant places whom I did not know, for whom I existed only as the words that spoke my passion, and perhaps theirs too: a voice that spanned the many-tongued night, the sundering seas, the long death of the heart.

In those first days of convalescence an unspoken amnesty seemed to come about between me and my enemies. I had some unlikely visitors as I lay on my day-bed, wretchedly weak still, shocked by the memory of that waxen mask I had glimpsed briefly, in the hand-mirror Praxinoa tried—with such clumsy tact and zeal—to keep from me. Andromeda came, as awkward and hoydenish as ever, with a gift of books and wine: I received her peaceably, we talked of trivial things, and Atthis was never once mentioned between us. Pittacus came, gouty and aphoristic in his retirement, offering wise advice and exotic herbal remedies, very full of some unofficial diplomatic mission he had been asked to undertake in Lydia. "Can't do without me, you see," he said, "even now—" And he wheezed, and chuckled, and told endless anecdotes, so that as I lay back against my pillows I wondered: Why was I ever afraid of this man?

So many others, too: Aunt Helen and Uncle Draco, who was then—though he did not know it—on the verge of his own last, fatal illness; Mica and Melanippus, elegant, childless, who filled my sickroom with great bunches of Lebanese roses and the latest smart social gossip; Telesippa, respectable, matronly, her once-blond hair flat and streaked with grey; Agenor, a middle-aged bachelor, fast developing old-maid-ish habits; Larichus, his Apollonian good looks blown now, like the summer rose he picked from my bedside table, fluttering its petals groundwards, blown with rich living and idleness and the indulgences of the Athenian heiress whom he had married. Last of all, Agesilaïdas and Ismene and Atthis came together from Pyrrha, and from Three Winds Ismene's son Hippias, now nearly thirty, with his sister's grey eyes and dark, coppery hair and sudden, dazzling smile, and the room swam in sunlight so that I seemed to float on a golden tide as I looked and listened.

While we were talking, Cleïs and Meg came in together, and I saw Hippias turn his head, and Cleïs pause, slim and white and elegant as a lily, while their eyes met and brightened in that sudden, momentous recognition. Then, I felt nothing but happiness, the filaments of love spreading out through my senses, the pattern of the future dancing before my eyes in a shaft of sunlight. It was only afterwards that the dark clouds gathered and the pattern was struck awry.

The last revellers have departed, the moon is down. Even the cats have fallen silent. Overhead I hear a mumbling snore, the restless creak of a bed as some unknown body thrashes on it in nightmare. Through the slats of the shutters a false dawn glimmers. I am alone here in Corinth, utterly alone, with a pen and a lamp and the past I carry in my head—luggage, passport, what you will—anonymous, unregarded, a middle-aged woman passing through Corinth to her elusive future, and now crouched over the table of a shabby, peeling room in a waterfront whorehouse. Making up her accounts.

Spring had come before I was fully recovered, bird-song and apple-blossom mocked my slow descent into angry melancholy, the sense of time irretrievably lost, the enchanted doorway now closed to me for ever. When the Coan surgeon congratulated me on my remarkable recovery—as complete a cure, he said, as he had ever assisted at—he also unwittingly pronounced my death sentence. Cheerful, kindly, insensitive, a still-young man who lived with death on too-familiar terms and therefore, perhaps, had become coarsened in his approach to life, he sat out with me on the southern porch, eating cherries and flicking the stones up at my poor nesting swallows, and gave me professional advice for the future.

"You've got to remember, Lady Sappho, that you're not a young girl any more, but a middle-aged woman. You've had an extremely serious illness which—I must tell you this—might well have proved fatal. In future you will have to make certain—adjustments to your way of life."

"Adjustments?"

He looked at me shrewdly from under those thick black eyebrows. "It would be most unwise for you ever to dance again," he said. "In fact, the strain, generally speaking, of your, ah, professional activities is something which, medically speaking, I must deprecate in as strong terms as I may."

I said bleakly: "You mean I should disband the House of the Muses."

He coughed. "Ideally, yes."

"That's out of the question. It's my whole life. Can't you understand?"

"Of course, if it were reduced to a small circle of friends again—" He looked to see what effect he was having, then plunged on: "But these endless pupils and guests—"

I shook my head violently. "You're asking the impossible, I'm sorry."

He said: "Forgive me if I seem presumptuous, but I believe your attitude is dictated, in part at least, by financial considerations?"

I felt suddenly deflated: "Yes. Of course. I can't afford to lose the fees." It was the most humiliating admission I have ever made in my life. This brusque, kindly, thick-skinned surgeon was perhaps the only person who could have wrung it out of me.

He said, in a cheerful, matter-of-fact way: "Well, there would be no harm in your under-taking commissioned work. And you could always get your brother to mortgage your share of the estate to tide you over any difficulty—at the beginning."

"You seem to have been investigating my affairs very thoroughly."

"Of course," he said. "I want to make sure I get paid myself: it's a purely selfish instinct." He flicked another cherry-stone up at the roof of the colonnade: it struck the pleached mud nest fair and square, and the occupant shot out with an indignant squawk.

I said: "I respect your advice, but I doubt whether I shall take it."

"I expected that. But don't be too sure. Other factors may be involved besides your will."

"What do you mean?"

He shrugged. "I never prognosticate too far in advance. Let me give you one last very conventional piece of advice, though: take a sea voyage as soon as you feel up to it. A change of air and scene is the best medicine for convalescent depression I know."

"I might."

"Your brother Charaxus did suggest a trip to Samos. I don't know whether that would attract you?"

I said carefully: "I have nothing against Samos."

He laughed. "Cheer up," he said. "We all have to make do with the brothers we're given, and yours—if you'll take my unsolicited private opinion—is a pleasanter fellow than you give him credit for being."

"I'm sure you're right," I said demurely. "Did he promise to underwrite your fees?"

The Coan paused, a cherry half-way to his mouth, and regarded me with a pensive professional eye. "I think," he said, "that your recovery may be progressing faster than I supposed."

But the House of the Muses, however hard I struggled to maintain it, was doomed. My illness marked the close of an era, and everyone, whether consciously or not, seemed to recognize this. Beauty, in every sense, was central to the life we made there together: these were the precious years of our youth, the days that were lit by passion, creativity, hope, when time seemed inexhaustible, the senses ran riot, and the deep well of physical well-being could never, we thought, run dry. The greying ghost who walked those corridors now had come back too late.

For a little while, loyally supported by Meg and my daughter Cleïs, I tried to defy the truth, call back the old days. It was useless. The stream of pupils became a trickle, the trickle soon dried up altogether. A shadow had fallen, and the air struck chill: I was no longer the ideal teacher and lover at whose feet young girls travelled half-across the world to sit, but a tired, impatient, semi-invalid woman of nearly fifty.

Newcomers were soon warned about my screaming, unpredictable rages, my occasional descent into tearful hysteria, my arbitrary whims and cruelties. Worst of all, never admitted consciously, was the dreadful sense of boredom that began to pervade me; pretty butterflies who once would have captivated my heart now left me wholly indifferent, or stirred me only to irritation and distaste. It was this, more than anything else, which hastened the end. Long before the House of the Muses ceased to exist, I had destroyed it in my heart.

Financially, I was almost bankrupt. I took the Coan's advice, and persuaded Charaxus to mortgage my share of the estate. I turned out wedding odes and epitaphs and hymns to order, but my creative gift, like my body, had been dulled by illness, and what I wrote no longer possessed that elusive vitality, even in the expression of commonplaces, which had made me so sought-after a poet during my Sicilian exile.

Yet I could not bring myself to abandon any part of my luxurious way of life: if anything I spent more, desperately staving off reality, running deeper and deeper into debt on bills that had little chance of being redeemed. I became obsessed by my own advancing age, haunted by images of death and decay, increasingly solitary: friend after friend was snubbed and alienated, it was as though I were trying to cut myself loose from life, to exist like a revenant in the place where I had once known happiness.

Sometimes, as now, in the clear-eyed moment after a long, sleepless night, I can face another daemon that prowls restlessly down the twisting, perilous corridors of my mind, a beast that squats at the labyrinth's core, the nightmarish monster whose bull's bellow echoes through my dreams while I fumble the thread in darkness, heart pounding, left hand, right hand, which passage to follow, what obscenity lies in wait for me, the cold sweat, the cankered fear in the skull, the ultimate, brutal, naked question—

Am I, could I be, insane?

Now, while I am alone, while I have a brief respite, I must consider this coolly. It is, after all, important.

In the end I followed the surgeon's advice, and took the voyage to Samos with Charaxus for my convalescence. It was dull past belief, and my brother, feeling he had me at a disadvantage, patronized me in the smuggest, most insufferable way. We stayed at the house of a merchant called Iadmon, a tall, thin man with a face like a mullet's: the same rough, reddish-blue complexion, the same sharp eye-teeth and recessive chin, the same dull, protruding stare. He and Charaxus were well-matched colleagues.

But the visit had odder consequences than I, for one, could have guessed at the time. It was here that my brother first set eyes on a pert, fair-haired slave-girl called Doricha, with the rosy complexion that afterwards gave her that more famous nickname by which she is remembered today. Preoccupied with my own problems, I scarcely noticed her—or the effect she had on Charaxus, which must have been devastating. But a year later she had been bought by some high-class pimp and established as a courtesan at Naucratis, the Greek trading-port in the Egyptian delta; and it was here that my brother, having successfully off-loaded a cargo of Lesbian wine, met her again, and proceeded—with that monumental recklessness of which only the habitually cautious are, on rare occasions, capable—to make her his mistress, squander vast sums of money on her, and even, if rumour was to be trusted, offer her marriage.

[259]

After my illness—I come back to this again and again—I became conscious of some fundamental, yet unrecognized change in myself. In ways (how can I describe the sensation without seeming fanciful?) it was as though I walked through the garden of the self and met a stranger there who bore my face, who stared at me blankly, whose actions were unpredictable and on occasion terrifying. Antimenidas once told me that among the Persians this duality is recognized and accepted. To me it was, and remains, something nightmarish, a usurpation. But how can a usurpation be from within?

First, during the difficult days of convalescence, I experienced—as the Coan surgeon told me I would—moods of black despair, when mind and body alike seemed to freeze in a long, dead midwinter, and my nerves were bare branches scribbled against a stormy sky. Then, slowly, despair was replaced by random explosions of anger, hysterical suspiciousness, the conviction that nothing was what it seemed, that behind a friendly social façade my undeclared enemies were working to destroy me.

(There: I think the Coan would approve of this analysis so far. We spent much time discussing clinical method: why should it not be applied to mind as well as to body? But I must not forget the triple golden rule. *Describe symptoms: diagnose disease: prescribe treatment.* The hardest part of my task is still to come.)

As my physical strength returned, I began to have a series of crude, unbelievably vivid sexual dreams, unlike anything I had ever experienced before. By day I was working, with an apathy I put down to my illness, on plans for the House of the Muses. But at night the dreams came: faces of sailors, of muscular porters glimpsed on the quayside, cruel, bearded mouths, hard bodies, eyes hot with lust, hands that seized my body, bruising, defiling; and with that defilement pleasure, secret, violent, shameful pleasure such as I had never known.

I dreaded the dreams, I longed for them, I lived in an endless, burning frenzy of desire. The stranger lusted in my body and soon was a stranger no more. The dividing line between dream and reality became increasingly indistinct. I found myself making excuses to go through the market, down by the harbour, past taverns, anywhere I could watch young, strong, animal-quick male bodies: the gleaming twist of a torso, muscles that bunched and slid under sun-darkened skin. I lived for days in an unspoken fantasy of lust.

Somewhere, somehow, this slowly mounting pressure had to find release. It may, or may not, be coincidence that about the same time

I caused much astonishment—not to say open scandal—by publicly circulating a series of the most abusive and indeed obscene verse lampoons. I pilloried the sexual habits of Andromeda, Gorgo, and their group with an outspokenness that raised laughter in the taverns, but embarrassed my friends horribly. It was, as they all said, so out of character.

I remember Meg wailing: "But I've never heard you use words like that in your *life* before, and to publish them openly—I just don't understand you, Sappho, it's as though you wanted to destroy yourself and humiliate us." And Alcaeus, back from his Boeotian wanderings now, hand a little tremulous, the network of veins visible now round eyes and nose: "Congratulations, my dear. You're being yourself at last. Better late than never." Then, with the cunning, sideways leer of the drunkard: "But you're mad, of course, you know that, don't you? Mad as birds."

Yet the scandal, in some curious way, failed to touch me. The more outrageous my behaviour, the greater my indifference to public opinion. I remained, I now realize, quite astonishingly blind to the degree of resentment I was stirring up among people of all classes and political views in Mytilene. I seemed determined to disregard every social convention which holds the fabric of our community together. The fact that my own private conduct was no better than that of my victims did not disturb anyone; it merely caused amusement. But my insistently public gestures—the lampoons, the fishwife arguments, one occasion when I nearly became involved in a brawl—these were regarded as intolerable, and all the worse because I was a famous citizen, whose acts would be reported in every barber's shop from Miletus to Syracuse. (Did *he* hear of them, I wonder?)

This leads me back to my brother, and his much-publicized infatuation for Doricha. Now, as all the world knows, I attacked Charaxus, when I heard about the liaison, in a series of poems that caused much unkind amusement at the time, but were thought—to say the least of it—lacking in taste and reticence. The truth is that if it had not been for me, Mytilene might never have heard of Doricha at all.

I have invariably maintained, when challenged, that I took this course to preserve our family honour: Charaxus ruining himself was bad enough, but the prospect of this former slave and prostitute coming back to Mytilene as his wife was quite unthinkable. Public ridicule was the only thing which might shock him out of his socially

[261]

and financially disastrous passion. (I have no doubt he is now enjoying our ironic reversal of roles.)

But even at the time I had serious doubts about my own argument. It is true that, in the event, my brother did *not* marry Doricha—or Rosie, as she was now known by every ship's captain on the delta run—but this, I suspect, was none of his or my doing. It seems clear, in retrospect, that Rosie herself had tired of him (who could blame her?) and was aiming a good deal higher than this ugly, middle-aged island wine-merchant. To judge from her present fame and wealth— it is not every whore who can afford to send offerings to Delphi— she would appear to have made a sensible decision.

No: my own motives can, all too easily, be fitted into that other, uglier pattern I have begun to sketch—a pattern in which conscious choice has little place, where freedom is illusion, and our most deliberate acts (as we think) are dictated by some capricious deity who, for his own pleasure, sheds a blinding glamour on our eyes. I disliked my brother, true, and was not slow to seize so perfect an opportunity of humiliating him. This, if not to my credit, is at least understandable, and leaves the will intact. But when I consider the way I behaved in the light of those other strange episodes, I feel the self dissolve, I hear the cold laughter of immortal, devious Aphrodite as she moves her pawn across the board. And now the game is nearly over.

That day, like any other, I walked slowly along the harbour-front of Mytilene, a small, thin, greying woman, no longer ill indeed, but still bearing the marks of my illness. The old man leaning against the bollard eyed me curiously as I went past—unescorted, another scandal for my aristocratic friends to chew on—with sad, hesitant eyes that had been blurred and paled by too many long watches, reefs awash to leeward in the storm-driven darkness, the Pole Star dancing faint above a stripped mast while men cursed or prayed.

When he accosted me it was with great respect and a natural dignity that I found both touching and impressive. He begged my pardon for the impertinence of speaking to so great a lady, but grief overcame his modesty. His son, his beloved son, had been drowned at sea ten days ago, and now his body had been washed ashore and given burial, all that the dead could wish for he had had unstintingly, but— And here the old man hesitated, cracking gaunt fingers, uncertain how to go on.

I smiled, guessing his trouble, why he had come to me. "You would like me to compose his epitaph," I said, and he nodded eagerly, still anxious, unable to believe that I would agree. "I have money," he said, "I can pay you what is fitting. And my sons' sons and their children after them will remember Pelagon, on whose grave are carved words by the greatest poet we have known. It is an honour to stand in your shadow, Lady Sappho." "It is a short enough shadow," I said, laughing, more moved than I cared to admit (yet would he have approached me at all if it had not been for the scandal?). "Very well: I will compose your son's epitaph."

He said, "You must come to my house, Lady Sappho. It is a poor home, but we will welcome you with the best we have, and my wife will speak to you of our son." So I went with him through the winding, sunlit alleys clamorous with children and women, till we reached the small harbour beyond the city walls, and the old man led me down a flight of worn, grey steps to a cottage on the foreshore, washed in blue lime, with a lean-to shed behind it, and red nets drying, and a pair of black-and-white goats tethered under a barren fig-tree.

As we stooped through the low doorway, a chicken ran out past us, clucking shrilly. My eyes, sun-dazzled, took a moment to adjust themselves in the half-light. I smelt the smell of fish and tar and masculine sweat, a clean rankness. Then my vision cleared, and I saw the man who sat in one corner, stripped to the waist, whittling, a bird-call, his heavy chestnut hair falling over one eye as he worked. He turned, and gave me a lazy, appraising smile. "This is my other son," the old man said. "This is Phaon." So we met for the first time: and from that first meeting all else followed.

Am I pursuing a phantom to Sicily, as Agamemnon pursued the phantom Helen to Troy? The lust for self-destruction; to be ravished by Death, what ecstasy!

When I took Hippias and made him the slave of my body, when Phaon burned me with that all-consuming fire of passion, was it I, or they, or Aphrodite who cast the spell? Where does the fault lie, who must bear the weight of it before Gods and men? Am I deceiving myself still, still anxious only to shift the burden from my shoulders, careless who may be compelled to take it up in my stead? The nightmare of madness, this sick frenzy in the womb, even Aphrodite herself, so cold, so capricious—may not these, too, be mere simulacra, the mind's last defence against surrender to the truth? How can I know? How can I ever be certain?

One way remains.

Westward from Corinth at dawn, with black wedges of migrant birds flying south to Egypt and the sun, and a cold wind blowing in gusts across the Gulf. The helmsman sniffs the weather like a dog, there are tiny white flecks on the water: the ship's bows dip and thrust, tackle creaks. Here am I, an unexplained traveller in a black cloak, propped against this handy bulk-head below the after-deck, out of the wind, writing, writing, scratching down my present and my past, using the one art that I possess still, the craft of words to which, ultimately, all else in my life has been sacrificed. Which was truth, the lover or the poem? This love endures, that is transient. Odysseus in the flesh must have been a devious, lumpish mercenary captain: it took Homer to give him immortality. Yet I ache for the flesh now, *his* hard body, where, where? Sprawled in some tavern of Syracuse? Handling tarry ropes among others of his kind, the men who live by boats and the longshore trade? Or—no, I must stop this, close the bright doors of imagination, shut out the light. Which can blind as well as heal. Apollo, be merciful.

So we have come here to harbour under the high white cliffs of Leucas, sailing north out of the Gulf by the scattered islands, past Cephallenia, with its high, ridged back, and Ithaca, where Odysseus returned at last after so many years and perhaps set his troubled house in order. We lie moored against a square stone quay, while sacks of food and water-jars are carried aboard, and friends exchange greetings. The dawn air strikes fresh: this is our last landfall in Greece. West of us lies the wide Ionian Sea, below that curving horizon rise the mountains of Sicily. We sail at noon.

It seemed somehow natural that I should hear his name: natural and inevitable. I looked and saw a knot of sailors on the quayside— our helmsman and several others I did not recognize, but my mind leaped, the blood cried out *Is he there?* seeing the dark merchantman lying beyond us with that well-remembered flag at its masthead, the cuttlefish emblem of Syracuse. What's the news? one said, and another, laughing, replied: You remember Phaon? Yes, I whispered, the unregarded shadow, a hooded woman standing alone in mid-journey, yes, I remember Phaon. And the first voice said: Who is it this time, then? They laughed at that, all of them, drinking hot spiced wine from the tavern, copper tankards aglow in the morning light, men among men, while I waited, waited. You can guess what happened, the Syracusan said. It was inevitable. Sooner or later. The helmsman wiped his mouth. Tell us, then, he said. You know Aristippe, the Syracusan said. Glaucus' wife? someone asked, and another cut in: Who doesn't know her? and the laughter broke again, till I heard a voice say: She's not as young as she was, and the Syracusan's reply: Phaon liked them ripe. Ripe and easy. *Liked?* That's right, let me tell this my own way. Glaucus came back from his last voyage ten days early—Some laughter, not much, and the first voice breaking in: And caught them? Pause. Oh yes, he caught them, said the Syracusan. There'll be no more stories about Phaon, so make the most of this one. Our helmsman hawked, drank his wine, said, falsely casual, a great lecher himself by the look of him: A knife in the ribs? And the Syracusan, swilling dregs, spilling the last drop for luck: What else? Scuffling of feet. So that's the end of Phaon. He had fun while it lasted. The Syracusan said: Here's something, now: they found it on him, and Glaucus sold it to me. Pause, whispers. Alabaster, eh? Beautiful workmanship. Looks like an ointment-jar. And the helmsman: What was in it? The Syracusan shrugged. Nothing, he said. It was empty. Another voice, cold, sniggering: Maybe Phaon kept his luck in it. They moved away down the quay, swaggering slightly like all seamen ashore, men from an alien element.

Here on this promontory, high above Leucas and the sea, the morning air strikes fresh. It is clear to the west still, the Ionian waters lie calm out and away over the horizon to distant Sicily, though eastward, above the high mountains of Acarnania, storm-clouds are gathering. As we sailed in, an hour, a life ago, the rising sun shone slantwise across these sheer, towering cliffs, tingeing their natural white a delicate rose-pink. It is two thousand feet from the edge down to that dark, wrinkling surface, where our ship, like some minuscule black insect, lies at anchor still by the stone quayside. A few yards behind me, white and peaceful, stands a small temple to Apollo. It is some grateful worshipper, the inscription tells me—yes, Menexus the son of Cratylus—who, in gratitude for the God's favours, set up the pleasant stone bench where I sit now and write these words.

When the captain asked me, in amused perplexity, why I wanted a mule, I said: "I must make an offering to Apollo." It was not what I intended to say, but it is true, and it is why I am here now. My mind is clear, no doubt remains.

After that first shock, reaching a nadir of despair, I wrote: "We are Aphrodite's playthings, there it begins and ends: our passions flare or fade at her cold whim, the self is nothing, the will is nothing, our splendid gestures contain the unconscious pathos and irony of a jerking puppet, that mimes—parodies—our human illusions. We laugh at the witless doll, with its all-too-visible strings, and bold, seeming-decisive movements: it is ourselves we see."

I, Sappho of Mytilene, daughter of Scamandronymus, deny, irrevocably, the words I have just set down. What I do now, I do by free choice and knowledge. My will is sovereign, and for all acts and decisions in my life I accept, without hesitation, the burden which that liberty imposes. No God, not immortal Aphrodite herself, can act through me if I will it otherwise.

Now I have set down these last words, I shall seal all I have written, the testament of my life, and leave it as an offering on Apollo's altar. Let the God and his priests keep it in their protection. Then I shall come back, alone, to this windy headland, while the sun is still bright, while no storm-clouds have yet overshadowed the western sky, and finish my journey as I must. Apollo, Lord of Light, accept my homage; Poseidon, sovereign over all seas and oceans, grant me a gentle passing.

μνάσασθαί τινά φαιμ' ὕστερον ἀμμέων

ON SAPPHO

Since *The Laughter of Aphrodite*, though a novel, attempts to re-create a famous historical character as faithfully as the evidence at our disposal will allow; and since the evidence is so mutilated and fragmentary that much invention has been necessary, while hardly one statement fails to involve historical detective-work; and since, lastly, the figure of Sappho is one round which curious myth and violent moral prejudice have clung since at least as early as the second half of the fifth century B.C.—for all these reasons it may be desirable to give the reader some idea of how much fact and how much fiction my novel contains.

The brutal truth is that we know rather less about Sappho as a person than we do about Shakespeare—another great collector of romantic or cranky adherents, and for very similar reasons. There is not one surviving ancient Life of Sappho, unless we count a wretched entry in a Byzantine lexicon. Our main primary source of Sappho's life is, naturally, her own poetry, and that of her contemporary Alcaeus —or such tattered scraps of it as survive in grammarians' excerpts and have been rescued on papyrus fragments: less than one-twentieth of the estimated whole.

I have done my best to put Sappho's life together in accordance with the evidence. My task has been rather like that of an archaeologist re-assembling some amphora from hundreds of sherds—of which more than half are missing. Only when historical evidence fails have I invented incidents or characters. I have been wary of modern myths, though I hope I have treated ancient ones with respect. For centuries, it has been a favourite pastime, among scholars and others, to prove (to their own if no one else's satisfaction) that Sappho could not have been a Lesbian, in the modern sense of that word; could not have committed suicide; and could not, for good measure, have had an affair in late middle-age with a boatman. A misplaced zeal for romantic truth has led men to maintain very curious arguments in this field: when all else failed, awkward or unwelcome facts were written off as misapplied mythology.

Sappho's life spans one of the most fascinating periods in all Greek history: the last two decades of the seventh century B.C., and the first three of the sixth. It was an age of transition—political, ethical, cultural—with a failing aristocratic ideal stubbornly entrenched against the rising flood of mercantilism. I have tried to take account of this conflict in my novel.

There is one other source of evidence which may, rightly or wrongly, be regarded as more beneficial to the novelist than the historian; and that is the island of Lesbos itself. Of all Aegean islands, this one has perhaps changed least since ancient times: it is, for instance, still very heavily wooded, with pine and chestnut forests in addition to the ubiquitous olive or ilex. Any permanent resident who knows his Sappho (and many Greeks do) will be struck, again and again, by climatic or topographical echoes of some striking image in the poetry: a 'rosy-fingered moon' after sunset will come as no surprise to an islander—nor will the 'down-rushing wind' that shakes the oaks.

Methymna, Lesbos   Peter Green

GENEALOGICAL TABLE

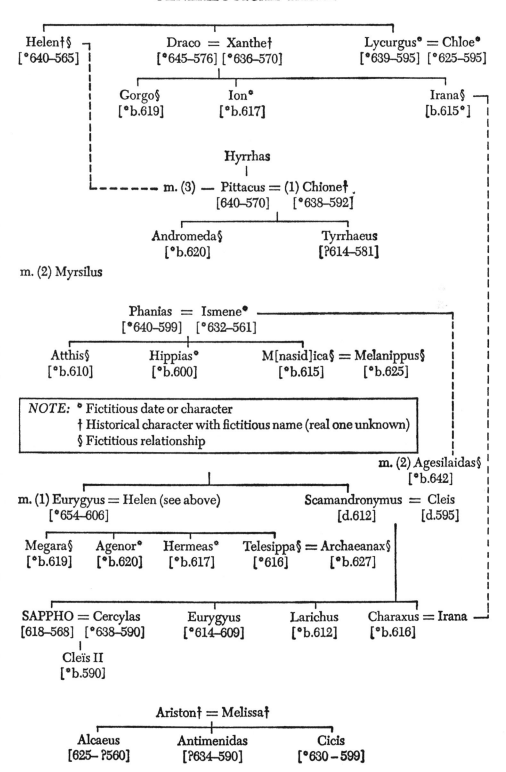

Helen†§
[*640–565]

Draco = Xanthe†
[*645–576] [*636–570]

Lycurgus* = Chloe*
[*639–595] [*625–595]

Gorgo§
[*b.619]

Ion*
[*b.617]

Irana§
[b.615*]

Hyrrhas

m. (3) — Pittacus = (1) Chione†
[640–570] [*638–592]

Andromeda§
[*b.620]

Tyrrhaeus
[?614–581]

m. (2) Myrsilus

Phanias = Ismene*
[*640–599] [*632–561]

Atthis§
[*b.610]

Hippias*
[*b.600]

M[nasid]ica§ = Melanippus§
[*b.615] [*b.625]

NOTE: * Fictitious date or character
† Historical character with fictitious name (real one unknown)
§ Fictitious relationship

m. (2) Agesilaidas§
[*b.642]

m. (1) Eurygyus = Helen (see above)
[*654–606]

Scamandronymus = Cleis
[d.612] [d.595]

Megara§
[*b.619]

Agenor*
[*b.620]

Hermeas*
[*b.617]

Telesippa§ = Archaeanax§
[*616] [*b.627]

SAPPHO = Cercylas
[618–568] [*638–590]

Eurygyus
[*614–609]

Larichus
[*b.612]

Charaxus = Irana
[*b.616]

Cleïs II
[*b.590]

Ariston† = Melissa†

Alcaeus
[625– ?560]

Antimenidas
[?634–590]

Cicis
[*630 – 599]

CHRONOLOGICAL
TABLE OF EVENTS

N.B. Fictional events (as opposed to historical hypotheses, or historical events for which no reasonably sure date can be argued) are marked with a star, thus:* Many birth-dates are highly theoretical; these, and other reasoned guesses, are marked with a query: ?

B.C.
640   Pittacus born
625   Periander succeeds to tyranny of Corinth
        ?Alcaeus born
618   ?Sappho born at Eresus on Lesbos
        Alyattes succeeds to throne of Lydia
616   ?Telesippa and Charaxus born
615   ?Mica born
614   ?Eurygyus, Sappho's brother, born; also ?Pittacus' son
            Tyrrhaeus
613   *Pittacus visits Scamandronymus and Cleïs in Eresus
        Alyattes, Periander, and Thrasybulus of Miletus in alliance
612   Melanchros, tyrant of Mytilene, overthrown by aristocratic
            coup: conspirators include Pittacus, Phanias, Antimenidas,
            Cicis, Scamandronymus
        Melanchros' deputy, Myrsilus, exiled
        ?Scamandronymus killed during coup
        ?Cleïs and her family move to Mytilene
        ?Sappho's brother Larichus born
610   ?Atthis born

[271]

609   ?Premature death of Sappho's brother Eurygyus
Death of Psammetichus I of Egypt; Neko succeeds him
608   Draco secures Pittacus' appointment as commander in Sigean War
*Praxinoa given to Sappho, Megara, and Telesippa as maid
607   Sigean War: campaign in Troad during which Alcaeus (aet.18) drops his shield and runs
606   Periander arbitrates between Athens and Lesbos in Troad
?Death of Sappho's Uncle Eurygyus
605   *Cleïs collecting conspirators
604   Return of Myrsilus from exile: successful coup; Council of Nobles overthrown
Defection of Pittacus
First exile of Sappho [to Pyrrha]
?Pittacus embezzles 2000 gold pieces from Alyattes of Lydia
601   Pittacus (aet.39) confirmed in joint power with Myrsilus
Nebuchadnezzar's campaign against Jehoiakim
600   *Birth of Atthis' brother Hippias
599   Unsuccessful aristocratic coup against Myrsilus
?Death of Phanias and Cicis
Alcaeus and Antimenidas captured
?Sappho and Cleïs arrested in Pyrrha, brought back to Mytilene
Second exile: Sappho to Syracuse[?] in Sicily, Antimenidas to Babylon as mercenary, Alcaeus to Egypt
*Sappho travels with Arion of Methymna, meets Periander
597   *Telesippa marries Archaeanax
595   Birth of Croesus
?Arion returns to Corinth: the dolphin story
?Death of Sappho's mother Cleïs
*Aunt Helen's second marriage: to Myrsilus
*Phanias' widow Ismene marries Agesilaïdas
*Charaxus marries Draco's daughter Irana
*Lycurgus and Chloe ambushed and killed in Sicily
594   ?Sappho marries Cercylas of Andros, returns to Mytilene
Sappho's brother Larichus cup-bearer in Mytilene City Hall
593   ?Sappho begins to establish group in Mytilene: Atthis (aet. 17), Megara (aet.26), Mica (aet.22), Telesippa (aet.23)
?Rival group led by Andromeda (aet.27) with Gorgo (aet. 26) and Irana (aet.22)

592 PAlcaeus (aet.33) and Antimenidas (aet.42) granted pardon, return from exile

*Death of Pittacus' wife Chione (aet.46)

591 PSappho pregnant with Cleïs

590 Death of Myrsilus [*and Cercylas] in ambush between Pyrrha and Mytilene

PArrival of Anactoria and Cydro

Pittacus elected *aesymnetes,* or constitutional dictator, of Mytilene

Death of Antimenidas; trial of Alcaeus

Pittacus marries widowed sister of Draco [*Sappho's Aunt Helen]

589 *Mica marries Melanippus

587 *Anactoria marries Iadmon, leaves for Lydia

586 PHouse of the Muses begins to crystallize as professional undertaking

585 *Agesilaïdas and Ismene move from Three Winds to Pyrrha

Death of Periander

582 First formulation of "Seven Wise Men" (including Pittacus)

581 Pittacus' son Tyrrhaeus murdered (aet.33)

580 Pittacus (aet.60) resigns tyranny of Mytilene

579 PAlcaeus exiled by new democratic Council; travels to mainland Greece

578 *Larichus marries rich Athenian heiress

576 PDeath of Draco (aet.69)

575 PAlcaeus returns to Mytilene (aet.50)

574 Croesus governor of Adramyttium

573 PSappho (aet.45) has serious breakdown and illness

572 House of the Muses dissolved; voyage to Samos; *affair

571   with Hippias

570 Charaxus' affair with Doricha-Rhodopis in Naucratis

Accession of Amasis as Pharaoh

Death of Pittacus (aet.70)

*Death of Draco's wife Xanthe (aet.66)

569 Sappho's affair with Phaon of Mytilene

568 Phaon removed from Lesbos [*at Charaxus' instigation] and sails to Sicily

PSappho takes ship for Corinth and Sicily; her death on the island of Leucas

ABOUT THE AUTHOR

Peter Green was born in London in 1924 and educated at Charterhouse and Trinity College, Cambridge, where he took first-class honours in both parts of the Classical Tripos, winning the Craven Scholarship and Studentship in the same year (1950) and subsequently obtaining a Ph.D. After a short spell as Director of Studies in Classics at Cambridge, he worked for some years as a freelance writer, translator and literary journalist and as a publisher. In 1963 he emigrated to Greece with his family. From 1966 to 1971 he lectured in Greek history and literature at College Year in Athens; in 1971 he came to the University of Texas at Austin, where he is now Dougherty Centennial Professor of Classics.

Sappho's Lesbos

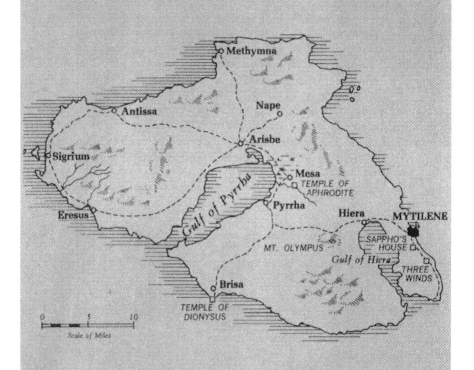

Methymna

Antissa

Nape

Arisbe

Sigrium

Mesa
TEMPLE OF
APHRODITE

Gulf of Pyrrha

Pyrrha

Eresus

Hiera

MYTILENE

SAPPHO'S
HOUSE

MT. OLYMPUS

Gulf of Hiera

THREE
WINDS

Brisa

TEMPLE OF
DIONYSUS

0   5   10
Scale of Miles

A e g e a n   S e a

Made in the USA
Columbia, SC
02 December 2020